A Penny Saved a Murder Earned

Book 1 of the Kelly Murder Mysteries

A novel

Written by S. G. Lee

First Edition 2016

SB

An imprint of *Shillelagh Books*

London, Ontario, Canada

Acknowledgments:

Sincere thanks to Jodi and Sydney, without your constant support and encouragement, this book would not be possible. You are the best friends a writer could have. I dedicate this book to my daughters, my son-in law and my husband; who have supported my writing endeavours with encouragement and love. Special thanks to my beloved mother in heaven, who taught me dreams, can come true with hard work, perseverance and patience.

Published at CreateSpace

Copyright © 2016 by Sheilagh G. Lee

ISBN (13) 978-0-9878420-4-6 (paperback)

ISBN-10: 0987842048

ISBN 978-0-9878420-1-5 (e-book)

Table of Contents

Chapter 1 - Bloody Shoes

"A penny saved is a penny earned" ~
Benjamin Franklin

The blood streaked across the floor, but

he had carefully sidestepped it. Stupid bitch! She got what she deserved. How dare she defile his Angel's property? He hadn't left a trace...had he? No, he was too clever by half.

A voice he didn't recognize interrupted his thoughts, "I didn't spot you entering. Working late, dear? Of course, I forgot; you have an early opening tomorrow."

The man strode closer to the killer and the body lying on the floor, "Wait a minute, you aren't the lady. Who are you? You shouldn't be here," the man continued clearly alarmed.

"You shouldn't be here either," the murderer insisted.

"You, you killed Megan. I'm telling."

"Really? You know this was something you shouldn't be allowed to see."

"I'm leaving. I didn't notice anything," the man lied, witnessing the blood.

"I'm sorry pal. Wrong place, wrong time!" the killer answered.

The homeless man ran dodging racks, finally deciding to hide behind some shelving. The killer ran after him, puzzled for a moment because he could see no trace of the homeless person. The murderer then laughed, as he realized how foolish the vagrant was being, his stench gave him away. He subdued the man with a Taser gun. Waiting seconds he then pulled the man from his hiding place. Taking ties from within his pocket; he fastened the man's arms and feet. Satisfied that the homeless person was now trussed up like a turkey, he smiled.

"P...P....P...Please! I don't want to die!" the man cried, visibly sweating and starting to shake.

The man tried to kick out his legs and arms but failed.

"You've heard about fate? Well sorry but this is your fate, buddy!" the murderer explained.

"P...P...P...Please, I'm begging you! Couldn't you let me go? I won't tell! I'll move to another city. Besides who would listen to a homeless man?"

"Someone would. My Angel would."

The homeless man then smiled as if to gain trust from this killer, "You won't hurt the lady who owns the store, will you?" he asked.

"I would never harm my Angel. How dare you?" the killer responded outraged.

"S...S...S...Sorry! I didn't mean to insult you! Please just let me go. I'm harmless ask anyone...."

"What is your name?"

"Why do you need my name?" He asked looking puzzled then reconsidering he answered, "My name is Al."

The killer put his gloves back on and smoothed them and then turned his back on his victim.

"You're going to kill me now. Aren't you? Just don't harm the sweet lady who owns this store. Will it hurt?" the man asked resigned.

"I would never hurt my Angel. She is sweet isn't she? Unfortunately that also makes unscrupulous people take advantage of her."

"I promise I would never take advantage of her kindness. I wouldn't!!! She's the best part of my day and this city, Happy Valley, Ontario. She picked me up from the gutter and helped me."

"I know you wouldn't and it hurts me to do this. Tell you what though, I'll make your death painless because I like you, Al," the killer offered, feeling suddenly sorry for the man. Then he checked himself. Living on the streets was hell; maybe he was doing the guy a favour? Yes, of course he was. Taking a pill bottle out of his pocket and opening the dispenser, he placed some in a coffee cup he took from the sideboard. He filled the cup with the tepid coffee from the coffee pot, stirring the pills in rapidly.

"C...c...c...couldn't you let me go? I won't tell and I'll watch over her when you're not here."

"Sorry, times up, Al. Here now, drink this coffee," the assassin commanded placing the mug at Al's lips.

Al tried not to drink and spit some of the coffee out, but the assassin plugged his nose and the cup was soon empty.

"Admit it Al, you had a crappy life. Just give in and go to the light. I hear good things wait there for people like you," the killer stated.

Al tried to fight some more, but he soon found it was losing battle. Al's breathing slowed as he slipped into a deep sleep and stopped breathing altogether. His age and living on the streets made the pills work fast.

Now what to do with the body? The killer thought. His Angel must not find this man's remains here, bad enough he left Megan's body here for his Angel to find. He couldn't hide Megan though she needed to be found. Every needed to know she suffered for her crime. Maybe even his Angel would see Megan's evil and protect herself from people like that. This man, Al however knew his Angel and she cared about him. It was so like her to look after the homeless. He could let her cry over Al. Where could he put the man so he wouldn't be found?

The dumpster of course...the perfect place for Al! The day after tomorrow was garbage day. Covered in garbage no one would find Al.

~0~

The next day

Lily

Ominous clouds replaced the

morning's sunlight turning the skies to shades of deep purple and navy blue, streaked with gray. Lily Kelly stared at the sky for moment, and then departed the courthouse doors in Happy Valley, Ontario, Canada, skipping down the steps. The city looked its age of over a hundred as the buildings downtown looked old and decrepit. If only the town could find some money to fix downtown Lily thought.

Then her mind turned to Amelia, her cousin and best friend. Amelia needed Lily to support her in her grief. Lily had a fight with her husband Horace again this morning about how much time he was spending at the office and how much time she spent supporting Amelia. Lily was always working, and so was Horace, so how much time was Rose their fourteen year old daughter really getting?

Lily had won in court, but all she could think about was her family. Everyone needed her and she felt like she was being pulled in three different directions. Something had to give and it looked like it was her job. She would have to cut back on some of her work. Her family had to come first.

Lily stumbled some more over the steps only stopping from hurrying across the courtyard to her office, when her heel broke on her shoe. Today was supposed to be about her victory after her win in court; but it appeared with her expensive shoe's heel breaking, she was mistaken. They ought to get the ruts in the paving stones fixed; that was her reflection as she cursed her bad break. What did they say about omens? Maybe she should have taken a hint from the heavens' darkening? She noted as her bad luck had seemed to get worse with the arrival of some reporters.

"Ms. Kelly, give us a statement about the Rockwood case?" yelled one reporter.

"Ms. Kelly, how does the Sulimani family feel about your victory?" yelled another.

One bold reporter stepped forward, "Crown Attorney Kelly, congratulations on your win. Was it hard to try a case which involved a council member?" asked Paul Knight from the local television station, thrusting a microphone in Lily's face.

"Anyone who commits a crime in Happy Valley will be tried by the Crown with the full force of the law, despite their office. So no, I did not find it difficult to do my job," Lily replied testily.

"Thank you, Ms. Kelly. What does the Sulimani family think about the judgement?"

"Amani Sulimani was five years old, when Zebadiah Rockwood's truck went through a red light. His truck struck the back of the Sulimani's SUV killing her. He then left the scene pursued by good Samaritans, who wished to stop Mr. Rockwood from continuing driving drunk: a pursuit caused by Mr. Rockwood's actions, which put a number of lives in danger."

"Will the family be comforted with this conviction?" queried another reporter.

"Amani Sulimani existed as their only child. Mr. Rockwood's conviction will not bring her back, but hopefully will bring some peace of mind to her family knowing he will be behind bars." Lily answered.

"Do you sense, given your own personal tragedies that you'll be able to get a sentence fitting the crime?"

"My family's history does not come into my trial cases, only the person's guilt."

"And when will sentencing take place?" asked another reporter.

"Sentencing will take place next month."

"Thank you Ms. Kelly. This is Paul Knight reporting, with an update on the Zebadiah Rockwood's drunken driving case. Zebadiah Rockwood was a long time council member here in Happy Valley. He took a leave of absence to deal with his legal issues. Mr.

Rockwood was charged with impaired driving causing death, two counts of failing to remain at the scene of an accident and dangerous driving last December. When asked about the conviction today Mr. Rockwood and his lawyer issued a no comment. We will have the complete story for you at six pm. Paul Knight reporting for CHPV-TV."

Lily hated speaking on camera, even though it was part of her job as the Crown attorney, so she was glad the scrum had been completed.

She hated sounding tough and unyielding but it was all in the description of her job title. She had fought difficult challenges to get this job and she had to work hard and fight hard to keep it. After all there were aspects of her job her she loved like putting the bad people that would harm others away. The press was gone and she was now free to go to her office to file her reports and leave early. She crossed the street, entered her building and went straight up to her office.

"Victory is mine!" Lily Kelly cried triumphantly as she walked into her office.

"So you won?" asked Colleen Finn, her administrative assistant.

"Yes, I bested that idiot, Michael Taylor. He thought he would beat me in court. He actually believed his client would win."

"Good for you, boss, I knew you would nail his lily white ass to the wall. He's such a scumbag lawyer all his clients seem to be as guilty as hell."

"Colleen! Language! But thank-you," Lily answered, showing pearly white teeth.

Colleen looked expectantly at Lily and she felt stupid did she miss something? Oh the joke! Lily hadn't laughed at Colleen's wit.

"Funny, I got it. Zebadiah Rockwood's sentencing takes place next month, but he will be held until then; no bail, no goodbyes to his favourite watering hole. As the Crown, I'll recommend the longest sentence I can get that he can serve. It's victories like these which make my job worthwhile. I don't know how much satisfaction this will give that little girl's family, but at least they'll know her killer remains in jail. He can't take another life again, because he will be incarcerated."

Lily went over to her desk and sat down.

"Can you imagine Michael Taylor, tried to use the defence that Rockwood was not drunk. Just tired? He claimed Rockwood drank only after the accident, while driving his company's truck; so the company couldn't possibly be responsible,"

"I believe you told me that before," Colleen commented, "However I'm glad you proved he'd drank so much before getting in the truck. That proved he was legally under the influence when the accident occurred. I hope I was some help in that aspect."

"Yes, you were invaluable."

A Penny Saved a Murder Earned

"Thanks, Lily."

"It's still early; only nine forty-five, and my day's clear until what, two-thirty?"

"That's correct." Colleen replied.

Colleen checked a day planner, frowning, "Is everything okay, Lily? You seem a little down."

"Everything is fine. Amelia's grand opening starts at noon, but I promised to be there sooner if possible. If I go right now, I'll surprise her," Lily grabbed her coat to leave.

"I'm glad she's doing so well. Although after what happened, Amelia needs the encouragement. Please tell her, I'll try to get to her store another day. I hope her store has great success."

"Thank-you, I will tell Amelia. Hold all my calls Colleen. Unless it's urgent then call my cell."

"I'll do that. What time should I say you'll be back?" Colleen responded to a departing Lily.

"Tell whoever asks that I'll be back after two p.m..."

"And if they ask where you are?" Colleen questioned.

"Tell them I'm meeting with a witness," Lily replied with a wink.

"If there's cake bring me back a piece. Please, boss?" Colleen begged.

"I ordered a cake, but it's not supposed to arrive until one thirty so we'll see. I'm leaving now. Remember only urgent calls to my cell phone." Lily cautioned, leaving through the front door.

She twisted her shimmering brown hair back up into its traditional bun. Pulling out her cell phone, she dialled Amelia's store. There was no answer. How odd! Amelia must be busy putting out last minute stock.

~0~

A few minutes ago

Alone male walked into the store. His left hand held a gun while his right hand steadied it. He strode in with caution. His dark brown eyes dart from corner to corner, searching for an assailant. His well over six-foot tall frame slouched. Ruggedly handsome, with dark brown hair clipped short to his head; he was dressed in a dark blue jacket and dress pants; a badge is also clipped to his belt buckle. Finding the scene secure he putting his gun away and pulled a pair of gloves out of his suit coat pocket and a pair of booties, which he slipped on his shoes.

He checked the victim. No pulse. Advancing forward, he bent down to check the second woman; her phone still in her hand, her head bloody. He noted the second victim was still breathing, though unconscious. He looked around, as if waiting for someone. Deciding they weren't coming yet, he took out a mini recorder. He started scanning the scene and speaking aloud.

"This is Sergeant Detective Emmett Rogers. I am at the scene of a homicide, at Quirks, one forty five Maple Street. A woman lays sprawled out across the floor. The woman's arms are positioned underneath her, as if to break her fall.

The back of her head and her long blonde hair are streaked in rusty-brown blood, as well as her clothing below the hair. Blood pools across the floor spiralling out in two long streams. Footprints are noticeable, as if someone stepped through the drying blood. The weapon appears to be a pair of scissors, found beneath the victim. I have marked both of these."

The man spoke aloud as he walked around, carefully avoiding contaminating the evidence, by stepping over a paper cup.

"A coffee cup... possibly one of those lattes is overturned. I'm sure the forensics team can determine this if necessary. Its contents are also spilled on the floor and countertop. Coffee is spilled at the front door and possibly on the shoes. The second victim's shoes are not on the bruised victim, but on the floor. The shoes can be found near an overturned ladder, at the front door. It appears the woman, who appears unconscious, may have been carrying a ladder and toy stock to place on the shelves, when she slipped in the blood.

The man paused to think.

"This might be a setup by the second victim to cover the actual crime. The woman, however, seems to have the victim's blood all over her clothes and hands like she crawled through the blood. I believe there are two possible scenarios here. One the owner of the shop, one Amelia Kelly (the unconscious person), murdered her employee or unknown victim and set this up to appear a perpetrator broke in and killed her accidentally hurting herself in the process. Or two... it is at it now seems that she stumbled on the crime scene and harmed herself."

He pulled out a notebook again and examined the room taking some more taking notes.

"Is it a robbery gone wrong? It is too soon to tell. The store owner will be en-route to hospital as soon as the EMTs have arrived. Interview to follow. The time is now ten twenty a.m.," he concluded turning off his recorder.

He examined the room scribbling on his notepad.

~0~

Now

Lily and Detective Emmett Rogers

T he man's eyes turn and his vision

focused completely. A woman entered the store. His eyes took in her tall and slender form and her long shimmering brown hair, pulled into a tight roll. He noted she was closely followed by the Emergency technicians and gave a sigh of relief. The woman entering the store had brilliant blue eyes. He had a feeling she often turned heads, even dressed as she was, in her business attire. But he noted something about the way she walked screamed money and upper class.

"Oh no, Amelia!" she screamed and tried to rush to Amelia, but was stopped by the man's arm.

"This is a crime scene ma'am. We don't want you disrupting our evidence. Let the EMTs and detectives do their job. Then you can go to ...you're er...friend?" Sergeant Detective Rogers commanded.

"Crime scene? What has happened?" Lily asked politely, wanting to be cooperative.

"Ma'am, I'll know better after I assess the scene. Until then, please remain near the front door." ordered Detective Rogers briskly.

"I promise I'll stay out of the way; but at least can I get her Adrienne Changs?"

"What or who, are Adrienne Changs?" said Detective Rogers looking totally perplexed.

"Shoes, those shoes right there!" Lily pointed to a pair of heels lying behind the yellow tape.

"You're worried about shoes? Woman! Do you have any idea of what's going on here?" Detective Rogers snapped, shaking his head.

"You sexist pig!" countered Lily under her breath.

"Men!" Losing her temper now and louder she continued, "Those shoes are worth five hundred dollars! And she probably wore them for what a half an hour? And you want me to walk away and leave them to be destroyed in some kind of liquid!"

"Liquid that's blood! And five hundred dollars for shoes? Is she crazy?" Detective Rogers asked dumfounded.

"No! She's not crazy. How dare you?" Lily asked suddenly outraged.

He was smug wasn't he? Handsome yes, but oh so smug, she questioned herself. That wasn't important. Amelia was injured on the floor and he questioned her? Instead of letting her go to her cousin! What was wrong with Lily? Why was she so worried and focused on the shoes? They were only shoes. Amelia was injured; who cared about footwear?

"Sorry, ma'am, the shoes are evidence now. Name? Occupation? Address?" Detective Rogers barked, ignoring her statement.

"I want to see your identification first, and then you'll get the information," insisted Lily.

"I am Sergeant Detective Emmett Rogers," the man revealed, showing his police badge.

"Oh that's funny," Lily uttered laughing, "If you and Amelia were introduced it would be Aem and Em."

Lily followed this up by hysterically laughing and then alternatively crying. What was wrong with her? She never lost it like this. She always appeared a professional. She had seen crime scenes. She could handle this. Couldn't she? Amelia would be okay. Wouldn't she?!

"Get a hold of yourself Lily. You have embarrassed yourself," Lily heard this voice in her head, she recognized as her father's. Odd how her Dad's voice, came back to her now, she rarely saw him, since he lived in Prague and he only called about twice a year.

"Ma'am, what you are saying is not remotely funny. Are you all right? Put your head between your knees if you feel lightheaded. I think your friend's relatively fine. She might have a head injury and possibly a broken leg, but she'll be okay." Sergeant Detective Rogers then turned to the Emergency technicians (EMTs) to seek confirmation demanded ,"Right?"

"Should be. But head injuries can be serious," the one EMT replied.

Sergeant Detective Rogers shot him a disapproving look.

"Yes, the Sergeant Detective is right. She'll be fine. She'll be taken to the hospital for treatment," the Emergency Technician agreed, finally.

"See...what did I tell you? Now that we have that out of the way; I need to see some identification and then get some answers to my questions. Name? Address? Occupation? The reason you are here?" Detective Rogers barked at Lily.

"Amelia's my best friend and more. This should have been the greatest day of her life, her opening of her new store; a one of kind toy and collectibles retailer. A grand opening and now it's ruined. Who did this to her?" Lily asked, uncharacteristically wringing her hands and still trying to regain her calm, as thoughts of Amelia's demise threatened to enter her mind.

"Ma'am, she slipped in blood. She hit her head on the floor and on the ladder. No one harmed her. She did this to herself," explained Sergeant Detective Rogers.

"I realize she's clumsy, but she didn't put blood there to trip in," defended Lily angrily.

"No, the blood was spilled by whoever killed the woman behind the counter."

"Someone is dead behind the counter?" Lily responded shocked and surprised.

"No comment; as I explained Ma'am this is an active crime scene. Now as I asked before what is your name?" Detective Rogers insisted forcefully again.

"Lily Kelly-Brooksfield. My husband is Horace Brooksfield, the mayor. We live down the street on Beaconfield. Do you want the number? It's nine hundred and sixty-two." she replied condescendingly.

"If you're Mayor Brooksfield's wife… then you're the Crown Attorney." Coming to this realization, Sergeant Detective Rogers hid a sigh.

"Please update me on this active crime scene, now," commanded Lily pulling back her shoulders.

Emmett Rogers put on his professional face and smiled. The smile was just so warm and inviting that Lily felt warm all over. Lily frowned back at him; she was just felt so angry. This cop who grinned back at her was the biggest reason. She was a married woman. She shouldn't be attracted to a cop who apparently existed to give her grief and solve a murder. She threw back her shoulders again. It was okay to look at someone attractive, she excused herself. Everyone looks, and most of the time it meant nothing. It's only if you acted on any attraction it became wrong. She would never act on the temptation. Besides he appeared to be the most annoying man she'd ever met.

"Ma'am, you know I can't fill you in on any of this case. You'll have to recuse yourself from this case, as you're familiar with the crime scene." Detective Rogers emphasized, once again interrupting Lily's thoughts.

"Why don't you just come out and say what you think. You consider me a suspect," Lily uttered.

"A lot of people are suspects in my book. I have to make a case for them committing the crime or I have to eliminate them as suspects. And don't attempt to solve this yourself; amateurs just get in the way." Detective Rogers explained, his eyes wandering.

Lily was slightly amused. Detective Rogers thought she wanted to insinuate herself into this murder investigation? She might not have before that comment, but she did now. He seemed to be focusing on Amelia or Lily as his prime suspect. Lily knew neither of them had committed this murder, so that meant she had no choice but to find out for herself who had committed this crime. She would pretend she wanted nothing to do with this situation, even as far as passing it off to her underling Barbara. After all she could always investigate behind the scenes.

Spotting the emergency technicians Detective Rogers exclaimed "Oh good, the ambulance has arrived to take the victim to the hospital. Now can we can get down to brass tacks; you can fill me in on these people and anything else you know or have held back from me."

"I want to go with her," Lily protested.

Lily pulled herself back taking several steps back putting distance between herself and this cop. It was odd, how alive she felt when she jousted with him. He was a cop investigating a murder and she was married.

"Stop this now Lily!" She told herself.

"Ma'am, I realize you want to go see your friend. Before I could release you from the scene, I need something from you. We need you to identify the other victim. Maybe you'll recognize her when I turn over the body." Detective Rogers explained, softening a little, as he slipped on another pair of gloves.

"Only if you'll stop calling me Ma'am. Call me Lily or Crown Attorney Kelly, but not Ma'am. It makes me feel eighty years old."

"If it will get you to identify the victim...thank-you Crown Attorney Kelly." "Let's look, shall we?" Lily agreed.

Lily took a breath as she gathered herself to observe who lay there dead. She gasped as she stared over the counter to see the back of the woman's head. She covered her mouth in horror.

"Good grief! I never realized they appear so alike from the back," replied Lily shocked.

"Who do you think she looks like ma'am?" demanded Detective Rogers.

"What did I say about ma'am? Don't they give you sensitivity training at Police College? You want to know who this is? This is Megan, Megan Fowler. She's an employee of Amelia's. But she works evenings she's...is....was a college student. I can't believe this is Megan. Megan is such a sweet girl and worked part-time to be able to go to school and support her mother. Why would someone kill her? Do you think it's possible someone mistook her for Amelia?" Lily rambled, tears slipping from her eyes.

"That's a possibility, ma'am. We will explore all aspects."

"I know the drill, Sergeant Detective Rogers." Lily gave the detective a mock salute, "Why can't you admit that they mistook Megan for Amelia?"

"We don't have any of the facts yet, Ms. Kelly," replied Detective Rogers.

"What about Amelia? Is she in any danger?" asked Lily. "If I were to speculate, I suppose that could be a possibility," Detective Rogers answered non-committally.

They both watched as the technicians gathered the evidence and blood samples and took pictures before the body was taken away.

"Will someone be assigned to guard her and keep her safe?" Lily asked getting exasperated.

"That's in motion, Crown Attorney Kelly," Detective Rogers explained, trying not to sound annoyed that she's telling him how to do his job.

Detective Rogers and Lily turned as another cop swaggered into the store. Burly and well over six feet tall, his hair was dark like Detective Rogers. Unlike Detective Rogers, this man preened like a peacock; Lily was aware of the type. Guys like him smiled with their mouths and not their eyes. They thought all women should admire them and only them. She noted his smile went as far as his lips.

"What have you got here, Emmett?"

"Nothing you need to be concerned about, Brad," Detective Rogers replied, obvious tension showing between the two.

"You should be able to get some great publicity out of this one," Brad said loudly to Detective Rogers.

Brad then strutted over to the murder scene.

"It's my case, Brad," Detective Rogers insisted.

"I'm not trying to interfere," Brad persisted walking around, "I just thought if you needed some help I would lend a hand. It doesn't look like something you could handle on your own."

"I don't need help, thanks, Brad. I don't need you messing up my crime scene." Detective Rogers declared "I've got it all under control.

"It doesn't look that way to me. I would solve this case quickly. You could use me in your corner," Brad continued.

"We don't need you. Now the Crown attorney is here, so I have it all in hand. Goodbye, Brad." Detective Rogers practically spat.

"Ah, the lovely Crown attorney Kelly is here. Can't go now," Brad exclaimed trying to sound charming but failing miserably.

"And you are?" asked Lily putting her full aristocratic chill in to her voice, "I'm Brad Owens, at your service, Attorney Kelly. Sergeant Detective Brad Owens. I use to be Emmett's partner," Brad explained smiling and pointing to Detective Rogers.

Detective Rogers rolled his eyes. "Thank God you're not anymore," He stated under his breath loud enough for only he and Lily to hear.

"So what do you think, Crown Attorney? Was it a robbery gone wrong?" asked Brad.

"I'm not sure. Why do I bother to tell you this? This isn't your case," Lily commented suddenly not willing to share with Brad.

She didn't know why. Something about his smile, and the way Emmett Rogers had reacted to him made her dislike him. Brad's smile was phony, like a used car salesman. It was slick and slimy. That wasn't fair to used car sales people. Lily was sure they were more honest than this phoney, Brad Owens. Lily had come across a lot of people in her job. She certainly felt she was a good judge of character. In fact, she could spot a phoney a mile away. Detective Emmett Rogers, unlike Brad Owens, appeared like he knew his job. She'd heard of him many times, but had never run into him on the job until today. Thank goodness for the Internet on her phone. He was a dedicated cop. He had done his time and had come up through the ranks, strictly on merit. Detective Rogers didn't seem to like Brad Owens and that was reason enough for Lily not to trust him.

Emmett Rogers had an exemplary record as a police officer; she trusted his instincts and knowledge over this smarmy, Detective Brad Owens. He'd get to the bottom of this. Lily wished he would let her leave soon and check on Amelia. They had spent their teen years together and were as close as sisters. She'd always felt responsible for Amelia, being two years older. She wanted to make sure Amelia was okay.

"Okay. Well if you don't need my help, I'm leaving because I have work to do. There are other crimes to investigate." Brad answered leaving, "See you around Emmett."

"Not if I see you first," muttered Emmett under his breath.

"So am I free to go?" Lily demanded.

Emmett then offered her his pen.

"I have your address, so as long as you sign here in my notebook. "You are free to go," he said gesturing.

Lily glanced over at Detective Owens and watched him leave before reaching for the book. She then signed her signature with a flourish. Detective Rogers scanned the signature, thinking momentarily it was just as elegant as Lily. He shook his head,

reminding himself to stay connected to
reality.

"So I am free to go, Detective?" Lily
repeated.

"I'll be checking in on your friend, of
course, and I may need to follow-up with
you later, but as of now, you are free to go."
he smiled, already exhausted.

"I would expect nothing else from you,
Detective Rogers."

As she got into her car, Lily breathed a sigh
of relief she had finally been able to leave
the store. She buckled up her seatbelt and
put her car in gear.

Backing the car up, Lily pulled out into the
street and narrowly missed getting hit by a
car, she didn't view. Luckily the other driver
slammed on his brakes. She noticed the male
driver shouting, "Stupid woman driver" as
she read his lips in her rear view mirror. He

was justified in his anger. It had been her fault, but she didn't have time to dwell.

She headed down the road toward the hospital; despite her resolve her mind wandered. She thought about poor Megan's mother getting the news of her daughter's death. It would kill Lily to get news like that about her adopted daughter, Rose. What kind of monster kills a young woman? Why did, whomever it was, have to kill Megan? It wasn't a robbery, she'd read in Detective Rogers' notes, when he gave his notebook to her to sign her statement. As Lily drove, more questions flooded into her head. Was Amelia the real target? Megan certainly appeared like Amelia from the back.

Amelia didn't appear too hurt. Maybe she suffered a concussion? Concussions could be serious; she knew from her readings. The EMT hadn't said Amelia was in serious condition though. Not that the EMT could explain before Emmett Rogers got on his case. Revving the engine, she waited impatiently for the light to go green. Once

Lily reached the hospital, she could reassure herself, Amelia was all right.

~0~

Chapter 2 - In Capable Hands

"Y ou're awake! I went out for coffee…I'm so glad you're okay," Lily exclaimed, as she entered Amelia's hospital room and sat on the edge of her hospital bed.

"Who did they find, Lily? Who was killed in my store?" asked Amelia, her eyes filled with tears and horror.

"I'm so sorry Amelia, it was Megan they found dead," Lily replied with great sorrow.

"Why would anyone kill Megan? I always told her if anyone ever wanted the money in the till, give the money to them. Why would they kill her for a few measly dollars?"

"There wasn't any money missing Aem."

"No money missing? But someone killed Megan. Why did they kill her, if not for the money?"

"I'm sure they'll find out who killed her."

"I'm so scared. I crawled in blood and then realized somebody lay injured... and I couldn't save her. Now that I know it was Megan, who was dead..., this hurts even more," Amelia rambled crying.

"I'm always here for you, Amelia," Lily affirmed hugging her. "I'm sure they'll fix up your leg and send you on your way soon. As for investigating the crime…they will be caught, whoever did this."

"That will be enough, Crown Attorney Kelly. Please don't discuss this with her until I speak to the witness," Detective Rogers announced from the door breaking in on their conversation.

Detective Rogers strode in and sat down in the chair next to the bed taking out his notebook; pen poised in hand he looked expectant.

"Witness to what? I'm no witness! I found my dearest friend and employee dead. It doesn't make me an onlooker to the killing! I didn't see the murder or the murderer."

"Ma'am, sometimes the little things help the most. Let me introduce myself. I'm Sergeant Detective Emmett Rogers and I am in charge of this case."

"Is it true someone killed Megan, but didn't take the money in the cash register?" demanded Amelia shaken.

"The victim is one Megan Fowler. Your employee?" questioned Detective Rogers, ignoring what Amelia said.

"Yes, but I have no idea why anyone would harm her."

"We'll get back to your ideas of who would harm her later. I need details. For instance what time did you arrive?" prodded Detective Rogers.

"About nine thirty I think! I'd gotten a coffee first; one of those cappuccinos." replied Amelia.

"This would be the coffee cup we found overturned and spilled all over the floor? Good! Now can we can discount the cup as not belonging to the victim."

"No, the coffee cup was definitely mine. I think I knocked the cup off the counter, when I fell."

"Did you perceive anything different, perhaps something out of the ordinary which had been moved?"

"Well, the door slightly ajar opened easily, but I didn't notice anything out of place. I did observe the mail had not only arrived early, but was also scattered in front of the door. That was weird," answered Amelia remembering.

"The mail arriving early; that stood out as a new occurrence? This had never happened any other time?" Detective Rogers noted.

"No, it wasn't a new occurrence. Philip, who's the mailman, cares about his job. He has a set schedule and he doesn't usually get to the store until about half past ten," Amelia explained.

"We did find mail scattered all over the floor. I thought maybe you'd dropped the mail, Ms. Kelly."

"Good detective work, I did drop the mail. I picked up the mail and I tripped and let go of the letters all over again," Amelia admitted.

"I see," replied Rogers writing this all down. "Did you have any differences of opinion with anyone recently? Remember before you answer the question, if you lie to a police officer this is a criminal offense."

"How dare you?! Amelia has answered all of your questions honestly," Lily responded, outraged on Amelia's behalf.

Lily thought at this moment she had been sadly mistaken. She wasn't attracted to this Neanderthal. He had no grace or couth, he acted like a relentless robot. Lily observed the way Detective Rogers grilled Amelia and she did not like it.

"I'm trying to do my job, ma'am. She knew the victim. She may have had words with Megan Fowler. Megan Fowler could have been a bad employee. Or Megan may have been taking money from the cash register; Amelia got angry and killed her. Then she staged the scene a little too well to cover her crime."

"You should do your job and realize Amelia was a victim here too. Whoever killed her employee managed to injure her, because she slipped in Megan's blood and hurt herself!"

Lily clenched her fists then hid them realizing she was showing him how angry he was making her. The radio on Detective Rogers' shoulder suddenly made a noise; a garbled voice, only Detective Rogers seem to understand.

"Rogers here! Yes sir, I am on my way," he replied into the radio. "I need to go. Duty calls. This conversation is not finished. I will return Ms. Kelly, Ms. Brookfield. Please, do not discuss this any further,"

Detective Rogers demanded, placed a card in Lily's hand and left the hospital room.

"What do you think the meaning of the call was?" Lily asked puzzled.

"Police business?" commented Amelia with a smile.

"Yes, I think so. At least the call wasn't about you."

"Why would he get a call about me? I've done nothing wrong."

"You're the prime suspect, until they clear you."

"Me? But all I did was find her," protested Amelia.

"That's right you found her!"

"He's insinuating that I am guilty? Oh no, I am a suspect. Aren't I? But what do they think I deliberately tripped? I hit my head and broke my leg, to look innocent?" Amelia realized.

"The person who finds the body is always deemed guilty first. They'll clear you," Lily replied, sounding more confident than she felt.

"They had better. Oh poor, poor Megan. Here I worry, I am considered a suspect, but she's dead," Amelia answered with remorse.

"Does she have any other family?"

"No, merely her mother."

"Oh no, her poor mother! Megan was barely twenty-one. And she's is or she was an only child."

"Doesn't matter whether you're an only child or not when a mother's grieving. As you are too aware," said Lily sadly, "Such a sweet girl. She always had a kind word for me when I called for you on the phone. I can't believe anyone would harm her, and yet someone did."

"I don't know what I would have done if you hadn't let me come live in your coach house, when Jack and Sam died. I nearly lost my mind and eating didn't even occur to me. If you hadn't brought me food and talked to me and given me a place to stay...," Amelia broke off, tears streaming from her eyes.

"You are my best friend and cousin; you would have looked after me." "You are always there for me. I'm the harbinger of death."

"Amelia, you know none of what has happened is your fault. Jack and Sam dying was an accident. Should I request an appointment for you again with Dr. Jones?"

"I'm not breaking down again. You need not worry. I'm coping, honest. If I wasn't I'd make an appointment. Thanks anyway, Lily, for caring and being my friend."

"Hey, want me to find out when they'll let you out of here?" asked Lily.

"Maybe they'll let me go home today… but I don't know how I am about to climb those stairs to my apartment in your coach house."

"You'll come and stay with us. We own an extra room on the ground floor."

"Are you sure Rose and Horace won't mind?" asked Amelia.

"Rose will love to have you in the house and Horace, well he always does what I want," replied Lily triumphantly.

"You sometimes take that man for granted."

"Never. He's always satisfied," Lily saucily responded.

"Too much information Lily! TMI !"

"The information made you smile didn't it? Now I'll go find a doctor and find out what's going on and how long you need to stay."

Lily walked into the hospital corridor, finding two interns. The first was a young woman, petite, five-feet tall, with a long white coat over green scrubs. A stethoscope hung gingerly around her neck. The second male doctor towers over her at six feet tall. He slouched to accommodate her. He too was dressed in a white coat over green scrubs. He looked nervous but tried to hide his unease.

"Hello. I'm Dr. Yvonne Stupna. I attended you, when you were first brought into the hospital. We are in charge of your case," announced the female doctor to Amelia.

"I'm Dr. Bob Stern," the male introduced himself, with confidence in his voice.

"Pleased to meet you, now can I go home?" impatiently, demanded Amelia.

"Not quite yet," replied Dr. Stupna.

"When can I go home then?"

"Let me put this in layman's terms. You've had a concussion…"

"A knock on the head." Dr. Stupna explained interrupting, resulting in earning her an annoyed look from Dr. Stern, who had tried to be subtle, but was unsuccessful in his attempt.

"A severe loss of consciousness." continued Dr. Stern interjecting, "You fractured your tibia and fibula. The tibia, a weight-bearing bone, supports the leg, so it is certainly a severe break. We put in a plate to reinforce the tibia. This is a dynamic compression plate and it will mold to the surface of your leg. This adapts to hold the tibia bone better. The plate is put in and screws lock it in place."

"You want to do surgery, on my leg?" Amelia asked sounding terrified.

"Yes, but this is simple surgery these days," Dr. Stupna reassured Amelia.

"I'm sure these doctors completed this surgery many times, to great success," Lily volunteered.

"We perform many surgeries of this kind," Dr. Stern agreed smiling.

Lily just nodded her head in Amelia's direction as if to say, see.

"These are serious conditions though. We'd like to go ahead and schedule the surgery. We will see how you are healing by keep an eye on you for a couple of days. Then if we believe you're in no danger we'll send you home," Dr. Stern explained.

Dr. Stupna seemed to take issue with this and took Dr. Stern to one side. Amelia and Lily watched them whispering. Dr. Stupna seemed to be the senior doctor and she tells him "You have a terrible bedside manner. You never tell patients there is danger. Your bedside approach needs a lot of work."

Lily and Amelia look at each other; then they both suppressed a chuckle.

"We do good work you'll be fine," answered Dr. Stupna, smoothing over Dr. Stern's blunder. She patted Amelia's hand and abruptly left taking Dr. Stern.

"Doctors they are all the same," Lily claimed "They always err on the side of caution. Why don't you just rest and I'll be back to see you tomorrow."

Lily looked at her watch, well aware she had to get back to work, but hated to leave.

"I hate hospitals," complained Amelia loudly.

"I understand. I hate visiting them too. There are too many bad memories in this hospital. I'll even bring you breakfast before I head into work tomorrow. Lily promised feeling guilty.

"I appreciate how bad the food can be here,"

"Thanks, Lily, but you better check first. I may be having the surgery tomorrow." Amelia replied yawning.

Lily left the room troubled and worried. After all, shouldn't there be a police officer guarding Amelia's room? Amelia may have been the target and she was unguarded.

Anyone could walk right in without being stopped. Shaking with anger, she took out the card Sergeant Detective Rogers had placed in her hand, picked up her cell phone, and called but was interrupted by Detective Rogers appearance outside the room.

"Why isn't there a guard on Amelia's door? Do you want Amelia to be killed?"

"Sorry, ma'am, I was overruled. I was told it wasn't justified."

"Not justified? That's ridiculous." Lily claimed, "Amelia could be in grave danger."

"I agree, but with the cutbacks, they decided the cost wasn't necessary," answered Detective Rogers.

"What kinds of idiots run your department?" Lily indignantly asked.

"I'm sorry, I really did try," Detective Rogers apologetically replied.

"Well you didn't try hard enough."

"There have been a lot of cutbacks, since your husband took over as mayor. You should take up the issue with him. We've been slashed so much our budget has to be kept for policing, not guarding, I'm sorry to say," Detective Rogers replied with a sarcastic tone.

Lily thought "Stupid jerk! Now he's bringing Horace into this. How dare he? What, did he think being the mayor came easily and making cutbacks to a shrinking tax base made Horace smile? Besides Horace found extra funds for the police department. He'd told her so. Who did they think they fooled with this 'we have no money stance'? She'd tell him, he lied.

"You don't sound sorry at all. I thought you might worry about Amelia. I know I am worried about her. What if the killer comes after her, will you cite your budget cuts?" Lily pointed her finger at him, but what she really wanted to do was hit him she was so angry.

This was ridiculous she wasn't a violent person. She didn't do things like that. Why was she allowing him to make her so angry? She had to start thinking more clearly.

"Look I said I'm sorry. I am. When we can't provide what the public needs, we are just as upset as you are, or more than you are. I have no control over this. If I did she'd be guarded. I've been told there's no money for it. I explained this. I can't do anything about it. I'm truly sorry, Ms. Kelly," Detective Rogers admitted, overly apologetic.

"Thanks anyway. I know you tried," Lily acknowledged, realizing Emmett Rogers could be telling the truth, but why had Horace lied to her?

She needed to talk to Horace later about this, but meanwhile she needed to make peace with Emmett Rogers. Being adversarial wouldn't help Amelia.

"I'm going to tell Horace his budget harmed policing and how he must find funding for the police department. But I'm not promising anything; Horace is his own man. Now I'll let you get back to the case. I do, however, want a full report to my office. The information has to be sent to my colleague, the assistant crown attorney Barbara Franks. She will be handling this case, since I can't."

"I'll send you the report to you for now. You can recuse yourself if necessary."

"Thank you, Detective Rogers. I appreciate you trusting me with the report." Lily answered surprised. "I will do everything in my power to show your trust was warranted."

"Goodbye, Ms. Lily Kelly."

"Goodbye, Detective Rogers!" Lily exclaimed firmly, shutting her cell phone and went to sit on a bench to think.

She wondered if the man flirted with her. The way Detective Rogers said Lily was oddly flirtatious. He knew she remained married, to a man she loved. He stood investigating a case; did she imagine he liked her? She hoped she was. She couldn't handle a flirtatious cop.

Lily loved Horace but they had their difficulties of late. He was so distant and aloof, the demands of the job. High pressured jobs like being the mayor of Happy Valley came with a lot of responsibilities and time required, and all those money woes the city was suffering wasn't helping. If she was patient and loving it would all work out. At least she hoped it would. Horace couldn't help the time his mayoral job leached from his family. She and Rose tried to understand but Rose suffered from Lily and Horace constantly working late hours.

Poor Rose. Lately she felt like they both neglected their daughter. Lily arranged with the office to cut back on some of the hours at work. Rose was a teen and some people thought teens could basically raise themselves. Lily knew that was ridiculous. Teens needed time and guidance. Good kids got in trouble too when they were neglected. If Lily wanted to be the mother (she promised Horace, Rose and Rose's biological mother) she would be, she must step up more and give Rose more time. Horace promised no more late nights when council wasn't meeting, but he hadn't lived up to his vow yet. When she confronted him about it last night, he promised he would fix the problem this week. She'd wait and see if he'd do it.

Should she call him and let him know about Amelia? She should call Horace, but Horace felt she spent too much time dealing with Amelia and Amelia's problems.

He'd changed so much since they got
married six years ago. He used to understand
and admire her devotion to her family. In
fact he said her devotion to her family was
one of the reasons he loved her most. Lately
however he seemed so cold and distant from
her; like he was mad at her. When she tried
to talk to him about what bothered him he
apologized and brought her roses and she
would let it go. She guessed all marriages
went through this. It seemed the honeymoon
was over for Horace and Lily. Could there
be someone else? No she wouldn't imagine
things an affair on his part; he didn't have
the time for someone else. He barely had
time for Lily and Rose.

Marriage was work people said, so a little
work was in order. They would be happy
again. What they needed was a family
vacation? First just a couple of days for just
Lily and Horace followed by a family
vacation? Why not? Summer was here and
she was owed time off... but what about
Amelia? Who would look after her?

Grandma Katha would! Yes, a good plan
and they would all be happy again. She
hoped Rose didn't find out at school what
had happened, for she wouldn't get home
until late. She must make up for the time she
took to go to Amelia's grand opening; that
didn't happen. She should talk to Horace
about taking time off and tell him about
what happened before he heard it from
someone else.

Lily dialed Horace's cell phone. There was
no answer, only his voice mail. Damn. Why
didn't he answer his phone? Lily then called
his private line in his mayoral office.

"Mayor Brooksfield's, private line. How
may I help you?" Horace's secretary Amber
Tate answered.

Something about Horace's administrative
assistant rubbed Lily the wrong way, but
Lily always found herself being polite.
Amber constantly forgot to give Horace
messages from Lily. This angered Lily.
When Lily complained to Horace, he said

the woman was a little ditzy and couldn't help it. Horace explained Amber needed the job, as she supported her widowed mother, so Lily tried hard to give her a little more slack. It was so hard to accept why Horace kept her as a secretary when she didn't do her job well.

"Hello, Amber. It's Lily, Horace's wife. Can I speak with Horace?"

"No, I'm sorry Ms. Brooksfield, you can't speak with him-I mean Ms. Kelly. Sorry, I forgot again what you wanted me to call you." Amber replied in her usual scatterbrained manner.

"It's just Lily, remember Amber," prompted Lily politely but hiding her frustration with Amber.

Sometimes it seemed to Lily all an act, but what would be the point of Amber faking that she wasn't intelligent?

"Oh yes, sorry, I forgot. Now, your question?" Amber absently asked.

"Is Horace there? I'd like to speak to him." Lily repeated herself, chill seeping into her voice.

"No sorry. He's gone for the day. He won't be back until later and he has tons of work to do. He told me I have to stay late and type notes from the council meeting last night," Amber whined.

Lily wanted to explain to Amber that gone for the day and coming back later weren't the same thing, but that would mean she'd be on the phone forever with Amber, so she shelved the impulse.

"I had a date too and I cancelled," Amber woefully continued complaining.

"Oh, okay, thanks for the information, Amber. Bye," Lily replied cutting off the call before she lost her temper.

What, did the woman think her job only took place between nine and five? Lily hadn't wanted to hear Amber's carping. The last time Amber had been bemoaning her life and job Lily was on the phone with her for a half an hour. Never again, that was one half hour; Lily would never ever get back. Lily reluctantly left the hospital.

She was still worried about Amelia. She couldn't leave her here at the hospital unprotected. What if the killer had been gunning for Amelia? But who was she to call?

Then she remembered Frank Hawk. Frank owned a security firm. Since Lily had been instrumental in putting a woman stalker who wouldn't leave him alone behind bars; they had become good friends. Frank tried everything to keep this woman from stalking him, short of taking the law in his own hands.

His stalker had been inventive and always
had a reason for being nearby. Lily had been
able to prove not only the stalking but Carla
Carmelo's plan to kill Frank's wife
Georgiana. Now his stalker Cara Carmelo
served ten years for stalking and planning to
commit murder. Frank was so grateful; he
said if she ever needed a favour call him.
This counted as a favour and Lily needed
someone right away. Surely Frank would
help Lily. She would happily pay a salary to
whomever he sent.

"Hello, Frank? This is Lily Kelly. I have a
job for your firm. Have you heard about
what happened this morning? Yes... the
murder at my cousin's store? Great... uh
huh, that's right; I do need someone to guard
her. You are a lifesaver, Frank. That would
be wonderful. He'll be guarding a room at
the hospital, and of course Amelia. Okay
thanks, Frank, I owe you one," Lily
confirmed before she hung up her phone and
breathed a sigh of relief.

A half an hour later while waiting outside Amelia's room, Lily was approached by a man with shaggy red hair, tied up in a ponytail. His arms bulged with muscles and he looked like someone she would have pegged as a biker. With his tattoos and long hair, she was sure he belonged to one of the numerous biker clubs. Could this man be the murderer? Could she be judgemental and showing prejudice? No, she felt she was being fair; the man appeared scary looking like a biker.

"Hello, I'm Zachary Buchanan, the man Frank sent to guard your friend," the man explained.

Lily was astonished; she believed he was a thug. She shouldn't have judged him so harshly she thought. She stared at his muscular frame, his arms bulging from his tee-shirt. He appeared big, to the point of covering the entire door while standing in it. It was a good thing he was a bodyguard and not the murderer. This man looked and felt dangerous. Frank had come through in spades. This man would keep Amelia safe.

Lily would relax and get her work finished, and she could go home to Rose. Maybe she could even have a late dinner with Rose. That would be time well spent. Family dinners had been falling by the wayside too. Rose shouldn't be so neglected, but no more of the neglect she thought. Well no more after tonight.

"I'll keep her safe. Don't you worry," Zach replied in a low gravelly voice, as if reading Lily's thoughts.

"I'll leave her to your capable hands than." Lily replied greatly relieved, with one last look at a sleeping Amelia.

~0~

Chapter 3 - Keep the Home Fires Burning

Lily drove home with her mind

wandering; she thought about Rose. She had talked to Rose earlier to make sure she'd arrived home from school, but she still wanted to see her after such a horrific day. Lily felt guilty about not going straight home and going back to the office earlier, but Horace would be home with Rose.

The vacation she was about to surprise them with would make it up to them. When she had them both in the same room, she would present them with the vacation plans. She'd been able to rent a cottage from someone at work, who wasn't using it for the month of July. The cottage was on the beach up north, near Parry Sound, at some place called Osler's Lake. Lily had seen pictures and it sounded like an idyllic place to spend a month. They would be able to go swimming, canoeing and traipsing about enjoying nature. It would be wonderful to share family time with just the three of them. She hoped they would agree to go.

What had she been thinking? Of course they would agree to go; they would be happy to have time together. If Rose wouldn't go, they could always take Carol to keep her company. Carol was Rose's best friend and constant companion. Lily would convince Carol's parents to agree. Lily parked the car in the garage and entered the house smiling, thinking about the vacation.

Rose, her teenage daughter, fourteen years old, lounged in her pajamas in the living room. She had a bag of chips in her hand, a pop in the other hand, as she waited for her mother. Rose turned, spotted Lily, and ran to her. She pulled back as if she didn't want to appear babyish. Rose's long blonde hair streamed down her back as her brown eyes glittered with unshed tears of worry.

"So, Aunt Amelia, she's okay? Like that was scary." Rose asked flippantly, as if she didn't care, showing her true emotional state.

"She'll be fine, a little care..."

Rose interrupted raising her chin a little, "Aunt Amelia's had too much stuff happen to her. I thought she'd die when Sammy and Jack died. She didn't eat, she didn't sleep. She looked like a zombie. You're sure she's going to be okay?"

"I know you are worried, sweetie, but you must not be concerned. Aunt Amelia will be fine. She's going to be able to handle this. She's been through a lot of therapy to learn coping techniques. She will be okay. She has a bump on her head and she broke her leg, so they want to keep her for a while, but she's going to be okay," Lily replied, as much to assure her stepdaughter as she did herself.

"You're sure?" asked Rose.

Lily nodded her head and Rose continued pretending she didn't care.

"Well at least we won't have to take care of her." Rose then showed her true emotional state looking scared and confused as she continued, "Wait a minute, if someone killed Megan, what if they come after Aunt Amelia?"

"How did you know it was Megan?" asked Lily surprised.

"The news reported the victim; a college student worked at the shop. Aunt Amelia only has one college student working at her shop. It isn't the fifties where you hear everything, what two weeks later, Mom?" Rose snapped rolling her eyes, "I must have had fifty texts, from all my friends. My Spacebook and Chatter accounts overflowed; even strangers talked to me. "They all think I should be able to tell them something. I should unfriend all of them. Except now I'm popular. I think one hundred more people following me on Chatter."

"The news does get out there faster via Chatter and Spacebook. I hope you are not mad at your true friends, and you use caution talking to strangers on Chatter," warned Lily.

"Like duh! I don't talk to people I haven't met in person. Carol was the only one who didn't bug me. She came over for a while. I hope that was okay?"

"Of course I don't mind Carol came to our house. Carol is a good friend to you."

"So do you think someone was after Aunt Amelia?"

"Don't you worry; I hired someone to look after Amelia. No one will harm her," reassured Lily.

"Who did you get and from where? I hope you didn't just pick one from any place. Not all those security places are legitimate."
"Who is the parent here?"

"I do grasp some things. Good grief! What am I four years old? Georgia Prentice's father hired this one firm and his place was still robbed," Rose announced as a matter of fact.

"Who is Georgia Prentice?" Lily enquired. "She's this girl in my English class. Her dad, like has this business downtown, Prentice Pampered Pets. They sell pet foods. I'm surprised you didn't read about this. It was a big crime spree. Anyway, they hired this security firm her dad found on the internet or something and next thing you know they are robbed. They complained to the security place and they demanded money from them. Georgia's dad complained to the cops and their place went up in fire."

"Oh I remember this one Barbara Franks handled it last year. The security guard at the firm shook them down for money. We convicted him of arson and robbery, "Lily interrupted.

"So I hope you thought about who you hired," Rose announced, in all seriousness trying to sound adult.

"This firm is good; don't you worry. I hired the guard from Frank Hawk Security. They are one of the top security firms in the city, with a stellar reputation. The guard's name is Zachary Buchanan and he is muscular, so he can hold his own. He looks rough, but he's one of the good guys," Lily explained.

"Good because I think someone is out to get her. I don't understand why anyone would hurt her. Because you know, Aunt Amelia is so sweet and she wouldn't hurt a fly. Maybe she was too polite to someone?"

"She's kind and people tend to take advantage of her, but neither of us has to worry she'll be safe now. Was that your dinner? Pop and chips aren't a meal. Didn't your dad make anything or at least order some food? He knew I would be late tonight. He promised he would be here for you. He is here, isn't he?" Lily asked dreading the answer.

"No he didn't come home." answered Rose, "When I was little, before my mother went to a jail, he didn't come home early either. I'm getting used to having my evenings alone."

"Damn him!" Lily angrily replied, under her breath. Worried Rose had overheard her she continued, "I'm sorry sweetie. Your Dad has been trying hard to get home earlier and I should have come home sooner too."

"He does try, Mom. It's his stupid job,"
Rose defended.

"It's not a stupid job, it just demands too
much of his time, and he promised to rectify
the problem. It's odd though, he told me
he'd be home by six, it's nearly eleven now.
Where is he? If you had called me I would
have been home sooner," chided Lily.

"I had some cereal. No biggie."

"It is a biggie! I'm sorry I wasn't here. You
are always the first priority with me and
don't let me forget. Now I'm hungry; do you
want to share a pizza?" asked Lily hugging
Rose.

"I could eat something." Rose admitted.

"Is pizza okay?" Lily asked picking up her
cell phone "Do you want a cheese pizza?"

"Yes, cheese pizza sounds good."

As they waited for the pizza they each
thought about Amelia and how much she
meant to them.

"I must find someone to work at Amelia's store. Do you think any of your friends would like to work there part time?" asked Lily.

"You've got to be kidding Mom! Someone was murdered there. I don't think anyone would."

"I guess I'll head over to the employee agency. First thing tomorrow morning I'll put in an ad."

"How much would you pay per hour? I mean Carol and I could use the dough, and you would understand we were safe. Right?" asked Rose. "Carol and I found a cute bikini. The bikini fit me like it was made for me, but it costs mega bucks."

"I don't think I want you and Carol working there."

"Mom, please!"

"Well, I did think of hiring a guard for evenings to protect employees, so I guess that might work. Be sure to tell Carol the job will be alternate evenings, until nine p.m. I don't want you to get behind on your homework though, and I'll be happy to pick you up or Carol as well," replied Lily realizing she sounded overprotective.

"Gee thanks, Mom. I'll ask Carol."

Rose rushed off to call Carol, coming back a few seconds later and declared, "Carol says okay, as long as I can hang out with her sometimes as well. In fact, would you pay us to work the same shift?"

"If I did how much work would you get done? You two forget about other people, when you are together. Would you still pay attention to the customers?"

"What a stupid question. It's a job and I think if you think I'm mature enough to work there, then I'm mature enough to do the job," Rose protested.

"Sorry Rose you're right, sometimes I forget you're nearly an adult."

"Well try to remember, I'm fifteen, not five!" Rose exclaimed outraged.

"Now I must contact an employee agency in the morning. I need to find someone trustworthy to run the store until Amelia is able to come back. I still have to prepare my briefs, to prosecute the Teflon man as well. Ugh, I can't let this man get away with his crime again. I'm prepared. It will work this time, Andrew Clayton will get at the least twenty years to life," Lily explained absentmindedly as she goes over her notes.

"Who are you after now, Mom?" Rose ventured to ask not catching the man's name. "You know I don't like to discuss my cases."

"Well excuse me for asking!" Rose muttered under her breath, and Lily ignored her as the doorbell rang.

The pizza driver arrived at the door and Lily paid him taking the pizza in. Lily glanced over at the clock noting it is now 11:30 p.m., "Dinner eaten near midnight? It was a wonder she didn't get indigestion," she thought.

Each ate their pizza, savouring each bite, both of them thinking their own thoughts, in their own little worlds. The second pizza, a pepperoni pizza was put aside and saved in the fridge for Horace.

"I have to call your dad and find out what kept him. He should have been home a long time ago," Lily repeated, becoming extremely worried.

"He probably fell asleep at his office. I told you, his job keeps him too busy," Rose complained.

"I'm sorry. I'm going to try to get him to do a little less of worrying about his job and more of spending time with us, like he promised. Would you be okay if I left you and went and check on him?"

"Mom, I'm not a little girl anymore. I'll set the alarm after you leave and then I'm going to bed. I can see Dad tomorrow. I've got choir and basketball before class tomorrow."

"Okay, sorry. Sometimes it's hard to remember you're not my little girl anymore," Lily commented.

"Try, okay? I'm growing up; I'm not a little girl anymore. You have to remember that and you don't need to keep saying it," chided Rose.

"I'm leaving the house. Lock the door and set the alarm."

"Mom!" admonished Rose, thoroughly outraged.

"Sorry."

"Okay, bye Mom," Rose replied as she watched Lily leave.

Rose went to set the alarm on the front door and the windows heading up the stairs to bed.

~0~

Lily drove quickly to city hall. She parked the car in underground parking. Lily remembered suddenly that she had forgotten to call Grandma Katha about Amelia. She would call Grandma Katha tomorrow. Grandma Katha would be a little annoyed, but she'd understand.

She rode the elevator to the first floor. She then exited and walked towards the elevator that would take her to Horace's office. In the hallway, Lily saw a security guard sitting at the front desk. He wore a blue uniform with yellow tassels on his shoulders. A badge is pinned to his chest. He was about fifty-five years old, or maybe sixty. His hair was white and his eyes blue and twinkly when he smiled and it was obvious from his wrinkles that he did it frequently.

"Hello, Mrs. Brooksfield. I believe the mayor is in his office. Working late tonight; isn't he?" commented the security guard.

"Yes, he works too many hours. Your name is Barney? Isn't it?"

"You remembered?" Barney replied surprised.

"You tell Mr. Brooksfield I said he should spend more time with his charming wife, before someone else snaps her up and takes her home."

"Okay, I will." Lily answered.

Lily laughed and waved goodbye to the guard. She got into the private elevator which went to Horace's office. As she pushed the buttons, Lily thought of how wonderful it will be to be with Horace. She blushed when she thought of what they did the last time she was in his office behind locked doors. Thank goodness for the lock on his door!

The elevator stopped and opened into the foyers leading into Horace's mayoral office. Lily turned the doorknob to Horace's office slowly opening the door. She was horrified to find a naked Horace on top of his also naked secretary Amber, directly behind his desk.

"Horace, how could you?" Lily shouted, with no corresponding answer. Lily stared at the pair confused.

Were they so into each other, they didn't realize she was there? How long had this affair been going on with Amber? Lily wondered, tearing her gaze away from their naked forms.

Puzzled she thought why didn't they bother to lock the door? Or respond, when someone talked to them?

Lily realized neither moved. Lily skirted the desk and felt Horace's wrist.

His wrist was cold and there was no pulse. She realized, with great shock, Horace was dead and so was his secretary, Amber. The whole world tilted on its axis for a moment.

She was cold to the marrow of her bones;
her feet remained frozen to the floor. What
sent all this into play? First Megan murdered
this morning, now Horace and his secretary.
Truly horrifying, this all seemed unreal. She
half expected Horace to jump up and yell
"I'm joking!" But as she gazed back on the
scene, she saw it was all too real. Horace
and his secretary had both been posed
naked, as if committing the act of
copulation.

Examining the bodies, clinically putting
aside her horror and disbelief, Lily noted
they sported identical bruises on their skulls.
Looking intensely at their heads, it occurred
to her this was the death-blow. This mark
was in the shape of the top of the nearby
lamp. She thought about it for a moment and
grasped that they had been posed this way.

Horace would never cheat on me with
Amber. How could I have though this for
even one moment? Lily looking closer at
Horace's wound there was matted blood.
Did this mean a lot of time passed since they
were killed?

She had seen other autopsy photos in her job; they had shown wounds such as these and they had been killed several hours prior. But how long ago were Horace and Amber killed?

She tried to put the sight out of her mind. She looked at Horace dead, but bile threatened at any moment. She swallowed, took a big breath, felt faint and yet cold at the same time. She needed to do something now. What did she need to do? Oh yes, she needed to call the police she reasoned.

Lily picked up her cell phone, gagged back the sourness coming up from her stomach and called 911.

"Nine one, one, what is the nature of your emergency?" enquired the dispatcher.

"My husband and his secretary have been murdered," Lily answered her voice shaking, and barely audible.

"Repeat yourself, ma'am!" The police dispatcher demanded.

"I am at City Hall. I am in the Mayor's office. My husband, Mayor Horace Brooksfield has been murdered, along with his secretary, Amber Tate," Lily replied enunciating each word.

Lily felt slightly angry at this dispatcher who didn't seem to grasp the horror of this all.

"Did I hear you correctly, ma'am? The mayor has been murdered, at City Hall?" asked the police dispatcher, gasping and losing her composure for a few minutes.

"That is what I said," Lily answered angrily.

Lily then wondered what kind of police dispatcher gasped at hearing someone's been murdered. The woman sounded like she lost her calm, what did this bode for Lily? A lot of help she would be someone who didn't even understand her job.

"Are you still in the office?" The police dispatcher asked.

"Yes," Lily replied, quietly thankful the woman sounded like she had gotten back her composure.

"Is there any way the perpetrator might still be on scene?" asked the police dispatcher, as if following a script.

Lily remembered the wound and the matted hair with blood on each victim. It was so awful, but didn't mean they were probably long gone. Lily looked around scanning the room, but comprehended with heart palpitating fear that the killer could still be there. She didn't think the killer would be able to hide in this office. She could see all the spaces and no one was hiding. Lily comforted herself. She was safe. If you

killed someone wouldn't you want to be
gone so you weren't caught?

"I'll check to find out whether they hid in
the inner room of Horace's office," Lily
volunteered and regretted the impulse.

"Where is this inner room?" asked the police
dispatcher.

"There is a small sort of vestibule off
Horace's office so he can...er...might leave
privately. It leads to his private elevator,
only he has um... had a key to fit the lock,"
Lily explained.

Lily trembled and she felt a tear escaping
her eye.

"Have you touched anything?" enquired the
police dispatcher.

"I don't know. I simply don't know," Lily
replied getting a little frazzled.

"Take a big breath and think. You came in the office and did what?" asked the police dispatcher.

"Ah… The door was slightly ajar. I touched the doorknob and turned it throwing the door open wider. I then walked across the floor to check on them. I touched each of their necks, checking for a pulse," Lily remembered.

"Was there a pulse? Should I be sending an ambulance?" the dispatcher demanded.

"No, there is no pulse, it's definitely too late. I can't believe any of this has happened…Why would someone do this?"

"I don't know, ma'am. We will find the perpetrator. Do you have anything else our officers can use?"

"I don't know. I think they've been dead for a while. What should I do?" Lily demanded choking back more tears.

"What I would like you to do is to leave the office and wait directly outside if it's safe to do so. Please wait there for the investigating officer," commanded the police dispatcher, "And stay on the line."

"Okay I'll do that, but hurry, please." Lily answered, shutting her phone without thinking.

Lily shivered uncontrollably. Finishing her report to the police allowed her to think now of the finality of it all. Horace was dead. Her husband of six years was dead. It was like the icy finger of death reached out and touched her too. She felt cold, like she would never be warm again.

Lily then remembered what the police dispatcher asked of her and backed out of Horace's office trying to pull herself together. Lily did not want to disrupt any of the crime scene. She also knew she had to get away from the horrible sight of the man she loved dead. If she didn't she would never be able to answer the questions the police detective would invariably ask. Her mind began racing.

Why had Horace been posed in such a defiling way? Could this be a warning to her? Was this a way to discredit Horace and make him appear as an adulterer in his final moments? Poor Horace; he was such a wonderful man... Okay, so he wasn't perfect, but Lily loved him. How could this have happened? During the day the place was filled with security.

Lily had no idea how many security officers were assigned at night, but Barney seemed diligent. Was the only security at night Barney? Why hadn't Barney heard anything? Barney made everyone sign in at night, so how did they get in past Barney's eagle eye? Who perpetrated these crimes? First Amelia's clerk was murdered, now Horace and his secretary, Amber. This seemed personal, like someone was targeting Lily's family. Could it have been someone she prosecuted who had committed these murders?

Lily looked back through the door at Horace
and Amber's bodies in totally disbelief.
Horace couldn't possibly be dead. This had
to be all a horrible dream. Lily pinched
herself and realized with trepidation, this
was no dream. Horace was dead, posed
obnoxiously draped on his secretary. It was
too awful to look at. If she closed her eyes
this would disappear, or maybe if she shut
the door? No, she would be tampering with
evidence. She wouldn't do that, as much as
she wanted to close the entrance.

Oh no, the press! If the press took this sight
in...No, she wouldn't let whoever had done
this defile his good name too, as well as
taking his life.

Why wouldn't her brain work? What did she
have to do? Oh yes! She had to somehow
get a media blackout on this. Should she
make a call to Judge Parker? No, that would
have to wait until she talked to the
investigating officer.

She couldn't believe the thoughts she had, she should be falling apart; her husband was dead...Murdered...with his secretary.

What was wrong with her? She needed to protect Rose. Oh no, what would she tell Rose? Rose who already lost her biological mother? How could she bear to tell Rose, her father was dead? Her mind sped from thought to thought, like a freight train going seventy-five miles an hour. She didn't want to think about what lay beyond the open door. Maybe she should call the police dispatcher back? They asked her to stay on the line and she accidentally hung up the phone. Lily heard a voice interrupting her thoughts and jumped a couple of inches.

"Ms. Kelly-Brooksfield. we meet again," Sergeant Detective Rogers announced, entering the foyer and spotting Lily in the office.

He noted she only seemed to be held up by the wall.

"Sergeant Detective Rogers. Why have Megan, Horace and Amber been murdered? Is there a serial killer on the loose?" Lily demanded.

Lily then covered her eyes trying to block out the scene in front of her.

"Hmm, you're on the sight of both my murder scenes. Do you have an alibi, Ms. Kelly-Brooksfield?" Sergeant Detective Rogers challenged from the door.

"I'm a suspect?" gasped Lily, while holding herself up against the wall. She felt nauseated, shaken and nervous. Lily breathed in a huge breath and realized how bad this all looked for her, but she knew she had not committed this crime.

"Well it looks you're husband, Mayor Brooksfield, stepped out on you. You picked up something and bashed their heads in and then admired your handy work," Sergeant Detective Rogers insisted trying to provoke her.

Lily held her hand over her mouth, as if to stall throwing up her supper.

"Don't you dare hurl on my crime scene!" Detective Rogers exclaimed, "In fact I think you should come out into the hall until the crime techs arrive."

Lily couldn't seem to take in what Detective Rogers said. None of what he articulated seemed to make sense. Shivering, Lily felt like she would throw up again. Lily then took a deep breath to keep from spewing and started to think about Horace. She wouldn't believe the husband she'd loved and had been married to for six years lay dead…brutally murdered. She couldn't get the picture out of her head, despite her closed eyes. Horace's glassy eyes wide open in object terror and the same subsequent look in Amber's eyes, were ingrained in her brain.

With Horace's hair bloodied and brain matter coming out, it seemed obvious to her, someone had bashed him hard on the head. That had to be just as clear to Detective Rogers. Yet Detective Rogers kept looking at her as if she had done this horrible deed. Why did he think she had done this?

Amber and Horace had been naked. Why? Why would someone pose them that way? When you examined them you could tell they died from head wounds, so why set them up that way? Why did they the need to stage their bodies? For my benefit, or to discredit Horace and embarrass him even in death? Lily wondered as she looked at Detective Rogers through her long hair, now hanging down in front of her eyes. And why did the annoying Detective Rogers, keep fidgeting so? Why did he hop from foot to foot? Did he think that would intimidate her, or was he nervous?

"So we get this straight, what did you do tonight after all the questioning?" Sergeant Detective Rogers demanded.

"Let see...after giving my statement to you, visiting my best friend in the hospital and arranging a guard to protect her because the police wouldn't... I went home to my daughter!" Lily replied sarcastically.

"At what time did you leave the hospital and what time did you arrive home?" Sergeant Detective Rogers asked pulling out his notebook.

"I don't know. It must have been about what ten or ten-thirty p.m.? My daughter and I ordered pizza from Pizza Pie. The pizza arrived about eleven-thirty p.m. and I left about midnight to come here. I arrived here about twelve-thirty p.m. Check with the guard Barney something. He can tell you."

"The statement from the guard, one Barney Terrell says you arrived here about twelve thirty P.M. Is that when you took the elevator up and bashed their heads in and then decided to pose them?" Sergeant Detective Rogers provoked.

"How dare you? Someone killed my best friend's employee today. Megan Fowler, a girl in the prime of her life with her future spread out in front of her, found cruelly murdered. Then I found my husband and his secretary, Amber, also brutally murdered...and you treat all of this like a huge joke?" Lily ranted angrily gulping back tears and wondering why she found it hard to breathe.

"Horace was the love of my life. I feel like I've been ripped in two. Do you want to know about Amber? Amber supported her mother. How many young people support their parent? I have known her for years. Why aren't you doing your job and finding the person who did this? Why do you stand there looking at me like I did this dreadful thing?"

"I keep looking into this, and two and two, equal the wife killed him," Detective Rogers explained. "You should have studied math a little harder. I think we are done here, Detective Rogers. I'm not speaking to you anymore without my lawyer."

Lily thought Sergeant Detective Rogers was an idiot. Why didn't he see Horace and Amber had been murdered by a person unknown? Why did he keep looking at her?

Yes, the first person the police always looked at was the spouse, but it should be obvious Lily hadn't killed them. Yes, someone staged the murder scene and posed them naked but he couldn't think she had perpetrated this crime. Of course he did and he looked straight at her for this crime.

Lily suddenly realized Sergeant Detective Rogers had said something else as she reflected on all that had occurred. Now for some strange reason he started to look blurry. Lily's chest was tight, not with unshed grief, but with some sudden strain in her airways. Why can't I breathe? Lily thought with fear. She decided to tough this out, not wanting to give Detective Rogers ammunition to use falsely against her.

"Mrs. Brooksfield? Did you hear me? I asked you to come out of the office." Detective Rogers insisted looking at her strangely.

"Would you stand still? It should be obvious even to you, the great detective, that they were obviously staged ... I don't feel so good," Lily muttered her hand over her mouth.

"I'm not moving." Detective Rogers insisted.

"Why are there two of you?" Lily managed to say aloud before falling unconscious to the floor.

~0~

Chapter 4 - Media Hound

Detective Emmett Rogers looked over

surprised. Did she think faking a faint would keep him from investigating? Or did her nerves get to her? The woman seemed cool as a cucumber. If she had killed three people he would be surprised, but Emmett had been burnt before and he wasn't about to let a pretty face fool him.

Crap!

Now he had to violate protocol to check on her. He should be wearing the gear, so he didn't leave fibres. He only hoped this wouldn't screw up any evidence. He should have gotten her out of the office sooner. He checked her pulse. Yes she had a thready pulse but it was there. She didn't seem to be faking this faint. Had the stress of committing the murder got to her, or was she an innocent victim like she appeared?

"Dispatch, Sergeant Detective Rogers here. We need a bus." he said into his radio.

Emmett stared at the woman on the floor. What the hell. Who perpetrated these murders? First this woman's cousin's employee was murdered then the mayor, Lily's husband. Were Amelia and Lily Kelly the victims, or somehow the perpetrators? Were these two women involved in these crimes? Or were they involved at all? He started to wonder why he hadn't come across Ms. Kelly. He had talked with her legal assistant, Colleen, and the assistant Crown attorney, Barbara Franks, in many cases. Now she was a piece of work. Barbara Franks. Little Miss, or should he say, 'Mrs. Butter don't melt in her mouth' Brooksfield better watch her ass. Barbara appeared to be gunning for Ms. Brooksfield's job.

This case might give Ms. Franks the opportunity for advancement. He hoped he wouldn't be responsible for that happening. He had heard good things about the job Ms. Brookfield did. She had a great reputation for working hand and glove with cops to get the perpetrator convicted.

He had been told (before being called to her friend's store) the jury had come in on the Zebadiah Rockwood case, guilty on all counts. The attorney had come through in a tough case. The slime ball, the defense attorney, Michael Taylor's reputation was for winning all his cases and people paid big bucks for him to succeed. Taylor must be spitting mad and that made Emmett Rogers smile.

This Lily Brooksfield didn't seem competent at the moment however; she had lost it this morning and now this? Of course her friend appeared seriously injured this morning...or was that now yesterday? And now her husband was dead? He should have cut her some slack, but damned if the woman didn't rub him the wrong way. She appeared incredibly beautiful, but off-limits. Not only was she married, but she stood married to the mayor. Of course she was a widow now. Emmett smiled again as he looked at Lily. What the hell was he thinking? He was on a case. She was a suspect!!!

He focused on the case again. The air appeared decidedly odd in here. The air stank like rotten eggs or something he couldn't quite peg. Maybe Lily had collapsed not from shock and his questioning, but from these fumes? Should he take the woman further out into the hall and shut the door? Why did this have to be his decision? Where in the hell were the emergency technicians?

Oh good! The EMTs had arrived, he thought as he heard the elevator ping. They would take Lily Kelly-Brooksfield to the hospital and take away this responsibility he didn't want. What could be wrong with him? He couldn't think clearly. He had to shake off the fog and start thinking with a level head. This was a big case. The mayor had been killed, and not only killed; but killed with his mistress.

What a mess; and the wife found them. Heaven knows the wife was blamed in these circumstances, so why did he have such a hard time believing Lily Brooksfield had committed the crime? Emmett watched as they took Lily Kelly-Brooksfield away. How odd, even though she still remained a suspect, he was strangely attracted to her. Something about her sassy attitude turned his insides to Jell-O. He'd had to get tougher with her, to hide the attraction he felt for her.

This wasn't right. How could he be attracted to a woman he just met, a woman who up until tonight had been married? A woman who may have killed her husband? What kind of man did that make him? Hell, if anyone knew he had this mind-set he would be a suspect. Emmett, get a hold of yourself! What could you be thinking? The woman's husband was killed violently tonight. Either the woman is a grieving widow or a ruthless killer, either way she's not for you.

Emmett looked up from his deep thoughts and saw Dr. Andrew Piper (the coroner) arrive. The tall and thin coroner had a shock of red curly hair with a streak of white right down the middle of his head. As Emmett looked closer he noticed Andrew's white hair starting to pepper throughout his hair. Why had he never detected his friend, Dr. Andrew Piper, getting older? He noted however, that Dr. Piper was jovial and smiling, even in the face of this gruesome death. Emmett wondered how his old friend could remain so cheerful.

"Say, Doc how do you stand this?" Emmett asked, "How do you stay happy faced with all these dead bodies?"

"It's either smile or cry. I give these victims their peace after such horrible acts. I help catch their killers. I must admit though seeing someone you've met is a lot harder."

Doctor Andrew Piper answered, motioning to Horace Brooksfield's body.

"It never gets any easier does it?" Emmett commiserated.

"You didn't suit up, Emmett?"

"There was time to suit up and then Mrs. Brooksfield collapsed," Emmett explained.

"At least you didn't let anyone else in .We should suit up now before entering again."

Emmett quickly suited up and followed Dr. Piper.

"Say, Doc, what's that chemical odour?" Emmett asked as he entered the office again.

"Here put this mask on your face, Emmett. We need to get the bio-hazard suits in here. Come on! Hop to it! We need to get out of here. We need to leave and not come back, until we wear the proper equipment." Dr. Andrew Piper replied "Any headache, nausea, faintness, shortness of breath?"

He then handed Emmett a mask and put a piece of tape across the office door that read Bio-Hazard.

"No, just a bit of a headache, but I had one before, I even whiffed the weird smell. We've been exposed to an unknown toxin? Is the chemical the reason why Ms. Kelly-Brooksfield went to the hospital?" Emmett demanded worried.

"I think there is a toxic chemical here, Sonny. I'll know better after some laboratory tests." Dr. Piper explained "but I suspect ammonia gas, mixed with bleach. So, I would venture to guess Chlorine gas.

You're lucky you appear to have no symptoms so far. In the meantime it's off to the chemical shower in the mobile unit that just arrived."

"Aw, Doc, don't tell me you're sending me to the shower. Do you know they steal your clothes and dispose of them? This is a brand new suit and those leather shoes cost me a hundred bucks," Emmett complained.

"Sorry, Emmett. We can't take chances with the toxins. I'm sure you can put a claim into the department," Dr. Piper sympathized, "If it's any consolation, I'm going to lose my clothes too."

"Have you seen the department budget? I'll be lucky to get enough money to replace my underwear. Why couldn't Brad answer this call?" Emmett complained, "This isn't my day."

"It wasn't their day either," Dr. Piper retorted, motioning towards the bodies.

"Sorry, Doc, you're right and I'm going to nail whoever did this," vowed Emmett, getting ready to leave to wait for the Hazmat truck.

Emmett and Doctor Piper went through the chemical shower and collected tee-shirts and sweatpants from a waiting colleague. Emmett left the tent to continue investigating, now dressed in a chemical suit, and ran into someone walking through the crime scene.

"Why are you here, Brad? Have you come to gloat about my loss of clothing?" Emmett asked sounding annoyed.

"I thought you might need a hand. I heard you got dosed with some strong chemicals. Those are not exactly clothes to wear in

front of the media. I could handle the case
for you."

"No, thanks."

"It's a real high-profile case. The mayor and
his lover were murdered, and the wife finds
them? It's a slam dunk case man. She killed
them," Brad continued, ignoring Emmett.

"Why don't you go home, Brad, and take
your media hound self with you. You barked
up the wrong tree. Crown Attorney Kelly
has an alibi."

"Try to do a guy a favour," Brad snarled.
"Don't let a pretty face fool you, buddy boy!
She knocked them off and gloated about it
thinking she has you fooled."

"Get lost, Brad. I don't need your kind of
favours."

"I pulled my weight as your partner," Brad complained. "I've heard what you've been saying about me. Why don't you like me? I'm a likeable person."

"I prefer being solo. You're a media hound and will always be a media hound, Brad Owens. Go take yourself away now. I didn't invite you and this is my case," Emmett announced, staking out his claim.

"As I said, try to do a guy a favour." 'Brad gripped as he left.

"Rentford, get over here," Emmett yelled over to another cop.

"What do you need, Sergeant Detective Rogers?" Constable Silas Rentford asked, all but coming to attention.

Emmett looked at his new partner with approval. He seemed to be eager; a good sign. Emmett watched Silas as he looked over the scene; Silas was quiet and methodical while he took in the entire crime scene Silas his brown hair, trimmed short to regulation style, towered over most at the scene, as his height topped out at six feet six inches. Emmett watched him and was sure this new partner would be a help to him in this case; at least he hoped so, but training new partners was never easy.

Silas had put on a protective suit and Emmett wanted to tell him the suit wouldn't be necessary. This wasn't where he needed him to investigate. Someone had to go talk to the victim's daughter, Rose Brooksfield, and inform Amber's mother, before the media got to them.

"Rentford, first I need you to start making calls and make sure I wasn't lying to Sergeant Detective Owens." Emmett commanded, "And find me a cup of coffee. This may take all night. I need you to send a cop over to inform Amber Tate's mother, one Agnes Tate, to inform her about her death. I want you to go inform the mayor's family about his demise."

"But you just told him..." Constable Rentford said hesitantly taking off the protective suit.

"I know what I told that media hound. Now find out the truth and try not to make me a liar!" Sergeant Detective Rogers barked.

"Training new partners is a pain," he muttered under his breath, but Constable Rentford heard and scurried to follow Emmett's orders.

A few minutes later he was back with a coffee he placed in Emmett's hand.

"Wow. You're good Rentford. This is exactly the way I like it, black; no sugar no cream, nothing but high octane."

"Thanks, boss. I'm off to check off the list. I'll check in later."

I can train a new partner. Emmett thought surprised. Emmett watched Rentford leave and he thought What if this is an act Rentford seemed so subservient; maybe a little too much? He had other partners and they all ended the same way screwing up and blaming Emmett. Why couldn't they just do the job? He found himself following Rentford through the building. Emmett obtrusively watched his new partner in action as Constable Rentford passed a CSI in the hall. Silas is stopped by her as she touched his sleeve.

"Hey, Silas. Is Emmett Rogers, your new partner?" The C.S.I. technician asked, through the mask.

Emmett noted the crime scene investigator
was dressed in space like gear as he hid
from their view. He watched as she took
head-gear off, revealing red-gold hair,
pulled back in a ponytail. Her green eyes
glittered with warmth and lust as she stared
at Silas, her tongue sliding over her lip. Well
what do we have here? Emmett wondered as
he watched her. Silas has away with the
ladies?

"Brandy?" Silas asked as he smiled with
approval.

"Yes, it's me. So Emmett Rogers, is your
new partner?"

"Yes, he is and his solve rate amazes me.
Although I hear his people skills leave a bit
to be desired." Silas answered "I've already
seen him in action. He's quite good."

Well, what an incredible compliment. This
guy might make a good partner after all. He

was on the right track. Emmett thought, as he tried to mold himself into the shadows.

"Yes, well, he's gone through hell the last year. His wife, Jenna died from breast cancer. She was his college sweetheart. I feel sorry for the guy; it would be horrible to lose the love of your life." Brandy replied. "I'd make a play for him, but the guy still drowns in grief. And don't get me started on his former partner, Sergeant Detective Brad Owens. The guy is bad news. The media is his bitch and he'll feed you to it if he thought it would get him press."

Emmett hated to be talked about in gossip. Where had this Brandy got information on him? How did she know so much about Jenna? Emmett kept to himself enough. He didn't want people to know anything about him. It was probably Brad. Why had he ever trusted his former partner? Brad was a partner but a leech who wanted all the credit for himself.

Damn, Emmett preferred to keep his information private. Last year watching Jenna die, had been the worst experience of his life, despite the impending divorce he had loved her still. Jenna had been ready to leave him, but when her lover (another cop) found out she was ill and dying, he'd dumped her.

He only hoped the gossips didn't know he had filed for divorce before that, or that she had been having an affair. He was glad Cameron Grenor had left the Happy Valley, Ontario police. Last he had heard was that Cameron had a job as a police officer, in London, Ontario. Brad would have a field day with the gossip that Cameron was Jenna's lover and he, Emmett, had been filing for divorce. Thankfully Brad hadn't known about the divorce, or that would be fodder for the grist mill too. Well good the kid liked him. He hoped he still did after his discussion with Brandy. Emmett thought.

"Brad's a bad cop?" Silas asked. "I thought he seemed okay."

"Oh, yes, Sergeant Detective Rogers pulled in all his chits to get a new partner again instead of being paired up with Brad again. You're his fifth co-worker since last year and his last for a while. His boss is fed up and declared he'll have to go solo if you don't work out as his cohort. Or maybe be assigned desk work."

"Wow, Brandy, you always know the skinny on everyone," Silas stated surprised "That doesn't sound good for me. I better get my ass in gear and get the job done. I wouldn't want to get tossed as his partner the first day."

"I guess I've heard enough." Emmett
thought leaving. The kid will do his job he's
even a little afraid of me and maybe that's a
good thing if it gets him motivated.

~0~

Chapter 5 - Crafty Old Ladies and Mouthy Children

Silas Rentford

Silas Rentford slipped into his patrol car. He took out his cell phone and called dispatch for information for the Kelly-Brooksfield residence. Getting the number he dialled.

"Hello?" answered a sleepy Rose, coming awake at the sound of the phone ringing.

"Is this the Kelly-Brooksfield residence?" demanded Silas.

"Yes it is," replied Rose scared, wondering who could be calling so late.

"This is Constable Silas Rentford. I would like to come by your residence in a few minutes. There has been an incident. We'd like to come over and discuss this with you," Silas explained.

"I'm fifteen years old. I don't let anyone in the house after midnight. If you'd like to discuss something talk to my mom and dad. They are at the Mayor's office downtown."

As the thought that something may have happened to her parents crossed her mind, she queried "Oh no, has something happened? Are my Mom and Dad okay? They are Lily and Horace Brooksfield."

"Is there someone with you, Ms. Brooksfield?" Silas asked.

"No but it doesn't mean you can dance around my questions. I want answers to them now," Rose insisted sounding like Lily.

"I don't want to get into this on the phone. I would like to come and speak to you," Silas maintained.

"You're not going to tell me anything except in person, are you?" Rose asserted adding "Okay fine, go get my Great-Grandma Katha O'Malley and bring her here. She lives three doors down at nine hundred and sixty-eight. I'll talk to you and not before I see my Granny. Bye now."

Silas perceived a click, as Rose hung up the phone.

"Cheeky little brat! She didn't even give me her address. I guess I can reverse directory the address from her phone number. Poor kid! I'll have to tell her about her mom and dad and that will hurt," Silas muttered aloud, while dialling Katha O'Malley.

"Hello? Who is this? Who calls at two o'clock in the morning? This is not a civilized time to call," the old and cranky voice answered. "It's Constable Silas Rentford, ma'am. Am I speaking to Katha O'Malley?"

"What would a constable, want with me?"
asked Katha half asleep. "Are you the
police?"

"Yes, ma'am. I am a police officer; there's
been an incident at the Mayor's office."
Silas began.

"Has that ass, Horace been caught with his
pants down and under a bed?" Katha barked.

"Ma'am!" Silas replied with censor.

"Ha! He has hasn't he? Poor dear Lily, she
has no idea what her man is capable of.
What has the heel done now? Wait a minute.
Is my adopted granddaughter Rosey okay?"
Katha asked.

"Ma'am, how did you obtain information on
a crime that happened this evening?" Silas
demanded surprised.

"Aware of what? I'm only going by your
conversation young man. Lily is so in love
with him, she can't see the forest for the
flowers." Katha explained, "He would wink
and flirt with other women. Schmoozing he
called it, but Lily didn't see the touching he
did and I didn't tell her. Why didn't I tell
her?"

"Explain your response to me. He assaulted women?" Silas asked excited.

"No, the ones he would touch liked it." Katha explained, "He seemed to touch ones that would smile at him afterwards. I wouldn't be at all surprised if he cheated on my Lily."

"That's impossible ma'am. Horace Brooksfield is dead. He has been murdered."

"Someone plugged him?" Katha asked proud of herself for using what she thought was police lingo.

"No, someone hit him over the head and poisoned him," Silas replied and realized he shouldn't have said the method of death before checking out her alibi. "Aw hell!"

"Young man, you watch your language. You will not speak to me in such a manner," Katha snapped imperiously.

"Sorry, ma'am," Silas apologized, and then thought Who does she think she is? The bloody Queen?

"I'm at your front door. Could I come in please, ma'am?" he begged.

"You wait right there, young man, while I throw on some clothes. I'm not coming to the entrance in my nightie. Keep your badge handy; I'm not opening up my door without it."

"Yes, ma'am." Silas agreed "I'll wait badge in hand."

"Well since you are so polite, I'll answer the door. This might take a moment. I have to make myself decent. It is the middle of the night after all."

Katha dressed quickly and came to the door in a lilac purple pant suit. Silas was amazed by the woman who answered the door. He had imagined a cantankerous old Biddy wizened and older than Medusa, but he found an older woman, her hair gleaming white perfectly coiffed, with brilliant sapphire blue eyes. Pearls adorned her neck. The woman could have walked out of the society pages he thought, as Katha smiled regally.

"Constable Silas Rentford I presume." She checked his identification and then waved him in the house.

"Yes, ma'am." Silas replied. "We should go to your granddaughter's home so I don't have to explain this twice."

"Lead on my good man," Katha replied.

Katha and Silas walked two doors down to a house shrouded in darkness. Silas knocked at the door with several loud wraps. Rose peered through the peephole. Seeing her Grandma Katha she opened the door.

"Grandma Katha, I think something terrible has happened. If this is Constable Rentford, he won't tell me on the phone what it is. Is that fair, just because I'm fourteen?" Rose complained loudly.

"Rosey, he's here now to tell you."

"But he won't! He's treating me like a child," Rose claimed stamping her foot angrily.

"Rosey, my posey, what have I been trying to teach you?" Katha prodded gently.

"A lady invites guests in, sits down gracefully and gently prods for information," Rose parroted what she was told.

"Good, dear, but remember next time don't repeat the information in front of the quarry," Katha corrected.

"I'll get it right next time, Grandma Katha," Rose replied smiling.

"Hopefully there will never be a next time," Katha admonished.

"Sorry, Grandma Katha."

Silas smiled at the banter between the two. They so obviously cared about one another. He thought that must be wonderful, to have someone care for you so much.

"Ladies, if you please, can we be seated?"

"Certainly, come this way, Constable Rentford? Please," Rose asked regally, assuming lady like manners.

Silas suddenly wondered what he had gotten into with these women. The older woman, Katha O'Malley, appeared charismatic and charming, but was also crafty. She had instructed her granddaughter to pump him for information, like he would soon be the interviewee not the interviewer. He had to take charge and take back the interview. Silas waited for Rose to be seated with her grandmother and then said, "There's no easy way to say this. I'm sorry to tell you your father, Horace Brooksfield, has been murdered this evening."

He watched as the child shrank pulling her legs up to her chin visibly shrinking in age. Katha held out her arms but Rose straightened herself up and exclaimed, "No, you are mistaken. He's the Mayor. He can't be dead."

"I'm sorry Miss Brooksfield, there is no mistake. He is dead."

"And my Lily? Is she okay?" asked Katha, trying to hide a tremble in her voice.

"Is my mom, okay?" Rose also asked shaking.

"Oh, I understood she was your stepmother," Silas replied, checking his notes.

"She is my mom. She adopted me. She's okay isn't she?" asked Rose again.

"You're an idiot! This child has just lost her father and you're quibbling about whether it's her stepmother or mother?" Katha O'Malley blurted.

"Ms. Brooksfield appears to have been exposed in the office to a chemical which killed your father and his secretary, but she is under medical care at the hospital," Silas explained.

"You are a horrible man. What away to tell a child her mother has been harmed. You, young man, should have told me immediately that Lily was harmed," Katha snapped. "Come Rose we should go to the hospital and be with your mother." she continued.

"I need to corroborate Lily Kelly Brooksfield's alibi first," Silas insisted.

"You overstep your bounds, young man. I'll have your badge." Katha asserted.

"You suspect my mom? You're crazy! She would never harm hair on my father's head!" Rose sputtered angrily "How dare you! Do you know she's the Crown Attorney?"

"I am well aware of Crown Attorney Kelly and her position, but I need to look into everyone's alibi. So where do you think Crown Attorney Kelly could be found between ten p.m. and midnight?" Silas asked Rose.

"We were together. We talked and waited for pizza, which arrived at about eleven-thirty. We ate it. What more do you need to know? I'm sure Pizza Pie would vouch for when they delivered." Rose answered.

"And before you ask me, Constable Rentford, I had a gentleman caller," 'Katha replied.

"Grandma Katha," Rose rebuked surprised.

"Who is it someone I know? I can't believe you did the nasty."

"Rose my love life is none of your business, please do not discuss this." Katha addressed Rose then turning to Silas she said, "Now look what you've done. You've made me shock my granddaughter."

"Well, don't you both be looking so surprised. I may be eighty or so but I'm not dead yet." she replied smirking "Would you like his name? It's Terrence Stewart, as in father of Chief Edward Stewart."

Silas blanched and then excused himself for a moment radioing the statements to Detective Emmett Rogers before stepping back into the room.

"I think I have enough information. I can speak to the chief's father later. Please, don't speak with him first ladies. Thank you both for your statements. I'm sorry for your loss." Silas said solemnly.

Silas worried he had been mean to a little old lady (one who had ties to the chief). His ambitions were on the line with this case he better pony up and act nicer, he couldn't afford to be in a bad light with the chief. Silas then offered, "Can I drive you to the hospital? My partner has asked me to meet him there."

"I'd appreciate the ride, young man. Thank you," Katha simpered. Rose and Katha then followed Silas to his car.

"That was incredibly masterful, Grandma Katha. Tell me how you did it later," Rose whispered.

"Quiet dear he'll hear you," Katha whispered back.

She had done it again. What have I got myself into with these two? Thought Constable Rentford, as he escorted the women to his patrol car and placed them in the back seat. These women were a lot harder to deal with then he thought they would be. The old lady appeared sharper than any young person. She seemed good at the manipulation technique perfected by the élite. He'd remain cautious with her for now. The girl was mouthy even for a teen. She obviously needed to take some more notes from Granny. He felt bad she had lost her father; especially given Ms. Kelly was her stepmother. Ms. Kelly might have committed the crime after all.

Lily Kelly was found at the scene of the crime and the wife remained the first suspect. Lily Kelly and her cousin Amelia looked good for these crimes at this time.

He would be careful with these people, however, if he wanted to remain Detective Rogers' partner; and he did want to remain his partner. Politics were always tricky.

Ms. Kelly, being the crown attorney, and now her Grandmother, being some kind of society dame, meant trouble with a capital T and then her relationship with the chief's daddy? Trouble he didn't need. Being Detective Rogers partner could be a step forward in his career and he was anxious for

advancement. He wasn't getting any
younger after all; he was twenty-nine years
old now.

He drove them in silence to the hospital. The
little girl, not like a teenager, seemed
subdued now like she now realized her dad
was gone. Of course she seemed worried
about her stepmother; Ms. Kelly obviously
held the child's affection. Mrs. O'Malley
still looked angry, like the world had better
get out of her way. Silas didn't feel like
stepping in her quicksand. His career had
seemed stagnant, as he played the politics
game, but now maybe he would see a rise in
rank. Silas wasn't about to let anything get
in the way of his occupation again.
Advancement would soon pass him by if he
didn't keep on his toes. He loved being a
cop and looked forward to the day he got to
be an inspector, even the youngest one ever.
A guy could dream and it could happen.

"We're here, ma'am, and Ms. Brooksfield."
Silas announced, stopping the car. Silas
opened the door to let them out, feeling
more like a taxi driver than a police officer.

"He sounds like a chauffeur, Grandma Katha," Rose commented snidely.

"Rudeness is not appreciated, Rose Brooksfield. The policeman has been generous giving us a ride to your mother," Katha replied giving Rose a censoring look.

"Sorry, sir," Rose stated looking embarrassed.

"That's okay," Silas replied mollified.

"You are gracious with a cranky old lady, and a wounded child. Thank you for your patience, Constable Rentford. You've been more than kind," Katha said as they parted.

As they walked away, Silas felt that he had judged the old lady too harshly. After all, she had made the teen be respectful, and that had to count for something. Didn't it? While they may not have been related by blood, they did act like family. Silas respected that.

~0~

Chapter 6 - Old Bones Rattle with Tempered Steel

Katha

Katha entered through the hospital

doors, going directly to the front desk to find Lily's room. Unfortunately no one was available at this time of night. Katha used the desk phone to call the emergency room enquiring where Lily had been taken.

A nurse appeared out of nowhere at the desk and said, "Please hang up the phone and leave. We are unable to confirm any information about Lily Brooksfield at this time. You can return in the morning."

"I beg your pardon?" Katha asked regally.

"I can't release any information," the nurse explained. "So you might as well come back in the morning with the rest of the press."

"I am her grandmother, not the gutter press," Katha announced leaving out the great.

"Sorry. The press called all night. Some of them are fine, but those tabloids... I guess then it would be all right to release the information, but we must be careful, like I explained. Please produce some identification. Miss.?"

"Yes, of course I do. I'm Katha O'Malley and this is my great-granddaughter, Rose Brooksfield, Lily's daughter. Rose, show them your student card," Katha commanded as she finished showing her identification.

"This would be so much easier if I owned a driver's licence. Why couldn't I be a year older?" Rose whined pulling out her wallet and showing her student card.

"Yes, your identification is sufficient. I hope you understand. The press tried to sneak their way in and we've got to be cautious. The police asked us not to release the information to anyone but family and there are privacy laws in this country which we strictly adhere to." continued the nurse, apologising some more and rambling, "I think we may have transferred her to the Medicine floor to monitor how much poison she has ingested. Let me find out all the information and get back to you."

A few seconds later after speaking to someone on the phone she said to Katha, "Yes, she's on the Medicine floor."

"Poison? She breathed in poison? I need the floor and the room number. Please?" demanded Katha sweetly, but clearly shaken by the news Lily had been poisoned.

Rose trembled, scared; as this was not the news she expected.

"The floor is the fourth floor, E-Wing; I'm not sure the room number. One moment please."

"Thank you, my dear," replied Katha as the nurse's desk phone rang. "I am so sorry. I've been called away and don't have time to look up the number," the nurse replied.

The nurse then she walked away.

"Totally unbelievable behaviour! Is this the way nurses behave now? Well how rude. Damn! Now what can we do? You didn't catch me swear, did you?" Katha cautioned.

"Hear what, Grandma Katha?" asked Rose. "I don't believe you shouldn't condemn all nurses for one nurse's actions."

"They are not helping their cause with this incident," Katha explained trying to find someone.

Katha looked around a look of dismay on her face. Rose worried Grandma Katha would have a heart attack because Grandma Katha was so upset.

"I can't believe this. Now there is no one to answer the phone. The nurses are unavailable and I don't know the room number." Katha ranted. "This hospital is badly run. Things have to change."

"Maybe we should just go to the floor and look for Mom?" asked Rose.

"Of course, I lost my facilities there for a moment. Thank you, dear. You are a smart cookie. Let's go find your mother."

Katha exited the elevator and started down the long hallway. She turned a corner with Rose in tow and then tramped loudly down the hospital corridor searching for Lily. Katha peered in rooms actively searching for Lily.

"I don't see her, Grandma Katha," Rose cried scared.

"Don't you worry will we find her. Grandma Katha will find her; never you fear," Katha replied determination showing in her face.

"Visiting hours are over until eleven a.m.," The nurse replied frostily. "You need to leave."

"Please I need to find my granddaughter," Katha stated loudly.

"Ma'am, you need to be a little quieter. Are you aware of the time? It is four a.m., the patients are asleep. Come back later in the morning," the nurse demanded.

"I am so sorry, these old bones rattle," Katha apologized, smiling a winning smile and then continued, "Please help me dear? We've news of a terrible tragedy tonight. My grandson by marriage, the Mayor Horace Brooksfield, was murdered. My granddaughter was brought here as well."

The nurse looked moved.

Katha took a huge breath and wiped away tears. "She was poisoned by the same awful person who did away with my grandson," Katha answered in hushed, anguished tones, wiping away some more tears from her eyes. "I must find her. I am so worried this poor child needs her mother after this horrendous night."

"Oh, you are the family of the mayor? It has been a dreadful day for you. Are you all right, my dear?" asked the nurse, suddenly seeming concerned with Katha's wellbeing.

"Yes, I'm sure we will be all right as soon as we know our Lily is okay," Katha continued.

The nurse at the desk looked up as they passed the desk.

"I'm sure I can help you find her. Noreen, take over here. I'm going to help this woman and her grandchild. They are the mayor's family," the nurse who had spoken to Katha said.

"I could help you find your niece. I was so sorry to get the news about the Mayor .I'm so sorry about your father," Noreen stated solicitously.

"Thank you. My father was a great man," Rose replied solemnly.

"He was indeed."

"I'm taking them to see Mrs. Brooksfield now."

"I'll hold down the ward, Linda," Noreen agreed.

"I believe the phrase is 'Hold down the fort'," Linda corrected.

"Fine, I'll hold down the fort!" Noreen agreed.

~0~

Rose

Rose wondered if she would ever able

to manipulate people to help her, the way Grandma Katha, always managed to get people to do exactly what she wanted. She wanted to be like Lily and Grandma Katha when she got older. They were smart strong women who seemed to get people to do exactly what they wanted in the nicest possibly way. They seemed to have a special power; people wanted to do things for them. Rose tried hard not to think Lily might not be okay.

Daddy was dead... Lily the only parent she had left...Deep down, she worried Lily would leave her too. Mommy (her real mother) was a drug addict and a murderess who only escaped a long prison sentence, because Lily hadn't asked for it. What kind of mother kills her drug dealing pimp in front of her daughter though? Daddy met Lily when Daddy asked for some leniency for her mother.

Rose had been terrified and wanting her mother not understanding why she couldn't see her. Lily had talked gently to her and her father, explaining it all. Lily had even hastened the trial because her biological mother, asked her to do so.

Lily even made a plea deal for Rose's biological mother which meant she'd be out in twenty years. She had offered her friendship to Rose. At first Rose refused to give her any affection, feeling she betrayed her mother.

When Rose started to realize all her real mother had done she started to think how special Lily was. Lily had been there for Rose long before she had married her father. Lily had kept up with everything a mother did. Lily had taken Rose to Brownie meetings. She had been there for school functions required of a mother, even baking cupcakes for a bake sale.

Rose thought back to when Lily said she wanted to be her stepmother and how she'd begged her to stay. She also begged to be able to call Lily, Mom. Lily adopted her, so surely that meant they couldn't take her away from Lily. Provided she was okay; after all she was in the hospital. They wouldn't take her away from her family now that her father had died would they?

"Don't you worry Rosey, your mom's going to be okay," Katha reassured seeing the thoughts going on in Rose's head flash in her eyes. "She has strong genes flowing through her veins. She can survive this and she has us."

Rose peered in the hospital room. She saw her mother, lying in a bed coughing; an oxygen tube ran into her nose. Mom appeared much worse. Rose thought. Somehow in Rose's mind she thought Lily would be coming home tonight, to look after Rose, in her grief. Rose took another look at Lily.

Mom looked small and broken, unlike the strong woman who took care of her. How could Mommy look after herself let alone me? If Mom is getting better; why does she look so bad? Is Grandma Katha comforting me, and lying to me, because she thinks I'm still a child? Rose then decided Grandma Katha was reassuring her, like you would any small child. I wish I could be a kid again and not understand someone had killed her father. I'm scared, what if the same evil

person comes after me as well? They hurt
my mom and dad they could hurt me too!
Rose looked over at her mother and thought
she needed her mother more than ever now.
She tried not to cry.

"I have to get home to my daughter; I can't
stay here." Lily cried, struggling with the
nurse who tried to keep her in bed.

"Lily, don't give the nurse trouble," Katha
commanded from the doorway.

"Grandma Katha. I'm so glad you're here
but it's so early. Lily then coughed and tried
to catch her breath "Rose should be
sleeping. Amelia's here too," Lily continued
as she struggled to talk, holding out her arms
to Rose. Rose threw herself gently into her
mother's arms and appeared happy for a
moment.

"Mommy, are you sure you're okay?" Rose
cried sounding like a small child.

"What do you mean, Amelia's here?" asked
Katha shocked.

"She had a little accident. I'll explain later," Lily mouthed over Rose's head, now on her shoulder.

"Rosey, my little Posey, I'll be fine. Lily then had a coughing spell. She then searched Rose's face and asked, "Sweetie, have you heard about your dad?" Rose began weeping as Lily comforted her and then cried with her.

"We'll get through this sweetie. They'll find out who hurt your daddy and he'll pay. God as my witness, he'll pay for what he's done," Lily vowed with a bitter tone in her voice.

"Now, Lily, they say 'Vengeance is mine saith the Lord.' therefore it isn't your job or this child's job to go after them. So don't you go tell her revenge is necessary. It is a policeman's job, specifically Constable Silas Rentford's job," Katha rebuked. "This child needs her mother, so don't do anything foolish."

"Don't you mean Sergeant Detective Rogers?" Lily asked, coughing again.

"No. Who is Sergeant Detective Rogers?"
Katha asked.

"I suspect he's Constable Silas Rentford's
boss," Rose replied knowingly, then dried
her tears.

"Yes, she's correct; I believe Detective
Rogers is his boss, because he is in charge of
the case," Lily countered.

"Will you be okay Mom?" Rose asked.

"Of course she'll be all right. She'll get
good care here and before you know she'll
be home with us. We will spoil her rotten.
Won't we?" Katha answered, as Lily smiled
her thanks at Katha for the reassurance.

"I think you ought to go. Ms. Kelly-
Brooksfield needs her rest." the nurse
commanded, coming back in the room.

"But they just got here," Lily protested
through another spout of coughs.

"And they can come back later today," the
nurse insisted.

"We'll be going. We came to make sure
you're okay. Don't you worry; I'll take good
care of Rosey,"

Katha reassured Lily, and then turned to the nurse. "My granddaughter recovers?"

"You should talk to the doctor about her condition," the nurse replied evasively.

"Listen here. I want to know now how my granddaughter really is!" Katha demanded with a no refusal attitude, as she stepped into the hall.

"She'll get great care. We'll move her to a normal room tomorrow. We will keep her a couple more days; until her lungs are clearer of the chlorine gas," The nurse explained gently.

"Chlorine gas? Isn't that substance rather serious?" asked Katha.

"Chlorine gas can be very serious when inhaled. The gas dissipated and she got a reduced amount, unlike the other victims. The doctor feels she got a smaller dose then would cause serious damage."

"Oh thank God."

"I'm so glad that Mom will be okay," Rose replied and then continued, "Do you think she might be moved into the same room with her friend and cousin Amelia Kelly?

"Why are you mentioning your Aunt Amelia?" Katha demanded.

"She's here too. Aunt Amelia slipped in some blood and broke her leg. She is concussed too."

"Amelia is in this hospital? She is concussed? When did this happen?"

"Grandma Katha, it's like this..."

"What do you mean she slipped in blood and broke her leg in blood? Do you people tell me nothing?" Katha demanded rapid succession from Rose and ignoring Rose's interjection. Then taking a breath, but not calming down, Katha asked, "Whose blood did she slip in to break her leg? Is it hers? Is she okay, Rose? Why didn't Lily call me?"

"It was scary. You won't believe this, Grandma Katha, Amelia's employee Megan..." began Rose.

"Amelia's employee, Megan bled all over the floor?

"What did she do to herself?" Katha interrupted seizing on the information "I'm always telling Megan she has to be more careful when she puts stock away. Stock we can replace. Megan we cannot."

"Don't you watch the news?"

"I was busy. I didn't have time to watch the news! I meant to get to Amelia's opening too, but for some reason I thought it took place tomorrow. All these meetings of the hospital board and I don't get called about my family?"

"It's worse than that, Grandma Katha. She didn't do anything to herself. Someone murdered Megan," Rose explained.

"I don't believe I heard you correctly. Did you say someone killed Megan?"

"I didn't believe it either, but Megan was murdered."

"But why? She is...was such a sweet girl," Katha said rhetorically wiping away a tear. "I don't know why or even how, but now Daddy is dead and Amber is dead as well. I hate this! I hate the world! I want to hurt someone! Why did they hurt my dad?"

"I agree the impulse to anger is there. I shouldn't be saying these things in front of you, but you are a teenager and I think you can handle it. I'm mad and I'd like to hurt someone too, but we have to let justice take the course and trust this person will pay. I promise you, we are safe though."

"I hope they find this person soon and we are secure. It feels like they targeted our family."

"I think you are wrong. I don't think it's anything but random, but I will make sure we are protected. I still think your mother should have called me though," Katha complained annoyed.

"I think she was busy with some policeman all day...then Daddy."

""I guess Lily did have a bad day to say the least. I don't know why you didn't call me though Rose. You have a cell phone." Katha stated reproachfully.

"Sorry, Grandma Katha," Rose apologised, trying to end the conversation.

Rose wondered how Grandma Katha made her feel so guilty. Rose's father had died, poor Mommy lay hurt in hospital, yet Grandma Katha had somehow made Rose feel like it had been their entire fault for not telling Grandma Katha everything. Like they had time to share anything with her! Oh well! Grandma Katha did love Rose like she was her flesh and blood granddaughter, and she never held what Rose's biological mother had done against her. That had to count for something.

"Now you will be able to arrange for Lily and Amelia to share a room with each other. Won't you?" Katha asked sweetly of the nurse, interrupting Rose's thoughts.

"I suppose but ...," the nurse replied as if she's humoured Katha.

"Oh I didn't introduce myself, did I? I am Katha O'Malley. I'm a chair on the hospital board," Katha stated, her voice sounding cultured and demanding "And I'm related to both women. In fact, I raised them from teenagers. So I want the best for my dear girls."

"Oh, then, I'm sure we can see to them rooming together."

"Thank you, dear, where would we be without such wonderful nurses? Thank you, for taking such wonderful care of my Lily and Amelia," Katha waxed smiling. "My pleasure." replied the nurse happily.

"We will come back after some rest to see them both." Katha told Rose "Now let's go find a taxi."

Katha and Rose went down to the lobby where Katha checked for signs against cell phones. Seeing none, she whipped out her cell phone and called for a taxi. The taxi arrived a few minutes later.

Outside of Katha's, Katha and Rose peered over at Lily's home, to the sight of press trucks and reporters camped out around Lily's house. They hurriedly opened the door and crossed the threshold into Katha's home before they were spotted.

"How long do you think those press reporters will be camped on our doorstep, Grandma Katha?" Rose asked looking out at the trucks disgusted.

"They will be out there until it is old news. Your father's death is big news. They don't want to harm us they just want to do their job."

"I wish they'd do their job somewhere else. Will they find us here?" asked Rose

"Not if I can help prevent them from doing their job."

"Oh, I hate it! I hate that Daddy died and these people act like vultures at our door," Rose cried, tears streaming down her face.

"I don't like them at the door any better. Some of these press people seem considerate but I don't want to talk to them either," Katha rambled, taking Rose in her arms and pulling back her hair out of her eyes, "I'm sure this is their top story, maybe you should leave the television off for a few days."

"I don't know if I can sleep, but I'm so tired. I want to go sleep in my bed but I can't. Where can I sleep, Grandma Katha?"

"Dear, the second bedroom is all made up with clean sheets. There are fresh blankets on it as well. You can find a nightgown to sleep in the top drawer of the bureau. Later, dear, I'm headed to bed too. These old bones do not like getting four hours of sleep," Katha replied yawning.

"Goodnight. Grandma Katha, I love you."

"Goodnight, dear, for what's left of it. I love you too, pumpkin," Katha replied as she too went off to bed.

Rose went up the stairs exhausted but thought I don't know if I'll ever sleep again. I wish I could go to sleep and this would all be a bad dream.

~0~

Chapter 7 - All Life's Journeys Have Secrets

Lily? I can't believe it! You're here

too? What happened to you?" asked Amelia surprised as the orderly and a nurse wheeled in Lily on a stretcher and helped her into a bed.

An oxygen tank lay beside Lily's arm on the bed.

"Yesterday was the worst day of my life," Lily exclaimed. "First I find you blooded and broken, and I find your employee murdered. I take a breather, go home and find out Horace wasn't home and hadn't given Rose dinner. Rose hadn't eaten anything but cereal all day."

"Horace didn't make it home by five p.m. like he promised?" Amelia asked, "But you said he had been so much better about not working too late."

"I know. That's why I was so surprised that he wasn't home. It was ten-thirty p.m. when I got home, and no Horace in sight," Lily said in a whisper.

"I thought he would live up to his promise. What's wrong with him? Doesn't he understand life is short?" Amelia asked.

Seeing emotions of sadness flash across Lily's face, she continued, "Something happened to you though, because you ended up here. What happened when you got home?"

"We ate pizza. It got close to midnight and he wasn't home. I told Rose I would get him. I went to Horace's office, to bring him home. I arrived at the office building and I went up in his private elevator and his office door remained closed. I turned the knob and...," Lily started crying.

"Oh no, Horace cheated on you? I'll kill the bastard," Amelia shouted.

"Someone already did kill him. Can you provide an alibi, Ms. Amelia Kelly?" demanded Sergeant Detective Rogers coming into the room.

"Gee, I don't know... my broken leg? I can't walk on it!" Amelia began sarcastically. "Wait a minute; why would I need an alibi? Oh no, Lily, is Horace dead?"

"Yes, Ms. Kelly, the mayor is dead," Sergeant Detective Rogers stated bluntly.

"You could have told her easier. She's my cousin and therefore Horace is her family," retorted Lily angrily.

"But she obviously doesn't like him. Now does she, Ms. Brooksfield? Why else would she threaten to kill him?" Sergeant Detective Rogers replied bluntly.

"You're a jerk!" yelled Lily. "Amelia thought I said Horace had cheated not that she killed him and you know it!"

"So you suspected Horace cheated on your friend Lily?" asked Sergeant Detective Rogers, zeroing in with a beady gaze.

"How dare you insinuate Amelia killed Horace!" Lily interjected shocked.

"Yes and no," Amelia answered.

"Which is it? Yes or no?" demanded Sergeant Detective Rogers.

"Yes, I suspected he cheated on Lily; but I had no proof and I wasn't about to get any proof. I didn't want to realize the truth, because then I would need to tell Lily," Amelia reluctantly admitted.

"So did she say anything about this to you?" Sergeant Detective Rogers asked Lily.

"No! Anyway, Horace wouldn't cheat on me. He loved me. I remained the wife he wanted and we were in a happy marriage. You've got to realize someone posed them like that," cried Lily protesting.

"Posed them? I don't understand. There is more than one person dead? Who is dead?" Amelia asked, trying to get more information.

"Horace and Amber are dead," Lily replied sadly.

"Horace and Amber, his secretary, are dead? Oh Lily, I'm so sorry," Amelia responded reaching for Lily's hand, then turning to Detective Rogers she asked, "Why would someone kill Horace and Amber?"

"Did you hire someone to kill them, Ms. Kelly and then pose them?" enquired Sergeant Detective Rogers.

"How could you think I had anything to do with this? Are you kidding me?" Amelia solicited shocked.

"You hide under an assumed name and I see there is an accident that occurred to someone close to you a year ago, still on the books. They never found him did they? The drunk driver who killed your husband and son were never charged."

"How dare you? The press proceeded to hound me day and night, so I took my mother's maiden name on my aunt's advice. It was my right. It is a family name after all. Do you understand what kind of pain I went through, you mean jerk?" Amelia snapped angrily and then started crying silently, hiding her face as she turned away.

"Amelia's right. You are a jerk. Do you comprehend how long it's taken her to come this far? A year ago I lost my cousin to her pain, my best friend, as well as my godson, and the best male friend I've ever known. She wanted to die too. She wouldn't drink, eat or sleep. The press camped out on her doorstep and demanded little tidbits for their daily news stories. And you throw their deaths in her face like this. That doesn't hurt her? Do have any idea what happens when you lose someone without warning? To want to die because you can't bear to feel a gut wrenching pain in the pit of your stomach any longer? Now do you?" Lily yelled at Sergeant Detective Rogers.

"I do understand that pain," Sergeant Detective Rogers answered quietly.

"You felt pain which hurts that much? I'm sorry for your loss. But nothing excuses what you've done to Amelia now. After all, you can appreciate how it is to lose someone you love, so you should be a lot nicer."

"Listen, you're the Crown attorney, so you must comprehend I need to do my job. As distasteful as the questions may be, I must eliminate or confirm suspects."

"I understand you're doing your job here so go ahead, but tread lightly," Lily cautioned. "And I remind you her lawyer is present."

"Ms. Kelly, I'm sorry if those statements hurt you. I'm also sorry I must bring up something else hurtful from your past, but I need to proceed with my investigation. Is it true when you were sixteen, your entire family was killed in a fire? No trace of anyone else found but you and your dead family at the scene? That the fire was determined to be arson and the culprit, or culprits, were never found?" Sergeant Detective Rogers continued.

"How did you know all this? How did you find out about this? It happened in a whole other city. My great-aunt adopted me and changed my name to her daughter's last name, my mother's maiden name." explained Amelia, "The publicity after the event was terrible. The pointing fingers, the pity, the ridicule, it felt like pieces of me dying. If my aunt hadn't come and rescued me and taken me into her home, I think I would have killed myself."

"No Amelia! You wouldn't have," Lily cried in a shocked voice.

"Not as long as I have you, Rose and Aunt Katha."

"Good, because we love you."

"I know, I love you all too," Amelia answered.

"Cue the hearts and flowers. While I'm enjoying this love fest; I want to get on with my questioning, Ms. Kelly. You were Amelia Cordova then weren't you?" Sergeant Detective Rogers prodded pulling out his notebook and reading.

"Yes, I was Amelia Cordova. I was sixteen years old and had a wonderful family. In one horrific night my family was wiped out, gone in an instant." Amelia stuck out her chin and steeled herself to tell the story. "My mother Aerilla was strict but always around if I needed anything. She worked part-time as a journalist for the Ravenworst Journal."

Amelia stopped to catch her breath then continued, "My mother was warm, funny and loving to all who saw her. She wrote stories in her spare time on little scraps of paper. She'd even read some of them to us from time to time. They were good and she wanted to get them published but they are all gone now. The fire took them and my families' lives. All I have left is memories and it is hard not to remember the bad ones."

Amelia hid her face under the sheet for a second, trying to regain her composure again.

"How I miss my mother. I'd give anything to see her again...the loving smile she offered us when we came home from school. She hugged me with arms that always reached me, even when they didn't physically touch me. That is what I would like to remember," Amelia sobbed, wiping away tears and continuing by telling Detective Rogers more of her family.

"My father on the other hand was a strict disciplinarian. My father, a product of his upbringing appeared cold and closed off to his emotions; though I understood he cared about me. He believed children should listen and obey their parents but he loves...loved us all," Amelia corrected, wiping away another tear.

"What did your father do for a living, Ms. Kelly?" Detective Rogers queried.

"My father, Robert worked in his own business. It was a bookstore, he inherited from his father. We all took a turn working at the bookstore during the time we weren't at school. We sold the books and cleaned the store. Daddy loved us but he expected us to pull our own weight and work hard. He always said, 'Work hard to get ahead.' He taught us a work ethic he was sure would stay with us through our lives."

"And your other family members, one Jerry Cordova and Grace Cordova? What were their personalities?" Detective Rogers asked curiously.

"My older brother Jerry was seventeen years old the summer they died. Jerry flirted and was popular with the girls. He was a bit what the kids today call a player, always with a different girl, but he was a good guy. He had a muscle car, a '67 Mustang he worked three summers to buy and fix the car. He didn't like hanging out with his younger sisters, but what seventeen-year old boy does?" Amelia voice broke here as she gulped to hold back more tears.

"Did you care about your sister, your other family members, Ms. Kelly? Or was all your love saved for your older brother?" Detective Rogers asked, provoking her.

"Are you always this cruel? Of course I cared. Grace was my baby sister. She was only fourteen years old. Of course I cared. Grace had her whole life ahead of her. She had discovered her first crush. His name was Billy I think... I remember how sweet she could be. But she also loved to torment me as little sisters do. She borrowed my best clothes without my permission."

Amelia smiled remembering, "Grace used my hairbrush, messed up my room, borrowed my make-up and she tattled to my parents about me; but I'd give anything to look at her sweet little face again and do any of those things to me."

"Isn't the truth you hated her? You said she annoyed you and told your secrets to your parents about you."

"Don't you dare twist my words! I said I'd give anything to glimpse her again and I meant every word. I loved her! I loved every member of my family! Is this all a game to you? Amelia looked at Detective Rogers beseechingly, begging him to believe her.

She couldn't understand what his problem was, why he didn't he see understand how it hurt her to talk about this.

"Oh, why don't you understand? My whole family died in a horrific fire; all of them...my older brother Jerry, my sister Grace, my mother Aerilla, and my father Robert. Everything was gone, my entire life up in flames in a matter of minutes. I awoke outside in my nightgown unconscious from smoke inhalation. I don't even know how I got outdoors. No one understood how I got out there. I wish I had protected them. I would have given my life to save them. It's like I'm still under a horrible curse and now I've let those I love most into the curse," Amelia answered, her voice filling with sorrow and horror.

She then exclaimed, "I am so sorry, Lily!"

"Weren't you suspected of committing the crime in which all your family died?"

"Not to my knowledge and certainly not by law enforcement; maybe in horrible whisper campaigns from people who love to spread unfounded gossip. Why would anyone suspect me?" Amelia asked dumfounded, "Whoever or whatever started the fire took all I loved from me."

"You were the only one alive, the only survivor. Why wouldn't they suspect you?" Emmett exclaimed.

"They didn't suspect me, because I didn't do it! You don't understand how nightmarish this was. I was a sixteen-year- old girl whose family had been ripped from her. My lungs were filled with smoke. They wheeled me down to the morgue. They made me identify the bodies. Did you read about that in your report? I stood up out of a wheelchair to stare at their bodies. People I loved. They were so burnt; I didn't recognize them at first. My mind told me I looked at cooked meat, but I soon realized with horror and dismay these were people. My family laid there, four hideous bodies, burnt beyond recognition. That was all that was left of my family. Their faces were unrecognizable. So why did they make me look at them?" Amelia asked, her face reflecting all the shock and horror of the moments so long ago.

"They wanted to see what your reaction would be; then they could decide your guilt," Emmett replied.

"Well then, they got a reaction didn't they? I collapsed and they took me to a rest home. I stayed in a rest home for six months until Great Aunt Katha came and got me."

"A rest home? Don't you mean a mental facility?" demanded Detective Rogers.

"Yes, I admit I stayed in a mental health facility. Are you happy? I suffered a nervous breakdown. Between the horrible sight of them dead and survivor's guilt, I checked out of life. I couldn't handle the stress," Amelia admitted.

"There no sin in illness, Amelia, Lily said then turning to Lieutenant Rogers she said, "Amelia and I are cousins once removed. Her grandmother is my great-grandmother's sister. That's how we became great friends when Amelia came to stay with Grandma Katha."

"All very sweet and nice, but getting back to your tragedies, how do you explain the fact you lost all the members of your immediate family? And you alone survived Amelia? Am I to believe that a year ago your husband, and your young son, died and you didn't simply because you were too sick to get into the car with them?" Emmett demanded to know, not truly listening to Lily

"I feel I'm under a horrible curse. Do you enjoy dredging up all this pain?" shouted Amelia.

"I'm trying to get to the bottom of this so-called curse," Emmett replied with force. "I don't believe in curses, only evil people, and it's my job to apprehend those people so they can't harm anyone else."

Amelia's face was as white as a sheet, pain etched deeply into it.

"I don't want to talk about this anymore. It hurts too damn bad. Please, Lily, make him stop talking about this," Amelia pleaded turning to Lily.

"You don't need any more information... do you Detective Rogers?" Lily demanded dismissively then started coughing.

"I'm done for now but...," Detective Rogers answered, as Lily interrupted her voice a little crackling from coughing.

"I know neither of us leave town. But you, Sergeant Detective Rogers, need to find the cretin who killed my husband Horace. I know it wasn't Amelia or anyone close to me. You need to find whoever did this without narrowing your field with false leads. I want to see whomever did this pay for this crime."

"Believe me, I always get my man, or woman, as the case may be," Emmett retorted.

"You just keep looking, Sergeant Detective," Lily said with a cutting glare. "My cousin and I are not your suspects."

"I'll be the judge of that, Ms. Kelly-Brooksfield!" Emmett exclaimed.

"People like you are always judge, jury and executioner," Lily sniped.

"Not in this country; there is no death penalty."

"No, you're like other cops and decide someone is guilty and build a case from supposition, even if they are innocent."

"Are you judgemental about all cops, Ms. Brooksfield, or just me?" Emmett asked surprised.

"So, you aren't going after my cousin for this crime?"

"I only go after guilty people, Ms. Brooksfield. I go where the evidence points me."

"I guess I was a little out of line, but the way you went after my cousin was cruel," admitted Lily.

"Sometimes you need to be cruel to be kind. I'd like to eliminate her from the suspect list, but I can't yet." Emmett explained, "So let me do my job."

"Fine. You do your job. Find who killed my husband," Lily repeated.

"Oh, I will, Ms. Kelly Brooksfield. You need not fear on my account." Emmett left for moment, coming back a few minutes later much to Lily's surprise. "I thought you said you hired someone to guard Ms. Kelly. Where are they?" Emmett demanded to know.

"He's out there isn't he? A big tall guy with shaggy red hair tied up in a ponytail, his arms bulging with muscles. He is kind of hard to miss as he looks like a biker," Lily stated puzzled.

"There is no one out here."

"That makes no sense. I'm paying him good money to guard Amelia." Lily said angrily, "I'm calling Frank."

"Who is Frank?" Emmett asked.

"Frank Hawk, of Frank Hawk Security, he sent over Zachary Buchanan to guard Amelia. I don't understand why Frank's man, Zachary is not in front of the door. Could he have gone for coffee?" Lily asked Detective Rogers.

Lily then dialled Frank on her phone.

"Frank, Lily here. What's up with Zachary Buchanan? He's not here. He's supposed to be guarding Lily and he's nowhere to be seen. What? I appreciate that, but if he can't do the job; frankly I don't want him back. No we'll manage without one Amelia and I seem safe now anyway. I guess that's why he left. You'll call around and find out where he's gone? Thanks Frank, but I still don't know. No, I don't want him back. I told you that. Okay, you can get back to me when you find out. Goodbye."

"So he's missing?" Emmett demanded.

"It would seem so. I guess he didn't like the job."

"Or one of you knocked him off. You seem to be good at getting rid of people," Emmett said his eyes narrowing.

"That's slander! How dare you? How did we kill him? Amelia hobbled on her crutches while I stopped every few minutes to cough, so I could breathe?" Lily replied sarcastically.

"So you hired someone."

"Did anyone ever tell you that you have a one track mind that's stuck on go?" Lily exclaimed.

"I'm doing my job."

"Fine! Go! Do what you are supposed to do. Find Zachary Buchanan. I'm sure he's wandered off from the job... and find my husband's killer," Lily demanded angrily. "While you're at it you can find the serial killer of three people!"

"Megan's boyfriend is a person of interest. We haven't been able to find him. So the two of you aren't guilty for the murder at her store, but I'm sure your friend Amelia would assist you in offing your cheating husband and his lover." Emmett taunted.

"You are on the wrong track. You know it and I know it. I loved Horace and I would have forgiven him about anything. That's what people who love each other do."

"You would have forgiven him anything, even cheating? Because if he left you he would have gotten full custody of your stepdaughter. Am I correct?" Emmett taunted some more.

"Nonsense, I don't know what I would done about his cheating, but I wouldn't harm him. We share custody of our daughter. That's right... our daughter, not step anything. I adopted her officially, right after we married. She's my child, as much as his!" Lily explained, ""Why am I continuing to talk to you? Go! Do your job."

"I'm going, but not because you tell me too. I have a great solve rate and you can bet these murders won't be any different. So if you are responsible, you better get used to those jail-bird duds," Emmett exclaimed as a parting shot and left.

"Arrogant troublemaker! You'll see we had nothing to do with this," Lily yelled after him and choked as she tried to gasp in some air, followed by coughing.

Lily then crawled back into the bed from the bedside chair. Lily had started to like him again and he thought Amelia was guilty? He believed Amelia and Lily killed all those people? Why did she remain so attracted to the man who wanted to find them behind bars? She loved Horace and he hadn't even been dead twenty-four hours and she stood attracted to someone else?

Disgraceful! She was a bad wife. Horace cheated on her, but they would have gotten past this. Wouldn't they? Lily tried everything to make this marriage work for Rose's sake. And if she didn't succeed she would have sued for custody of Rose. After all, she legally adopted her, so she had as much right to the child as Horace did. Tears slipped out of Lily's eyes. Horace died; there would be no making up for this cheating he had done. He was gone forever. Her husband was dead!

Lily sobbed quietly into the pillow lying back in the bed, finally falling into a fitful sleep. Amelia stared at her cousin. Poor Lily; she would help her deal with all of this. Even if that stupid detective thought they had done the killings. Amelia would help her, the way Lily helped Amelia when Jack and Sam were killed, but for now...sleep.

~0~

Chapter 8 - Keep to the Motto

The Killer

W hy are there trucks and cars and

other news vans outside of Lily Brooksfield's home? Where are Lily, Rose and my Angel? All this noise must be disturbing their rest. How dare they bother her? I had killed to protect my Angel, but I forgot how much the newsmakers were like predators. There were real journalists of course; those who acted with grace and dignity to those they interviewed. I used the predators always on the lookout for stories. I manipulated them with stories I wanted them to present, but these reporters seemed like real vultures. But maybe that was good? I certainly didn't want them to discover my part in this, but what about my beloved? The stress these vultures would cause to her made him so angry.

Huh? There's Rose, with the O'Malley woman.

Where was Lily? Was she at the morgue visiting Horace? I thought she'd be with her daughter! I had done all of this so they could be together after all. Lily personified being a good mother and deserved to keep her daughter. Horace even in death remained an unnatural father and terribly neglectful. He hardly ever spent time with his daughter. He stayed too busy with work or Amber, or both at once. He deserved his end. I did well in ending those two, now they would never harm my family again!

Why did the press continue to still linger? Did all of them want a story because of his position as mayor?

That must be it. I suppose, or was it the O'Malley woman's fault? She was in a relationship with the chief's father. What was his name...oh yes, Terrence Stewart. Surely Terrence would put an end to this fiasco and demand his son remove the trash.

Should I make an anonymous call and stop
all of the noise and aggravation for my
Angel? No, if I did make a call I would
reveal my hand. I'd stay in the shadows,
continuing to watch, only taking action if it
remained completely necessary. Safety first;
protecting yourself, that had to be my motto.
So for now I'd watch and wait. No one
would harm my beloved Angel. No one!

~0~

Chapter 9 - Slander and Lies

Katha O'Malley's house about eight hours later

G randma Katha, do you think mom's

going to be okay?" asked Rose fearfully.

"Rose, she'll be fine. And so will you. Don't you worry, my pet. You're family and we take care of family. You're a Kelly/O'Malley/Brooksfield now and don't you forget it," reassured Katha.

"Do you think Amelia's cursed and it's rubbed off on Mom?" asked Rose.

"Rose Brooksfield! Amelia, through no fault of her own, has had a lot of sorrow. It's not a curse. Don't ever let me catch you saying that again. I'm so sorry your father died, but it is not some conspiracy or a curse; someone with evil intent killed him and his secretary Amber. The police will find whoever did it," Katha claimed.

"Daddy's dead...he's never coming back," Rose exclaimed tearfully, coming to a realization that hadn't quite hit her until now.

"I'm so sorry, sweetie. I understand you're hurting. You should see a counsellor, so you can talk about what you feel," Katha insisted, concerned.

"I'm fine. I'm angry. You should be angry too! I would like to see the person who killed my Dad die, slowly and in lots of pain!"

Katha looked at Rose, gravely alarmed and frowning.

"Don't look at me like that! I'm not about to do anything stupid! I'm going to stare at some television," Rose replied stomping into the living room.

She then turned on the television to block out any follow-up conversation.

"Rose, my dear child." Katha began before a special bulletin came across the television.

"Naughty Mayor dies in sex scandal with secretary." A voiceover said..,. "This reporter has learned Mayor Horace Brooksfield was found murdered in flagrante delicto with his secretary Amber Trent yesterday. Amber Trent worked for Mayor Brooksfield for the last two years. There is no comment from Crown Attorney, Lily Kelly-Brooksfield or family. Sources close to the mayor say Amber Trent had been having an affair with the mayor for the last year. The police have no comment at this time about the cause of death. Unconfirmed sources tell this reporter they died from poisoning... the same poisoning which is believed to have felled Crown Attorney Lily Kelly-Brooksfield, who is now in hospital in satisfactory condition. Mayor Horace Brooksfield leaves behind a fourteen-year - old daughter Rose and his current wife Crown attorney Lily Brooksfield. Our deepest sympathies go out to the mayor's

family. On another odd note, the Crown attorney arrived at the scene of a murder at her cousins' new store Quirks yesterday."

"Store clerk Megan Fowler was found dead earlier today in an apparent robbery. Store owner Amelia Kelly was also hurt and is in the hospital. Were the two connected? Stay tuned to this station for more updates and tune in at six p.m. for News Hour for all the latest stories. Paul Knight reporting for CHPV-TV"

"In flagrante delicto? Do they think by disguising it with their fancy language, I won't know what they're talking about? Daddy did not cheat on Mom! How dare he say Daddy cheated? It's slander. We can sue him right Grandma Katha?" Rose asked.

"Right," replied Katha, not wanting to disillusion Rose and recognising she too had heard rumours of mayor's infidelity.

"Damn reporters. I can see them in front of our house," Rose said looking out the front window.

"Rose, please guard your language. I can discern these muckrakers are a pain in the neck, but we must act ladylike," Katha explained. "Besides, you have to remember there are always reputable reporters who get the story correct."

"Sorry, Grandma Katha. Oh no, I think one of them is headed to your front door."

"Dear, I think it is your friend, Carol Banks."

"Wow, I can't believe you recognized Carol before I did. Do you think she can tell I'm here?" asked Rose.

"Since she's coming up the walk. Yes, I believe your friend seemed to have figured out where you are. She's an intelligent young lady and polite," Katha declared.

"Carol is crafty; she ferrets out information. One time we tried to figure out what George Prinze hid. Carol figured it out before anyone else. He rifled through lockers, stealing the valuables and hawking them for cash. He also rifled through some teachers purses and broke into the principal's office and took some cash. Carol nailed him to the wall. He got suspended and he's in reform school now."

"What kind of school are they running? Are you sure this school is a good place for you?" asked Katha worried. "If you'd like to get out of that school I will pay for boarding school."

"I don't want to go to any boarding school; all my friends and family are here. Carol and I got rid of the riffraff, so I go to a good school now. Besides, stuff like that happens everywhere."

"Riffraff? I didn't think anyone your age recognized such an expression."

"I learned it from you," Rose replied as Katha laughed. Rose peered out the window through the curtains. "She's taking a long time to get through those reporters, Grandma Katha."

"Yes. I should shout out the door for her to run."

"Yes, go ahead, Grandma Katha," Rose agreed.

"Come on, Carol! Run!" Grandma Katha shouted.

Carol blonde-haired and blued-eyed had her long blonde hair cascading in waves down her back.. Tall and model slim and only fifteen years old she felt overwhelmed by male attention, but when standing next to Rose who could command a room, Carol felt invisible and she liked that. Rose didn't even seem to notice the admiring looks she drew; or at least she pretended not to but maybe that was better because was shy. Standing five foot eight inches Carol wore a tee-shirt with a popular television character on it. Her bottom half was covered with black boot cut jeans. On her feet are well worn black Ugg boots with three buttons on the outsides.

Carol heard Katha's call and tried to get by the reporters .She shoved through the gauntlet of reporters, jostling them with her shoulders. Carol sprinted while being bombarded with questions the whole way to Katha's house.

"Are you Rose Brooksfield?"

Carol shook her head at the reporter and
continued going to the door of Katha's
home. If it were anyone but Rose she would
have stayed at home instead of fighting
through these crowds, but Rose needed her.

*"Hey kid, do you know The
Brooksfield's?"*

*"Do you have any comment on the fact
Mayor Brooksfield had an affair?"*

*"Do you have any more information on
Lily Brooksfield's condition?"*

*"Do you think there is a Kelly curse and
are we all at risk?"*

Carol breathed a sigh of relief as Katha
ushered her in the house.

"Hi Rose. I'm like so sorry to hear about
your dad. I can't believe someone tried to
hurt your mom too! Billy Carter said you

were dead. I had to come see you and make sure they hadn't hurt you too," Carol fired rapidly at Rose. She then turned to Katha she said..."I hope you don't mind Ms. O'Malley."

"Billy Carter is stupid," Rose exclaimed.

"Yes, he is. I'm glad you're here and safe," Carol said with relief than embarrassed to be showing her feelings she added "With whom else would I watch soaps and Vampire Diaries?"

"It's more than okay, dear. I'm glad you came for Rose's sake," Katha interjected smiling. "You are a good friend to come when she needs you."

Carol blushed and replied, "She'd come to me if I needed her."

"I'm glad you're here, Carol. It has been so horrible."

"I can't imagine what you're going through with these killings. I thought it was bad when my Dad left last year, but this is so much worse."

"Thanks for reminding me," Rose replied snarling.

"Gee, I'm sorry, Rose. I don't know what to say. Please give me another chance to make it up to you. I'm stumbling here; I want to help you get through this but I don't know how," Carol said contritely. "Nobody I ever knew died except my grandmother, and she had cancer, so it was like expected.

"I'm sorry too. I don't understand why I was so angry at you. You didn't do anything. You come over here to be nice to me and I snarl at you. Sorry."

"It's okay. I'd be angry too. Someone killed your father and hurt your mom. You have a right to be angry."

The doorbell pealed loudly.

"Thanks, Carol, Grandma Katha's right; you are a good friend."

"We'll ignore them and they'll go away," Katha insisted to Rose, and Carol as the doorbell repeatedly rang.

"I want to talk to my Grandma Katha for minute...could you?" asked Rose, motioning with her eyes for Carol to go upstairs.

"I'm going up to your room now," Carol replied understanding.

"Grandma, do you think these reporters will ever go away? And why haven't they found Daddy's killer yet? It had to have been an escaped killer or something," Rose enquired angrily.

"Dear, they'll go away when the next story hits, and yes, I believe they'll find your Daddy's killer soon, but we will have to be patient awhile. They won't rest until they find him or her. Don't you worry."

"Daddy and I were so lucky when he married Mom."

"Your dad hit the jackpot when he won my Lily. Never you fear; Lily will take care of you now. She adopted you, but you are her daughter even without those papers. You are safe with your family."

The doorbell pealed again.

"Dratted people! Why won't they go find another story," Katha asked no one in particular.

"Katha it's me, Terrence. Let me in the house!" demanded the voice at the door.

"Terrence who?" asked Katha playing it dumb.

"Terrence Stewart, your beau, hopefully the love of your life," the voice answered.

"Why Terrence, come in here, quickly. Vultures are out there."

As Rose looked out, she saw several trucks, camera operators, and reporters with microphones in the distance. She tried unsuccessfully to block out the shouting.

"Ms. Brooksfield, Ms. O' Malley, any comment about the fact the mayor was found naked with his secretary?" asked one voice, as another asked, "Any leads on the killer er... killers?"

Katha ushered Terrence in and closed the door quickly. Terrence looked back at them like he escaped tigers and asked while glaring at the crowd, "Do you want me to call my son and have all of them removed?"

"Well I don't want to make difficulty for you, dear. It might be too much trouble," Katha answered demurely.

"Why my dear, it would be my great pleasure to have them removed. After all if the police chief's father hasn't the influence to get rid of those people, who does?" Terrence asked.

"Why, thank you, Terrence. A lady does appreciate such heroism," Katha said, fluttering her eyelids like Scarlet O'Hara.

Rose looked at the man in surprise. This six-foot white-haired coiffured gentleman, being manipulated into doing exactly what Grandma Katha wanted, appeared intelligent. How did Grandma Katha always manage to get what she wanted? He stood tall, about six feet, and for an older man, quite good-looking. He appeared trim, and

for a senior, strong. He looked younger than
Grandma Katha but Rose couldn't guess his
age or Grandma's for that matter. Grandma
insinuated she was eighty-five or eighty-six,
but she certainly didn't appear that old.
Grandma certainly understood how to pick
her boyfriends. He appeared to be the police
chief's father, Police Chief Edward Stewart.
Rose wasn't completely surprised that he
had connections. No doubt about it,
Grandma Katha held a position as a mover
and a shaker, and this guy was top-notch. He
seemed to like Grandma Katha too. Maybe
Grandma Katha would be happy again?

When she lost Grandpa Kieran she seemed
so lonely. Grandma Katha lost all her spark
and only recently she seemed like she had
her spirit back. Did this man make her
happy again? Would Mom lose all her spunk
like that, now that Daddy was gone? How
could Daddy be dead? Murdered! This
seemed all unreal.

Rose watched as Terrence put his arm
around Katha hugging her for a moment.
Terrence stopped and picked up a phone and

called his son. He better not hurt Grandma
Katha, or she'd make him sorry.

"Yes, son, they are surrounded Katha's
house. No, son, I haven't. You'll be the first
to know when I'm ready to marry Katha.
Sorry, so you'll remove the paparazzi?
Okay. Thanks, Neddy. Goodbye, son."

"The scum should be gone within the hour.
My son sent police to disperse them."
Terrence told a smiling Katha, "The
reporters should leave soon." "So what will
your son do about the murder of my great-
grandson by marriage?" Katha demanded.

"He has his best man working on the case.
My son gave me the grilling of a lifetime of
being your alibi, dear. He asked me if I
would make you an honest woman."

"Sorry, dear! When, Police Constable Silas
Rentford demanded my alibi, I had no
choice, but to tell him I spent the afternoon
with you. I'm embarrassed. I understood it
would get back to your son, but with Lily
and Amelia hurt, it went out of my head to
call you," embellished Katha.

"Oh, my dear girl, I'm so sorry. How incredibly selfish of me not to think of what you had suffered. It must have been nerve wrecking and heartbreaking for you. Are you okay, dear heart? Are your chicks okay now?"

"Chicks? I think that word might be politically incorrect now."

"It's so hard to keep up with what is acceptable language. The thing is I never use the word the way they think it means."

"You'd think you would have learned in your job, Terrence."

"I'm retired from that job, which gives me a lot more leeway. Now about your girls, are they okay?"

"Lily is still in the hospital, but they say she'll get better in a few days. Amelia has a broken leg and a concussion and she is staying too."

"I'm so sorry, my dear. Neddy will get to the bottom of this don't you worry. He is the police chief after all." Terrence reassured.

"Neddy? You call a grown man Neddy? Be careful not to do call him Neddy in public, dear, it might embarrass him as chief of police." Katha cautioned, and then tempered it with praise "But I am so lucky that I can always count on you, dear."

"And this is this Rose, your great-great-granddaughter?"

"Yes, Terrence."

"It is lovely to meet you, Rose. I hope you don't mind me calling you by your first name."

"Not at all, Mr. Stewart. It's a pleasure to meet you too," Rose replied ladylike. "Well, such exquisite manners; a credit to my dear," Terrence said to Katha.

Speaking with Rose again he asked, "Would you like to call me Terrence? Mr. Stewart is quite a mouthful. And perhaps someday I'll convince your lovely grandmother to marry me and I can be your Grandpa Terrence."

"Terrence, don't put ideas in her head," Katha rebuked.

"I'll think about it," Rose replied, smiling.

"This one is a definite keeper, Grandma Katha," whispered Rose.

As she walked towards the stairs she retorted "I'm going to leave you kids alone while I watch television in the guest bedroom upstairs... with my friend. Don't do anything I wouldn't do," she said saucily, as she bounded up the stairs.

"Rose Brooksfield, you behave," replied Katha waving her finger.

"Sorry, Grandma Katha; I'll see you two later."

"I like how that child thinks," Terrence stated and kissed Katha's neck.

"Terrence, there are children in the house. Rose's friend is upstairs as well," Katha scolded.

"Sorry dear, I forgot myself in your loveliness. Are you okay Katha?" Terence asked searching her face, "I've been worried sick. Should I stick to your side like glue?"

"I'm sure you have been; I have been too; they have to catch the evil person or persons who are behind these murders. Soon!! Drat now I better admit I'm scared and I don't scare easy. Why did people close to my girls get murdered?"

"I don't know, my darling, but I'm going to protect you and your chicks. I already asked Edward for a patrol car to swing by regularly and I'm going to hire a guard to protect your girls in the hospital," Terrence replied fiercely.

"It is sweet of you. Don't worry about the guard. Lily has already hired one. I called too. Her close friend said he already sent one. He runs some big security firm downtown."

"As long as your chicks are safe and you are safe I'm happy."

"That's why I love you. Even though you understand I can take care of myself and my love ones you step up to do so."

"Did you get any sleep last night?" Terrence asked looking worried. "You won't be any good to them if you don't rest too."

"Not a lot of sleep." Katha admitted. "Why don't you rest up against me, sweetheart, close your eyes and I'll watch over you and Rose and Carol."

"I think I might take you up on your offer," Katha replied closing her eyes and sounding extremely exhausted.

~0~

Terrence

Terrence stared at Katha's sleeping form. How did he get so lucky to meet such a dynamite lady? The woman was quicksilver when it came to pinning her. She already refused him several times but he hoped she would relent and marry him now, especially now that she saw him with her family. She worried about the age difference, but so what?

Age meant nothing. Terrence was seventy-four years old to her eighty-one. In relative terms this was not a big deal. It seemed funny how she let people think she was older and looked good for her age. Even for an eighty-one-year-old she looked far younger than she should. In truth Terrence felt she looked way younger than him. A few times people teased him saying he was a cradle robber. They were equal when you considered that according to the actuarial tables men didn't live as long as women. He would show her tender care and that despite her strength, she needed him as much as he craved her gentleness and her loving touch.

This business about the murder troubled him. Some awful person had gotten awful close to Katha and her chicks. Well they had better think again if they think they will harm anyone else his Katha loved. Katha was prideful and she worried about her reputation. Katha wouldn't let him stay. Someone had to protect them. Neddy promised him he would have a guard on the house for a few days. Surely that would give them time to find the killer.

He hoped he got to meet Amelia soon. He had met Lily a few times when she came into his court. He presided as a judge on some of her cases, but he didn't know her well. He understood how passionate Lily prosecuted the guilty, but he'd also seen her understanding for those who made a mistake. She always felt they could be rehabilitated.

He had seen a lot of those same
characteristics in Katha and realized Lily
absorbed them from Katha. Katha was the
first woman he fell for immediately after his
wife's death. It was like he had known her
all his life.

He felt sure she existed as his soul mate, the
woman he'd been waiting for all his life.
She was the one, the original incredible,
irascible Katha. The woman he always
dreamed there for him. She remained a
woman of immense emotions and pure
pleasure to spend any time.

She was the woman he wanted to marry and
be with her for the end of his days. If only
he could convince her marrying him
wouldn't kill him. She truly believed she
held a curse on her which killed her
husbands. How foolish that notion was. At
first he mocked her concerns.

Katha truly believed however that her husbands, all three of them died before their time, simply because they were married to her. Even though none of what she said was true, Terrence discerned to spend even a short time as Katha's husband, a man would be extremely lucky.

All those years on the bench told him neither of Katha's girls had perpetrated these hideous crimes and there appeared something more sinister behind all this. How were the three murders connected? Terrence wasn't sure, but he knew he had to protect Katha's family. No harm would befall them while he watched over them.

Terrence heard the soft voices of Carol and Rose talking upstairs and listened in over the soft breaths of Katha sleeping. Terrence stared up to the now quiet upstairs and hoped Rose slept. This new murder sounded like someone strongly targeted Katha's family, but was it for protection or harm? He would protect his Katha at all costs. He would protect them all. Katha loved fiercely and she put everyone but herself first. This was what he loved most about her. That and her zest for life.

Katha entered a room and everyone seemed brighter, happier. She had a ready smile and a big heart. Her little courtesies, the compliments she gave out, the willing ear she lent, all of these attracted him. People would smile when they saw her coming. Total strangers would confide in her and she would listen and give advice.

Someone so giving like Katha, deserved all the happiness in the world and Terrence wanted to give the world to her. He would convince Katha that she would be the wife for him and he could be the husband she deserved. Katha Stewart had a lovely ring to it after all, and it would give her his power to protect her.

~0~

Carol and Rose a short time ago

"So what happened with your dad the other day?" asked Rose.

"I don't understand!"

"He showed up to the soccer match and you quit. Why?" Rose asked.

"Oh that," Carol said. "He didn't want to be there. So I quit, then he grew angry because I did. He said I am a disappointment. He said quitters never prosper. Blah, blah, blah."

"I'm sorry; your dad said all the wrong things. He loves you despite his attitude. At least your dad is alive and you two could mend your relationship."

"You had a better bond with your dad then I did. You had lots of years of wonderful memories."

"My dad did like to do things with me, when work didn't take him away."

"Yes, but your dad did make time for you. When did mine, except for that one time he came to my soccer game? Let's be honest, I think my dad wanted an athlete, not a daughter. Nothing I ever do or did meant anything to him. When he discovered I play soccer, he felt he could be proud of me. He would have an athlete for daughter. It's never about me."

"I think you are wrong and he loves you and doesn't understand how to show it."

"It doesn't seem like he does," Carol replied sadly.

"Adults aren't perfect. They are human and they make mistakes; besides parents always expect a lot out of you."

"Where did you get that from? Your mom? My dad wishes I would have been a boy," Carol whined.

"No, he might say it the wrong way and show you awkwardly; but he loves having a daughter," Rose reassured.

"How do you know what he thinks?" Carol sniped.

"He brags about you when you're not around. He told me you're an A-plus student and he hoped I was too."

"He did?" answered Carol surprised but happy.

"Yes, I heard him talking about you with Mrs. Pelland, the guidance teacher as well. He bragged about how smart you were."

"Here I came over to help my best friend, because she's lost her dad and she helps me. How did I get so lucky to pick you as a friend?" Carol exclaimed.

"I thought I picked you," laughed Rose.

"Remember how we met?"

"I remember those dancing toads harassed you at school. We were ten years old," Carol started.

"Yes, Priscilla, Daria, and Tina," interrupted Rose.

"They were mean," Carol admitted.

"You paid them back though. You stuck a frog, which had been preserved in formaldehyde, in Priscilla's favourite purse. What did you do to Tina and Daria?" Rose asked.

"Tina's brother put the fear in her. He liked me, so he stood up for you. He told her he would tell their mom, how she'd been bullying you. Tina's mom hated bullies and would have severely punished her."

"And Daria? Why did she stop?"

"I told her if she didn't, I would beat the snot out of her," Carol replied.

"You didn't?" Rose asked incredulously.

"I did! She backed off didn't she?"

"Thanks for sticking up for me Carol. I don't think I ever thanked you."

"Sure you did! Every time I ever needed you, you were there for me;" Carol exclaimed. "So let me help you now. Tell me about your dad."

"Someone killed him," Rose replied in a quiet voice.

"I heard that on the news," Carol insisted, "But tell me anyway."

"My dad was found dead with Amber, his secretary. Mom and Grandma Katha tried to keep it from me, that he was found naked with her. But I understood that's how they were found even before the newscast."

"It's embarrassing, but it's your father, not you," Carol insisted.

"He wasn't having an affair with ditzy Amber," Rose protested. "She couldn't even put a single sentence together. My dad likes...liked smart woman, like Lily and my mother."

"Well d'oh you'd know he didn't cheat. If someone killed him they were smart enough to pose them together," Carol agreed.

"That's what I thought, but those awful reporters made things up to report. That why you are my best friend. I knew you'd understand the truth without me even saying anything. Why can't other people realize it was staged? It's horrible that someone killed my father, but all they seem to care about is he was found naked. What about finding his killer?" Rose explained.

"Reporters are supposed to be objective. Any good reporter checks their facts."

"How do you know so much about reporters?" asked Rose.

"I want to be one someday."

"What kind? Print? Radio? Television?" Rose asked.

"I'd like to be an entertainment reporter, like the host of Entertainment Tonight," Carol explained.

"I would never do a job that you need to speak in public. I hate speaking to people and to be affected by people staring at me all the time."

"I know Rose. I think it would be a fun job for me, obviously not for you," Carol explained "It is hard work too. People don't realize how much work it is."

"I haven't a clue what job I want to do in the future," Rose explained.

"There's plenty of time. My mom says that all the time," Carol reassured "You'll figure out exactly what you want to do."

"Good imitation of your mom," Rose said giggling.

"I thought so," Carol replied looking serious. "If you need anything, I'm here."

"Thanks for realizing I can't talk about my dad yet. I'm kind of going screen saver here."

"When you want to start talking, I'll listen."

"So did you see Barry ask out Emily?" Rose asked changing the subject.

"Yes, they make a cute couple."

"Barry has liked Emily forever."

"Matchmaking again?" asked Carol smiling.

"Yes, Barry needed a little push."

"So how did you get them together?" Carol demanded.

"Barry hung out near Emily's locker again and I said to him. 'Why don't you ask her out for and cut the damn-a-rama?' " Rose admitted.

"And that worked?" Carol asked.

"Not exactly. He asked me where he should take her," Rose admitted.

"Gee, clueless much?"

"You'd think hanging around her so much he'd realize she wanted to watch she wanted to watch *Star Trek Into Darkness*. She loves *Chris Pine*," Rose replied.

"I want to see *Star Trek Into Darkness* too. So did you tell him?" Carol asked.

"I did and he said, 'But the movie is a drama and a travesty of the older version," Rose laughed.

"He didn't. What did you say?"

"I said it's a great movie. Check out the trailer. He liked the trailer. He said, 'I'm wrong it really takes it back to the Star Trek series, and then he decided to ask her to the movie." Rose laughed.

"I'm glad he took your advice. Like I said, they are cute together."

"They are cute," Rose agreed. "So can you stay over later tonight or do you need to bounce?"

"I can stay; my mom said I could, as long as it's okay with your Grandma Katha," Carol replied.

"It will be. Grandma Katha will say yes."

"Good. Now let's watch some *Much Music* unless you have some recorded old episodes of *All My Children*."

"You're in luck Grandma Katha has a lot of old tapes of it. I wish they hadn't cancelled *All My Children*. Hopefully they'll put it on the internet again at some point, but it's not looking good, though that could change. Grandma Katha's tapes and recordings are nice and clear," Rose said putting *All My Children'* on the television set.

Carol replied sadly, "We should watch one of the really old tapes of the show. Why isn't it on the air anymore? I miss it."

"I agree. I miss it too. Maybe we could watch some of the really older stuff later. I'm just going to close my eyes for a minute but keep talking." Rose answered.

"So I think J.r. and Annie are delecto. They look like they'll mack on each other any moment," Carol replied still watching.

Carol glanced over and realized Rose had fallen sound asleep. She covered Rose up and climbed into the other twin bed. Turning the close captioning on and muting the sound, she turned off the PVR and turned on the television setting. As she did that she saw a scroll come across the screen. Terrence also watching television silently downstairs saw the same scroll.

Fourth murder this week. Local security expert Zachary Buchanan found murdered. Story at 11p.m. with Henry Roberts. Breaking news story: Local reporter Paul Knight reported missing. If you have seen him please call your local police station with any information.

This town is damaged. Four murders in two days? Now a news reporter had gone missing? This is whack. Is this related? Poor Rose. I hope she doesn't find out her dad was such a dirty dog and cheated with Amber. I should have told her, but she was already wigged out. What kind of friend would do that? She has always been there for me. I'll be there for her. I'll beat up anyone who gets up in her grill. Carol thought, closed her eyes and went to sleep.

~0~

Chapter 10 - A View to a Kill

Earlier that Evening

A man passed in front of the television screen pacing. He turned on a DVD recording of the news.

"This reporter has learned Mayor Horace Brooksfield was found murdered in flagrante delicto with his executive assistant, Amber Trent yesterday. Amber Trent worked for Mayor Brooksfield for the last two years. There is no comment from Crown Attorney Lily Kelly Brooksfield or family. Sources close to the mayor say Amber Trent had been having an affair with the mayor for the last year. The police have no comment at this time about the cause of death. Unconfirmed sources tell this reporter they died from poisoning... the

same poisoning which is believed to have felled Crown Attorney Lily Kelly-Brooksfield, Lily Kelly who is now in a hospital in satisfactory condition. Mayor Horace Brooksfield leaves behind a fourteen-year- old daughter Rose and his current wife Crown attorney Lily Brooksfield. Our deepest sympathies go out to the mayor's family.

On another odd note, the Crown attorney arrived at the scene of a murder at her cousins' new store Quirks yesterday. Store clerk Megan Fowler was found dead earlier today in an apparent robbery. Store owner Amelia Kelly was also hurt and is in the hospital. Are the two murders connected? Stay tuned to this station for more updates and tune in at six p.m. for News Hour for all the latest stories." Henry Roberts reporting for CHPV-TV."

He screamed in anger at the television, picked up the phone and called the hospital. He wanted to discern that she remained okay.

"Please tell me about Lily Brooksfield, and Amelia Kelly. What is their condition?" he asked politely and sweetly.

He composed himself as the voice on the other end said, "I'm sorry we can't give out any information at this time."

Slamming down the phone in anger and ranting aloud, as if talking to the announcer on the television he began..., "How could she be hurt? The plan wasn't that she should be harmed. I had done it all for her. Every breath I took existed for her, my sweet Angel. Oh how I missed her. I missed looking at her lovely face. Some people can stare at a lake, watching every ripple every nuance. I look at her, and view the ripples of her emotions. Her sweetness, and kindness, the onc I saw the most. How I loved her. So much so it hurt. Her happiness remained my only goal," he ranted then continued..., "You behold a great beauty. You should be bowing to her greatness."

He looked over at the man lying on the
floor, duct tape over his mouth and rope
over his hands and feet connecting both. He
pulled the duct tape from over the man's
mouth.

"Yes, she's beautiful and going to be fine,"
the man replied muffled licking the lips,
which had held the duct tape.

"Don't get any ideas. She's mine!" the man
snarled, his eyes glaring.

"Of course she's yours," mollified the man.
"She must care deeply about you."

"Not yet, but she will once she knows me."

"It's like that? I loved a woman once, but
she started going out with some other guy.
She left me high and dry," sympathized the
tied up man.

"It's not like that. I must show her I've
changed and am worthy of her. I made a few
mistakes in my life. Those other women
enticed me to their beds. Who doesn't sow a
few wild oats in their youth? I got my life
back together for her. I wanted to be near
her and take my rightful place at her side but
others kept getting in the way. Damn them!"

"No control! Control, control! No one must comprehend this side of me. I have fought long and hard to hide in plain sight until my plan was completed and my goddess would be every day by my side," he muttered, then said louder..."You didn't hear that, did you? Let me compose myself. I'm good the interview can continue."

"Hear what?" the prisoner stated, agreeably.

"She will have my children. We will truly be happy in her home. I will allow her cousin to remain in her life if the cousin behaves. We can grow old together, just the two of us; with her family, no...our family surrounding us."

"Of course you will."

"Don't pretend to humour me. The damn doctor was wrong; I stand in control of my life. I'm in control of everything and everyone. I will have my lady by my side. My lady has shown herself to me. I will have her heart, once I revealed myself," he muttered some more.

The man began pacing back and forth, but smiled like he saw the object of his affections before him.

"She glows with a light, that beholds the goodness in everyone and oh how I need such a light. How I love her. I remembered the first day I met her. She smiled a beckoning smile at me; the smile that told me she remained mine, and mine alone. She pulled her hair back from her face with one hand and the other held lemonade for me. She cared enough to give me drink, when I was thirsty. She existed as a sight of beauty in a pale yellow sundress, with those lovely sandals on such delicate ankles. A lady of high calibre and she looked at me and smiled!"

"She sounds lovely," the captive man commented.

"She is lovely. Such beauty and warmth, my Angel has always projected. I had stared a little too long and she blushed, such an innocent. I loved the way she kept herself to herself. She captured my frozen heart on that glorious day."

"I can understand that"

"Her father, the cheap skate, paid me a mere five dollars to cut the lawn. I wanted to decline and punch him in the nose, when he refused to pay me more-than I saw her, my Angel. She came home and she brushed by me, saying sorry, swiftly entering into the house. Like a ray of sunshine, she appeared smiling moments later. A glass of lemonade clutched in her hand, offering it to me, when I stood dying of thirst."

"You mentioned the lemonade already," the man replied.

"Oh do be quiet while I give you this interview."

The hostage immediately zipped his lips with his fingers.

"Much better now where was I? Oh, how she smiled, demurely and sweetly. Her eyes cast down and she blushed. She ran back into the house putting distance between us because of her modesty. I went home and told my dying mother I met the girl of my dreams. Mother smiled. Mother glowed in happiness, as I described my Angel. She said she hoped my Angel and I would be happy together. It was meant to be. You believe me now? Even mother understood my Angel should be with me."

"Of course I believe you," the prisoner agreed. "But how did you know she was the one?"

"Terri, my former girlfriend, had also smiled, but without the blush and the honesty of my Angel's smile. Terri grinned at me, but she betrayed me instantly. She earned the punishment she received. I get turned on just thinking about it. Her body lush and willing cried out to me. How she begged for her life, pleading with me so prettily. Terri even said she had loved me. But I understood the truth, she had been with him. She offered herself to the football jock Henry. Did Henry treat her like a queen? No! He soiled her forever marking her as easy. I caught Henry bragging about it."

"Shame on Henry," the captive replied and then seeing the man's face he added, "And Terri, of course."

"Mother told me about girls like that, who put on airs of innocence but are at their hearts whores. They are liars and whores, sluts, who say whatever you want to hear. Terri had been one of these. Hadn't she offered herself again to me, to save her life? I told you I took what was offered and how she cried. She begged me to spare her."

"So you did. Right?" the hostage asked hopefully.

"No, silly! She had said we were joined as one. That I would be killing myself if I killed her. She insisted it over and over like a buzzing bee, but I understood the truth about her. She contained evil and had to die, and I cleaned myself with bleach to get her taint off myself. The blood on the power saw cleaned up nicely as well. I disposed of it and my clothes, and of course all those lovely little pieces of her body. Those delightful little pieces of flesh, I had placed so lovingly in garbage bags, for the trash she was!"

"You killed her?" the captive man exclaimed paling.

"Of course I killed her. I truly expected them to find her body but they still haven't. Foolish aren't they? You'd think they would do their job and be productive police officers. But back to my Angel, you wanted to hear all about that didn't you? Of course you do! It's your job."

"It is my job; now fill me in on your beloved Angel," encouraged the captive trying to remain useful so he wouldn't be killed.

"Now don't get ideas she's my Angel. I saw everyone mourning a whore, not knowing where she lay or how she met her fate. It was so delicious. I truly loved keeping a secret of this magnitude. I even went to the funeral and no one suspected me. Well no one except my father who hustled me off to a clinic and a doctor. My father hadn't admitted to the doctor I had killed a human being. No, Father had only said I loved to kill animals. Personally I think he was in denial but it served my purposes. He didn't stop me."

The man continued to pace wildly moving his hand while telling the story. "You know the type of father don't you? You do?" He said.

Noting the captive's nod of his head he continued, "Oh good, it shouldn't be as hard for you to understand all of this. My father abused me. His belt told me all about his displeasure. Even the doctor said that father shouldn't have struck me, or put me in the closet...that it was wrong."

"You told a doctor about your murderous tendencies and they didn't stop you?" the hostage blurted.

"Hah. good one. I do like you. The doctor wouldn't, or couldn't, understand about the murders if I told him; so I hid the real me. I learned well from the doctor how to hide in plain sight. I learned how to hide my true self, from those who would condemn it. I'd learned control, so those around me saw only the agreeable young man they wanted to view. Not even my eagle-eyed father penetrated into my core. The foolish doctor told my father I was much better with the drug and the psychotherapy I received. If people did see through the façade, I would deal with them. I've dealt with you. You understand my position right? I didn't mean to hurt my Angel. It wasn't my fault."

"You hurt your Angel? Where's your doctor now?" asked the hostage.

"Don't say that I hurt her."

"Sorry, of course you didn't hurt her," the captive agreed.

"I did kill the doctor, but only when he got to close. He wanted to lock me up in a padded cell! Me!"

"Well of course you had to. Locking you up would have been bad for you."

"You do understand. Wonderful! Now to continue with my story, my father came to me and said he knew I had killed the doctor. He didn't turn me in, but he said he could no longer pretend his son appeared normal. Normal? As if! If normal was like my mealy-mouthed father, I never want to be him."

"Who would?" agreed the captive.

"Exactly! My father told me the next day we would be going to a private clinic in Brazil, because there was no extradition there. Like I would ever be extradited; no one guessed my crimes but my hawk-eyed father. Mother had been right when she said all his cheating with his secretary made him stupid. How dare he cheat on the lovely lady, my mother? He never guessed what I planned for him. Too bad he died so quickly, clutching his heart. I felt bad for a few minutes. I even sought help after the incident. I listened for hours on end to a simple-minded shrink who blamed all my woes on my father. Why didn't he understand I loved my Angel? She makes me whole, instead of the shattered pieces he made me without her."

The man then clutched his hands to his heart and seemed to be carried away with his thoughts. His captive grew alarmed he had to keep him talking. He smiled at the man hoping to connect with him.

"Where was I? You are listening, aren't you, Paul? I love your newscasts by the way, even when they anger me by mentioning my Angel. Of course those same stories brought my Angel back to me, so I forgive you. I understand you have to do what you are told. It's your bosses I blame. But enough about you, back to my reasons for all I'm doing."

"Thank you... I think you were speaking of about your shrink and your father...," Paul commented, but was interrupted.

"I think you need the tape back on your mouth. You're ruining the interview," he exclaimed, placing duct tape over Paul's mouth again.

"You understand why I had to do this. Don't you? Why all this was necessary? Why I had to bring you here? After all you get a great story out of it. Enough, enough about your story though, and of course dwelling on my conquests, my triumphs, I need to focus on the work at hand and getting my beloved to love me. I think she will finally perceive me as the man she wants as her partner. Don't you, Paul? My psychiatrist was wrong. He said my Angel was an unattainable woman. Silly man! What did he know? But I believed in my Angel; all she needed was to meet me again. Then she would smile her smile and love me. I will be the man she will call her hero, her knight in shining armour."

"No, I'm getting ahead of myself. Quit making me rush, rush and ruin my plans. I need to stick to my plan, slowly advance and win my fair maid. This interview is over, Paul. I have a lot of work to do. A man like you should understand."

Paul couldn't conceal the angry look which came over his face. Paul knew what this meant if he didn't get the interview, he would be killed.

"Don't you dare make angry faces at me! I'm doing my job, you just do yours!" Paul tried to signal that he would do his job by bobbing his head but the man ignored him and he was forced to watch as the man called the hospital yet again.

His Angel lay injured in a hospital room. At least she had her cousin for company. She was safe. Take a deep breath, the man thought and he began to pace and rant out loud again.

"Those damn girls. Those whores! They tainted both sweet cousins. It is why they were in the hospital; I shouldn't blame myself. Should I, Paul?"

Paul nodded.

"I tried to save the innocents from the taint. Hadn't I slain to get rid of the taint?"

Paul nodded again and hoped to once again convince him the interview was necessary.

"Okay Paul, you want an interview on why I killed?"

Paul nodded frantically.

"Certainly I'd be happy to give you an award-winning interview. I am so careful after all this. These stupid cops will never discover me. What? Well certainly I killed. I didn't leave any evidence of myself there. I snuck up when her back was turned to me. Megan! What a slut. I had viewed how she let her boyfriend in after closing hours. How they had soiled the countertop at Quirks. How dare they? She had to die. She fought back too easy and I had to kill her brutally... all that blood."

"It was her fault my Angel slipped. The boyfriend will die too. His turn will come. Slowly and more painfully, it won't be as easy as her death. I saw him take from the till while the slut cleaned up herself at the store. First, though, I plan to let him suffer, mourning the whore. I'll bide my time and kill him too. Or I'll let the cops think he committed the murders. Oh the irony that would be. You agree, Paul?"

Paul tied with rope, sat somewhat slumped in a chair, directly in front of the killer. Duct tape now covered his mouth again, but he nodded.

"Of course you do! I'm brilliant. He will pay... oh yes... he will pay for his treachery. The whore Amber, who screwed Lily's husband in his office? She deserved what she got. What, you think she was just his secretary, Paul? Oh no, she was his paid whore! I watched as she strutted and tempted Horace; but he was married to sweet Lily. So why did he cheat? Some men don't understand how fortunate they are."

Paul shook his head trying to get free of the duct tape.

"Don't shake your head at me! What? You want to understand why I wasn't identified? No one saw me arrive through the basement. The guard during the day is an idiot. I snuck up the back stairs and spotted them. Those two rutting like farm animals. I waited patiently, until they stopped falling all over each other; snuck up and first hit him on the head, then her. She shook then. Oh I truly scared her! I loved that part! It was so delicious! She ran but I caught her and hit her on the head. I posed them so everyone would recognize their crime. I was simply brilliant."

Paul moved his head; he was finding it hard to hold it in this position listening to this man drone on, but the killer moved his head back and forth as if Paul was agreeing.

"Why thank you, Paul. Yes, I have to admit it was brilliant. So you wanted to see how I created the gas?"

Paul bobbed his head in agreement, anything to keep this man talking.

"Chlorine gas is such an easy fix for me to make. After all, I excelled at Chemistry in high school. So, I remembered the quantities. Like I said, I my memory is excellent. They used this substance in the First World War. Our poor troops were harmed irreparably. Some of them out right killed with various gases they used. But why am I telling you this? You are a journalist and well-educated; you'd comprehend all of this information.

"Now where was I? Oh yes...in fact, if truth were to be told, I have a photographic memory. Like my Angel, these were truly a match. It was so much fun to mix and watch the chemicals take root. I cleaned up at the scenes, leaving no trace of me. I'm good at cleansing. I still can't quite believe the Ravenworst police haven't clued in about the chlorine gas."

 Paul struggled to get some more to get free at this point, but the killer took it as if he'd asked him a question.

"What? You want to know why they didn't clue in Paul? The investigators in Ravenworst were underfunded and too proud to ask for outside help. Lucky for me! It does seem the Happy Valley Police investigators are more thorough. They identified the gas. Damn that Coroner Andrew Piper. He is too smart for his own good. As for the investigating officer,

Emmett Rogers, scrutinized too close at my Angel. As long as he doesn't threaten her, I will allow him to pretend to investigate. The widow Lily likes him despite her protests. But believe me, Paul, I will fix him, or any police officer who threatens what is mine. I noticed the way he looks at Lily Kelly, when no one is looking. Don't you think it would be kind of funny if he became a relative and never discerned any of my crimes, Paul? Oh how glorious that would be, flaunting my crimes in front of a police officer. Now wouldn't it, Paul?"

Paul tried to nod but his head wouldn't bob anymore.

"You understand how it is, being in front of the cameras all the time. Emmett Rogers is an upstanding man, fit for a family member. So I think he would be acceptable for her. Don't you?"

Paul managed to nodded again, trying to make himself agreeable once more to the killer.

"Well, of course I was worried about my dear, sweet Angel and her cousin, though it hadn't occurred to me though that Amelia would slip and Lily would be gassed. I blamed those whores just thinking about it again. Yes the whores are to blame; at least now their taint is stopped. They can't harm my Angel. I'll continue to watch over my sweet Angel keeping her safe. Those damn paparazzi stalk my Angel's house. Can't you do anything about the paparazzi, Paul? I appreciate you hate their ilk too. They give reporters a bad name. If they don't leave her alone, they will suffer the consequences. And you know what that means, don't you Paul? And if the cop dares to threaten my Angel, I'll stop him. One day soon my Angel will appreciate me and she will comprehend all I had done for her."

"Quite the story," Paul retorted as the killer took the tape off his mouth again and offered him a lukewarm coffee.

Paul readily drank, his throat parched from the exposure to the tape.

"Do you want me to feature you on the news? We should get this all on camera for a special series. It will be on tomorrow."

The killer didn't respond and Paul grew frightened.

"You will you let me go now?" asked Paul.

"No, we may need to have another interview. Aw, I can't lie to such a trusting face. The truth, though, is now you know about me... I can't let you go," the killer answered putting the tape back on Paul's mouth, "It's too bad you won't be available for the story at six p.m. Isn't it, Paul? It's too sad; you are so much of a snoop, you caught onto me. You'll have to explain how you did later, when I return. In the meantime, those pills I slipped in your drink should be taking hold soon. Nighty, night, Paulie. Oh, and sorry about the tight space. You can't be found. Don't think about making any noise. I've soundproofed my apartment, including this closet."

The killer upended Paul like he weighed next to nothing and placed him into the hall closet.

"Please..." Paul begged groggily through the new duct tape, begging for his life.

"Sorry, Paul, I'm going to the hospital. Nothing and no one will get in my way. I must grasp for myself, my Angel is okay. I can't have done the unthinkable and seriously hurt my Angel. I would never harm her, ever. I blame those evil people who made me kill them. Why did they get between us?"

He shut and locked the door to his apartment after changing into the police uniform. That uniform would make them tell her how she was. He got into his car, driving straight to the hospital. When he arrived at the hospital, he became angry to find a man standing guard outside her hospital room door. Who is he? Why did he keep me from my Angel? How dare he come between us? He thought.

He went to the cafeteria and purchased two coffees. Taking two stir sticks, he placed sugar and his. He reached into his pocket for the pill bottle he no longer used. With no one watching, he put pills into the other coffee and waited as they melted into the cup. It was ready. He went up in the elevator to the floor he seen the man on. Making small talk, he began..."I'm Detective Barnes sent to protect Ms. Kelly and you are?" he lied.

"Zachary Buchanan, I work for Frank Hawk Security Services. I was told there were cutbacks and you weren't able to guard the lady." protested the man.

"We'll get this killer, you need not worry. But it certainly is a relief to find Ms. Kelly is protected. The station sent me to check on Ms. Kelly."

"But that isn't what you said a minute ago." Zachary Buchanan protested.

"A slip of the tongue, forgive me I've had a long shift today. Now you were hired by whom?"

"Lily Brooksfield hired me. I know what that's like to work along shift, I was supposed to get some relief an hour ago so I could get lunch."

"Oh, where are my manners? I have two coffees, here have one." the killer offered.

"Thank you. That hits the spot."

"Listen, see that cop down the hall?"

"Yes," Zachary answered.

"Excuse me for a minute while I'll speak to him and get him to take over while you go to lunch."

"That would be great."

The killer went down the hall and appeared to speak to the cop then returned, "We can go now. Come on I'll treat you to lunch."

"Wow, they pay you that much?"

"No, but I won fifty bucks in the office bet, so I can treat you."

"Well thanks; I'll take you up on that." Zachary gulped down his coffee in the elevator and the killer pretended to get a call, which he had to answer in his car.

"Say, can you go to my patrol car for a minute, I have to check in before lunch.

"I could just meet you in the cafeteria."

"I might be called away and then I couldn't tell you. Come on it will only take a few minutes," begged the killer.

"Okay, sure." Zachary agreed.

How easy it was to trick someone using a police uniform. It just initiated such trust. At least someone had the use of those pills, he thought laughing to himself ...two some ones. He chuckled. How he hated that they clouded his mind. He led the man to his car.

"Wait a minute I feel dizzy. What did you do to me?" Zachary asked already swaying on his feet.

The gun was stuck in the man's side with no resistance, the drugs already cloudy the man's mind. He made the man get in the trunk and slammed it shut. At first he heard banging then silence as the man succumbed

to the drugs effect. He was mad at Lily
before, but he understood now. She took
steps to protect his Amelia. How could he
fault her for helping his Amelia?

The killer drove, thinking about the man in
his trunk. Obviously Lily had hired him
sight unseen, a repulsive brute which could
harm my Angel. If he hadn't shown me his
security badge, I would have thought him
the dregs of society or one of those gang
members.

My Angel shouldn't be tainted with such
burgeoning evil. I must get rid of him before
he blemishes her, or makes a move on my
poor Angel. In her grieving state she's fair
game for predators like him. Don't worry
my darling; he shan't get near you again.

He reached his underground parking spot
and opened the trunk. Damn the man wasn't
moving yet another body to get rid of. He
drank down the coffee in one gulp and
reached for the protective suit in his back
seat putting it on.

Oops, I must have put too many pills in to the cup.

Who understood that many pills would kill? That damn doctor! He had been trying to kill me? Well, I'd fixed him first. I'd have to remember that for future reference those little pills did so much. But it meant the body must be dumped sooner.

Where could I put him? Think. Somewhere he wouldn't be found too soon? The Beyer building downtown? Undergoing renovations to be sold... it would be perfect! I will find some place to hide him somewhere in the building. The car rocked and he worried about the body in his trunk.

Watch the road and follow the laws. I must not give the cops a reason to stop me. Good, I'm here at the rear entrance of the Beyer Building and no cop in sight. I must not leave evidence of myself on him. After planting him there I must strip him bare than redress him.

Damn! There is someone there. That asshole real estate agent, Herbert Weatherthorpe prowled around the building. Guess it's a dumpster for old Zachary Buchanan. There's one nearby. I'll strip him, then redress him with the clothes I brought and toss him in the bin. I hope this would be a lesson to those who would try to take advantage of my Angel's good nature.

Her cousin obviously shared some of her good nature or she wouldn't have hired this man sight unseen. If she caught sight of the man she wouldn't have hired him. Lily had been there when he couldn't be for his Angel and he wouldn't forget the cousin. She deserved his familial devotion. He would grow to care for her. She was like a beloved sister-in-law. After all, she would soon be family. There, no one saw this remote location of the dumpster and pick up is tomorrow. Zachary would soon be lost at the dump, like Terri.

I'll throw away the plastic liner and vacuum the trunk when I get home. No fibres could be found from Zachary Buchanan. We are safe, my Angel, safe. He tidied himself, took off his protective suit, and then placed the suit in the back seat. He had to clean the police uniform at the cleaners. He then got back in his car and peeled away quickly from the curb.

~0~

Chapter 11 - Family Ties

"The ad should read ...SALES

ASSOCIATE WANTED MUST BE
PREPARED TO WORK EVENINGS AND
WEEKENDS. RE-ENUMERATION
ACCORDING TO EXPERIENCE...and the
phone number I gave you," Lily repeated
still with oxygen in her nose.

"Lily shouldn't you be resting? Who did you
call?" asked Katha, coming in their hospital
room.

"I was calling to place an ad, so we could
reopen Amelia's store again." Lily
explained, "I thought Rose and Carol could
work at the store, but I'm not prepared for
the girls to work there anymore. Not after
the guard disappeared which I had hired to
look after Amelia. I called the office to take

over my cases for a while; a month or two until they figure out who killed them."

Katha noticed Lily was careful not to mention her husband was one of the victims and Katha worried about Lily. Katha recalled how Lily avoided grief, by keeping busy and fretted this time she would not be able to do avoid the inevitable.

"Lily, I already hired someone. I interviewed earlier today for the position. There were several excellent candidates, but the best one was a lovely college girl Susan Terrell. She's the daughter of Barney, the security guard at City Hall. She is a black belt and experienced in sales. She worked all through high school at George's Toys."

"Didn't they go under?"

"Yes, unfortunately the toy shop was taken over by a big conglomerate and they closed it when George died, a few weeks ago. So she needs a job. I offered her the job and she happily accepted. Today the cleaning crew came in to fix the place, so the store can open tomorrow. I think the store should be strictly a nine to five operation for a while, until Amelia can be more hands on at the store."

"You hired someone to work at my store, Aunt Katha?" Amelia asked with a touch of anger and surprise, "And now you're setting the hours in my store?"

"I hope I didn't over step my bounds," Aunt Katha countered innocently.

"No of course, you didn't overstep," Amelia claimed swallowing her anger.

"Thanks Lily, thank-you, Aunt Katha. What would I do without you?" she said sarcastically under her breath, but Katha heard her anyway.

Amelia then hugged Katha despite her misgivings.

"You'll never find out, because family is always here for you honey," Katha replied taking it for a compliment, then turning to Lily she said. "Do you want to talk about Horace?"

"I don't want to talk about this!"

"Lily, you like to avoid things you don't want to face," Aunt Katha began.

"I'm grieving, that's how I'm doing. I'm madder than hell, that's how I am," Lily cried.

"You won't do anything stupid will you?"

"I never do anything stupid. I'm the poster child for good behaviour," Lily replied.

"No, you do go off the rails from time to time. You bumble into places no one should go. Like last year with that horrible man who threatened you, and years ago with that other man." Katha commented, "They could have killed you."

"Ian Turner was a maniac. I think he would have killed you. Thank god he's in jail. Horace was terrified for you. Oh I'm sorry, Lily, I shouldn't have brought up Horace," Amelia apologized.

"No, it's good for me to catch his name. I can't believe he's gone. Horace was so wonderful. He was a good father and a good man. I'll be damned if I let his murder, take all those memories away from him and his family," Lily cried, wiping tears away from her eyes.

"Let the police handle this." Katha begged,
"They will work hard to solve this crime.
They'll find out who did this and they'll
pay."

"She's dating the police chief's father,"
Amelia announced conspiratorially to Lily.

"And you didn't tell me? When did this
start?" asked Lily looking surprised.

"Oh about two months ago I think. I came
over early one morning and he was still in
her house," Amelia replied smirking.

"I'm still in the room girls. Do you mind not
talking about my love life? It's unseemly,"
Katha retorted annoyed, "And we've been
dating for a year."

"Is he handsome? I've never met him, only
his son Edward," Lily asked of Amelia,
ignoring her grandmother.

"He is extremely handsome. He's kind of
Sean Connery meets Edmund Gwynn,"
Amelia commented, "He wears top of the
line, fitted suits too."

"He is a hottie, isn't he?" Katha agreed.
"And he's got charm to spare."

"Well he better understand what he has in you," Lily commented.

"He does," Katha admitted.

"Ladies, good afternoon," Sergeant Detective Rogers exclaimed, stepping in the hospital room. "Better now ladies?"

"Hello, dear. You solved the crime all ready?" Katha asked innocently.

"We are still actively looking at the crime scene, ma'am," Detective Rogers admitted, then turning to Lily he demanded, "I'd like to talk to you alone, .Ms. Kelly-Brooksfield."

"'I don't think so. Lily, don't speak to him without us, or at least another lawyer," Katha claimed angrily.

"Don't say a word to him, Lily. He wants the crime to be committed by one of us, so he can close the book on this case!" Amelia agreed.

"I am a lawyer, remember?" Lily answered.

"Listen to me, Ms. Kelly. You're still a valid suspect in my book."

"You will not bully my cousin! Is that clear, Sergeant Detective Rogers!" Lily demanded, "My husband has been murdered and we had nothing to do with either murder!"

"Then you won't mind answering a few questions will you?" Sergeant Detective Rogers commented.

"Fine, I'm innocent, so go ahead," Lily said.

"I believe your first husband died in a car accident? Sorry, correction, I understand the investigating officer believed it to be a drunken driving accident?"

"Dredging up what you think are skeletons will not solve my husband's murder! My first husband died crossing a street. The police thought someone leaving the bars had too much to drink and had killed William. One day we will find the drunk driver and he'll pay. William Wentworth was a great man, a great Crown attorney. I became a Crown attorney based on my own merit, after his death," Lily cried. "My life is an open book. I have no skeletons."

"It would seem to me you're a black widow and so is your cousin. Wasn't there gossip that he had been cheating on you?"

"Do you believe everything you overhear? That must be a real drawback in your job," Lily snapped sarcastically.

"So was he?" Sergeant Detective Rogers demanded.

"No, he wasn't. I'll never believe he cheated on me," Lily shouted.

"I found documented proof he was having an affair with one Cecile Grimes," Emmett confirmed.

"I don't believe any vicious gossip. She's a lawyer in my office. He spoke maybe two words to her."

"The affair has been documented, I'm sorry to tell you. It's too bad you're a head in the sands kind of girl. We've confirmed Horace had a long-term affair with Amber by the way. Two husbands, two cheats, two dead men! Suspicious wouldn't you say?" Sergeant Detective Rogers needled.

"I think you've said enough young man. I'll be talking to your superior about this!" Katha spit angrily.

"You go ahead, ma'am, but I need to solve a murder. I am looking at every angle to solve the case," Sergeant Detective Rogers explained.

"Well since you've now discovered I had nothing to do with the crime, you can now move on and figure out who killed my husband," Lily demanded.

"Goodbye, Sergeant Detective Rogers," Lily dismissed him.

"Goodbye, for now, Ms. Kelly-Brooksfield," Sergeant Detective Rogers retorted, than added as a last parting shot, "We'll be in touch."

"That man is rude. I don't like him!" Katha bristled, "How dare he talk to you like you were a suspect?"

"He's doing his job. You do understand that, don't you, Grandma Katha?" defended Lily.

"I may perceive he has a job to do, but I don't need to like the way he does his job," Katha grumbled, "I have half a mind to complain to his superiors."

"Don't worry, Aunt Katha, it will all blow over once he realizes he's got the wrong person."

"If you say so, my darling Amelia, but if you change your mind let me know. I'm heading out my dears. Get some rest."

"We will. Goodbye, Grandma Katha," Lily replied.

"Goodbye, Aunt Katha," Amelia added. "I got strange vibes from Detective Rogers; despite his bringing up all that garbage, the man likes you," commented Amelia smiling knowingly after Katha had left.

"Oh be quiet!" replied Lily only half kidding.

"Well he is kind of cute; don't you think?" asked Amelia.

"He is positively handsome in a rugged sort of way." Lily replied, then thinking of Horace, she continued, "He's also looking into two murders and seems to think we had something to do with the crime. Besides, I'm not looking at any man. I lost the love of my life to murder."

"Sorry, Lily, losing Horace must hurt like hell. The only thing which got me through, when my husband and child died was you, so lean on me, cousin, I'm here, bum leg and all."

"Thanks, Amelia. Do you think Horace cheated on me?" asked Lily.

"I'm sorry Lily; I didn't know how to tell you," Amelia explained.

"Did you see something which made you think he had an affair?"

"I saw him kissing Amber at a local restaurant. I followed them when they left right to a motel," Amelia admitted. "I had planned on coming over to tell you today."

"I can't believe this. I thought he loved me. Why did you do this Horace? Why?" Lily asked.

"If it helps in his twisted way, Horace loved you Lily. You were the woman he held on a pedestal. He loved you."

"Yes, he loved me enough to sleep with Amber," Lily said bitterly, "Was she prettier than me? Is that the reason why?"

"No and I take what I said back; Horace was a fool. You did everything for Horace and he didn't appreciate any of it," Amelia exclaimed fiercely.

"Thanks, Amelia. What would I do without you?"

"You'll never need to find out how to live without me."

"I seem to have heard that," replied Lily smiling.

"We're family and we support one another through thick and thin right?" Amelia answered. "Right! We keep having these weird tragedies though. Could Sergeant Detective Rogers be on to something?" asked Lily.

"People die. We can't read things into this. It's not mysterious. We are not cursed. At least that's what Dr. Jones has been telling me."

"But most people don't have two dead husbands at the age of thirty. Do you think William was murdered like Sergeant Detective Rogers suggested?" Lily asked.

"No, some idiot with too much to drink killed him. It was unintentional, unfortunate, and tragic, but not a deliberate murder."

"I understand he has to investigate, but I wish he'd quit bringing up the past and all it entailed. I hope he doesn't mention Rose's mother in front of her," Lily commented.

"She still doesn't know does she?"

"No, she has no idea her mother is in a mental facility for the criminally insane," Lily replied.

"Do they treat her well?" Amelia asked.

"Yes, I check up on them all the time. She's treated with gentle care. She's been there six years now. The doctors have great hopes she can be cured. But I've seen no sign of her recovery."

"What exactly is wrong with her?"

"She doesn't recall her crime. It's a self-defence mechanism. She thinks she works at the hospital and Rose is a doll she carries around with her," Lily explained.

"Oh how awful, to live with the knowledge you killed someone; even to defend yourself and your daughter."

"I tried my earnest to get her off, but my supervisor overruled me. I had gotten her a twenty-year sentence when she became catatonic. She was languished in a jail cell, neither eating nor sleeping. She didn't respond to anyone. I finally got them to move her to the centre with the judge's permission."

"If Rose knew she would be grateful that you'd looked after her mother so well. So what happened since then?"

"Cordelia started responding to voices but she didn't recall me or her crime. Horace took her a doll of Rose's to remind her and snap her out of her fugue, but she declared Rose was a doll. Horace didn't want Rose to have any knowledge of her mother's condition. He made me swear only to tell her about her mother, if necessary. Horace didn't even want his mother or anyone else to know she wasn't in jail but in a forensic psychiatric facility."

"That's like a jail thought too. Right?"

"She has access to her shrinks; but yes she's kept securely so she can't harm anyone."

"Why are you worried about that? Do you think she'd harm Rose?"

"Horace thought there might be more to the story. Something may have happened to Rose, but we could never get the story out of her. Rose doesn't remember that night," Lily admitted.

"But what did you tell Rose?"

"Rose thinks she's in jail and she isn't allowed to visit. I hate lying to her, but as I said Horace insisted she should never comprehend what her mother did."

"Isn't it better Rose doesn't know? She's already had a difficult life and now losing her father..,." Amelia asked.

"Yes, that what I thought too." Lily replied, "But I still feel guilty."

"Don't beat yourself up about protecting Rose. You are the best parent you can be."

"Thanks, I love my little girl, okay not so little girl, so much. I hope I can be the best parent for her now she doesn't have her dad," Lily replied sounding worried.

"You will be Lily. You mother everyone, even me. Rose is the luckiest kid alive. She has you!" Amelia reassured.

"I love you Aem."

"Enough with the mush. I'm tired; I'm going to take a nap now. You should get some rest too."

"Goodnight, Amelia." Lily replied closing her eyes.

Then sneaking a glance under her lids, Lily smiled. She noticed Katha watched and listened from the doorway. Amelia closed her eyes and she thought, how she'd like to go back to that time when they were the teenage girls Katha raised. Those rebellious young teens Katha took in had bonded like sisters, through the tragedies that touched their lives. The bond was still tight and would remain so. They would all get through this. They were Kelly's and family was there for each other.

~0~

Chapter 12 - Ghosts of the Past

The next day Lily awaited the doctor.

She had to get permission from her physician to leave the hospital. She had a lot to do. Horace needed to be honoured befitting his status as mayor, but she wished she could have a funeral for family only. Well why not? Rose had been through enough, so she wanted a simple funeral. Others who wanted to give their respect would come to the wake and do so. She would make a quick appearance at the wake and leave. There. Plans made, unless that stupid cop Emmett Rogers decided to arrest either her or Amelia. He wouldn't, would he? No, he had no grounds.

A model thin woman polished looking, with honey blonde hair in a twist at the back of her head entered the room. She wore a dress which would be worn to high society tea. She was followed by an older woman about sixty-five years old, with short dyed black hair. She too, was dressed in a high society tea dress.

"I found you! You rotten bitch! You thought you could hide and play the poor grieving widow. But I know what you did it and you'll pay."

"What?" Amelia answered.

"I warned him my poor Horace. I knew you'd be the death of him. How could you?" demanded the first woman bitterly.

"Why haven't you got on handcuffs? You did this, Lily Kelly. I warned my son about you. I told him you were trash! After all, you are related to Katha O'Malley, and Lord knows she's a piece of work!" the older woman yelled, "Katha O'Malley goes after anyone in pants. I understand she's after Terrence Stewart now. God save the man!"

Lily sitting in a chair beside her hospital bed, looked up in surprise.

"Who are these people Lily?" Amelia asked.

Lily smiled a bitter smile and narrowed her eyes. and then smirked, "You've met my mother-in-law Cheryl, Amelia, and this woman is Horace's first wife Renée,"

Amelia caught on quickly and asked acting puzzled, "But I thought his former wife rotted in jail for life?"

"Oh Amelia, I do love you. No, you're thinking of his second wife, Cordelia." Lily replied laughing, "Cordelia is Rose's mother."

"You killed him, you evil bitch. Don't think you can get away with this act pretending you were poisoned!" Cheryl commented viciously. "I warned Horace he shouldn't marry you. I told him you were a black widow."

Cheryl then paced near the hospital room door.

"Oh gee, where have I heard those lies before? Have you talked to Sergeant Detective Rogers recently?" Lily asked sarcastically.

"We weren't about to let you get away with killing dear Horace. He chose to take sustenance elsewhere because he wasn't satisfied with you. You evil bitch! That didn't mean you had the right to kill him," Renée sneered.

"I talked to a pleasant young cop. I told him what kind of woman you are," Cheryl expounded. "He won't let you get away with this."

"You two are so repetitive it's boring. As to this cop what did you say? Did you tell this cop that your son didn't talk to you anymore? Did you tell him you assaulted your son? You have a file? Did you tell him you aren't allowed to associate with your granddaughter, because you obtained a record? That you are forbidden to associate with children less than sixteen years of age, because of a conviction for child abuse? Isn't that right, Cheryl? You have a child abuse record dating back to when Horace was young?" continued Lily twisting the screws.

"Simply a misunderstanding!" Cheryl complained.

"I don't call a child of three, getting a broken arm from his mother a misunderstanding!" Lily replied angrily.

"Horace lied. I never touched him! That wicked nursery school I sent him to made Horace tell such wicked lies." Cheryl whined.

"Right and your husband didn't divorce you and sue for custody to get away from you and protect Horace," Lily said bitterly.

"If anyone has motive here, it's you two. I should enlighten the police officers about you two. Right, Renée? Funny how you were charged with stalking! Didn't your dad get your record expunged?"

Renée's face grew purple and looked extremely angry. She stalked to Lily, raising her hand as if to hit her.

"I wouldn't do that, Ms. Harrow," demanded Detective Rogers coming upon the scene. He pulled back Renée's hand as she was about to hit Lily.

"I wasn't doing anything!" Renée protested.

"Would you like to lay charges against this woman, Mrs. Brooksfield?" asked Sergeant Detective Rogers.

"No, I think I'm okay for now. But I'd like them to leave," Lily replied forcefully.

"Not before I speak with them. Ms. Harrow, Ms. Waverly if you please, I'd like to speak to you both in the hall?" demanded Detective Rogers.

"I guess we can discuss this in the hall. I can give you an earful about this evil siren," Renée replied to Detective Rogers, then turning to Lily she shouted, "But this isn't over bitch. We know you killed Horace. You wait, you've got a whole lot of hurt coming your way."

"I said enough, Ms. Harrow. You can go out into the hall instantly or I can file a harassment charge against you, and perhaps throw in a stalking charge," Detective Rogers commented.

"Renée we must not sink to her level," scolded Cheryl.

"Thank you, Mother," Renée answered sweetly.

"But I'm worried about him, Detective Rogers. He's taking her part. What about justice for our Horace?" Renée continued motioning at Detective Rogers like he was a chair.

"Got another man twisted in your web, do you, Lily?" Cheryl cried viciously, "Is he the reason you killed my boy? He waited in the wings? What do they see in you?"

"Enough! You two leave this instant. I'll be back shortly, Mrs. Brooksfield," Detective Rogers exclaimed.

"Wow! He does like you. I told you so. Did you see how he defended you with those witches?" Amelia commented, "His kind of chiselled good looks make you warm all over."

"Amelia, quit trying to set me up with him! I just lost my husband. Or did you forget I'm in mourning?" Lily protested, "I loved Horace."

"Horace wasn't good enough for you. I'm sorry to say. You deserved a hell of a lot better than a man who cheated, using you for a place to eat and sleep and a mother for his child," Amelia retorted angrily.

"Amelia, please, I'm begging you, I just lost my husband."

"Sorry, Lily, I understand how awful it is to lose someone you love. I want someone I consider closer than a sister to be happy." Amelia commented, "I wish you would get over the hurt faster."

"I love you too, Aem," Lily responded.

"You're closer than a sister to me too, but I loved Horace and I need time to grieve."

"I want to know what they are saying," Amelia insisted.

"Okay, then will both listen," Lily replied.

Amelia then used her crutches and went
with Lily to hear the interrogation from the
doorway.

"So, Ms. Harrow, where were you between
hours of eight p.m. and twelve a.m. on June
fourteenth?" asked Detective Rogers.

"We're suspects? Try looking beyond your
hormones. That bitch killed my Horace, just
when he decided to come back to me,"
Renée screamed loud enough for Lily to
overhear.

"It would have been so wonderful when
Horace married you again. I'm sure you
would have talked Horace into talking to me
again," Cheryl said regretfully.

"Ms. Harrow, is this all your imagination?
Or did Mr. Brooksfield say he would leave
his wife to return to you? And remember
this is an official police statement, which
means if you give me false testimony, you
can be charged! Are we clear?" Sergeant
Detective Rogers demanded.

"Well, he hadn't come right out and said he was coming back to me, but I read between the lines he would have come back to me. I know he loved me. Even my brother said so," Renée claimed.

"And who is your brother?" asked Detective Rogers curiously.

"Sergeant Detective Brad Owens. We had different fathers so he's sort of my half-brother," Cheryl explained "I'm sure you've seen him, he's a cop too."

"Renée," cautioned Cheryl but didn't elaborate.

"Well isn't that interesting," Sergeant Detective Rogers said slowly drawing it out, empathizing it didn't matter to him. "Now your alibis, ladies?"

"Well I chaired an event. The People Against Drunk Driving charity ball. I lost a child to a drunk driver! My sweet, Cheryl-Lynn Rose. I went out of my mind when she died. I admit I was a little too forceful with Horace but I regretted it," Cheryl admitted "I attended from six p.m. until after two a.m. I'm sure many people saw me as I spoke as the main speaker at the podium. Roberta

Anderson, Barry Pike, and John Nevelson.
Oh, and Gregory Hanks will vouch for me.
I'm sure you're familiar with Greg; he is the
CEO of Hanks those grocery stores across
the country?"

"And you. Ms. Harrow?"

"Well I watched television, by myself.
That's an alibi. It was *The Bachelor* on
TiVo. I had to catch up on a few episodes,"
Renée expounded.

"Sorry, but unless someone can substantiate
your alibi, it won't convince me. Now will
it?"

"But I watched television. Can't you just
check my *TiVo* and tell?" Renée stammered.

"No, Ms. Harrow. You could have left it
playing while you went out and murdered
Horace and Amber," Detective Rogers
declared.

"Why aren't you observing Lily Kelly? She
had more of a motive. He cheated on her.
Glare at her! The woman is a black widow!
Her first husband died mysteriously. Look at
her, not me!" whined Renée stamping her
foot.

"We are looking at everyone at this point, Ms. Harrow, but you just moved up on my suspect list," Detective Rogers declared.

"Me? I moved up on your suspect list? I didn't kill him. I loved Horace. I hate you! I'm going to tell my brother about you and then you'll be sorry," Renée whined, stamping her foot like a child.

"Don't leave town Ms. Harrow. Now I expect you both at the police station, you and Ms. Waverly, at one p.m. to sign your official statements."

"I'm not coming. I refuse. You can't make me. You just want to grill me," Renée complained. "I could arrest you now."

"No, please," Renée begged.

"If you're not there at one p.m., I'm issuing a warrant for your arrest," Detective Rogers declared.

"You will be so sorry! I'm going to get my brother to get you fired. He's popular and he'll make you pay," Renée threatened.

"He's already tried and failed big time, but please, be my guest, go whine to your brother," Detective Rogers replied breezily.

"Come on, dear, drop this tact. You'll just rile up the officer. Once he understands what she's like, he'll go after Lily; you wait and watch. He can't be blind to her evil, even Horace wasn't. was about to drop her like a bad shoe," Cheryl insisted pulling Renée's arm and leaving.

~0~

The next day

Emmett

Emmett stared after the departing women. How did a caring person like Lily Kelly-Brooksfield get mixed up with two witches like those two? Horace must have been a piece of work. Being involved with that woman Renée, and being brought up by Cheryl Waverly, probably made him the person he became. He learned some bad things about Horace Brooksfield in his investigation. The man collected women like they were disposable; nevertheless he obtained a loyal wife like Lily Brooksfield? He must have entertained some decency and yet someone murdered him.

Those women were piranhas. The way they were involved with Horace Brooksfield, made them definite suspects in his mind. He'd check out the mother's alibi, but Renée's alibi couldn't be verified. It didn't make her necessarily guilty, but she did have a strong motive. She was the jilted ex-wife, after all. What a story! Horace planned on getting back together with Renée? Given a choice, what man would pick that shrew Renée? But the victim Horace sounded like an idiot. He had been having an affair with Amber, when the woman was by all accounts mindless. The story that Renée told bore checking. Brad was not a good source. The man remained treacherous; it didn't matter if he was a cop.

He'd lie to back up his sister. He wanted to believe her cousin, Amelia, hadn't done this; but the first rule of being a cop in homicide, suspect the spouse. He needed to make a quick trip to visit Dr. Piper. He would get the autopsy reports and then he would check out Ms. Waverly's arrest warrant and her alibi. He had begun to experience something for Lily Kelly Brooksfield a little too much.

He must get back his objectivity. What if she and her cousin were serial killers in those sweet packages?

~0~

Chapter 13 - Home Sweet Home

Amelia slipped her crutch up higher,

trying to balance on her crutches, as she entered the foyer of Lily's home.

"So great to be home, I won't even complain it's your house," Amelia commented, stepping into the living room and settling into the dark blue sofa, propping up her leg.

"My casa is your casa. Besides how will you get up those stairs anyway?" Lily asked. "The guest room is down the hall there."

"Thanks again."

"Consider this your home."

"Have you talked to the funeral home yet?" Amelia asked.

"Yes, I arranged a simple private service Friday morning at ten a.m. I can't bear to have all those people there," Lily answered.

"I can understand you wanting a quiet funeral," Amelia replied.

"A good thing I've already changed the arrangements for the funeral," Katha commented coming in the room.

"You did what?" Lily screeched. "You didn't! Did you Grandma Katha?"

"I had to, dear. If you have the small simple service you want, everyone will think you're guilty and you'll lose your job," Katha explained.

"She's right Mom. Some of my acquaintances called the two of you, the Cousin Killers. I say acquaintances, because I no longer consider them friends. Some would call them frenemies, but they are just a bunch of haters," Rose commented.

"I'm sorry honey. None of this is fair. You lose your father and they now blame your adoptive mother for killing him. For the record, I didn't kill him. I loved your father."

"I know you didn't kill him Mom," Rose replied sounding annoyed. "Why do you think I was so mad at my so-called friends? Carol has stood by me though. She's shown she's my true friend. She came over to Grandma Katha's last night and spent the night."

"Carol is a true friend," Lily agreed.

"It's going to be a little rocky for a while, but we will get through this. At least school is out for the year. I'm glad school started in August last year. We should go away, somewhere fun. But where?" asked Lily

Mom!!!" Rose protested. "We can't leave! Are you cray, cray?"

"Cray, cray? Does that mean crazy?" Lily asked, amused by the slang.

"Lily, think of how guilty you'll appear." Katha complained, "Partying, vacationing while your husband is dead."

"Grandma Katha, I would never...," Lily protested, hurt by the accusation.

"That's what people will say and think Mom. People like to gossip," Rose agreed.

"Do you think we are not aware you would never do that Lily? People judge others; it's not fair, and not right; but you're in the public eye as Crown attorney. They will be scrutinizing your every move," Katha explained.

"I guess you're right, but I don't have to like it."

"I love you all and I will do all in my power to protect you from the paparazzi and keep all three of my girls safe. We are strong and we are Kelly's, descendants of Boudicca and her name means..?" Katha demanded.

"The word means Victorious," all three women answered in unison.

"That's right. We shall triumph. We shall overcome adversity and no man shall ever dominate a Kelly woman!" Katha announced

"Amen to that!" all three women replied.

"The funeral is Friday at ten a.m. just like you wanted. Now, though, there will be some dignitaries and some other prominent people."

"Thank-you then," Lily commented meekly.

"Now that's settled, my story is on and you know I love my soaps, I missed it yesterday. *General Hospital* is okay too but it isn't All My Children. *Young and Restless* is fine, too; but *All My Children* was my soap," Katha complained. "So wonderful, seeing some of the actors from my favorite soap on *The Young and Restless*, and sometimes *General Hospital* though. I'm so glad they are still working."

Rose meanwhile was surfing her computer and watching the television at the same time.

"Oh no! Grandma Katha, Mom, and Aunt Amelia; the news on Chatter is mindboggling. You'll never guess the terrible thing that has happened," Rose interrupted.

"Are you sure you're reading a reputable source?" Katha asked, "I'm forever reading some celebrity died when they didn't because of some hoaxer."

"No this is being widely reported by news organizations, I'm afraid," Rose commented.

"What has happened now?" asked Lily like she doesn't really want to know.

"They found a body in the dumpster near Aunt Amelia's store this morning. The body has been there since the first murder. They only found it because they came to pick up the garbage today and one of the garbage men noted blood under the dumpster," Rose stated shocked.

Lily gasped and held her hand to her mouth. Amelia also, gasped.

"My store? They found a body at my store, again?" Amelia exclaimed, shocked.

"You read that on-line? I try to only read the only headlines on Chatter; all the rest of the stuff is too depressing. In my day you'd read that kind of bad news the next morning in the paper. Now when your mom was young, you'd see a special bulletin on the television. Another body found? What in the world is going on in this town? I'm going to get Terrence to get his son working on this a little harder," Katha rambled, "So we are all safe."

"Why didn't anyone call me? It's still my job! Does Barbara think I'm unaware that she tried to make people think I'm the guilty party? I know Barbara is after my job. She's not fooling me," Lily angrily shouted, then coughed.

Katha glared at Rose for telling Lily and Amelia bad news.

"Don't you dare get yourself all worked up and tied up in knots Lily. She won't succeed. You have something she doesn't, common sense, decency and morals," Katha stated consoling Lily.

"Grandma Katha's right; besides she's weird," Rose exclaimed.

"Rose, we don't call people weird," Lily admonished.

"Even when they are?" Rose exclaimed.

"Hush Rose, don't upset your mother .Our world has been turned upside down. I can't believe there has been another murder in this city!" Katha continued.

"Why would someone kill and put them in the dumpster near my store?" Amelia asked.

"It is so bizarre," Lily commented.

"It's the curse; it has to be the curse," Amelia announced.

"Amelia, what did Dr. Jones say about curses? There are no such things. Isn't that what you told me?" reminded Lily.

"But if that is true, why do I feel like I am under one?"

"Sweetie, there is no such things as curses. Life gives us challenges. Sometimes too hard to bear and get through; but we soldier on and live our lives. Now put all this curse talk aside," Katha explained.

"Yes, Aunt Katha," Amelia meekly answered.

The doorbell pealed loudly. Rose looked out the peephole in the door to see Sergeant Detective Rogers on the doorstep.

"Mom, Sergeant Detective Rogers is here and he doesn't look happy," Rose said in a sing-song voice.

"Hello Ms. Brooksfield, is your mother, and Ms. Amelia Kelly, here?" Sergeant Detective Rogers asked stepping into the house, as soon as Rose opened the door.

"Mom, Aunt Amelia, he wants to talk to you," Rose yelled. Lily walked over and Amelia hobbled over on her crutches.

"We just heard the awful news," Amelia commented. "So the murderer killed twice?"

"Yes, the murderer did. I'm sorry Ms. Amelia Kelly but you are under arrest. You have the right to remain silent, anything you say can be held against you in a court of law. You have the right to consult with an attorney, and to have that same attorney present during questioning. If you are unable to afford an attorney one will be provided for you," Sergeant Detective Rogers announced clipping a handcuff through her crutch and onto her one wrist.

"What? You're arresting me? Lily he's arresting me. Help me!" Amelia screamed, horrified and turning to Lily.

"Don't say a word. I'll take your case until we can get you another lawyer. Now, Sergeant Detective Rogers, who is Amelia supposed to have killed?" Lily demanded.

"The charge is murder in the first degree of Megan Fowler and Albert Young," Sergeant Detective Rogers answered.

"Quit kidding! It is not funny! I didn't kill Megan and I don't know any Albert Young," Amelia protested.

"Quiet Amelia! Don't volunteer anything." Lily cautioned, "As your lawyer, I'm telling you don't say a word."

"But I don't know any Albert Young!" Amelia protested again.

"Ms. Kelly, you're going to lie now?" Sergeant Detective Rogers commented with disgust.

"Albert was his name?" Amelia questioned. As a thought crossed her face she continued, "Oh no, not Al! It's Al? Al's dead?"

"Ms. Kelly that's an award-winning performance, but we have you dead to rights," Detective Rogers replied clapping.

"Sergeant Detective Rogers, I advise you to keep your opinions to yourself. My client is innocent!" Lily demanded and turning to Amelia she cautioned, "Are you okay honey? You can tell me later who this Al is. But don't say another word in front of this police officer, do you understand?"

"Did anyone tell you Al was homeless?" Amelia angrily asked. "I helped him. I offered him a job but he wouldn't take it. He said he would watch over my store. He was so sweet; he just needed a little help. I used to give him money for breakfast every morning. How can Al be dead? Who could do such a thing?"

"Homeless? The guy was homeless and no one thought to tell me any of the information?" Sergeant Detective Rogers commented sounding shocked.

"It looks like your department isn't being entirely helpful. Listen to me please. Look at my cousin. Amelia is innocent. She would never hurt anyone. She doesn't even have a record," Lily protested. "She likes to help people though and she helped Al. Just because she is a good person, it doesn't mean she's a murderess."

"Counsellor, you are aware people can surprise us; but I'm inclined to believe you, something about this doesn't add up to guilty. She doesn't have a clear motive. I thought when I came in here that Ms. Kelly was guilty but...," Detective Rogers began.

"You say they think my client is guilty? Tell me what you evidence you think makes her a suspect as a favour. Please?" Lily begged.

"I shouldn't be telling you this, but I think from my own instincts and her reaction she's being set up for the crime."

"So tell me."

"She was aware of both victims, but that shouldn't get a person convicted. The reason the assistant crown attorney made me make an arrest..." Detective Rogers began before he was interrupted again.

"The assistant crown attorney? My employee who works for me? Barbara Franks?" Lily interrupted, "I was appointed by the attorney general, not her."

"I am well aware of the way you were appointed, but Ms. Franks insisted to my boss that I had to arrest Ms. Kelly. I had no choice," Detective Rogers explained.

"On what basis did she want you to make an arrest? Was it because my husband was the deceased?" Lily asked continuing, "Or because Amelia happened to be near the murder scene and she had seen them both?"

"Amelia's hair was on the Mr. Young's body," Detective Rogers replied. "I'm sure the hair got there as transfer, but Ms. Franks insisted it is crucial evidence, and proof of Ms. Kelly's guilt."

"Well of course my hair was on him. I hugged him yesterday. He was such a sweet man. He always looked out for me." Amelia explained, "I can't believe he's gone."

"All of this is circumstantial evidence. Don't worry Amelia. I'll get you out on bail by this afternoon." Lily replied, "And you, Detective Rogers, you know this is a bad collar; so why are you listening to Barbara Franks?"

"Ms. Kelly-Brooksfield, she might be safer in jail. I think someone has set her up and possibly you for murder. I think you're both in danger until we catch this killer," Detective Rogers commented sounding worried.

"Why do you say we are in danger?" asked Lily.

"It just feels too personal, these killings. Call it a hunch, but I feel like someone is watching my every move and yours too. This killer is smart and seems to be one step ahead of us."

"You think someone watched your every move? Don't you think you're being a little paranoid?" Lily asked.

"No, I don't. It's only paranoia if you're wrong and I'm not wrong. Someone is pulling the strings, but whoever it is I will find them. Now I'm sorry Ms. Kelly, but we need to go. I must take her in; it's my orders."

"And you always follow orders," Lily replied grimly.

Emmett looked at her apologetically and said, "You can follow my car if you want Ms. Kelly, or meet me at the main police station." he explained. "That's where I'll be taking her for the booking."

"Grandma Katha, will you watch Rose? I'll be back soon."

"Mom, do remember I'm not two years old, but bring back Aunt Amelia," Rose commented.

"Of course, go!" Katha answered.

"Adults, you're such a pain sometimes! I'm fifteen," Rose stated to Lily's departing back.

Detective Rogers, Amelia and Lily left through the front door. Emmett placed Amelia into the back of his patrol car and drove away as Lily followed.

"Grandma Katha, will Aunt Amelia really be okay?' asked Rose after they leave.

"Of course she will child. Your mama is a bulldog as a lawyer. She'll get Amelia, home by dinnertime," Katha reassured Rose.

"I'm kind of worried about something Detective Rogers said though. He said he thought someone set up Aunt Amelia."

"Nonsense! Why would anyone set up Amelia?They've made a mistake and they'll rectify it. Amelia will be home tonight. You just wait and see."

"He also said the person pulled the strings behind the scenes and was one step ahead of him. Are you sure we are not in danger?" asked Rose looking around as if to see the person.

"Not to worry dear, whoever it is doesn't know who he or she's dealt with; we are the Kelly's and we triumph over adversity and evil."

"Thanks, Grandma Katha. That does make me feel better."

~0~

Chapter 14 - Your Place or Mine

Violet and Brandy

Violet a tall thin woman resembling Olive Oyl with glasses, sat at the front desk of the Happy Valley police station. She perused the police roster on her computer, only looking up as Constable Brandy Calders came through the metal detector at the front door.

"Where's Rentford today?" Brandy Calders asked before she had even reached the desk.

"Rentford? Who is that?" Constable Violet Garden enquired.

"Silas Rentford, the cute new cop, who works with Sergeant Detective Rogers," Brandy Calders answered stopping at the desk.

"Oh, that man. He's not new. He's been around for years. I just didn't recognize his name when you said it. He called in sick. Must be a bug going round. Sergeant Detective Brad Owens called in sick too," Constable Violet Gardens commented.

"Oh? Do you know if he has a girlfriend?"

"You like him too? What does Brad Owens hold out the *'I'm available'* sign?" Violet probed.

"Not Sergeant Detective Brad Owens! I'm speaking about Constable Silas Rentford. He's cute and his eyes are like a puppy dog, all soft and sweet," Brandy replied dreamily.

"Silas Rentford? You like Silas? But he's so shy."

Violet looked at Brandy, a pale red-head, slightly overweight, dressed in a police officer's dress uniform. If only she wear some make-up and lose some weight.

"He's not gay is he? My Gaydar did go off like it usually does." Brandy asked.

"No, I don't think so. I've seen him ogle Tricia, when he didn't realize anyone looked."

"Tricia, who's she?" Brandy probed, nervously shifting from foot to foot.

"Constable Tricia Peters. She has all her uniforms form fitted so her assets are observed," Violet replied cattily. "Let us not forget Kendall, the iron lady, I won't get into her."

"Kendall sure has been promoted a lot. Has Silas Rentford been here long?"

"He's been here for a few years. I think he came here, what about six years ago?" Violet replied. "Or was it five years?"

"He has been here that long? I didn't realize."

"He is kind of cute, I guess if you like that type," Violet admitted, "So you like Brad?"

"Yes," Brandy responded.

"But I thought you dated someone else," Violet commented.

Violet then looked around as if she was being watched, as if she was afraid she'd be seen slacking off.

"I was, but it didn't work out because he wasn't exactly faithful. You had better be careful; Brad changes partners all the time. He might not be any better with you."

"I think people misjudge him. He's sweet and just a little insecure," Violet exclaimed. "But any woman getting in between us, had better watch out; I'm a little possessive."

"Do you think he'd like some chicken soup if he's sick?"

"Brad or Silas, or both?"

"Both," Brandy answered.

"I think they would. Do you think we could get a discount at the soup place around the corner, the Soup Queen? I'd like to take some soup to Brad after my shift ends," Violet requested.

"When is your shift finished?" Brandy asked.

"I'm off in a half an hour, but if it's busy at the desk I'll need to stay longer to work.

"Well if you give me Silas' address, I'll go get us both some chicken soup for our guys and when you get off you can give it to him. I'm sure he'll love you for it," Brandy offered smiling widely.

"I'm not supposed to give out any personal information, but I guess I'll make an exception. Seeing as you're not after my guy. Thanks. This might be my chance to win him. We girls have to stick together against women like Tricia and Kendall."

"Thanks, I know this will help," Brandy answered, pulling out her notebook and a pen to write.

"Just go get the soup, here's the address for Silas."

Violet wrote out the address and gave Brandy the piece of paper.

"Good, I'll be back shortly with the soup. Bye now! See you soon."

Brandy excitedly looked forward to bringing
Silas his soup and making him feel better.
Granny Calders always said the way to a
man's heart was through his stomach. Now
if you provide a man with medicine and
chicken soup when he's sick, he would love
you forever. Brandy would be that woman if
it killed her. She would get chicken noodle.
It was the best soup for cold and flu. Should
she pick up some medicines too? No, she
didn't want to look too obvious. Soup would
be enough. When he was well again, she
would make him her raved about famous
turkey lasagna. Everyone loved her lasagna.
Silas would too. She had him in the palm of
her hands; he would be hers soon. She
wished Violet as much luck with her
delivery.

~0~

The Killer

In the shadows in his apartment a man

listened to a radio, *"And in local news, Reporter Paul Knight, remains missing. Anyone who has information is asked to call your local police station. In other news Amelia Kelly, owner of Quirks and cousin of Crown Attorney Lily Kelly, was taken in to custody today as a person of interest in the murder of Megan Fowler and Albert Young. Megan Fowler and Albert Young were found murdered near Quirks two days ago. Crown Attorney Kelly's husband, the Honourable Mayor Horace Brooksfield, was found murdered in his office two days ago. Police Chief Edward Stewart has told this reporter an arrest is imminent."*

What!?What!? Were these police officers fools?

His Angel, and her cousin, were the victims.
Yes he killed, killed to protect his incredibly
lovely Angel's innocence. These people
were vermin and vermin you killed. They
blamed his beloved Angel and her cousin? If
they looked at them they would know they
were angels sent from above for him. It had
to be all the fault of the assistant Crown
attorney's fault. She wasn't like his Angel's
cousin. A pit-bull when it came to her job.

Barbara Franks, even her name, ugly, not at
all lyrical like his angel, or her cousin.
Barbara coveted Lily's job. Don't think he
didn't understand her motives, but she
wasn't going to get the job.

He suspected she wasn't strictly on the up
and up, but she hid it well. Barbara,
extremely sneaky, managed to elude him, an
unheard of occurrence in his world.

No one eluded him, until now. She appeared
up to something again. When he found out
what he would use it to his advantage.
Barbara better watch her step. She annoyed
him, her constant barrage of Lily, one more
step out of line and it was curtains for her.
Curtains…

Ha, Ha, Ha! He'd use the curtains to strangle
her in her office... er Lily's office. Wouldn't
it be funny, even ironic? She was totally out
of line; that bitch Barbara Franks. Her
britches were too big, his daddy always said.

He awarded Lily a job, to benefit his
beloved Angel and her beloved cousin. He
rid the world of a crooked Crown attorney,
who cheated on Lily. Lily still did not
understand the lengths trash like Barbara
could do, but he did. He protected her from
that knowledge too, but maybe he hadn't
done her a favour by protecting her from
William Wentworth's cheating ways. Lily
had found another man just like him in
Horace. It had been simple matter to tamper
the car of the stranger and make it appear a
drunken driving accident. Lily trusted just

like her cousin. In some ways she exuded
the same innocence, so he protected her. Her
bad choices should not harm his beloved
Angel.

He had arranged a simple accident, and poof
Wentworth appeared a traffic statistic. A
reason pointed out not to drink and drive.
The bottle of scotch he offered the driver
convinced all, the driver drank and drove
and ran over Wentworth. Okay, so he put the
bottle of scotch within the man's reach. The
drunk driver had chosen to drink it after all.
He didn't feel any remorse. Why should he?
The driver deserved to die anyway. He'd
seen him two days before driving drunk.

The driver sat before the wheel, striking an
old lady crossing the street. The man left her
to die, broken and battered in the street. The
man had explained to the killer, he needed to
drink, but he promised he wouldn't again.
He would go to rehabilitation. And the killer
let him go; thinking he would give the man a
second chance, but the man threw it all
away. So the man sobered up for two days.
So what!

The man fell off the wagon again. The man
would have killed someone else, once more!
He patted himself on the back. After all,
hadn't he just saved a lot of pedestrians and
other drivers from Wentworth and this drunk
driver? A vermin like William Wentworth,
out of Lily's life, and the drunk driver killed
himself. All painstakingly tidy, he was good
at his craft.

Wow! It was surprising that it had been
seven years ago. Seven years ago, Lily, the
brave little widow. She lobbied for the
Crown attorney. A word here, a word there,
and he got a lot of people to rally for her.
Her success hadn't been totally on her own
merit. She remained, however, the perfect
woman for the job. Despite worrying
someday she might be obligated to arrest
him, he respected her. She stood tough on
criminals, something he admired. He wasn't
a criminal, just a person who acted as a
judge and punished the wicked. He did
something valuable for society. After all,
society needed judges to keep order when
the courts failed. If it wasn't for his feelings
he had for his Angel, she might hold his
heart. She needed as much looking after as

his Angel did. She was a great mother to
Rose.

Rose existed as a testimony to her. A modest
girl, not flashy, and given to flirting with the
opposite sex. Lovely girl Rose! Kind and
sweet, everything a girl should be. Lily? She
trusted too easily. She got mixed up
alongside Horace Brooksfield, right after
that disaster William Wentworth he excised.
It must be the kid which made her fall in
love with such a cretin. She was a natural
mother who needed a child. Neither of those
two worms gave her a child of her own.

Lily treated the child as if she was her own.
He hadn't been able to stand for such a
sweet trusting woman, as Lily lived, to be
cheated on repeatedly, while she mothered
that lovely little girl. More women should
mother as she did. Simply put...Horace had
to die.

Look how Lily looked after his Angel. Oh
sure, Rose's real mother Cordelia was no
prize, but then she obsessed over drugs.
Cordelia did the right thing and protected
Rose from danger. He respected that about
her. Lily took the child after the incident,
right after the poor deluded woman Cordelia
lost her mind. Lily made sure the child felt
safe and loved. He felt sorry for Cordelia.
She lost her child. He understood sometimes
people needed a break from reality after a
great loss. He needed one when Sam died.

No, concentrate; don't go to the bad place. It
wasn't your fault. The fault lay at Amelia's
husband. Jack's door; he shouldn't have
taken Sam in the car. He started humming. It
calmed him. He didn't want to think about
Sam anymore because it hurt too much. He
needed to think of something else. The time
came to put his plan into action. The
boyfriend would be blamed.

Albert the homeless man had gotten in the way. Albert would have told Amelia. One plus one equals two; simple arithmetic. Albert had seen the murder, and Albert died painlessly. He was homeless after all and he probably wouldn't have survived long anyway. He was guiltless in Albert's murder too. That made him feel much better.

Planning was always crucial. The culprit was all picked out for the other murder of Horace Brooksfield, ready to be framed. He'd kill two birds with one stone, as well as get rid of that insipid ex-wife of Horace's, Renée. Or should he go with the mother-in-law; after all, both of them dared to threaten Lily? How dare Renée threaten his real family? After all when he married his beloved Angel, his darling Amelia, we would all be family.

Amelia needed family, with all her losses to be made whole again. He would be her rock. She would be his family, the one he'd always needed, and he would be hers. He'd planted Renée's hair at the scene. He wondered whether they'd tested the hair yet and if it would be traced back to Renée. The trashy, vulgar woman thwarted him at every turn. He thought about killing her, but this was so much more delicious. She would go to prison for the murders, and the inmates might even take the job of killing her for him. If not, then she would suffer. Truly suffer, like she made Lily, his Angel's cousin suffer, through her vulgar accusations and her constant attentions to a married man (Lily's husband).

If Andrew Piper stood truly as good as he claimed, he'd find the hair. Renée, such a bitch, with a wicked tongue; Daddy would have called it forked. She lied as easy as she breathed.

They had better free his Angel soon. If they didn't fix that rapidly, Assistant Crown Attorney Barbara Franks would see some roses too and a tombstone together with her name on it.

How he hated that horrid woman Barbara! He'd like to rip her head off like you would

a Barbie doll. Wouldn't it be a lovely sight
for Andrew Piper, or a sight for the lovely
Brandy Calders? He put Rogers off his trail,
but he should be polite and ask his help.
Yes, the plan would work.

The doorbell rang. Who could be at his
door? They found him out and knew his
crimes? No he remained far too clever for
that.

Dimwitted Barbara Franks and the idiot
Emmett Rogers thought they were so smart.
Luckily Paul had been disposed of in a place
that wouldn't be traced back to him for the
murder. No trace of him left here. How dare
he deny him exclusive control of the
interview, after everything he contributed to
his career?

He should have supported the woman
reporter. She did her job better. What was
her name, Holly Hollis? She was just so
forward and in your face, qualities he
disliked in a woman. Holly Hollis wasn't a

female he trusted, but then he should never have trusted Paul Knight.

Oh well, live and learn. Sadly, he hated to take care of Paul. He had drugged him and then disposed of his body.

He would just be another celebrity who died tragically by his own hand. Paul's body had no restrain marks, the special cream he'd put on first before the ropes, erased all traces of the restraints. Chemistry never failed him. Only the track marks from the drugs remained. Paul's stint in rehab a couple of years ago might convince them. Stupid ass!

Why did Paul make him take this step? They could have had a long profitable relationship. If only Paul hadn't wanted an exposé on all his crimes. His Angel must never find out all he had done until she married to him. Why couldn't Paul have understood? He paced a little; checking once again; to make sure the place remained clean of any traces of Paul Knight.

Damn! The doorbell rang again, and he
didn't answer it. No, don't get angry. He
mustn't show any anger to whomever
appeared at the door. He'd better answer the
door quick, though, and find out who was
there. He wouldn't want to be too obvious.
He hurried to throw on a robe over his
boxers. He answered and found a woman
holding soup.

"I brought you chicken soup." she cried, "I
hope it makes you feel better." "I'm sure it
will but I wouldn't want you to get sick."

"I'm hearty. I hardly ever get sick. Let me
come in and help you."

"Thanks, but I'd never forgive myself if you
did." he said gently, "Besides I'm sleepy.
It's the cold medication."

"Yes, right, see you tomorrow." He said
quickly, closing the door and thinking 'In
your dreams honey."

Soup! Yum! He loved chicken noodle; too
bad the woman longed for him. She stood a
sad, pathetic, sort of thing. He couldn't be

mean to her. She wasn't one of those women to betray him. No, rather like his deceased mother, she was sweet, down trodden and perhaps a little forward but not too forward. Kind of like a puppy dog you wouldn't kick when it was down and injured. He had standards after all, rules to follow. One of his rules was to treat women who are chaste and innocent correctly. If he wasn't so sure his Angel remained the one, this woman might have been a good substitute. But that would never be... He would never betray his Angel.

~0~

Chapter 15 - The S.O.L.F.B.O. Club

"Amelia Kelly is out on bail. Wow that was an incredibly quick release from jail yesterday. Must be nice to have connections," Violet exclaimed straightening the front desk of the Happy Valley Police station.

"The Crown attorney was her lawyer though," replied Police Constable Fourth Class Jenni Hayes, getting ready to leave.

"Nepotism!! Told you so! So did any more evidence come in on the case?" questioned Violet.

"No, the hair is hers, Amelia Kelly; but it could have been transference exactly as she said. She met him every day and hugged him, which might have ensured hair transmission. It's not like homeless people change their clothes frequently."

"If Amelia Kelly didn't kill Albert Young, Megan Fowler, Amber Tate and Horace Brooksfield, who did?" queried Violet.

"Damned, if I know!"

"Anything I should be on top of today?" Violet asked.

"No, the duty roster is done," Jenni replied yawning. "I'm so tired, I think I'll walk home, but I'm going to shower first. I don't think I'm awake enough to drive."

"Good thing you live close to the station. Why do you drive here anyway?"

"Sometimes I like to go to the place around the corner for breakfast. It's too far by foot."

"I wonder how Brad is today. Have you heard from him?"

"Brad Owens? The hottie? Brad, the guy who all the recruits, straight and even those who weren't drooled over him? What's his name...Brad Owens?" Jenni joked.

"Right, make fun of me. I took Brad some soup last night. Poor thing; so sick, all he wanted to do was sleep. He was in his bathrobe when he took the soup and then just said goodnight."

"It worked. He's on the duty roster and he hasn't called in sick."

"Well good," Violet countered, not sounding so sure.

"Here he is now." Jenni commented, "Good day, Violet, and if you get a date later, don't do anything I wouldn't do!"

"Jenni quiet! He'll hear you," Violet admonished.

"No he won't. He only has eyes for you."

"Hello Violet. You look lovely today. Did you get a new hairstyle?" Brad flirted.

"Why yes, it is," Violet replied her eyes shining and happy.

Brad responded playfully. "I feel so much better, where did you find such ambrosia?"

"You're welcome. I made it by my own two hands," Violet lied blushing.

"Later Vi," Brad replied smiling and going went into the locker room.

"Wow, he called me a pet name," Violet said to herself aloud.

"Are you okay? You are speaking, but you make no sense, Violet!" Brandy queried, coming into the locker room.

"I'm fine. Brad called me a pet name."

"I'm impressed, what did he call you?" Brandy solicited.

"He called me Vi."

"Oh how sweet. So did you get Silas to notice you last night?" Violet queried.

"No! He liked the soup but he took it and sent me away in his bathrobe no less," Brandy replied. "But I hope to meet him today. Even get him to like me as Brad did you."

"He'll remember the soup you brought. He is on today's roster."

"Oh good! They'll remember we brought them soup and then we'll be their girlfriends," Brandy claimed.

"Granny always said the way to a man's heart is through his stomach."

"I certainly hope Granny's right," Violet remarked.

"I think he liked it, and he's better today, but let's not get ahead of ourselves."

"Ladies, if someone does appreciate you for yourselves they aren't worth it. I don't know what you want with them," Jenni commented coming out from the shower area.

"I thought you'd gone home," Violet admonished.

"Besides didn't you also take soup to a certain male someone yesterday?"

"I took a sick friend soup, which just happened to be male. He's much too old for me. There's nothing romantic about that. Barney Terrell used to be a cop and he was sick. I'd do it for any fellow officer. I'll go home in a moment. My shower's broke and the landlord hasn't fixed it yet. I need to be awake enough to walk home anyway." Jenni answered, "You two need to value yourselves more. Let the guys run after you. Bye now."

"Good grief! She insists we are running after guys, but she's not?" Brandy whispered.

"Just ignore her. That's why she doesn't have a guy... she lies," Violet answered cattily.

Jenni gave Violet a dirty look as she left the locker room, and as a parting shot she said, "Try to lead a horse to water..."

"Why did she call us horses?" questioned Violet, "Is she insulting our appearances?"

"No, she's not insulting our looks. It's an old saying;" Brandy explained. "She may be right about letting them chase us."

"Oh no, he spotted me alright. He called me a pet name. He remembered the soup; it won't be long before he starts thinking of me in a different light," Violet replied with a dreamy appearance on her face.

"Well I hope Silas thinks of me too."

"Silas will think of you. When we land those two you and I can double date."

"I'm sure it will be fun," Brandy replied.

"We will go to the movies and dancing. You will be the maid of honour at my wedding," Violet waxed dreamily.

"And you can do the same for me."

Brandy then began twirling around like she was dancing with a partner.

"Someone will see you!" hissed Violet.

"Sorry, guess I was carried away," Brandy commented. "I'm just so excited."

"It's a great plan," Violet agreed. "But I think you'll need to lose a little weight to fit into your wedding dress or my maid of honour dress. I don't think they sell size sixteens, and the way you're putting on weight that's all you're going to fit in."

"Forget about being my maid of honour. You're fired!" Brandy retorted angrily.

"Like Silas would ever marry you anyway. Brad, on the other hand, would love to marry me."

"Dream on Violet. He thought to be kind. More than likely he threw the soup away in the garbage."

"You take that back bitch!" Violet shouted.

"No, I won't! He's stringing you along; he doesn't give a damn. I have seen him with many women within the last year."

"He didn't recognize me until now," Violet claimed.

"You need to go on a diet for your own good and none of the purging I observed you doing earlier."

"I don't purge. Something I ate disagreed with me," Brandy explained. "Besides Silas likes me the way I am."

"Yes Silas does. Sorry if I was harsh. People commented on my being too skinny and I hated it."

"You were too skinny last year, so I said so I said that you didn't look so hot and you appeared sick," Brandy commented.

"I appreciated your concern. That's why we are friends. You were the only one who was honest. Everyone else just said you are too skinny. Or wow, you lost weight, which I took to me you look great. Anorexia deceives you," Violet admitted.

"I'm glad I helped you."

"You should recognize just because your
guy, Harold dumped you as his mistress,
doesn't mean you need to let your body go
to seed," Violet continued.

"I've never been anyone's mistress. Why
would you say I was someone's mistress?
I'm insulted!" Brandy cried angrily. "And
I'm not fat."

"You can hide it from some people but not
from me honey...oh no you're not fat you're
pregnant! How far along are you?"

"This time you are wrong. I'm not pregnant.
Do you honestly think that? I know I put on
a few pounds but..."

Violet looked Brandy up and down as
Brandy straightened her dress short the short
gaping at the bust line. She noted Brandy
left her top button undone on her dress pants
and then threw a jacket obviously too small,
over the shirt to try to conceal all.

"Sorry, but you know I can help you get a bigger uniform without anyone knowing."

"The uniform fits fine. I must go get ready for roll call. Sorry about earlier, are we still friends?" Brandy asked mollifying Violet.

"Yes, sure we are friends. If you need help let me know. Silas is one of the good guys; he'll still like you even if you are pregnant."

"I am not pregnant!" denied Brandy.

"Sorry. I sometimes let my mouth get away from me but I mean well."

"Okay, I'll forgive you too. Don't spread around the rumour I'm pregnant though. I must go before the big boss gets mad," Brandy explained.

"Yes, you better. Chief Stewart gets angry when you're late for roll call. Besides I need to go too. My phone will be ringing off the wall," Violet explained, "Everybody wants to know when we will catch the mayor's killer. What about the other two women? Why aren't their killings important to the people? The same person likely killed them."

"You think the killings are connected?" probed Brandy. "From the paperwork I saw the homeless man Mr. Young. Amber what's her name, the mayor's hottie, and the store clerk they were all murdered by the same person."

"Wow, that's weird. Honestly, a serial killer? What a difficult case. I hope my Silas solves the crime. I'm reporting for duty before I'm late. Later," Brandy replied, checking her watch and opening the door to leave.

"Silas won't solve the case, and don't count on that nitwit Rogers. My Brad will run rings around both of them and solve it first. You'll find out and apologise," Violet yelled after Brandy.

Detective Sergeant Emmett Rogers walked in to the police station in time to overhear this but preferred to ignore it. "Hello Violet how's things?"

"Fine," Violet informed him. "Did you hear they found the news anchor Paul Knight dead?"

"Paul Knight? Was he murdered? Who got the case?"

"No, can you believe it? He hid; that he was a closet junkie. He more than likely offed himself, but Brad Owen nailed the case, so he'll find out the truth."

"Hmm," Emmett replied trying hard not to comment and say what he really thought of Brad.

"Oh, I forgot Alan Barnes tried to find you earlier," Violet remembered.

"Alan was looking for me?" queried Emmett

"I don't know. You should be careful talking to him. He deserved to be demoted last month. He didn't show up to the job and blamed his partner Brad Owens," Violet cautioned. "What a nerve he has. He is a backstabber, so watch your back Emmett."

"Violet, you should be a better judge of character." Emmett explained, "Brad isn't who you think he is."

"Brad is a great guy," Violet protested.

"Sorry, I haven't seen the great guy. The guy is a hotdog and he always wants the press to write him up, just so he can advance his career," Emmett said angrily.

"And if anyone gets in his way say goodbye to your job."

"You aren't being fair Emmett. I'm surprised at you. I thought he offered to help you with the murder of the mayor."

"He wanted to help himself right into the press. The mayor's murder is a high-profiled case, but the joke is on him. Chief Stewart handled the press aspects anyway," Emmett said angrily.

"You can't know him all that well. He loves helping."

"He was my partner. I recognize him better than you do Violet. Be careful that you don't cut off more than you can chew," Emmett cautioned.

"I think you've read him wrong, but I am aware this comes from a mistaken place, so I'll let it go," Violet retorted, but still gave him an angry glare.

"I tried Violet. You need to learn to think for yourself."

"Hey buddy, I've been searching all over for you," Alan Barnes cried, walking in to the station.

"So I hear," Emmett answered. "How can I help you?"

"Can we discuss this where we can't be overheard?" Alan whispered.

Alan motioned first to show Emmett; Violet listened in and then gestured to the men's locker room.

"Sure," Emmett replied.

They both walked into the men's locker room and sat on the bench.

"My career is in the toilet and I hoped you would give me some tips on how to fix it," Alan explained.

"How did you get demoted? Did this have something to do with that asshole, Brad Owens?"

"It's a long complicated story but I'll shorten the tale. I'm too damn trusting and I shouldn't always trust and cover for my partner."

"So what did 'Mr. Hotdog' do this time?"

"He kept disappearing and I'd cover for him. One day I went to look for him, but Brad overheard that Chief Stewart was at the crime scene so he hurried to the call. He got there before me. He told Chief Stewart that I was late because he searched for me. Brad went on to say he'd been covering for me. The lying bastard! He convinced him easily. Chief Stewart bought his act. The Chief thought Brad had an exemplary record. He said I should be grateful he covered for me. What did he discern of me? Only what Brad told him. Brad even backed up this position by writing vague reports, like he had been covering for me. Of course the Chief believed him."

"Wow, that's rough. If I didn't distinguish all the bad points about the guy, I'd be tempted to believe him too."

"How can I rectify the chief's opinion of me?" Alan questioned,. "I don't want to be a patrol officer forever."

"Keep your nose to the grind stone. Accept all calls and all requests. Sooner or later Chief Stewart will comprehend your worth in the department," Emmett counselled.

"I hope so."

"Later, Alan."

"Have a good day Emmett, and call me please if anything breaks on the case. I recognize I'm hot dogging, but I need the collar," Alan pleaded.

"Don't worry, I'll call you. The guys in the club, meaning us, need to stick together," Emmett replied cryptically getting up to go.

"You mean the blue-collar?" asked Alan.

"Yes the blue-collar too but I'm taking about the S.O.L.F.B.O. club."

"I still don't get understand," Alan stated puzzled.

"I'm talking about the Shit out of luck from Brad Owens club," Emmett explained, laughing as Alan joined in.

After they left Silas Rentford stepped out of
the shadows and went to his locker to get his
report book. Silas glared at their retreating
backs. He then left to get on with his day.
Brad Owens too has also been hiding in the
corner and he laughed. They talked about
him.

"Too funny," he spoke aloud, "You'll be a
patrolman forever Alan; you might as well
accept your future. And latching your star to
an idiot like Emmett Rogers will get you
nowhere .Why do you think I'm not his
partner anymore? I'm going places neither
of you will ever be able to achieve. So play
your games, but I'll still be chief one day.
You'll grasp how you should have revered
me. Did you tell him about your
disappearances Alan? I don't think so. Let
Rogers realize what a backstabbing little
know-it- all you are. Then he'll appreciate
what a worm you are." Brad laughed when
he realized he was talking to himself. He
then left to get in his squad car.

~0~

Chapter 16 - The Kelly Curse

Lily paced back and forth in her room

trying on one garment after another, as she prepared for Horace's funeral anything to postpone the moments ahead.

"Lily, you saved my life," Amelia pronounced while she put on a black dress that Lily handed her.

"I still need to get the charges thrown out of court," Lily declared, finally settling on a black suit.

"Mom, Aunt Amelia's right. You rock," Rose articulated as she entered the room without knocking.

"Glad you think your mother did well, but we must do more to do to get Amelia free," Lily answered.

Lily then checked her notes on her dresser.

Exiting the bedroom they went into the living room; Rose following behind them. Amelia sat down on the sofa, slipping her foot into one shoe and then trying to manoeuver into the other one.

"Do these look all right?" Amelia asked. "I can't wear heels with my broken leg, but these slip-on shoes are easier to walk in and get on."

"They look fine Amelia," Lily answered.

"I've been thinking about my dad recently, Lily. Do you remember much about him?" Amelia enquired changing the subject.

"I remember him being strict and having a bit of a temper," Lily cautiously replied. "But I also remember he loved you so much."

"The one thing I remember about my dad is that he had this money clip. He played with the money clip all the time. He'd rub his fingers along the gold inscription of the R. Do you remember?"

"I do remember. Uncle Robert used to strip dollar bills out of the clip and hand them to us for the ice cream man."

"Did you realize my Grandfather Cordova made the piece for him? I think it was the last gift he ever gave him. I still remember the stones, all our birthstones. Mine, Grace's and Jerry's birthstones were all on it. Dad treasured that money clip."

"I loved when my dad and Grandma Katha let me stay for the summer to spend time with your family. Your mother, Aunt Aerilla, used to make us picnics," Lily recalled.

"And Grace always imitated us." Amelia revealed sadly, "I still miss them."

"I know. I miss them too," Lily replied softly.

"Your dad, Uncle Peter, is still at the embassy in Prague?" asked Amelia changing the subject.

"He focused heavily on his career. His job was all he had after Mom disappeared."

"He had you too. I know you don't like to talk about this, but do they have an idea what happened to Aunt Heather?"

"I went to school. We lived in Prague and I attended an English language school. Dad's job played big bucks for me to be there. Mom dropped me off at school," Lily replied.

Lily paced a little and she sniffed back tears threatening to surface.

"You were how old? Nine or ten?" prodded Amelia.

"I'd really like to know what happened. No one ever told me and you don't talk about it."

"I was nine. Excited about a part I had in a play. I had the part of Wendy in Peter Pan. Thrilled to play, but I never got to portray the part." Lily's voice broke, but she continued, "Mom drove me to school and dropped me off after kissing me goodbye. I observed her drive away her little Volvo. My dad came by at noon. He took me out of the classroom, and at first gently asked me when I'd last seen my mother. I told him I had seen her in the morning before school. He told me not to worry; she must be shopping and hadn't gotten in touch. We got in the car and we went to our house. Time went by quickly that day and my father paced back and forth, waiting on a phone call that never came. They discovered her bloody vehicle the next day. The police came and I caught the whole story, despite their hushed tones. My mother wasn't in the car but her purse remained and there was a lot of blood. Her blood was throughout the car. There were bullet holes in the driver's side door panels. They had no idea whether she was alive or dead, but they insisted there was so much blood she couldn't be alive.

Amelia gasped.

"You can't imagine how scared I was, Amelia. We were all devastated. No one told me anything. My mother was missing, feasibly dead, and my dad didn't say anything to me, not even an encouraging word."

"Not one word?" Amelia commented. "Uncle Peter must have been out of his mind with fear."

"My dad appeared shell-shocked. I swear he kept expecting Mom to come back through the door. Sleep appeared to be the last thing on his mind. He made me food, but I don't remember eating much. The first week went fast. I was sure she would come through the door. Grandma Katha finally came to us. Dad had broken down and called her explaining about my mother being missing. Grandma Katha comforted me. She made me eat even small amounts of food and put me to bed at night."

"Where was your dad?" Amelia asked.

"Dad spent more and more time at work. The police came to the house, his office, and took him in for questioning. They seemed so focused on my father. They kept him for hours, questioning and re-questioning, but

Grandma Katha hired a terrific lawyer and he came home, set free."

"Why did they suspect your dad?"

"They always suspect the spouse first. It's the first rule of police work. Anyway, they seemed to stop focusing on my dad once he proved he had an alibi. Dad became lost in meetings amongst fifty people the morning Mom disappeared. They understood he couldn't have done killed her, at least not by himself."

"Well of course not. I knew part of the account, but not the entire story. Uncle Peter wouldn't have harmed Aunt Heather! Stupid cops, always judging others!" Amelia exclaimed.

"You know that and I know that, but they didn't seem to believe him innocent. One cop insinuated he had hired someone to murder her, but the lawyer made short work of him. Grandma Katha consoled me, talked to me, stayed by me in Prague about six months. My mother never reappeared. My dad became more and more immersed in his work. I saw little of him, but lots of Grandma Katha. Grandma Katha thought my dad should pull himself together and take care of me. Dad stated he didn't understand how to look after me. Grandma Katha talked to my Dad. Ill-equipped to keep me he gave me to Grandma Katha who took me to Happy Valley. You know I only saw him about once a year. Grandma Katha has truly been like a mother to me since all of this happened."

"Me too! What would we do without her?" asked Amelia.

"I remember when she brought you home, and even though I lived in Ravenworst and you lived here, we've acted like sisters ever since, in every way. Indeed, what would we do without Grandma Katha?"

"I don't ever want to find out how being without Aunt Katha would feel," replied Amelia.

"Mom, is our family cursed?" asked Rose.

"No, we've had a lot of tragic things happen, but it doesn't mean we are cursed. Bad things happen to good people once in a while. We are strong Kelly women," Lily reassured. "What doesn't break us makes us strong."

"But I was not born a Kelly," Rose protested.

"You are my daughter! I have the adoption papers to prove you are a Kelly! You couldn't be more family, even if I gave birth to you," Lily admitted.

Katha and Amelia then left the room a moment to give Lily and Rose some time to talk.

"So you don't regret you adopted me? I mean you had Dad before and he's gone," Rose whimpered before breaking into tears.

"Never ever doubt that I love you. You are my daughter in my heart and mind. Adopting you and making you officially my daughter was the best thing that ever happened to me," Lily fiercely replied.

"I love you, Mom. I'm sorry you lost your first mom too."

"Thanks honey. We miss them they are still in our hearts and it is okay,"

"So you don't mind that I think of her as my mom sometimes?" Rose timidly asked.

"Of course not I'd be disappointed if you didn't."

"I do love you, Mom," Rose articulated again. "I love you too, pumpkin."

"Mom, I want to go to the mall today and meet my friend Carol after the services and the Wake for Daddy. Daddy wouldn't mind that would he? I need to get away and go out with my friend Carol," Rose enquired.

"Rose, if that will make you feel better then I think you should go be with Carol. Your dad would tell you the same thing," Lily replied, dabbing her eyes and pretending she had something in them instead of tears.

"He was always a great dad. He always went to my plays and my games. I miss him too, Mom," Rose answered, trying hard not to cry.

Rose adjusted her pantyhose and her dress and then put on high-heeled shoes.

"Is this outfit okay? Would Daddy like this dress?" Rose asked while smoothing her skirt.

"Yes, the outfit is perfect. I can tell you do but we're going to take one day at a time starting with this ordeal today. We're about to put on our manners and mourn your father."

Katha entered the room and surveyed their outfits without saying a word. Katha then smiled and Lily was relieved that she found them acceptable.

"Will there be a lot of people there?" asked Rose.

"There will be. Your father was well-loved."

"He could be a little gruff at times but a decent person. Other people ought to have seen that in him. Do you think they'll talk about the way he was found?" asked Rose.

"Crass people will talk about him, dear. The thing to do is hold your head up high and pretend you didn't hear them because what they need to say doesn't matter," Katha advised.

"Aunt Katha is right! Ignore any ignoramuses," Amelia counselled.

"See, we all agree," Lily replied smiling.

"I love you all! I'm so glad I made you my family." Rose declared looking around at the three strong women in her family, "With Daddy gone you are all I've got."

"You always have me. We love you too!" Lily reassured.

"Make that three," added Amelia.

"No, four," replied Katha interjected, "One for all and all four one!"

"That's from The Three Musketeers Grandma Katha," protested Rose.

"My dear haven't you seen the movie with Chris O'Donnell. There are four of them!" Katha explained winking. "Chris O'Donnell is still hot. Have you seen NCIS: Los Angeles?"

"Grandma Katha," admonished Rose.

"Well, I may be older, but I'm not dead yet."
Katha laughed and then continued, "Okay
then, one for all, and all for one. Ladies,
time to put on your best manners. We will
do Horace proud."

Katha then put on her coat as she steered the
women out to the waiting limousine to travel
to the funeral parlour.

~0~

Chapter 17 - Goodbye Is Not a Word I Want To Say

Arriving, the women faced a huge room filled with people. Lily felt surprised, since the funeral would not take place for another half hour. The big, accommodating, funeral home held all the dignitaries who arrived for Horace's funeral. The men wore black suits with sombre ties, the women black or navy blue dress. Lily found this all so surreal. How could she be at a funeral for Horace? It seemed not long ago she attended a funeral for her first husband, William Wentworth. How could she have lost yet another husband, in such a short time? And Horace had been found in such a way?

Horace had an affair with his secretary? Amber seemed like a lovely woman...ditzy, but polite. But does a courteous woman sleep with your husband? Lily hadn't wanted to believe it, but Emmett Rogers confirmed through his investigation Amber had been having an affair with Horace. Why Horace? Why did you do this? Why wasn't I enough? Who killed you? No one, not even someone who cheated on me like you did, deserved to die.

Unbelievable, how had women in her family lost all their husbands in such a short time. Was there a curse at work here, or something more sinister? Odd how both her husbands were dead! Two mysterious deaths, one deemed a traffic accident, the other murder. Would they ever find out who killed Horace and Amber? How did these murders relate to Megan's killing and the homeless man Mr. Young? All these questions raced through Lily's mind. She looked around noticing a lot of people here, to say their final goodbyes to Horace. There must have been two or three hundred people there. A lot of them were politicians wanting publicity, understanding the press would be here, always ready for the photo opportunity, a sound bite to get them elected or re-elected.

Lily noticed the awful Harold Crimshaw.
How dare he? Horace hated him.

He said the only reason he ran for mayor,
was to keep an opportunistic bastard out of
the City coffers. Horace also said if Harold
Crimshaw ever got to be mayor, there would
be a lawsuit from every female employee in
the mayor's office vicinity. She thought
Horace had been exaggerating, but the man
did seem a little smarmy. She only hoped
the people there, would give her a few
minutes alone at Horace's grave to say
goodbye.

Both she and Rose needed privacy to say
goodbye. She wanted a private graveside
ceremony, not a photo opportunity, to
observe the grieving widow and her
daughter splashed on television and the front
page of the paper.

Lily sat down with Rose and Katha and
Amelia followed. She found her mind
wandering to wonderful times with Horace.
She remembered times when she and Horace

went on holidays at the beach with Rose. He
encompassed all the qualities of a good
father, but had he been a good husband?

So many times she complained to him that
he needed to spend more time with her and
Rose. She remembered all their holidays as
wonderful, but had she idolized them? She
recalled the first Christmas they spent
together when Horace, not realizing Rose
was too old to believe anymore, dressed up
as Santa. Rose guessed at once her dad was
in the costume. Rose went along with the
disguise, realizing how much it meant to
him. Rose was such a thoughtful child, even
at nine years old. It was a good memory and
the memory she wanted to keep of Horace in
her head. Not the image of the way she
found him. Lily realized with a start the
service had been concluded. It was time to
say goodbye.

She wasn't ready. Would she ever be ready?
Oh how weary, she felt, like she was cold
and would never be warm again. She
shivered pulling her coat she hadn't taken
off, closer to herself. Did Rose appear cold

too? Lily thought, as she glanced at Rose and leaned in hug her.

"Thank goodness the service is completed," Lily said aloud.

"Excuse me, dear, but you need to go up and announce the wake afterwards," Katha whispered, prodding Lily.

"I'm so tired Grandma Katha. Do I have to go to the wake?" Lily whispered back.

"I know, sweetie. The worst part is near over and you can soon go home, take a hot bath and rest," Katha promised.

"I don't ever think I'll sleep again," Lily whispered.

"It will get better Lily. Do you want to go visit my Doctor? He can help. I can call him for you," Amelia whispered.

"No, but thanks, I appreciate the thought Amelia."

Lily sauntered to the podium and spoke to the room, "Everyone please feel free to join us for a celebration of Horace's life, at the Pope Hotel, in the Rose Room. Light foods and refreshments will be provided. We will be holding a private graveside service for Horace, for family only. Thank you all for coming; this concludes the service for today."

People slowly wandered out making their goodbyes. The four Kelly women also left, and headed for the graveside ceremony.

At the cemetery, after getting out of the limousine, Lily looked around at Horace's grave site. This was a lovely spot to be buried in, even if the cemetery at the edge of town marked the official end of Happy Valley. Lily wiped away a tear as she felt guilty for even thinking of this. Horace need to be buried, whether she liked the thought, or not and this spot had been carefully picked. Lily glanced around and saw a lovely full-grown maple tree nearby, with a bird's nest. She noted it also held a bird feeder. The other graves close were well-

tended and flowers were on them. The
graves adjacent to those that crept up a tall
hill were well tended as well. Lily wandered
how they mow the grass, so evenly when it
went up such a huge hill. Those graves were
cheaper but not ideal. They hadn't sold the
ones higher. The fact that some of the graves
would be situated beside the fence next to
the Canadian Shield rock face high above
the hill made them undesirable. The igneous
(pink and some say red in colour) Canadian
Shield face rock flowing from the great
lakes to western Canada resulted from
volcanic ash which had covered the area
eons ago. The Canadian Shield rock face left
a gap in the cliff face above, where a chasm
would make anyone climbing there, fall
about one hundred feet to a valley below.

The fence preventing that from happening
was often broken and defaced by the town's
teenagers, making the place dangerous.
Horace had campaigned to have them build
a better fence and hired guards after one of
the teens fell and needed to be rescued. The
teen was lucky; he survived the fall and
spent two weeks in the hospital.

The minister began to say a few words over Horace. Lily felt cold and out-of-place. It was like she wasn't at this tomb. She understood unfortunately this remained the truth not an illusion; she stood beside Horace's final burial-place. A tear slipped from her eye and she wiped it away before anyone could notice. The coffin hung on winches about six feet above the ground. Lily watched them get ready to lower the coffin.

"May we take a couple of minutes before you lower it?" Lily inquired.

The one man looked reluctant and frowned. Lily looked at the other man expectantly, hoping he'd change the other one's mind.

"We can give the lady ten minutes, Bob. The body is the mayor. How much time do you think the lady has had without prying eyes to grieve?" declared the other man, "Besides, it only takes one of us to lower it."

"Fine. I will come back in ten minutes, Mrs. Brooksfield. We are so sorry for your loss," Bob replied.

"Yes, Bob can do this on his own," the other man replied.

Then the two men walked away towards the chapel on the grounds.

"Mom, someone is watching us," Rose fearfully retorted.

"It's probably one of those muckraking reporters from the tabloids. We'll say goodbye quickly and leave. Then they won't have a story," Lily explained annoyed.

Ten minutes passed quickly and Bob returned. As they watch the coffin being lowered into the grave a shot was heard. All the women duck for cover. Bob, who had been lowering the coffin by machine, jumped out of the cab of the backhoe and ran for cover as well.

"Keep down all of you," Lily commanded taking charge and dialling her cell phone.

"Nine-one-one. What is the nature of your emergency?" requested the voice.

"I need the police. Now!"

"Police operator, what is the nature of your emergency?" solicited the police dispatcher.

"Shots fired at Westside Cemetery, the south side of the cemetery. We're under fire here, please hurry," Lily screamed into her phone as a bullet whizzed by her.

The bullets rang out fast and furious. Lily found herself pushing Rose into the open grave under the still hanging coffin. She took one arm of Katha and one arm of Amelia and pulled them both into the burial plot, dropping her cell phone, and hanging up the phone by accident. Just as she did so a bullet pinged overhead. It had hit the metal wench holding the coffin. The coffin was now hanging precariously over their heads in a downward angle.

"Mom, someone shot at us again! We're all going to die."

"It will be okay honey. The police will come and stop whoever this is. And we will be protected here under your dad's coffin," Lily reassured her daughter, while still searching for the cell phone she dropped.

More bullets rang out over their heads. They heard poof sounds; as the bullets hit the dirt and some of them narrowly missing the coffin above them.

"Yes right, keep telling yourself we'll be fine. Bullets are coming our way, there isn't a cop for miles, and only Daddy and his coffin is all that protect us. Oh no, they'll put holes in Daddy's coffin. Daddeeee," Rose complained hysterically. "And his coffin is falling down on our heads."

"Your dad is protected us even in death, Rose. The coffin won't fall. Now pull yourself together. You can't fall apart now. We will beat this gunman," Lily answered.

"Rose is correct, we're all going to be killed, Lily," Amelia cried.

"Oh, for Pete's sake pull yourself together, Amelia. Set a better example," Lily sniped.

"You're squishing my foot," Katha complained to Amelia.

"My leg, oh my leg. The crutch stuck into the dirt and I'm falling over in soil," complained Amelia.

"Good grief, someone's shooting at us, we could all be killed and you two complain about being cramped?" Rose shouted annoyed, "Get a grip people! We could be killed here."

"Well if she'd get off my foot with that crutch...,"Katha replied annoyed.

They heard sounds of running across the graveyard and then more shots ringing out. Lily picked up the phone and went to dial the police again and realized they were still connected.

"Hello, ma'am, are you still on the line?" enquired the police dispatcher.

"Quiet. I can't hear the police operator," Lily cautioned.

"Can you spot the shooter ma'am? Is it just one shooter?" probed the police dispatcher.

"No, I can't glimpse the shooter. We're trying not to get hit by the bullets," Lily explained exasperated.

"No need to take that tone, ma'am; you demanded my assistance. Please stay on the line. Police are on the way," the police dispatcher cautioned.

Lily tried to quiet her family, "Quiet all of you. Would you all quit squabbling! I must hear this woman. I told you all that."

"You've taken cover? Where can the policemen find you when they arrive?" demanded the police dispatcher.

"Believe it or not, we've jumped into my husband's grave to get away from the shooter. His coffin dangles above our heads and it could fall with the right shot." Lily explained, "Please hurry! My daughter is here, too, as well as my cousin, and my great-grandmother. And my cousin has a broken leg from last week."

"They're on the way, ma'am. Do you hear the sirens?"

"I hear them mom," Rose claimed.

"Yes, I do now. Thank you so much." Lily answered.

"As long as it not an ambulance!" Katha announced.

"Why would it be an ambulance? None of us are hit!" Amelia stated.

"Please give me your name for the officers," demanded the dispatcher.

"I didn't give you my name? Oh, I am sorry, this is Mrs. Horace Brooksfield," Lily replied proudly. "And what is your name, so I can thank you later."

"No, thank you is necessary ma'am, but my name is Violet Garden. I believe we spoke the other day," answered the dispatcher.

"Thank you, anyway, Violet. We appreciate all of your help."

"Mom, they take forever and you thank her? What if the shooter comes here and shoots down at us. We are sitting like ducks waiting to be plucked," Rose complained.

"More flies with sugar Rose," Amelia muttered under her breath.

"We're being shot at here, not throwing a tea party," Rose exclaimed.

"My hip, oh dear it's stuck again. I don't know how I'll ever get out of here. I don't think they made artificial hips for crawling into graves," Katha complained, trying to distract Rose.

"Are you okay, Grandma Katha? I've never known you to complain. I guess it would be okay if Daddy protected us up in heaven like Mom said," Rose said pointing to her father's coffin.

"Daddy won't let anything happen to us."

"That's right sweetheart," Lily agreed approvingly.

They listened intently but heard no more shots filling the air with sound and fury.

"Do you think it's over, mom?" Rose asked.

"Mrs. Horace Brooksfield?" a voice asked, hovering above the grave.

"Yes?" Lily said cautiously, hiding her daughter beneath her just in case.

"Police, ma'am."

"Can you pass down your badge?"

"Lily, just let the man help us out of here. I'm getting filthy," demanded Katha. "I don't know how we can go to the wake like this."

"I agree with Mom. Don't listen to the two whiners. Mom, please, just take a look at his badge before we trust him," Rose insisted.

"I did, Rose. His identification is legitimate."

The policeman reached down and helped them up out of the small space pulling Lily up first, followed by Amelia and Rose and Katha.

"Why Brad Owens, is that you?" questioned Amelia surprised as the police officer pulled her out gently.

"Amelia Cordova! As I live and breathe. It's wonderful to see you again," Brad Owens said sounding pleased.

"You know Sergeant Detective Owens?" asked Lily shocked that Amelia had smiled at him.

"Brad used to come by my house when I was a teenager before the...before the accident," Amelia stuttered.

"So you were aware of my cousin as a teen?" Lily enquired.

"Did I? We were all in love with Amelia. She was the prettiest girl in Ravenworst. She was the one who got away." Brad answered, with deep feeling in his voice turning to Amelia he said,

"So this is where you got to, I was so sad to hear about your parents and your siblings."

"Thanks. I moved in with my Great Aunt Katha when they died," Amelia explained, trying to change the subject.

"I've been here about six years," Brad commented.

"Six years? How odd, I've never even run into you."

"A police officer has a busy job. We don't have a lot of time for anything else. It is a bigger city now," Brad explained. "It's wonderful to see you," Amelia said sweetly. "I'm so glad you answered our call. We're safe now aren't we?"

"I sent another cop to check the perimeter, but we should probably take cover until he comes back." Silas Rentford appeared suddenly looking haggard and with his gun still drawn.

"For Pete's sake, put your gun away. You could harm the ladies. Did you find the shooter, Rentford?"

"Yes and I called it in, she's dead."

"What? How can the shooter be dead? You say it's a she? Did you return fire?" enquired Brad puzzled and angry.

"No sir, I did not," Silas denied. "But she's dead all the same."

"People don't up and shoot themselves. It has to be another shooter, or she shot herself," Brad insisted.

"Why, what is this old home week?" Amelia said suddenly, looking up after hearing Silas' voice.

"Silas Rentford, is that you?"

"Amelia Cordova?" Silas asked looking surprised, "Wow, it's so incredibly wonderful to meet you again."

"It's lovely to see you too, Silas," Amelia replied blushing. "Did you know someone shot at us from the graveyard?"

"I was sent to find the active shooter here in the cemetery. Are you okay? You don't have any wounds do you?" probed Silas worried, looking like he wanted to personally check her over for bullet holes.

"No, I'm fine, and is everyone else here," Amelia answered.

"Gosh, it's great to spot you, Amelia. When you disappeared after the fire we were heartbroken at school," Silas continued, grinning wildly at Amelia.

Lily looked at both men. They seemed enthralled with Amelia; no one else existed for them.

"Silas talk with the lady on your own time!" Brad then mouthed 'Sorry' to Amelia and then ordered, "Back to your report Rentford. Did you examine the body?"

"Yes sir, she's dead. Woman about sixty, sixty-five years old, dyed short black hair, society matron? Wallet in her purse says she's one Cheryl Waverly."

"No, it can't be Cheryl. You have to be mistaken. She's my mother-in-law. She wouldn't shoot at me. Not while her granddaughter was nearby," Lily protested shaking her head, "Even she would shoot at family."

"Oh no, you are wrong. It couldn't be Grandma. She wouldn't shoot me or anybody," Rose cried, also shaking her head.

"No, I'm not sorry, Ms. Brooksfield. She looks like her driver licence picture. No room for doubt about the shooter, it was the deceased woman, Cheryl Waverley," Silas replied unequivocally.

"Excuse us ladies we'll be right back we need to check the perimeter again," Sergeant Detective Owens said frowning at Silas.

Silas and Brad then left.

"Good Lord. What kind of people do I come from that my grandmother shot at me?" demanded Rose disgusted.

"Watch your language, missy. We do not take the name of the Lord in vain," Katha retorted.

"She was my grandmother and she shot at us. I have a right to be angry," said Rose dejected and hurt, "She could have killed us."

"Obviously, the loss of her daughter obviously broke her mind and Horace's death (before she could make up with him) put her completely over the edge," Lily agreed. "If she had been truly thinking I know she would never put you at risk. The woman adored you."

"Is it true she broke his arm when he was little?" Rose probed, "Do you think she killed Daddy?"

"I know she didn't kill him. She loved him, no matter what. Yes, it's true she broke his arm. She became unhinged slightly when she lost her daughter, but losing your father must have made her even more unbalanced.

"I hate her! How could she do this? And at Daddy's grave! It's like slapping Daddy. I don't want to be a Brooksfield."

"You are upset dear, but you must not talk that way. As for the people you come from, you are of my blood now, so you come from good Irish stock," Katha expounded.

"That's right, Rose. You are a Kelly woman remember?" Amelia agreed.

"I remember."

"Come on Rose; we have to go."

"Great, now I've got dirt in my hair. Must we still go to the Wake? I've already said goodbye to Daddy," questioned Rose, changing the subject.

"Yes, but only for a short time. We need to leave now," Lily explained.

"I need a drink," Katha announced. "Preferably a gin fizz, or a fuzzy navel."

"Me too!" Amelia agreed.

"Me three," Lily exclaimed.

"I need one too," Rose announced.

"I hope you're talking about pop, because you're getting a drink over your mother's and my dead body. Oops, poor choice of words, but you get the drift right, Rose?" Katha exclaimed.

"I do, Grandma. Pop sounds good. I feel like I must have a ton of dirt in my mouth. Ooh, decaying body dirt. Yuck!" Rose fretted wiping her tongue.

Amelia hid a laugh. Suddenly Sergeant Detective Owens appeared again at Amelia's elbow. Silas looked chastised Lily noted as if Brad had yelled at him.

"Can I escort you ladies to the wake?" asked Sergeant Detective Owens sounding boyish and nervous.

"I'm finished all my paperwork and I'm off duty. Can I escort you Amelia?" requested Silas, also smiling "And we could catch up on old times with you?"

Brad frowned again at Silas.

"While you gentlemen made kind offers, it wouldn't be seemly for you to escort me to a wake," Amelia answered prettily, side stepping both offers. Amelia turned to each of them and smiled a sweet endearing smile, "But please, feel free to come to the wake."

"We'd be happy to. Wouldn't we, Brad, I mean Sergeant Detective Owens," Silas chimed.

"Correct. At least let us see you safely to your limousine?" agreed Brad, "You are lucky the chauffeur guy didn't panic and take off when he overheard the shots. He called us too. He is still parked over near the front gates of the cemetery."

"Seeing us safely to the car would be wonderful. Thank you gentlemen," Lily agreed, but neither seemed to register that Lily was even there, until Amelia nodded her head.

The chauffeur then drove away with the ladies inside only after a lecture from Brad and Silas about keeping the ladies safe.

"Home please," Lily requested from the driver.

"We don't have time to go home," Katha stated annoyed.

"Well I'm so glad you're done with your cops," Lily said cattily to Amelia.

"I can't believe they were more interested in you, Aunt Amelia, than the fact that Grandma tried to kill us. Did they really say Grandma was dead, Mom?"

"I'm sorry, sweetie," Lily replied sadly.

"This is ridiculous. I can't believe any of this happened. If Grandma tried to kill us, then who killed Grandma?" asked Rose.

"I don't know. The whole business appears strange and the body count keeps rising," Katha exclaimed.

"There's a lot of stuff going on in Happy Valley I don't understand. I understand the news anchor Paul Knight killed himself. I for one do not believe it. I met him once; he seemed like a focused man and not the type to kill himself."

"Paul Knight the television anchor?" Rose queried, "Who cares about him? Grandma tried to kill us. Why?"

"I don't know why. She must have a screw loose. I met Paul Knight a couple of times. He seemed like a nice young man. I can't believe they are reporting his death on Chatter," Katha explained holding up her I-phone.

"When did you get an I-phone? Mom won't buy me one of them. She claims I'd always be on the phone. And you own a Chatter account?" asked Rose surprised.

"Doesn't everyone have a Chatter account? I'll get an I-phone for your belated birthday present and the data plan as well. Then you can use Chatter a lot more," Grandma Katha offered whispering.

"I already have a Chatter account, but I'd love an I-phone," Rose exclaimed.

"Don't encourage her, Grandma Katha. She's not getting an I-phone, as much as she wants one. She'd never get her homework done, always surfing on the thing," Lily admonished.

"Yes, I will. Please, Mom?"

Katha gave Lily a look that conveyed to Lily that this could make Rose feel better.

"Well if Grandma Katha chooses to give you one for a belated birthday present and you don't abuse it, I guess I won't stop her."

"Thank you, Lily. Now I hope it won't upset you but, we just do not have time to stop at home. We are late as it is. We'll need to stop at the washroom and tidy up before we go. I own a lint brush."

Katha held up the lint brush from her purse and began brushing off soil from her dress. She then passed it to Amelia.

"A lint brush? You're going to clean yourself up and go to the wake? My husband's been murdered. We've been shot at by his mother, but we're still going to hold up appearances and go to his wake?"

"Mom is correct. Let's just go home."

"Lily and Rose, this has been hard on all of us, but we can't let the murderer win. If we don't go to Horace's wake then we haven't truly said goodbye. I know it didn't really make me start to feel better until I realized how many people loved your great grandfather."

"Fine, then! Can I borrow the lint brush after you, Amelia?" requested Lily.

"So we're going?" Rose asked her mother.

"Yes," Lily answered.

"We can all use the lint brush," Katha replied generously. "I think some soap and water is also in order for our faces. You have a dirt mark, all down your neck Rose."

"Why didn't you say something sooner? What if someone saw me like this?" Rose replied sarcastically.

She then scrubbed at the dirt despite what she said.

"Quit rubbing it in, Rose. It makes it worse." Katha claimed.

"Who cares? I'm sick of this all. My dad is dead. My grandmother is dead. I just want the world to go away." Rose answered.

"It will get better," Katha stated.

"How can it ever? My mom is in jail...my family is gone."

"No, it is not. You have your mother, Lily me and your Aunt Amelia and we are your family Rose and we love you."

"I love you too, Grandma Katha. I'm sorry I'm such a pain," Rose replied wiping tears away.

"You're never a pain. To me, your aunt, and your mother, you are our pride and joy. Now, dry your eyes. I have some wipes in my purse, I'm sure they will do as well, to wipe the dirt off."

"Always prepared aren't you, Aunt Katha?" Amelia stated.

"I certainly am," Katha replied and then turning to Rose she asked, "Are you okay now?"

"No, but I want to forget about all of this and just remember Daddy for a while."

"You do that Rosey," Amelia, Lily and Katha all said.

"Please, stop near here," Rose instructed the driver, "It's City Hall. It has a washroom, a huge one, where we can clean off the dirt...Oh no, we can't. Daddy was killed upstairs,"

Rose remembered and bit her lip so she didn't cry. But it didn't work as tears escaped from her eyes and she rushed to wipe them before anyone noticed.

"Your father would understand and want us to get cleaned up to represent him best."

"Okay, I do look bad. Daddy would hate my dress appearing dirty," Rose said dabbing her eyes.

"We'll make it through this," Lily insisted taking Rose's hand.

"Driver, stop here, for a few minutes,"
Katha advised.

The driver parked the limousine in front of
City Hall. After the ladies excited the
vehicle, they entered the City Hall foyer
where Barney Terrell greeted them.

"What happened to you all?" Barney asked
and then observed, "You are all covered in
dirt. It's obvious something happened, but I
thought you'd all be at the wake by now."

"We had a little incident at the gravesite.
Someone shot at us," Lily replied not
admitting it was Cheryl, her ex-mother-in
law.

"Someone shot at you? Good lord, are you
all okay? Should I call the police?"

"Not necessary. The police have been
informed, and other than a lot of dirt, we are
fine."

"Mrs. B., sorry that happened to you, especially after Mr. Brooksfield's death. I wanted to go to the funeral but I don't get off for a few more minutes. I did plan on paying my respects at the wake. Horace Brooksfield was a fine man and deserves my respect," Barney explained.

"Thank you, Barney. Horace was fond of you. He spoke highly of you."

"Thank you Mr. Terrell, Daddy spoke well of you. He said you were the best at your job here," Rose responded, changing the subject.

"I believe Mayor Brooksfield was a lucky man. He has a lovely wife and daughter. He spoke lovingly of you, Miss Rose. He said you played basketball like a pro and had a real talent for mimicry and acting."

"We need to get cleaned up before we go to the wake, Barney, but since you're off in a few minutes would you do us the honour of accompanying us to the wake?" Katha invited impulsively.

"I would be truly honoured, ma'am," Barney replied smiling.

"Please excuse us now while we clean up the dust," Lily said.

"Sure. I'm sorry that I kept you, ma'am."

Barney watched their departing backs, his gaze never leaving them until they went into the washroom. This made Rose feel slightly uncomfortable, but since she didn't want to upset her mother she said nothing.

"You were awfully good to him, Grandma Katha," Rose said.

"Well he seemed like a pleasant man, and your father liked him, although he didn't like Amber..."

"How do you know that?" Lily asked.

"I came to visit Horace to arrange a surprise birthday party for Lily last year and I saw him glance at Amber with such malice when she flirted with him," Katha admitted.

"Are you sure you didn't imagine it?"

"No, she brushed him and he pushed her away and then he yelled at her to quit flirting with every guy who had legs," Katha admitted.

"We should tell Detective Rogers," Lily insisted.

"Fine, I'll do that after the wake." Katha exclaimed continuing to brush her hair and replace her make-up, "There, all fixed. We all look decent now. Let's go, girls."

~0~

Chapter 18 - The Awakening

Arriving at the Pope hotel they entered

into the Rose ballroom for the wake. Barney helped Amelia in, earning a dirty stare from both Silas and Brad.

"Hello, Lily. I'm so dreadfully sorry about Horace. He was a lovely man," Colleen Finn lied.

"I know you didn't like him much, Colleen, although you never hesitated to put him through to me on the phone at work," Lily replied.

"I'm still sorry he's gone, Lily. I recognize how much you and Rose truly loved him," Colleen answered.

"I appreciate you coming, Colleen. How is the office?"

"I'd rather not get into it; you have enough to worry about today," Colleen commented.

"Is Barbara that bad?"

"She is different than you are to work for in the office. But you quit worrying about the office. I'll manage until you come back," Colleen explained.

"I appreciate you holding down the fort until I return." Colleen scanned the room and seeing a crowd gathering waiting to speak to Lily she said, "I better let you go; it appears like there's a line of people who want to speak to you."

"Thank you again, Colleen, I'll see you later," Lily answered.

"If you need anything you tell me, Lily," Colleen insisted touching Lily's arm, and then walked away.

"My dear Mrs. Brooksfield, I am so sorry to hear about your loss and troubles," Gregory Hanks said as he came up to Lily and took her hand. Gregory Hanks was a tall gentleman, whose blue eyes sparkled with life.

"Have you met Mr. Hanks, Rose?" Lily asked politely.

"Yes, of course, Mom. You own Hank's, a huge grocery conglomerate across North America, don't you Mr. Hanks?"

"Yes, little ma'am, I do," Gregory Hanks admitted.

A man came up and whispered in Mr. Hanks' ear and Lily discerned the man objected to Mr. Hank's speaking to her. He must be his campaign manager. Lily had been told he ran for parliament. Why had he even allowed him to come here? Was it because Horace had been the mayor? Lily wondered.

"Should you be seen speaking to me?" Lily asked, "I understood you thought of running for office. A member of Parliament wasn't it?"

"Wow, you certainly have great sources, my dear. My mind isn't made up yet. I've known you since you were a child, at one time I had hoped to be your great-grandfather. Of course, I can be seen with you. I would never turn my back on you, parliamentary seat or not," Gregory Hanks expounded.

"Thank you, Mr. Hanks."

"My dear, call me Greg," Greg Hanks replied congenially.

"Thank you again, Greg."

"Your grandmother appears so sparkling and extremely lovely. Like a fine wine. Does the woman never age?" Greg stated with a leer in his voice.

Lily was always amazed at how easily Grandma Katha seemed to collect eligible, interesting admirers. She only hoped she'd be able to do the same in her old age.

"No I don't think Grandma Katha does age. It's part of her charm."

"It certainly is. I've missed the dear lady."
Greg announced, "Damn Kieran for
swooping in and grabbing the prize. A blast
from the past and then he pounced regaining
her heart."

"Speaking of the love of my Grandma
Katha's life; if you recognize what is good
for you, you'll guard your tongue around her
when you speak of my great-grandfather
Kieran."

"Who's hanging around her now?" asked
Greg, sounding peevish and jealous.

"His name is Terrence Stewart. He's the
police chief's Dad," Lily explained.

"Oh..." Greg replied sounding dejected.

"I'm sure she'd love to hear from you," Lily
responded devilishly.

"I think I'll go speak to her." Greg
announced, "My nephew took over the
business, so I'm going to have a lot of time
on my hands."

Katha spotted Greg, smiled, and waved.

"Look, she's smiling. Go talk to her."

Greg sauntered over to Katha as Terrence frowned. Lily watched from across the room, trying not to laugh. She scrutinized around for Rose, only to find her standing behind her.

"Mom, where is Aunt Amelia?" asked Rose. "I don't see where she went."

"I can't tell," Lily answered and looking around she added, "Oh there she is."

Lily pointed. Rose then walked over towards her Aunt Amelia. As Lily gazed around, she was happily surprised at how many people came to honour Horace. So many people kept coming up to her and telling her how sorry they felt that Horace was gone. No one mentioned the way he was found, although Lily had caught some quiet whispers stop when she circulated the room.

A few people had offered to start a scholarship in Horace's name for law students, a wonderful idea and something she had planned on doing for Horace's memory. Rose would be happy to have her father honoured this way. Rose wandered back to Lily's side interrupting her thoughts.

"Mom, Aunt Amelia is embarrassing us. You'd think this was a party not my dad's wake. Look at her; the men kowtowing to her every wish or command."

"Why, whatever do you mean?" asked Lily.

"Look over there, Mom, near the window. Those two police officers grovel all over her every word, and observe how they keep chasing the other men away. There's something odd about them."

"I'm sure you are mistaken. Why would they grovel? They hardly know your Aunt Amelia."

"Watch them. The guy in the blue suit came over to speak to her. He speaks to Aunt Amelia and bam he's turfed," Rose stated watching intently.

"Sweetie, Amelia said she met them when she was a teenager. Aunt Amelia lost her family to a fire; this has brought back some lovely memories for her, instead of the horror of their deaths," Lily explained, not believing this but trying to appease Rose.

"But, Mom, I don't think she has a clue those men like her."

"Rose, you're quite right, she doesn't have a clue, but it is harmless enough. I do however appreciate you watching after your Aunt Amelia. We both understand she is a special person."

"Mom, I love Aunt Amelia. I'm not judging her when I say this, but she's awful naïve for her age."

"Aunt Amelia is inexperienced. Despite all she's gone through, she trusts like a child, "Lily agreed.

"I understand, mom. She doesn't see what is right in front of her." Rose explained, sounding worried, "And sometimes people take advantage of such trust."

"We can all be blind to other's motives. I hope Amelia never loses her zest. Sweet people like Amelia lose their innocence becoming bitter, confused and lost," Lily reassured. "But I promise I'll keep an eye on that pair. Thank you for letting me understand."

"So you'll keep an eye on her too?"

"Yes, I promise I will, sweetie," Lily agreed.

"Will you be okay?" Rose asked searching Lily's face.

"We both will, sweetie, but I want this wake finished," Lily admitted.

"Can I go, Mom?" Rose asked. "I need to get out of here."

"Going to the mall with Carol?"

"Yes, she's over there," Rose pointed to Carol, who was flirting with a waiter who couldn't have been more than eighteen years old.

"Okay, take your cell phone and make sure you are home by four p.m. Promise me, no flirting with older boys. They can't be trusted."

"Good grief, Mom. Can you be any more embarrassing? A. If I was to flirt with older boys I don't think it would be your business, and B, I'm not the type to flirt with older boys at the mall. Don't you understand your own daughter?"

"Sorry, what could I be thinking?" Lily replied sarcastically.

"Mom!"

"Fine. Do you need any money? Of course you need money. Here, is a hundred dollars. Spend the money and find something lovely to wear, but nothing too short or too trashy. Got it?" Lily ordered knowing that she gave Rose too much money.

"Thanks, Mom. You're the best," Rose replied, changing her tune and hugging her mother.

"Like, I'm so sorry, Mrs. Brooksfield, you know about your husband. And I don't believe what the press said," Carol proclaimed as she stood in front of Lily.

"Hush, Carol," Rose exclaimed, poking Carol in the ribs.

"What? What did I say?" Carol asked dejected.

"Ah, thank you, Carol," Lily said a little flustered.

"Don't you worry! Rose and I will go hang out at the mall and do some window shopping. Retail therapy is good for the soul," Carol explained.

"It is, isn't it Carol? Have fun at the mall you two," Lily laughed.

Carol had been hanging around so much for years. She was like part of the family, so it wasn't a stretch to say she'd changed a little. Lily thought. Carol appeared more outgoing now she had turned fifteen, more so than Rose. But wasn't that a good thing? Rose needed to come out of her shell and not worry so much about what people thought all the time. Carol would distract Rose although she should worry about Carol.

Carol seemed a little more boy crazy than Rose. She hoped Rose would stay as sensible as she was now and not follow Carol's lead. This was difficult for them both to bear and Rose had already been through so much in her short life. It was good Carol and Rose would go to the mall. A little retail therapy would distract Rose, for a few hours. Lily looked forward to a little shut-eye while Rose was gone, if she ever got away from this wake and never-ending crowds.

"Lily, check out Amelia. Those policemen are a little too forward with her," Katha interrupted Lily's thoughts.

"You want me to check on her too? It is harmless enough, Grandma Katha. She's just chatting with some old friends."

"She might think of them as old friends, but those boys have designs on her and I don't trust them," Grandma Katha replied perceptively.

"Fine, I'll check on her then," Lily answered, appeasing her Grandma Katha.

Lily went over to Amelia and listened to part of the snippets of the conversation, going on with the two policemen. Barney Terrell stood nearby, fingering a money clip in his pocket and listening to the conversation.

"Do you remember when your dad hired me to cut the lawn?" Brad said touching Amelia's hand and fingering a money clip in his pocket as well.

"You cut the lawn too?" Silas blurted frowning. He too fidgets, fingering a money clip in his pocket.

"You both did," Amelia admitted.

"I used to slip out and bring you lemonade. Daddy used to get mad. He said it was wasted on the help. I'm sorry he was mean to you."

"He was a tartar wasn't he?" claimed Brad.

"He was abusive; I saw him hit you," Silas insisted.

"I did too," admitted Brad.

"My father had the right to discipline me." Amelia defended, "He didn't like it when I talked to boys."

"Do you remember when you slipped out to the dance?" asked Silas

"Do you mean the one where I danced with both you and Brad? It was such a magical night, until I got home. I went to sneak in the window and my dad caught me. He was so mad. I barely sat down for a week. He wouldn't let me out of the house for a week either except to go to school," Amelia remembered. "I thought he would kill me. He was so mad."

"I wanted to take you to the Prom, but you disappeared," Brad explained.

"I did too!" Silas piped in like he didn't want to be forgotten.

"I was ill after the fire. It was a terrible time. You understand I don't want to talk about it," Amelia explained quietly, not elaborating.

"So gentleman, how do you know my cousin?" Lily interjected, changing the subject.

"Yes," both answered in response to Amelia, not hearing Lily.

Both men continued to stare at Amelia. Lily noted that Barney Terrell stepped a little closer, trying not to appear like he was listening as well. All these men seemed too interested in Amelia. Amelia suddenly seemed to be a man magnet. Amelia had been sending out vibes she wasn't interested, since Jack and Sam died. Now it was like some kind of light switch had been turned on and it was on high neon.

"Thank you for allowing me to honour your husband, Ms. Brooksfield. Like I said Mr. Brooksfield was a fine man that will be greatly missed. I need to take my leave now. I wasn't feeling to well the day before yesterday and I'd like to go home and rest," Barney exclaimed taking Amelia's hand, earning a frown from Brad and Silas.

"Goodbye, Barney, and thank you for coming," Lily commented.

"Barney, did I meet you before today?" asked Amelia.

"Yes, I used to live in Ravenworst and we may have run into each other a time or two then as I use to come to your dad's store; but my daughter Susan also works for you now." Barney answered.

"Oh, so that's it. Susan is wonderful, a simply fantastic help to me at the store. But you look too young to be her dad."

"She was my wife's daughter. My wife was considerably older than me. Before she died, I adopted Susan," Barney explained.

"Oh, how sweet," Amelia stated earning Barney another frown as he sent a triumphant grin their way.

"Well, it was lovely to be with you again, Ms. Kelly. Goodbye, for now," Barney replied.

Barney kissed Amelia's hand and left. Lily was disturbed that was kind of weird. Why were all these men fawning over Amelia? And why did they all come from Ravenworst?

"Awfully presumptuous of him," Brad complained, watching Barney's departing back like a hawk.

"Yes, I don't like him either. Are you okay, Amelia?" asked Silas solicitously. "I don't understand what you are asking, but I'm fine."

"So gentleman, how do you know my cousin?" Lily asked again, this time a little more forcefully.

"I met her a long time ago. She lived in Ravenworst. Silas and I grew up in Ravenworst," Brad answered, as Silas jabbed him with his elbow.

"It's been a long time. We did some catching up of old times and memories," Silas answered, smiling at Amelia.

"It must be enjoyable to meet with an old friend," Lily replied gauging them.

"Yes, it's always wonderful to be with an old high school classmate," Silas answered, taking control of the conversation.

"We are sorry about your husband, ma'am," Brad stated solemnly.

"Please call me Lily," Lily said speaking to both Silas and Brad.

"Thanks, Lily," Brad and Silas stated at the same time.

"I'm so sorry you were harassed at the station," Brad exclaimed.

"And I for one don't believe you're guilty of anything, other than being at the wrong place at the wrong time," Silas cried, as Brad glared at him.

"I tried to get on the case, but Rogers has it in for me. I know you are innocent Amelia. I was so angry, when I heard he had arrested you," Brad announced smiling and offering his hand, earning him another elbow from Silas.

"Can I get you something to eat?" asked Silas of Amelia.

"No please, let me."

"No thank you, Brad, Silas. I don't feel well," Amelia stated appearing wan and limped on her crutch. She then asked, "Can we leave soon, Lily?"

"Oh, I'm sorry, Amelia." Brad sympathized, "We are awful of us not to realize how tired you would be standing on your bad leg."

"Let me say goodbye to Grandma Katha," Lily said solicitously, walking away for a moment.

"I will drive you home," Brad offered as Silas glared.

"Thank you both. Lily and I would love a ride home, but first we need to go make sure Aunt Katha doesn't need a ride."

"Okay, then," Brad replied smiling. "Let me do the chauffeuring."

"Thank you, Brad. I'd be happy to take you up on your offer," Amelia answered.

Lily approached Aunt Katha, who held court with her current beau Terrence Stewart; beside him his son, the chief of police, Edward Stewart, and Greg Franks held a deep conversation.

"Grandma Katha, we're going to head out now," Lily announced.

"Oh well, I guess I should be leaving now. Excuse me, gentlemen," Katha retorted.

"Please, couldn't you stay a little longer?" asked Greg, "This is truly a wonderful conversation."

"You just remember she's my woman now Greg!" Terrence said glaring.

"I don't see a ring so she's fair game," Felix challenged.

"Gentlemen, I'm right here. As to staying I don't know. Terrence and I had some plans too," Katha answered.

Terrence grinned, because Katha made it clear she was with him.

"Well played, Terrence, well played," Greg exclaimed.

"I believe you and I need to talk about this kind of behaviour, Terrence Stewart," Katha admonished.

"Sorry, dear. You are correct; I'm acting like a cave man. Forgive me?"

"Since you ask so nicely, I will."

"Grandma Katha, please talk with your friends and have fun. I'm going home for a nap. I'll see you later, Grandma Katha," Lily said ready to walk away.

"All right, you can come to supper. Terrence and I will bring something to eat at six p.m. So don't you dare cook."

"Thanks. I don't think I have the energy or inclination to cook, so your offer will be wonderful."

Lily then walked across the room taking care to walk beside Amelia in case she needed help with her crutches. Lily and Amelia climbed into the car with Brad to drive home. Silas and Brad, Lily noted,

A Penny Saved a Murder Earned

continued to chatter all the way home to
Amelia, like two old friends, but Lily noted
each one persistently vied for Amelia's
affections.

Arriving at the front of Lily's door, Amelia
got out of the car first. Amelia scrambled for
her crutches. Brad assisted her placing them
carefully under her arms. Lily climbed out
feeling totally ignored by all of them.

"Please come in Lily's house for coffee,"
Amelia invited Brad and Silas with a smile.

Entering the house ahead of the party, Lily
noticed disarray. She could not believe it,
but it was obvious someone had been in the
house. She was terrified. Someone had
broken into the house. Everywhere she
stared things were moved, and thrown
around the room. The sofa cushions were
shredded and their contents spread across
the carpet. The lamp had been thrown on the
floor; its cord appeared frayed and broken.
The kitchen was not much better she noticed
as the fridge door was open and food had

been flung all over the countertops and floor. Why? Why would someone do this? Lily thought with great dismay.

"And they say you can never find a cop when you need one," Amelia commented looking at the mess.

"We'll be happy to call this in Amelia," Brad reassured.

"Thank you so much, Brad. We would certainly feel so much safer," Amelia said.

"Who could have done this?" asked Lily, still in shock.

"Sorry, Ms. Brooksfield, I mean Lily. People read about these things in the notices and break in when people aren't home. We should have thought of this and posted a guard. I am so sorry the police department failed you," Silas apologized.

"I can't believe this. First the cemetery where people shoot at us and then this? Are we safe here?" Amelia asked, sounding scared.

"Don't you worry, Amelia. We will keep you safe won't we, Silas," Brad reassured.

Brad then put an arm around Amelia, which earned him a frown from both Lily and Silas.

"Thank you. I feel so much better now. Don't you, Lily?"

"Yes, I guess. Thank you, gentlemen. Now could you call this in while I check to see what appears to be missing?" asked Lily, wanting them to be gone and for this to have never to have happened.

 A few minutes later a team of police officers arrived to check for fingerprints, but Lily began to think it was odd she couldn't find anything missing. Why had someone broken in if they didn't want anything here? Had someone slipped out the back door when they arrived? As the policemen scurried around, Lily realized how tired she is. She wished the policemen would all leave, so she could sleep. All the sleepless nights she'd been having had caught up with her. She wanted to have a short nap before Rose came home. They take forever to make a simple report, she thought. Amelia had already gone to her room. Amelia got to sleep. Lily wished she was.

"Are you finished yet?"

"We have completed our investigation, Ms. Brooksfield. You seem tired. I'm sorry we kept you," Brad stated solicitously.

"Good. I'm glad to hear that. It's been a trying day with little sleep."

"We will check back later, but for now we leave," Silas announced.

"Thank you, and good afternoon," Lily replied; shutting her front door and breathing sigh of relief to have them go.

~0~

Chapter 19 - Stirring the Pot

Flashback to the morning before the funeral

Cheryl Waverly and the Killer

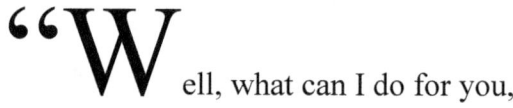**W**ell, what can I do for you,

officer? Come to grill me some more? Why you police officers need to ask and re-ask all your questions, I don't know! Well don't stand looking like a hound dog, come in the house," Cheryl Waverly retorted, opening her door to a police officer in uniform.

"Thank you," the policeman answered. The police officer unconsciously fingered a money clip engraved with the initials R.C. in his pocket.

"Would you like coffee? Here," she said, shoving a cup at him without waiting for an answer "Cream or sugar?"

"Nothing thanks, I like my coffee black," the policeman responded. "I prefer it cold, but this will be fine."

"Well, I don't hold with those newfangled drinks. I think cold coffee is so disgusting. Now what do you want from me?"

The police officer didn't answer quickly enough for the impatient Cheryl so she snapped at him, "Spit the information out! What do you want? I'm a busy woman. I've got a club meeting to go to and tomorrow I have my son's funeral. Lily Kelly or not, I'm attending the service. He was my boy and that bitch killed him. You know she did, so why haven't you arrested her?"

"Lily Kelly will not be charged with killing your son," The officer began before being interrupted.

"And why not? She's as guilty as sin. The black widow killed my boy. She did! Even if she has political connections, does that mean she should get away with murder?"

"I agree her family always uses clout to get out of crimes. They are criminals, those Kelly's; I have no doubt. Are you aware years ago Katha O'Malley ran over a little girl while drunk and she got away with the crime?

"What do you mean? When did this happen? Why wasn't she charged?"

"In the summer of nineteen hundred and sixty eight, a child played out the front of her home. A car came out of nowhere, mounted the curb and struck the little girl. The mother had stepped in for a second to get her child a drink. The mother came out and found the car gone, her little girl lying broken, dead in the grass," The police officer explained, deliberately creating a picture of the day to invoke anger.

"No! The bitch and her evil spawn killed both my children? How did you become acquainted with this knowledge? Where's your proof?" Cheryl demanded suspiciously.

"Your daughter was Cheryl-Lynn Rose Brooksfield?" asked the officer consulting his notes.

"Yes, my baby was only three years old
when she murdered. She was Horace's
twin," Cheryl explained dabbing her eyes "It
was July the eighth, 1968. They told me she
was killed by a drunk driver. My Cheryl-
Lynn Rose lived as an angel, such a sweet
good-natured child. She obeyed without
question. I thought she would be out of
harm's way, but she wasn't. She stepped on
the road. She was so good. Not like her
brother, Horace. I loved Horace, but he
loved being a naughty boy. Horace had such
bad taste in women, although he did give my
granddaughter his sister's middle name."

"Hmm, the date of Katha O'Malley's
drunken driving cover-up is the eighth of
July nineteen hundred and sixty eight," the
police officer lied, pretending to consult
records; Katha O'Malley went to a party.
She was seen inebriated, stumbling around
and entered a car taking the wheel; not more
than a block away after the accident. Her car
appeared on the stolen vehicle list the next
day."

"You believed Katha O'Malley killed my
baby Cheryl-Lynn Rose? Lily killed my
other baby, Horace, and neither paid! There
can be no justice when they get away with

killing my babies," Cheryl begged crying loud sobs, "Why does an evil family like the Kelly's get to exist? Why? Someone should stop them."

"There is no accountability if someone isn't charged, ma'am. A person who abused their power to get away with killing a child is beyond comprehension," the police officer waxed. "If I had a child that was killed by a drunken driver, I think I would want revenge. I'm not advocating taking justice in your own hands though; that would be just as wrong."

"You're a good boy. Your mother must be proud," Cheryl replied, wiping her tears away.

"I hope so ma'am, but my parents died a long time ago. I grew up in foster homes, and a good family took me into their hearts and adopted me," the police officer confided, fake tears falling from his eyes.

"Oh you poor dear boy! Horrible places those foster homes, and cesspools for the worst dregs of life. Were you aware Horace was removed from my home and taken until his daddy was found? Why they thought I broke his arm, I'll never know!" Cheryl raved.

You did break Horace's arm, you monster. You go through life harming others and think no blame should come your way. You did not get your daughter a drink, but got yourself a snout full of booze. Cheryl-Lynn died because you are a neglectful, unnatural mother. Why shouldn't there be payback? Payback is a bitch, and you'll get yours. You dare to insinuate I'm not good enough for your company, simply because through no fault of my own, I was in a foster home. Of course I'm lying, but you don't know that you arrogant, rich, bitch!

How dare you go through life judging others? 'Judge not lest you be judge' is what the good book you carry around says. Well, you've met your judge, jury and executioner, and she's starring at you in the mirror. Be

*careful, son, you're in the home stretch now;
don't show your thoughts on your face and
tip your hand. He thought.*

Cheryl looked at the police officer as if he
wasn't listening to her but continued
anyway, "Did you ever hear the like of it?
They pointed the finger at me! Would you
believe it? They accused me...of harming
my child. I would never harm a hair on his
head even though he was a worthless
wastrel."

"Why anyone could see you would never
harm a child. But I thought Horace had a job
as the mayor? A job so prestigious doesn't
make him a wastrel!"

"Quite true, I certainly would never harm a
child. As for him being the mayor...well I
had to use all my connections to get him
such a prominent position. A good mother
does what she can for her child. "

Liar! Even though your son was a cheat as a husband, he earned his position as mayor.

"Well you'd never be aware of your upbringing; obviously someone did something right by you. You certainly act like you have breeding. Such a kind man, you should meet my ex-daughter-in-law Renée. She's a delightful woman," Cheryl ranted on oblivious.

Anger flashed briefly across the police officer's face but then he smiled sweetly, "Why thank you, ma'am. It wasn't my fault or my parents' fault; a drunk driver killed them."

"Oh, you poor, dear boy. Did they find the evil person who killed them?" Cheryl asked, offering him a fresh-baked chocolate chip cookie.

"Yes I found her, but the crime was swept under the rug. Katha O'Malley drove drunk and she killed them too," He answered nibbling the cookie edges.

A Penny Saved a Murder Earned

"You are telling me that Katha O'Malley, or her family member, has killed three people and no charges have ever been laid? Katha O'Malley's family continued on living their lives, like nothing ever happened being happy and earning lots of money? Katha O'Malley and her family have much to answer for their crimes," Cheryl demanded angrily.

"Katha O'Malley and Lily Kelly might have much to answer for, but their family is blameless in the crimes. If only I had the guts, I'd make the two of them pay. I would..."Cheryl finished.

"Someday...,"The police officer said sadly shaking his head.

"Someone should make them suffer. They are totally evil. Katha's spoken to me many times over the years, no hint of the evil she has created. She saw me grieving and said nothing," Cheryl snarled under her breath.

The police officer heard this and hid a smile.

Cheryl pounded the table in anger, and then composed herself dismissing him, retorting loudly, "Are we done here? I'm sorry, but I must not be late for my committee meeting."

"Yes, sorry, ma'am. I needed to confirm your alibi."

"If you did your job, you'd know I signed a form yesterday to confirm my alibi. Nail Katha O'Malley, she most likely helped kill my boy too," Cheryl said firmly, walking the police officer to the door.

"Thank you, ma'am. I can't tell you how much I'd like to make them pay. If there is any way I'll try, but she has political clout...Well I've made it my life's mission, but she still gets away with her crimes," The police officer replied, in a last parting shot, leaving the house.

He got into the car and smiled. His plan appeared to be working. The silly woman had fallen for the scheme, hook, line and sinker. She believed Katha had harmed her child, not only that but both of the Kelly's had killed her children.

A Penny Saved a Murder Earned

It was simple physics you stir the pot and
the pan boiled. Cheryl Waverly appeared
sensible, even normal, but she was an evil,
vindictive bitch. She thought she loved her
children, so to sooth her moral compass she
must seek revenge. She thought it okay to
harm her own child, like his father had done
to him.

He remembered how his father had locked
him in closets and beat him black and blue.
He had told him to keep all the abuse a
secret, or he'd find himself back in the
closet or in one of those foster homes again.
The dark still held great fear for him. He still
slept with the light on because of the
monsters in the dark. His doctor had tried to
tell him nothing would harm him if he
turned out the light, but the doctor had never
seen the demons which came in the night.

The doctor hadn't had the devil wage war
against him, in the guise of his father. Call
him names he'd like to block out and burn
his ears with them. He didn't feel the soft
whispery breath of the demon's drink, as he
lashed out, and smacked you against the

wall of the closet. He hadn't caught the
sound of the door's lock click, and
understood the door wouldn't open for
hours. No parent should harm their child.

Even if Cheryl hadn't been such a threat to
Amelia's beloved cousin, he would have had
to stop her. She would have harmed others;
this behaviour was her way. He felt justified
in his actions. Much like an avenging angel
he righted wrongs and protected his Angel.
If Cheryl Waverly took the bait and came
after Katha, she had signed her own death
warrant. It would then be a necessity to kill
her. He wouldn't let her harm one hair on
any of his Angel's family. Cheryl Waverly
was an insipid woman who believed the
world revolved around her. Well, she would
soon found out it did not!

He would be merciful, however. One quick
shot to the head provided she didn't try too
hard to kill Katha. She had better not move
one strand on that shock white head of hair
.Any endangerment of his sweet Angel, in
any way, or her family, all bets were off and
she would suffer a fate worse than death.

She'd die sooner and less humanely. They would soon be his and no one harmed his chosen clan.

Never ever again would he sit back and let the demon win. People would not push his family around anymore. He would keep following his plans. Soon, his sweet Angel would be all his.

~0~

The afternoon before the funeral

He stood outside the house listening to

the bug, he had planted. She had swallowed
the bait and ran with it. He listened as
Cheryl picked up the phone.

"Bob, do you still own a twenty-two rifle?
Why? Oh I thought I'd go away for a few
days after the funeral and go on a hunting
trip in Saskatchewan. Piffle, no I don't
possess a licence but you'll loan the gun to
me, won't you? You won't? Please, Bob,
can't you expedite a permit for me? You
will give the rifle to me? Fantastic! I knew I
might count on you. Thanks, Bob, I'll owe
you. Goodbye, dear."

The bullets she obtained would all be
blanks, but she would never find out that the
gun wouldn't harm anyone...at least until the
last-minute. He would never take the chance
she could harm his beloved Angel, or her

family. He'd watch her and when she shot at
Katha, like he understood she would, her life
would be extinguished. He would claim he
shot her in the line of duty. Threatening his
Angel and her cousin was not to be
accepted. He read the transcript. She had
gone too far. The woman was dangerous. He
stopped the other woman Renée. The police
would soon find Renée's hair in the samples
taken at the murder scene; but this woman
would not, could not be tolerated any longer.

No doubt of the signs; she would snap and
harm his Angel. The seeds planted, she
would come after Katha. Killing Cheryl
would be no great loss.

The woman annoyed everyone and was an
evil child abuser. She abused her own son.
She was not fit to be near his Angel or Rose.
So she would not live another day. He
listened into the chatter at his cousin Lily's
house, well... not his cousin yet, but soon.
The bugs he planted worked perfectly; even
if they were the bugs the department
classified, as out of date. The bugs would
never be missed and the wiretaps still

worked like a charm. He enjoyed spending
time amongst his family, even if he only
heard their voices.

He would get someone to break in while
everyone attended the funeral and remove
them. No he decided he should do it
himself! There'd be enough time before he
went to the Wake. He'd be on duty and slip
away. They must not be found in the house.
As much as he wanted to leave the wiretaps,
if he didn't find all the bugs, all would be
lost. He might get someone to remove the
bugs, but then someone would enter the
home and he couldn't allow them to soil his
Angel's domicile.

The only solution was for him to do the job
himself. He would see the way his family
lived and touch their things.....touch
Amelia's, his Angel's things.

~0~

One half hour before the funeral

"**G**ood, the family is gone. Time to put the plan in place," he muttered to himself as he entered Lily's house.

He searched eagerly for the wiretaps he had planted. He took the bugs out of the phone, but the lamp would not be found. He searched frantically for it. Where was it? He could not remember where he had placed some of the other bugs. Could he find them all?

Where did he leave them? What if the wiretaps were found? He searched frantically while his fingers lovingly touching the money clip in his pocket. Calmness filled his body as he fingered his trophy. His Angel was nearby, he felt her, as long as he had her father's money clip. He

thought the token wasn't needed anymore,
and yet knowing her birthstone was on it,
filled him with such happiness.

All he could think about when he touched it
was her beauty... her eternal goodness filled
him with such joy and euphoria. Peace! He
felt an utter calmness come over him. He
then touched a scarf belonging to his Angel.
He pulled the stole to his nose smelling the
garment. A sweet floral scent filled his
nostrils. The scarf smelled of her. How
glorious! It was like being next to her in a
meadow of flowers.

His other hand stayed on the money clip, as
if transferring her being into the clip. He
closed his eyes and remembered dancing
with his Angel; only in his dreams, but soon
this would be reality, in his visions, his
beloved wife and she adored him, a dream
come true. All he needed to do was follow
his plans. He must protect his Angel at all
costs. She would be his family. Her cousin
and her daughter would welcome him into
their family; especially after they knew the
lengths he went to protected them all.

However, if her cousin found those bugs, she would misinterpret what he meant to do for her, his Angel. She would seek to turn his Angel against him.

Where were those damn wiretaps? He manipulated the money clip, not finding the smooth gold comforting. The bugs traced to him, so it was imperative that he find them all. He continued frantically searching for the bugs. Finally he found a bug in a lamp. Had he found them all?

Of course he did!

Breathing a sigh of relief, he slipped his hand out of his pocket and got ready to leave before the family came home. What the man did not realize was that when he pulled his hand out of his pocket the money clip fell out and then he inadvertently kicked it under the sofa. He completed his sweep for his bugs, tossed the rooms in anger, and then headed to the funeral and his Angel.

~0~

Chapter 20 - Caught In the Wake

Rose and Carol

As Rose and Carol ate at a table in the food court, Rose decided to bring up something that was bothering her.

"Did you get creeped out at the funeral, too?" Rose asked. "Those two cops threw themselves at my Aunt Amelia like they were her last meal."

"I saw them. Yuck! I like Bobby Bradford, but you can bet when I'm as old as your aunt, I won't remember him. Or if I do I won't be hanging all over him," Carol replied.

"It's gross when old people drape all over each other. Your Grandma Katha had men fawning over her too."

"I saw Gregory Hanks of the Hanks grocery stores; he was all over Grandma Katha."

"Your Grandma Katha sure has some choice guys for older men though," Carol answered.

"She does. Aunt Amelia on the other hand ought to be careful. I think those two cops were creepers," Rose responded.

"But they're cops, so that makes them okay," Carol protested.

"Just because they have a badge, that doesn't make them perfect. I'm getting bad vibes from one or both of them. Remember when I got bad vibes about the new kid Kyle, and it turned out he was an arsonist?" Rose asked.

"Like intuition?"

"Yes, like intuition. I keep getting a creepy feeling something is wrong with them. I want to check out more about those two cops. It's strange they ended up in the same town as Aunt Amelia, when she used to live thousands of miles away," Rose explained. "You should leave it alone. "No harm and no foul, as the saying goes."

"I would if it weren't for those bad vibes from those two," Rose continued. "Besides don't you find it odd they end up in the same place as my aunt?"

"So they moved here. Just because they lived in the same town as your Aunt Amelia, that doesn't make them guilty of anything."

"I should tell you about my aunt. Can you keep a secret?" demanded Rose.

"Sure, I'll even pinkie swear," Carol promised and then upon Rose's hesitation to speak, Carol pressed, "Spill it already, would you?"

"Well, okay, but it is a bit of a long story. My aunt grew up in a town about one hundred kilometres from here, a place called Ravenworst. She had an ideal life, two parents and siblings; her younger sister Grace and an older brother Jerry."

"She has siblings? I was never told she had siblings. Where do they live?" Carol then looked at Rose hurt and angry.

"Don't look at me that way. I'll explain."

"Then do so, Rose."

"Anyway at sixteen, or seventeen years old, Aunt Amelia had taken a babysitting job. She was supposed to babysit overnight. All went well until she became sick. She threw up and stuff. She came home after calling the parents of the kid and went to bed shivering and sick. She fell into a deep sleep, after taking cold and flu medicines of some sort." "Something weird happened; when she woke up she was outside in her nightgown."

"Whoa! What happened? Did she like, sleepwalk?" Carol asked, popping a French fry in her mouth.

"No, she wasn't sleepwalking. Let me finish the story please. Aunt Amelia found herself choking. She felt the grass underneath her. She opened her eyes disoriented and looked around and saw her home burning and huge flames shooting from the roof. The house was ablaze and burned quickly to the ground. She tried to crawl back to the house, but she had inhaled smoke and her lungs felt like they were burnt. Aunt Amelia collapsed and when she woke up again she was in the hospital. She was told her whole family had perished in the fire. Her father Robert, her younger brother Jerry, her sister Grace, and her mother Aerilla could not be found. The puzzling thing for her was she wasn't aware of how any of it had happened."

"How was that even possible? Shouldn't she have felt someone carry her outside, or did she go on her own?" Carol demanded, enthralled by the tale as she ate.

"She still doesn't remember. Anyway, someone had called an ambulance for her. The police interrogated her since she was the only survivor. They even made her look at the remains."

"Well how cold. It's not like she could identify them, might she?"

"No," Rose stated. "And to this day no one knows who it was that called the ambulance either."

"What a bizarre story!" Carol said while finishing her taco meal. She then reached for her share of the fries.

"Where do you put all that food? If I eat tacos I gain weight," Rose stated.

"I think you worry too much about calories. You're way too skinny."

"No, I'm not." Rose rolled her eyes at this comment.

Carol then retorted "So tell me more of the story. There is more isn't there?"

"Poor Aunt Amelia lived through all of the tragedy. Last year she lost her husband and her son to a drunk driver. And now her employee Megan and a homeless man were murdered. My dad and his secretary are also murdered. What does all this have in common?" asked Rose mysteriously.

"Amelia Kelly?"

"Right again. People get stalked. Anyone who they feel tarnishes their obsession is just in their way," Rose said knowledgeably. "I think someone fixated on Aunt Amelia and will keep killing until she's with them."

"Rose, how do you come up with this stuff? Don't you think that's an exaggeration? I mean, just because she has a few bad things happen to her," Carol insisted, "And would you eat some fries? I can't eat them all myself."

"I'm not hungry, but I'll take a couple of fries."

Rose picked two of the smallest fries on the plate and tossed them in her mouth. She then raised her brow and said while chewing, "There, are you happy now?"

"No. I'm worried you make up stuff to distract yourself from your dad dying."

"I'm not making up any of this story. I've snuck into my Mom's office and read some case files over the years. These things happen. Crazy people get fixated. I think that's the word and they think the person loves them. You know how those Hollywood stars get stalkers? Well, I think Aunt Amelia has one. I know she does," Rose explained with confidence.

"Didn't your mom get mad when you snooped in her office?" asked Carol.

"No, silly! She thinks it is all password protected. Too bad she uses such an easy password," Rose boasted.

"You better hope your mom doesn't catch you. If my mom caught me snooping on her computer, I'd be dead meat," Carol exclaimed. "My dad uses complicated passwords you would need to hire a cryptographer to figure out."

"What or who is a cryptographer?" Rose asked.

"So you don't know everything. A cryptographer deciphers (figures out) his password. During the Second World War, they used them to keep secrets from the enemy with passwords," Carol explained.

"How did you find out the information and I didn't?"

"As I said, you don't know everything, Rose! Just because you do well at school, you think you know all. My great-grandfather told me all about cryptographers. He said he dated one, but she wouldn't talk about her work, so he married her."

"He sounds interesting."

"He is," Carol answered proudly. "And so was my great-grandmother, but she died."

"I am sorry, but she must have been mega-old."

"She died when I was little, so I don't think she was that old though she was older than him. And my great-grandfather is only seventy-four," Carol commented. "He married some other woman. I didn't like her, but they are divorced now. Thank goodness."

"Oh, well, I got into my Mom's files and there are lots of crazy stalkers out there."

"If your mom catches you using her password you'll be in so much trouble, I'll never see you again."

"I'm careful. Mom hasn't a clue I read her files."

"If your aunt has a stalker, how will you realize who he is?"

"I think the stalker is one of those cops. They are here from Ravenworst. They creep all over here and they seem predatory."

"Predatory? They didn't seem that way to me," Carol said faking, as if she actually understood the word.

"Hmm, you don't even understand the word. They want Aunt Amelia completely to themselves. You only exist in their eyes if you are in their view of her... that is predatory," Rose insisted.

"They did drape themselves all over your aunt, but they are cops. Cops aren't criminals; you are imagining things," Carol protested.

"I'd like to believe that, I really would. But I've seen in my mom's cases, people whom you would never suspect of being criminals. The worst of the worst ones are those who hide in plain sight," Rose explained.

"You mean like the janitor at our school last year, busted for being a pervert?" asked Carol.

"Yes, exactly like him. So I figure I need to access information about these cops. We need to find out where they were born, who their families are; or whether they've ever committed a crime, even if it's been sealed."

"Sealed?"

"Yes, when you are under age, sometimes you can get your record hidden, so no one can find out," Rose explained reaching over and ate another fry. "We must find these things out to keep my family safe. If what I suspect is true that one of those cops is a serial killer."

"I don't want to be involved in this."

"Well d'oh, who else can help me, Carol?"

"I don't want to get in trouble. We shouldn't be involved," Carol protested. "You won't get in trouble."

"Fine, but I think you should check out the security guard who found your dad .I saw him watching Amelia too. He's a creeper too."

"Okay, I'll put Barney Terrell on the list."

"How will you find out the information?" Carol asked.

"I'm going to sneak into Mom's office downtown and you're going to help me so I am not caught."

'I am not sure that's a good idea. I don't think I want to go to your mom's office. You should tell your mom what you think," Carol advised. "Besides, I'm supposed to be home soon. I'm going to get in trouble."

"Come on, Carol, don't be such a chicken. Please, you can be a heroine!"

"Would you please just tell your mom, Rose?" Carol pleaded.

"My mom would not believe vague suspicions, especially about a police officer," Rose explained. "If I can get the information we need, she will believe me. Grandma Katha dates the police chief's father."

"She is? Really?"

"Grandma Katha can do something, or at least look into his background more. Please Carol, help me. I'm begging you."

"Wow, your grandmother dates the police chief's father? I've met him; he's an interesting guy but I'm still not doing this," Carol laughed, like she understood something Rose didn't.

Rose looked hard and long at Carol with a beseeching stare.

"Fine, I'll help, but we better not get caught. It won't look good on my college transcript," Carol reluctantly agreed.

"We won't get caught. We will be careful," Rose promised. "Okay, let's hurry. I have to be home at four p.m."

"Fine, it shouldn't take long. Besides, you owe me. Remember when I snuck out to your locker, and got your homework. I have gotten a detention." Rose replied, piling on the guilt,"We aren't supposed to go to the lockers during class, but I did for you."

"I said I do it, now quit making me feel guilty. Let's go already." Rose and Carol waited patiently for the bus and got on.

Arriving at the city hall building housing the Crown Attorney's Office, Rose and Carol entered the building. The guard passed by into the other part of the building and they snuck down the hallway. They quickly hid behind a pillar at the sound of the guard coming back.

"We're going to be caught," Carol whispered.

"Quiet or we will be caught." The guard passed by again.

Rose breathed a sigh of relief and uttered, "My mom's office is down there, around the corner. We will make it."

"We almost bit it there," Carol complained. "But we didn't get caught. We are safe as long as you watch while I go in my mom's office," Rose claimed.

Rose crept to the office door. Finding it locked Rose frowned and jiggled the door.

"Don't shake the door. It's locked and the guard will know we are here. Do you have a bobby pin? I think I can pick the lock," Carol explained.

"You can pick a lock?" asked Rose.

"Sure, my dad taught me how to pick a lock."

Rose pulled a bobby pin put of her long hair and handed it over to Carol. Within five minutes of Carol attempting to pick at the lock with the bobby pin, the lock made a clicking noise. Carol turned the knob of the door, ushering them in the dark room.

"See, I told you I could do it," Carol boasted as she turned on a lamp.

"You keep watch while I check out the files and once the computer is on, we turn off the lamp."

Carol kept watch for the guard as Rose peered at the computer screen. Rose keyed in her mother's password and began searching through files. Soon she realized it might take a while.

"Sorry, I realize I'm taking time, but I'm scanning through a lot of files," Rose explained.

"Hurry! I think I heard the guard again. I don't want to be caught." Rose finally managed to access the file on the fire in Ravenworst.

"Here it is. I found the file," Rose cried loudly.

"Hush! Do you want him to hear us?" Carol stressed.

"Hurray up and find the information."

Rose scanned quickly through it realizing nothing jumped out at her. She ran another program to access police sealed juvenile records, on both policemen and Barney Terrell. Carol glanced in.

"I'm still looking. Keep watch," Rose demanded seeing Carol out of the corner of her eye.

Looking intently at the screen, Rose unrelentingly searched for the information. She gasped as she found something. Continuing to read she printed off a copy of the record.

"I found the information. Come on Carol, we have to get the evidence to my Grandma Katha," Rose insisted, as she dialled her cell phone "Drat! No answer. I'm going to try again."

"Tell me," Carol demanded. "I put my neck on the line. Share with me."

"There's nothing bad on Barney Terrell, but you won't believe what I found on that police officer! It's like this…" Rose lifted a finger while she dialled her Grandma Katha's phone number again. She then spoke into the phone and left a message, "Grandma Katha, I'm coming over there. I must talk to you! Don't open the door to anyone, except Terrence or his son."

"You should call your mom and your aunt," Carol demanded. "The man could be a serial killer, and he's a cop. He's dangerous."

"No. I'm going to Grandma Katha's. I can find the spare key, let myself in and wait for her. Thanks, Carol. You should go home. I promise I'll tell you before anything happens."

"I don't think it's a good idea to leave you to tell your Grandma Katha alone. What if she doesn't believe you? I should go with you," Carol insisted.

"You will get in trouble if you are not home in time, I'll be fine."

"I can't ditch you. My dad will have to wait," Carol asserted.

"It's perfectly safe. All I have to do is to get to Grandma Katha's and she'll get her boyfriend's son to send out the other police officer to nail him," Rose contended. "Now go. You know how your dad gets when you keep him waiting."

"Okay, fine! But call me in a half an hour okay? I have to know you are safe."

"Don't worry, I'll call you. Hurry, so you are not in trouble."

Rose left to catch her bus, leaving Carol to go home on her own. Carol knew she had to be home on time. Her mom insisted she be early the nights her Dad, Gerald picked her up to go to his house. Carol began to worry though. Should Rose be going to her Grandma Katha's by herself? Rose should have shared more information with me. If anything happens to Rose, what am I supposed to say? It's short trip to Rose's grandmother's house, so she'll be okay. Wouldn't she? Carol then felt that she was just being a worry wart. He mother always accused her of being one.

"Rose will be just fine," Carol thought out loud. Yet the idea to go find Rose still lingered, even as Carol boarded the bus to go home.

Carol rode the bus, all the while feeling that Rose could be in danger. What kind of a best friend remained more concerned with herself getting in trouble than protecting her friend? Carol was a terrible friend. She checked her watch and decided she should call her friend and thought, Rose should be there by now. Rose's phone rang four times and then went to voice mail. Carol then decided that she could not allow Rose to remain in danger while she rode the bus home.

Carol got off at the next stop. She was determined to find Rose. She would go to her best friend's house and then Rose's grandmother's house. If Rose was in trouble she would save her. If she wasn't in trouble, then why didn't Rose answer her cell phone? Carol contemplated; I'm going to back up Rose's story to Uncle Edward and help apprehend this awful person. Carol had never told Rose that the police chief was her great-uncle. Maybe it was too late to tell Rose, but Carol felt that her Uncle Edward would listen to her. As Carol walked down the street she heard the wail of a car horn. She turned around and noticed her mother's

car pull over to the side of the road next to
her.

"Carol I've been looking for you. You were
to meet your father over twenty minutes ago.
Now get in this car now," demanded Carol's
mother, Francine. "Are you aware of the
grief I would get if you weren't there on
time? Your father will lecture me. Ever
since he's been dating Alana, he's been
impossible."

"But, Mom..."

"Get in this car now! Don't argue with me!
If you get in this vehicle now, we might be
in time for your father."

"Mom, please," Carol begged.

"Did you hear anything I said? He blames
me when you're late and keeps threatening
to take custody of you. He could go to court.
See how much attention you get from him.
Your father has the attention span of a gnat,"
Francine complained.

"Fine, I'm coming," Carol retorted angrily under her breath and then stated, "It's on your head if anything happens to Rose."

"What did you say?" Francine asked, her eyes narrowing like she thought Carol had something bad about her.

"Nothing," answered Carol.

Carol prayed nothing would happen to Rose. She would go along with her mom, but as soon as her dad's back was turned, she would leave to look for Rose. Nothing and no one would stop her from saving Rose.

~0~

Chapter 21 - "Mom It's me, Rose"

Lily rose slowly from her bed. She had
been so tired earlier, she had lain down and
fell straight asleep, but somehow she still
felt exhausted. Getting Silas and Brad to
leave hadn't been easy. The two policemen
jumped into action, after finding Lily's
home tossed. Lily thought about how odd it
was. There appeared to be something
suspicious about the break in at the house,
though nothing seemed to be missing. All of
this was strange and the two police officers
acted odd. It was strange how the two
policemen continued to fawn over Amelia
and never once spoke directly to Lily about
the break in at her house. They kept
reassuring Amelia, like Amelia's house had
been broken into instead of Lily's.

Amelia's coach house hadn't even been
entered. All of this seemed surreal, like Lily

didn't exist as the homeowner or even in their minds, in any form at all. The two of them didn't seem to want to leave Amelia's side either, but Amelia inviting them to dinner this evening seemed to work. Amelia also said she felt tired and suddenly they had been all solicitous, saying them later. Weird and yes a little creepy, how much they fawned over someone they hadn't seen in years.

The pair of them needed looking at closely. She hated being suspicious of people but so much had happened lately. Those two cops set off warning bells inside of her. Amelia didn't need to be afraid on top of everything else. Did Amelia have a stalker, or two? Wait a minute...would a stalker explain everything that had happened?

These men had recognized Amelia, from a town one thousand miles away. How unusual that they should appear in the same town as Amelia... hmm at the same time things had happened to her and her family? Lily felt like she might be onto something here. Amelia came to Happy Valley as a teenager. She changed her last name, so people would not connect her with her family tragedy. She now shared the same name as Grandma Katha. So what were the odds they'd show up in the same place and find her? One of them stalked her? Had she missed something here? The tragedy! Of course someone killed them. Those men knew Amelia's family. They said they'd cut her lawn for Uncle Robert with disgust in their voices. Had Uncle Robert done something to start all of this? Might it have been some little thing Uncle Robert did, or didn't do? A normal every day thing people did, which triggered something only a psychotic person would take offence to and react?

Aunt Katha said the police had always questioned how Amelia had gotten outside in her nightgown. What if her stalker saved her?

Amelia had been safe at the Freidman's babysitting; he wouldn't comprehend she had come home. So he might have set the fire thinking she was safe. If the killer did, which one of these now police officers had done the crime or crimes?

A year ago Amelia lost her husband and
child. A stalker killed them and made the
crime look like a drunk driver? That was
certainly a bit of a stretch to think the crime
happened in that manner. Although, trying
to connect all of the murders were as well.
Even a crazy serial stalker wouldn't kill a
child. Would he?

And what motive did the stalker have for
killing Megan? And the homeless man, Mr.
Young? And if she followed the reasoning a
stalker had killed them, might she take the
deduction one step further and suggest the
stalker killed Horace and his secretary?
What could connect complete strangers, who
were now gone...murdered?
Amelia...Amelia appeared to be the
connection. No wonder the acting Crown
Attorney had gone after her. If Lily had been
thinking clearly, instead of focusing on her
grief, and protecting Amelia she would have
seen the associations. Barbara didn't
understand Amelia the way Lily did.

She hadn't seen the connections Lily now looked at in retrospect. She needed to get to her office tomorrow and research those two. Until she could do the research, she would pretend she didn't suspect them and keep smiling in their presence. Don't alert them or make them suspicious in any way, which might be dangerous to them all. Hmm, what was the saying? Oh yes. "Keep your friends close, and your enemies closer." The Sun-Tzu Chinese general and military strategist from four hundred B.C. sure had that right, she thought looking up in her favourite quotes book.

She wondered what time the clock said. The sun appeared down in the sky a lot lower than four p.m. It couldn't be so late, could it? She glanced over and noticed the power had gone off at some point as the numbers flashed on her alarm clock. How odd. She pulled out her cell phone. Remembering she had turned off her phone earlier for the wake, she turned it back on glancing at the time. Good grief! Six o'clock. They'd all be here for dinner soon. Good thing Grandma Katha always brought enough food to feed an army.

"Rose?" Lily called aloud, looking around for her.

Where could that girl be? She should have been home two hours ago. Lily fiddled with her cell phone and realized she missed a message.

"Mom, it's me, Rose. I shouldn't have, and you can get mad at me later for my actions, but I accessed some records at your office. We're all in danger. Those two cops Constable Rentford, and Sergeant Detective Owens, I thought both of them were trouble. But only one of them is a serial killer, who stalks Amelia. I'm on my way to tell Grandma Katha. She can do something, her or her new boyfriend's son, the chief of police. By the way the man I suspect is...the phone message broke off here.

Lily tried urgently to call her daughter back, but only got the call answer feature on Rose's cell phone. She repeatedly called getting the answer machine. She stared at her phone in disbelief. She had missed an important message from Rose. Rose didn't go after them herself did she? No, Rose said she went to Grandma Katha's, but that was hours ago. So why hadn't she called since the first initial call? As the dawning realization Rose might have gone after them herself, Lily became frantic with worry. Katha entered the house, her hands filled with food from a takeout Chinese food place. Grandma Katha was here. Rose would follow Grandma Katha, Lily thought breathing a sigh of relief. The minutes ticked by and still no Rose. Lily's heart turned over, but she dared ask, "Isn't Rose with you?"

"Why would Rose be with me?" enquired Katha.

"She said she was headed to your house in a message I received about two p.m.," Lily answered.

"I wasn't home all afternoon. I got in some afternoon delight at Terrence's place," Katha replied winking and setting down the food on the kitchen counter.

When Katha realized Lily appeared serious she asked, "You haven't seen Rose at all?"

"No and I'm worried."

"This is not like her. She usually comes home promptly. And why did she tell you she came to my house?"

"I promise I'll explain later Grandma Katha. Right now please call those two cops, Constable Rentford and Sergeant Detective Owens."

"Reporting Rose missing?" asked Katha.

"No, I won't explain anything to those two men. Please just tell them Amelia has a headache and get rid of them. Just get them not to come to my house," Lily begged urgently.

"I don't understand what's going on with you. Why don't you trust them? Is Amelia okay?"

"Amelia's fine. I promise I will explain fully later. Right now I'm going to your house and see if my daughter is there," Lily said, hoping her maternal instinct which told her Rose was in danger, was wrong.

"Okay, honey, I'll do as you ask," Katha
promised.

Lily left immediately, going out the front
door, hoping to find Rose next door. Lily
hurried to Katha's house and let herself in
the domicile. Everything looked normal. All
looked untouched. Nothing looked
disturbed, oddly though the phone was on
the hook. But where was Rose? Why had
her message stopped? Had Rose's cell phone
simply died? Was Rose in the spare room?
Lily ran down the hallway and opened the
closed-door to the bedroom of the spare
room. She found a perfectly made bed. The
spread, a beautifully crochet blue and white
blanket, lay thrown pristinely across the bed.
The pillows were fluffed and the sheets light
blue in colour, crisp clean, and nothing
appeared disturbed.

No one had been here since this morning.
No one slept in the bed. So where was Rose?
Panic seized Lily as she thought of what
may well have happened to Rose. Was it one
of those policemen, a serial killer? Rose was

in grave danger; though her mind refused to go there.

She needed to do something, but what? How could she keep her daughter safe if someone took her? Grandma Katha...she needed Grandma Katha. Rose's voice was all she could think about hearing. Lily dialled Katha.

"She's not here!" Lily screamed in horrified tones, "I can't find her."

"I'll be there in less than ten minutes. You can explain to me why you sound so frightened, and what happened." Lily paced the floor waiting for Grandma Katha to arrive.

It seemed like an hour before Katha arrived, however Katha arrived in less than five minutes and immediately hugged Lily.

"Amelia will keep the food hot. Now tell me what happened?" Katha demanded.

"My phone was turned off, but Rose called me. I fell asleep when she needed me. I'm a terrible mother." Lily cried. "Grandma Katha, what will I do if anything happens to my baby?"

"Lily, the first thing you will do is pull yourself together and make some sense. What did Rose say to you? And I want it word for word!" Katha demanded.

"Rose phoned me and because my phone was off the cell phone went to voice mail. I got a voice mail from her." Lily explained and played the message as Katha listened.

"Mom, it's me Rose. I shouldn't have, and you can get mad at me later for my actions, but I accessed some records at your office. We're all in danger. Those two cops Constable Rentford and Sergeant Detective Owens, both of them are trouble. One of them is a serial killer who is stalks Amelia. I'm on my way to tell Grandma Katha she can do something, her or her new boyfriend's son the chief of police. By the way the man I suspect is..."

"Oh my God! She didn't! She broke into your computer? The child is in danger. You think she didn't get here?" Katha asked shocked. "She seemed to think she discerned who the killer was. Was it one of those two policemen? Policemen have guns... Oh no, my great granddaughter is with a serial killer."

Katha took a huge breath and closed her eyes. Opening her eyes she said, "Sorry, I lost my calm for a moment, Lily. We will get her back safely. It has to be something simple, like she went somewhere else, because I wasn't home."

"Perhaps she left a message on your phone? May I?" Lily asked, reaching for the home phone.

"I'm sure that's true. She's at Carol's house," Katha repeated, breathing sigh of relief.

"There are no new messages, no saved messages," a computerized phone message said.

"But that's impossible! I left a memo to myself. A reminder about picking up the food in case I forgot. There were saved messages. I saved one from the funeral director about the costs, a few messages from friends and condolence messages from the hearts of our friends. Someone has been here and erased my messages. But why would they do that?" Katha asked puzzled.

"Oh no! You don't think Rose..."

"Left a message on my machine?" Katha completed Lily's thought.

"Yes, and whoever has erased the message has Rose?" Lily finished, her voice breaking up in fear.

"Why would someone who's stalking Amelia take Rose? I'm sure she's fine. She forgotten to tell us she went to Carol's," lied Katha unconvincingly.

"Didn't you hear the message? She suspects both police officers, but she understood one of them was the serial killer. Do you think she was talked about Megan Fowler; Mr. Young's and even Horace and his executive assistant, Amber,as his victims?"

"Rose says in her message a police officer is a serial killer. How can a serial killer be a police officer? Serial killers don't start as adults, do they?" Katha asked.

"No, the studies I've read said they start in childhood."

"And those two said they had known Amelia since she was a teenager."

"You mean she thinks one of them killed Uncle Robert, Aunt Aerilla, Jerry and Grace?" Lily demanded, getting more horrified by the minute, "And this person might have my little girl? Oh no, my baby. What can we do?"

"First of all we remain calm and don't jump to conclusions, Lily. Like I said, perhaps she's at Carol's house."

"Yes, right! She must be at Carol's house. Someone broke in to your place and erased your messages and they didn't take my daughter," Lily replied sarcastically.

"Sarcasm is unnecessary and beneath you, Lily. We will find her."

"She may already be...," Lily's voice broke off and she started crying.

"We'll find her. Terrence will help us. He's a retired judge. And as you well recognize he's the police chief's father," Katha insisted positively. "He has to be careful. If one of them took my daughter, and a police officer understands we are on to him, the man might do something drastic before we can find Rose."

"I know that, and somehow we must protect Amelia without letting him know. Because if Amelia even suspects one of them it will show all over her face," Katha cautioned. "Now I'll call Terrence. He should be to your house anyway."

"Call Terrence. I'm going to use your computer and access my files. If I can find what Rose found, maybe I can pinpoint which one is the killer," said Lily excitedly.

"Okay, Lily. Please, go ahead, dear." Katha agreed, "We will get Rose home safe; believe me, Lily."

"I know we will," Lily agreed, clicking with her mouse as she started to search files on the computer.

"Terrence, dear, can you come to my house before we go to Lily's? I need to talk to you privately and urgently," Katha requested on the phone. "Oh thank you, my dear. See you soon."

"He's coming, Lily. He'll be here soon and our little girl will be safe," Katha reassured Lily.

"From your lips to God's ears," Lily replied.

~0~

Chapter 22 - Keep Your Enemies Closer

Rose and the Killer

At the killer's home, Rose was bound

and gagged. Her feet were fastened tightly to the chair with yellow household rope. Her arms and hands were also bound with the same type of cords. She had a white tee-shirt gagging her mouth. Rose began rocking back and forth attempting to knock over the chair to no avail. Her eyes searched for him, as the door to the bedroom opened.

"You are a clever girl aren't you?" He retorted chuckling, "You tried to get free? You are so like her, my Angel. Odd, considering you don't share the same blood. I'm not going to harm you. I promise you. Don't struggle now. I'll remove the gag and you won't scream. Nod yes or no." the man demanded.

Rose ignored him struggling to get free but her head moved slightly.

"I'll take that answer as a yes. Sorry, but I'm not going to untie your feet and hands yet. This should make you more comfortable."

"So where did you take me? Will you kill me?" probed Rose bravely.

"Kill you? Why would I kill you? You are family," declared the man astonished.

"Oh, okay then. Good," replied Rose, trying not to appear puzzled.

"Oh you don't understand? I thought you would. It's okay though, I'll explain. It's quite simple."

"Explain what? You executed my great-uncle and his family? They were kinfolk."

"No, no they were not. They didn't act like family. They only pretended to share the same blood. They didn't protect Amelia, not like your mother and you do," The kidnapper explained.

"Family doesn't harm you."

"Why did Aunt Amelia need protection? What happened to her that was so bad?" solicited Rose, trying to get him to talk and see her as a real person.

"She was a little older than you, and her father would beat her...every day. I noticed the bruises. I know teachers did too." The man exclaimed, "No one helped her, my poor Angel. They turned their eyes away and did nothing to aid her."

"Her father hurt her? What a rotten creep! What kind of man was Uncle Robert, that he would beat his own child?"

"Yes, you understand?" he asked with a smile and cocked his head. "Somehow I knew that you would."

"No one should harm a child, let alone their own child. Poor Aunt Amelia, what a horrible thing to be raised by a parent who would stoop to harm their own child."

"You are like my Angel. I thought so. She defended her dad. She would tell people she bumped into doors. But it was her father. Do you want to understand about her brother Jerry? Why he had to be killed?" His voice drifted, as if weighing whether or not he should tell her.

"What did Jerry do?" Rose inquired, trying to get him to talk.

"I love that you call him Jerry for he doesn't deserve the title of honorary uncle like my Amelia being your aunt. That scum defiled women!" The man said with anger, "He had sex with my girlfriend, after Henry did. He slept with many innocent women at school."

"I'm sorry, that must have hurt. What a dreadful man Jerry was. You must have really loved your girlfriend. How could she have done that to you?"

"I did love her, until I saw her for the woman she was. Amelia showed me that she alone was the real thing, an angel and vision of kindness and sweetness, untainted by evil surrounding us."

"Aunt Amelia is special. So you protected Aunt Amelia? How did you defend her?"

"I watched over her. I saw what they did to her. I told Jerry to leave her alone. I told him he was not to raise his hand to her again. He looked at me with scorn as if I was beneath his notice."

"What a jerk," Rose commented.

"Yes, he was a jerk and I lost my temper and struck him. I was skinny and had no muscles then and Jerry snorted with laughter as I didn't hurt him at all. Jerry pummelled me, knocking out my front tooth. He told the principal I started it all. They believed him, not hearing me at all."

"How awful."

"The fight resulted in a punishment...mine! I got two weeks suspension and a beating from my father. I spent three days in a closet."

"Closet? You were trapped in a closet? Who put you there? Was it your father?" Rose asked

"I don't want to talk about the closet. The only thing that matters is that when I got out, I vowed revenge. I planned on telling his father what Jerry had done .I went over while Amelia wasn't home."

"What did Uncle Robert say?" Rose asked, trying to get the rope off her wrists without him noticing.

"Don't call that cretin uncle!"

"Sorry," Rose apologised.

"You'll understand why when I finish this story. Robert Cordova laughed at me and applauded his son. He congratulated him for knocking me down. He called me an interfering wimp! He thought I was lying that Jerry had been sniffing around your sister. He threatened that Jerry would knock my block off in the next five seconds if I didn't get out while I could."

"Did Jerry attack you?"

"Jerry raised his fist again and knocked me off my feet breaking my nose. Do you notice the scars?"

"Is that why your nose is a little crooked?"

"Yes it is," he admitted. "I grew even angrier, when it took my nose so long to heal."

"Is that when you decide to kill them?"

"Of course it was. Her family didn't cherish and protect her, my poor Amelia, my beloved Angel was in torment and I could save her. Amelia at her babysitting job, I made my plans to pay them back for their treachery. I started a fire and to get rid of her family. I dispatched Grace first, smothering her, as she lay sleeping in her bed."

"Why did you kill Grace?"

"I eradicated Grace because I had seen her evilness. She'd kick Amelia, hit and lash out at her. She deliberately told lies about Amelia to incite her father Robert to hit Amelia. That wasn't what a sister did."

"No, she didn't act like a sister, but Aunt Amelia must have loved her."

"Amelia was better off without her. I saved her," he protested, angrily.

"Of course you did. I'm sorry." Rose replied, worried she'd angered him, "Please, tell me more."

"No, I need to think."

The man then paced the floor, stroking his fingers through his hair.

Rose was sure that the man was now convinced she didn't believe him, which meant any bond she had made with him would be severed. She couldn't allow him to think she didn't believe him her life depended on this.

"Please I'd like to hear more. I think I'm beginning to understand." Rose insisted.

"Okay, but don't interrupt me again." the killer said tightening the bonds on her feet.

Then he sat down in a chair near her and began his story again. "I crept up the stairs to Jerry's room. I hit him over the head with a lamp as he slept and smothered him in his bed. Maybe I should have harmed him more, but I didn't have the heart."

"Of course you didn't you are a good person," Rose said mollifying him.

Rose was rewarded with a smile from her kidnapper.

"I went to her parents' room. I gagged Aerilla and tied her to the bed he slept on, the demon who called himself Amelia's father. Aerilla begged me with her eyes to spare her. I ignored her. I clobbered that devil, Robert over the head. When he awoke, I had tied him to the bed hand and foot. He begged me to let him go kill Aerilla and the rest of his family and let him go."

"No, a father wouldn't!" Rose exclaimed, then seeing the sad shaking of the killer's head she replied shocked, "He did? How truly evil!"

"The arrogance, the selfishness Robert displayed made me realize he had to go. I asked him if he wanted me to kill Amelia. He said go ahead, like to him she was a worthless daughter, no better than a piece of trash. I told him she was worth hundreds of him. I hit him on the head again for the pain it caused him."

"And then what happened," Rose probed softly.

"I don't want to talk about this anymore. I only want to talk of my Angel. All of this reminds me of how she disappeared after the fire."

"Please, tell me what happened?" begged Rose.

"Talking is good for the soul," he quipped.

"So true... please continue."

"You are a good listener. As much as it hurts, I'll continue. The pain was my punishment for starting a fire that might have killed my Angel. Luckily I got her out in time, and then I hid after calling for an ambulance. They had to take her to the hospital and I couldn't find her. When she reappeared six years ago, it appeared a sign

from God that my Angel needed me. I
watched from afar and she looked happy.
Truly happy! How could I interfere with true
happiness? If she had remained that way I
wouldn't have. If he had been good to her I
would have left them alone. I would have."

Rose tried not to reveal the revulsion she
was feeling, but her up-curled lip gave her
thoughts away.

"Don't look at me that way."

"I know you would have let her have her
happiness. You love Amelia," Rose agreed
trying to appease him.

"Please tell me more."

"Okay, that husband of hers, Jack, the lucky
man who held her heart, cheated on her. He
told her he went to work and he ducked into
a motel with his mistress, a married woman.
I wanted to kill the evil woman who dallied
with him through carbon monoxide
poisoning. She had hurt my Angel, even if
Amelia remained unaware. The woman lied
to her husband so I should have slayed her,

but I recognized her all too well, so she lives still."

"Uncle Jack? You murdered him too? But you didn't kill the woman because you recognized her?" Rose inquired, trying to keep him talking to make sure he identified with her as a person.

"I admit it. I felt angry with him. He had a treasure beyond measure, and yet he had cheated on an Angel. Why would anyone hurt her like that?"

"I don't know why anyone would hurt Amelia. Uncle Jack cheated on Aunt Amelia? I don't believe it," Rose retorted shocked.

"I saw them together so make no mistake he cheated on Amelia. Jack had been blessed with a child with her; the child should have been ours...and he did that? Amelia's beloved son Sam was his to cherish and love. Sam was such a cherub. How could he? Sam should have been mine and Amelia's."

"But he wasn't."

"I thought Sam had stayed with her when I tampered with the car and I drove my car right into Jack's. The child went with Jack in the car, to my ever-loving shame and revulsion. Jack deserved to die. Amelia's son Sam did not. I took his life. I am a horrible person for murdering a child."

"You killed Sammy. Little Sammy?" Rose cried covering her mouth in horror.

"I blame Jack! He made me do it... If Jack hadn't cheated and made me punish him..."the killer sobbed, "I cried so much and my Angel, Amelia was devastated to lose her son. I became overcome with shock and pain to find out what I had done. I had to rest in the hospital after the accident."

"You stayed in the hospital? You sought help from a shrink?" Rose inquired surprised and feeling sick, but wanting to keep him talking to her, so he would see her as an extension of Aunt Amelia.

"I wanted to die when I discovered how I harmed my Angel. But the drugs and the doctor convinced me it was all an accident. I hadn't made her sick with the flu after all. The flu had made her unable to look after Sam, not me. Jack had taken the boy. He hadn't properly strapped him in his car seat, so he murdered him, not me," The man rationalized.

"You told the doctor what you did and he let you go?" demanded Rose, now wondering what doctor in his or her right mind would let this nut job go.

"No, it is my secret, and you'll keep my secret won't you?"

"Of course I will, you didn't mean to harm Sammy," Rose lied.

"I didn't tell the doctor. He wouldn't understand. I only said I felt unhappy. I said I had hurt the one I loved, and I wanted to die," he explained.

"Aunt Amelia wanted to die. She didn't sleep and she didn't eat. Do you understand how you harmed her?" Rose exclaimed angrily, "I thought she would die and that would have been your fault."

"I understand she hurt from the loss, but she found Doctor Jones. Now I can forgive you and thank you for talking to me in such a stern way because of Doctor Jones. Doctor Jones is a genius. I love everything about my Angel. We even shared the same shrink," he boasted.

"How sweet!" Rose replied sarcastically, without thinking.

"I love how you stood up to me for Amelia," he replied thinking what Rose had said supported his position. "Family is so important. You'll be my family too and you'll love and support me."

"Why did you kill my father?" inquired Rose in a small voice. "I didn't want to at first. I wasn't going to harm him, for your sake, but he wanted to leave your mother Lily, for a slut. Yes, the one I executed him with Amber. Silly, stupid Amber."

"Amber wouldn't do that and neither would my father," Rose protested.

Rose realized with surprise she had the ropes off her one hand. She ducked her face down to hide her triumphant smile.

"Oh dear, I shouldn't have said such a word in your presence, little Angel. I'm sorry for sullying your ears Rose. Forgive me, little Angel," he said thinking she hid her face because she believed him. "Now back to my story about Amber. She had convinced him to leave your mother Lily. Your mother is a divine woman. She's a woman of exceptional strength and character. She is more a mother than the woman who bore you, and yet he took up with that slut Amber. He was an evil bastard not fit to be your father," he said manically.

Rose couldn't help the tears that ran down her face. Rose feared that she would never get away from this madman and that she too would die.

"Please don't cry, Rose. I'm sorry I made you sad. I never wanted to that."

"I'm sorry but this is just all so sad," Rose responded trying to stop crying.

"Please, you don't know everything!" He protested as Rose couldn't stop two more tears from falling, "He had decided to take you from Lily and that would take you away from Amelia. You are more Lily's child than his."

Rose shook her head.

"No, he really was going to take you, Rose, and divorce Lily. Allowing him to go ahead with his plan, he would take your home away and you. So I'm sorry, but he had to die," he explained and smiled warmly at her.

Rose found it very creepy; it appeared he thought he would now be a father figure to her.

"But Daddy loved Lily," Rose protested, before she stopped herself.

"No, he didn't. He loved himself. I told you why aren't you listening? Pay attention to me!" he yelled. "Horace planned to leave Lily and remove you just to hurt her because if he cared about you he would have made more time for you. Amelia loves you, and Lily does too. If he took you, he would be hurting her."

The man paced back and forth swinging his fists into the air which scared Rose.

"And Amelia's store clerk, and the homeless man...why did you kill them?" questioned Rose trying to hide her fear and revulsion, worried he would become more agitated.

"She dared to defile Amelia's store. Al said he would tell everyone I killed Megan. Now was that fair? He had to go. You know he did. I killed him humanely. He was collateral damage," The man screamed. "It wasn't my fault. It wasn't!"

He then stomped his foot like a child.

"It's okay; of course you had to kill them. They tried to harm those you loved," lied Rose, trying to get on his good side and calm him.

"Do you mean what you just said? You don't think it's my fault?" the man replied excited.

"Of course I don't .We must protect Aunt Amelia," Rose reassured, as the man smiled at her.

"We can be family. But forgive me if I must keep you here for a while tied up to the chair. I trust you, I do, but we must convince your mother you are safe. Once Lily is convinced she likes me, Amelia will love me, too. I am convinced she will. And we will be family. You will be my honoured niece. You can be the flower girl at our wedding," the man replied beaming.

"Aunt Amelia will be upset, because they can't find me!" protested Rose.

"We must make her believe you visit a friend or something won't we? Now you will write out a letter for her, exactly as I tell you to write it. We wouldn't want Amelia to worry, now would we?" the man commanded expecting an of course we wouldn't.

Rose nodded her head in agreement.

"Here you go," he said handing her a pen and paper, "And tell your mother to tell Amelia not to worry on this one."

He then untied Rose's hands, but not her feet.

"I can't write two letters. My mom would be suspicious if I sent two letters," Rose complained setting down the pen.

"Fine then, write one, but remember no funny stuff. I will be reading it," he cautioned.

He smoothed out the paper and placed the pen in Rose's hand.

"Don't worry; I want you to be my uncle," Rose lied again.

"Good, now write," he demanded.

~0~

Chapter 23   - The Best Laid Plans

Lily and Katha heard the front door open of Katha's house and close and at first they hoped that Rose was somehow safe and coming in the door but they knew that was impossible. They had to search her whereabouts.

"Oh, hi, Lily, I just came from your house. No one answered," Terrence stated entering the kitchen.

"Sorry dear, I should have told you the plans changed," Katha apologised.

"Quite alright, my dear. By the way, I found this letter addressed to you on your stoop, Lily," Terrence said, noting Lily's tears he turned to Katha and probed, "Katha, my dear, what is the matter?"

"You found a letter? May I see the letter, Terrence?" Lily demanded, holding out her hand and all but snatching the letter from his hand.

"Sure here you go. Now as the kids say, spill it. What has happened?"

"The letter is from Rose. Why didn't she text me? She wouldn't send a letter. This makes no sense," Lily cried.

"She's okay. The person who broke in here...didn't take her?" probed Katha, ignoring Terrence's question.

"Someone broke in your house?"

"Yes, but the matter is handled," Lily claimed.

Terrence bent over and began to look under furniture and under the lamp shades.

"What is wrong with you Terrence?" asked Katha.

"Nothing! I'm sitting down and resting. But maybe I'll walk around and get the kink out of my leg," he said with a finger to his lips.

Terrence continued complaining about his leg as he walked. Using nonverbal clues, Terrence showed Katha and Lily a listening device he had spotted under a table. He continued to search for more and found one in the phone. He also found one in the kitchen cabinet and one even in the bedroom lamp which the killer had somehow missed. He put all of them in a glass jar he filled with cotton balls.

"Read the letter quickly and then we will spin it differently to whomever listens," Terrence requested whispering.

"What if he already knows we think he took her? Lily and I talked about Rose," Katha answered worried.

"We'll convince him, but first, as I said, I must read the letter," Terrence reassured.

Lily read the letter aloud, "Mom, I sent you a letter to tell you and Amelia that I am at my friend, *Daisy Adair's*. You remember her. Don't you, Mom? Please reassure Aunt Amelia, all is well. Oh and *Daisy's* friend *George* says ' Hi.' I'll be home tomorrow."

"Daisy Adair? Wasn't that a character in the show *Dead Like Me?*" Katha queried. "It's one of Rose's favourite shows. I bought the DVDs for her for Christmas. *George* is the main character."

"Yes, Daisy Adair is a character from *Dead Like Me* which means she is sent me a message that she is with one of these men. I think I know which one, but proving it will be difficult. We set a trap. But what can we use to trap him?" enquired Lily.

"Did you lose your money clip, honey?" Katha questioned Terrence as he spotted and picked up a money clip off the floor.

"It's not mine," insisted Terrence.

"Oh my, you found Uncle Robert's money clip. How could it be here?" Lily asked puzzled.

"You don't think the person who took Rose killed Robert and the others do you?" asked Katha.

"Nonsense! How do you know it's your Uncle Robert's?" commented Terrence.

"All my cousins' birth stones are on it. Grandpa O'Malley fashioned the money clip especially for him. Remember, Grandma Katha? I recall Uncle Robert taking it out to buy us ice cream (a rare occurrence) from the ice cream truck the week before he was murdered," Lily explained.

"The money clip has stones on it," Katha agreed.

"Are you saying the man who murdered your uncle, aunt and cousins kidnapped Rose?" Terrence queried.

"What can we do?" demanded Katha. "We need to save Rose."

"Follow my lead. We will catch him in the act. As soon as he claims the money clip, we can name him as the murderer," exclaimed Lily.

"We will find our Rose." Terrence took the listening device out and all of them gathered around it.

Lily read aloud the letter again from Rose.

"Well isn't that lovely, Rose is visiting her friend **Daisy**. It is lovely she can have fun with friends. She went through such trauma today. She deserves some fun."

"It was bad enough we buried her dad today, but her own grandmother shoots at her at the cemetery," Katha exclaimed. "It's good that she can spend time with her friend **Daisy** and forget all of this," Lily continued.

"Yes, it's pleasant for kids her age to have friends," Katha improvised.

"I found this money clip outside in the street. I wonder to whom this money clip belongs," Terrence said offhand with a wink.

"We should place an ad in the paper," said Katha continuing to improvise.

"The law states you must call the police and report found money, especially if it's more than twenty dollars," replied Lily.

"We need to go now?" asked Katha.

"No, it can wait until later tonight."

"I guess I could take the clip to the police in the morning. For now let's go to my house and eat dinner. The two fine policemen will be coming for dinner. We could give the clip to them," Katha retorted.

"Sounds good to me." Lily answered.

"I did try to cancel because Amelia seemed tired, but I wasn't able to get in touch with them, so the two men should be arriving soon," announced Katha.

Katha mouthed to Lily, Sorry I didn't cancel.

"Okay, let's go back for Chinese food. Amelia's at my house," Lily declared, sounding a little wooden.

"Yes, let's go. I'm hungry," Katha replied.

Katha, Lily and Terrence left through the front door of Katha's home.

"Do you think who ever planted those bugs listened to us?" queried Katha, while walking over to Lily's house.

"No doubt about it. I'm sure they eavesdropped," Terrence said.

"I want Rose back," Lily cried.

"We will get her back. He has made a mistake dropping the money clip and we will find out where he has Rose," Terrence reassured.

"Excuse me while I bring Edward up to date on this," Terrence explained, as he entered the kitchen of Lily's home.

Amelia, oblivious to the conversation in the kitchen or their suspicions, answered the doorbell the trio failed to hear. Emmett Rogers was ushered into the house. Amelia then went back to her room.

"Hello, Ms. Kelly, Ms. Mallory, Mr. Stewart," called out Sergeant Detective Emmett Rogers, as he walked into the kitchen and they all seemed to jump a foot.

"Why are you here?" asked Lily puzzled. "We didn't call you."

"Rose called me. She said she had something to tell me and she invited me to dinner," Sergeant Detective Emmett Rogers replied smiling.

"You can't be here, you'll spoil it all young man," Katha retorted.

"I think he can be a big help, dear," Terrence exclaimed as he turned to Emmett.

"So you see, Emmett, we believe this money clip belonged to the dead man," Terrence tried to explain.

"It's simple; I believe it is a clue." "But we're not sure which of them has my great-granddaughter," Katha interrupted.

"You alleged one of two policemen committed a horrific crime. A money clip is all you require to find him guilty? Lots of money clips are similar," Emmett protested. "I think you need more evidence if you want to find Rose."

"This money clip is special, Detective Rogers," protested Lily, showing him it wrapped in a Kleenex as to not pick up fingerprints, "You see, this clip was specially made for my Uncle Robert by a jeweller, my Grandfather O'Malley. Grandfather O'Malley made this money clip and a jewel encrusted tie clip to complete the set. The tie clip also has a ruby, an emerald, and peridot for my Uncle Robert's children's birthstones. Amelia has the clip in her jewellery box. I've seen it," Lily replied, continuing to show him the clip.

"You said you believe the clip is the same one...the money clip that belonged to your Uncle Robert? You're speaking of Robert Cordova, who was murdered in a fire in Ravenworst?" Emmett demanded.

"Yes, and one of those policemen dropped this when they grabbed Rose. You have to do something to save her," Lily commanded.

"I'll help find Rose and if it is one of those two we'll find her. Now I know I've seen a tie clip like that and recently. But where, and whom?" Emmett probed thinking hard.

"You have? You've seen the clip then, young man? Where did you see and who had it?" inquired Katha.

"Grandma Katha, please be quiet. Let the man think," Lily snapped exasperated. "I don't want to believe a cop could do all this, but cops are people too. People are flawed, so cops can be too. I do recall seeing a money clip recently. It had been held in either Owens' or Rentford's hands. They rubbed the clip, like the clip held a magic Genie or something. That is why I remember the incident. I saw the clip in one of their hands, but I'll be darned if I can remember which." Emmett retorted.

"We'll figure out which one it is. We have a plan," Lily explained.

"Plans are good and if I think your plan is a solid one, we will go ahead," Emmett replied.

"I'm glad we have your approval but son, your boss, Chief Edward Stewart has already approved my plan. Your agreement is just a formality," Terrence announced, grinning to take out the sting.

"Fine! Then we'll go ahead. But call me Emmett, please, all of you, since I'm working with you."

"Please, Emmett, just get my daughter home safe." begged Lily, not even realizing she called him Emmett.

"One more thing you need to know, Amelia doesn't know anything about our suspicions. Don't let on to either of them before the trap is sprung."

"It is about time you called me Emmett, Lily. It sounds nice from your lips." Emmett replied smiling then turning to Terence he agreed though he sounded annoyed, "Don't worry, since you got my boss to okay this action and this is highly unorthodox, I will follow the plan to the letter."

A Penny Saved a Murder Earned

Emmett quietly found a place to hide in the house, cautiously avoiding any recording devices.

~0~

Chapter 24 - A Penny Saved A Murder Earned

A half an hour later Emmett waited in

place for the culprit to come, so the trap would be sprung. Lily jumped up to answer a knock at the door.

"Where is Amelia?" Brad Owens asked, as he was ushered into the house.

"I'm sure she feels better after her rest," Lily answered.

"I'm so glad Amelia is rested," Brad replied.

"Me too!" replied Silas who had arrived as well.

"But where is she?" Brad demanded like he'd said nothing.

"She'll be down in a couple of minutes. Please, come in and take a seat. Can I get you a drink? Tea coffee, beer?" Lily offered.

"Beer, please and thank you," They both answered.

"We're off duty now."

Katha limped into the room and took a seat in the living room in a swivel chair.

"Oh how lovely to visit with you both again," Katha exclaimed.

"I don't understand why you'd say it's lovely to visit with us again. You saw us a few hours ago at the wake," admonished Brad.

"Oh so I did. Forgive my forgetfulness in my old age," Katha explained preparing to spring the trap.

"It's okay old...er...people forget," Brad replied "Excuse me a moment, I need to use the facilities," Silas commented, but Terrence didn't catch the words.

"Talking about people forgetting, you'll never believe what I found out in the street," began Terrence.

"So what did you find?" asked Brad.

"I found a money clip, and look...someone's money." Terrence said pausing for effect and trying to appear normal, "I know what you're thinking. Don't you worry; I'm turning it into the police station. I'll go down to the station after dinner and give it to them."

"You don't need to take it to the station," explained Brad. "It's mine, I must have dropped it at some point."

Brad took off his coat, revealing a tie clip, a ruby, an emerald and peridot stone, glinting in the light.

"Brad?" asked Amelia, as she entered from the garage.

"I thought Lily said you were upstairs?" Brad commented puzzled.

"Why, Brad, where did you get that tie clip? It's just like the one Grandpa O'Malley made Daddy to match his money clip," Amelia's face contorted by confusion.

Brad looked horrified and in the next instance grabbed Katha. Pulling a gun out of his holster and held the gun to her throat.

"Brad! What are you doing?" Amelia cried out, oblivious and confused, "Why are you holding a gun on Aunt Katha? You'll hurt her!"

"I don't want to hurt her. I understand Katha's been good to you, and like a mother. But I need you to listen to me Amelia."

"Don't listen to him, Amelia!" Katha screamed, "He's not who you think he is! He's a serial killer!"

"Shut up you crazy old bat! What I did, I did to save Amelia," Brad shouted.

"I don't understand. Why are holding a gun?" inquired Amelia, still appearing perplexed.

"Oh, my darling, my Angel, of course you don't understand, but you will," Brad promised. "Do you remember the summer I cut the lawn?"

"I do, but what does that summer so long ago have to do with you holding a gun on my aunt? Why are you arresting her? She didn't kill my family!" Amelia cried, still sounding puzzled and sitting down on the sofa.

Terrence whispered to Lily, "Is she really that stupid?"

"Quiet! She knows what she's doing," Lily whispered back.

Brad focused so hard on Amelia and her reaction that he didn't hear Lily or Terrence.

"No, of course I'm not. Katha hasn't done anything wrong. I know how loving she can be to you. She tried to look after you years ago. She even went to the police about what your father had done to you. She told them he beat you! She even sought out a lawyer and tried to get custody. Unfortunately no one would listen, as the cops were friends of your father. You need not worry though; I've dealt with those police officers."

"My father lived as a good man and father, so he disciplined me. I wouldn't listen to him. I was a know-it-all teen," Amelia exclaimed defending her father.

"When he called you a slut, because you spoke to Silas and me, then he thrashed you! Did that show fatherly love? He left bruises on your beautiful skin! Was that discipline?" questioned Brad angrily.

"He was my father." Amelia exclaimed, "He had the right."

"He was a terribly abusive man and father. Your mother didn't stick up for you. Instead she avoided it all, by falling into the bottle," Brad complained.

"I loved my parents."

"I understand you felt affection for them, but it was so hard to see them harm you day after day. I couldn't bear to see them hurt you anymore," Brad begged Amelia by his eyes to accept and praise him.

"You killed my family? You murdered my mother, my father, my sister and my brother?" Amelia demanded, tears pooling in her eyes.

"I didn't know had come home! I had made sure you went to your babysitting job, but I didn't see you come to the house. I would never have hurt a hair on your head," Brad apologised.

"You killed my family? Why?" demanded Amelia.

"They harmed you! Your father beat you, while your mother drank. Your brother brought his slutty women home, and your sister hit you, belittling you, calling you ugly. This was not a family for an Angel. This family came from hell. You deserved better, my Angel, my pet. I couldn't allow this anymore, and when your father came out to me and said..."Your money for cutting

the lawn, five dollars, in pennies. I grew
angry because he owed me for the summer.
He owed me ten weeks, at five dollars a
week and yet he had offered me a total of
five dollars for an entire summer's work. He
even laughed at me as he stated 'A penny
saved is a penny earned. Save your pennies
and you'll have more money!'"

"Daddy gave you five dollars for the whole
summer?" Amelia asked astonished.

"Yes, in pennies. Do you believe it? He gave
me five dollars' worth of pennies. He threw
the money at my feet... like I was an animal.
He laughed at me again. He told me to stay
away from you. He'd seen the looks I'd
given you all summer. He saw how I felt.
But he said you weren't for the likes of me.
He had sicced Jerry on me. Jerry beat me up
as he, your father, held me down on the
ground. Jerry broke my nose, the bastard . . .
oh, forgive me, my Angel! I should not use
such foul language in front of you." Brad
began to pace… "I waited for you...When
they were all in their beds, I started my plan.
I snuck in and tied them to their beds. I
won't sully your ears with your sister's and
your brother's killings, except to say, I
remained merciful."

Amelia gasped but Brad didn't hear her and continued explaining what he had done.

"I tied your parents to their beds too, but mercy was not on my mind. Not with those excuses for parents. They begged for their lives, not yours, or your siblings, theirs! She offered up herself in exchange for her life, not his. I mentioned your sister and your brother were easy prey. She didn't seem to care. She told me they didn't matter. I grew so angry, I dispatched her first.

"You killed my mother?"

" I told you I had to dispense with her. I talked to your father for some time before I took his life. After all I had to give him a chance to tell his side. I won't tell you what he said about you. That would be too cruel. I did however tell your father my new saying, before he died."

"You had a new saying?" enquired Amelia, trying to humour him and keep him talking.

"I did indeed. Your father inspired my new saying, *'A Penny Saved A Murder Earned'*. I told him my new saying as he slithered and writhed beneath the pillow I held over his face. He stopped fidgeting and I left the room."

"You smothered my father?"

"Of course I did. I smothered them both."

"You smothered them both?" Amelia cried.

"But they really deserved it!! You know they did. They were so evil. I then set up the chlorine in the house. The chlorine caught on fire much too soon though. It burnt much too bright. I ended up burning the house down to the ground," Brad waxed bragging. "The flame was so beautiful; I watched as the colours of the fire rose so high in the sky. I seemed to touch it."

Brad seemed to go into a trance talking about the fire.

"How did the fire occur then?" demanded Lily, but he ignored her and she motioned to Amelia to ask him.

"How did the fire happen then? Did you find me and save me from the fire? Is that how I got outside the house?" inquired Amelia.

"Yes, but the fire didn't happen until after I took you out of the house. I couldn't believe it. You'd come home when I had killed them. You slept in your bed and you were unconscious. That was my entirely my fault," Brad responding to Amelia's voice.

"Tell me, Brad, why did the fire start?" Amelia prodded. enunciating each word.

"I set the fire to cover my crime, but you were safe. You didn't burn. I'm so sorry about your accident. Chlorine got into your lungs. That too was entirely my fault."

"So I got on the lawn, because you carried me?" Amelia softly requested.

"Yes, my Angel. I became scared because you vanished. They took you away from me. My punishment for my miscalculation was the absence of your beautiful smile. Lost, so totally lost, as if I was put in the closet again, by the devil himself, I tried to be

good, like you'd want me to be. I did try
hard, Amelia, my beloved Angel," Brad said
mournfully.

"You tried to be good for me?" replied
Amelia, still in shock how Brad had fooled
her and murdered her family, but somehow
she wanted this monster to explain it all.

"I joined the police. I went to the police
academy in Ravenworst after I got out of the
hospital. For once father had pride for me. I
had joined the side of the good." Brad
explained, "My father claimed you were my
curse. But I was so miserable without you.
Working for the Ravenworst Police force
and not being near you, my beloved, sweet,
Angel, seemed the curse."

"You worked for the police force there too?"

"Yes I did. Like a sign right out of blue you
appeared in front of me. I had found you
without even trying. The story appeared on
the news all about Lily, and you emerged
there, Amelia, comforting her. My dear
Angel, my dear Amelia, helping her cousin.
You needed me so I came to Happy Valley."

"You saw me and found me from a television story?" Amelia asked shocked.

"Of course I did. A single glimpse of your cousin on the news, and I found you. Some guy kidnapped Lily; poor Lily, working as a lowly employee in the Crown attorney's office. In the background of Paul Knight's story, you cried hugging Lily. I wanted to take you in my arms but you were here and I resided there. I thought and I applied to the Happy Valley Police Department."

"They were anxious to get someone like me. They needed skilled police officers. I moved up quickly through the ranks. The department was damn glad to get someone of my calibre here. I could be happy; I could watch over my Angel again."

"Six years ago? You've been a cop six years?" demanded Amelia, connecting the dots in horror.

"Maybe a little less time, than six years; but enough about me you were residing with your husband Jack. You didn't even take his name, but you had the boy Sammy. So if you loved him, why didn't you?" Brad said accusingly.

"I loved him, but I didn't want to change my name again," Amelia claimed softly.

Brad eased up a little with the gun, but still held the gun to Katha's side, as he paced across the room.

"But he didn't love you, the bastard. If he had I'd let you go...even if it hurt, just to make you happy," Brad coldly exclaimed. "But I watched him. He cheated with another woman in a motel."

"How dare you! You're lying! He would never cheat on me. He loved me," Amelia protested.

"You and Lily both know her. The woman he cheated with was Renée Harrow," Brad said smiling.

"You believe he slept with Renée?" Amelia protested. "I don't believe he would cheat with her. Why do you continue to lie to me?"

"Believe me, he slept with her. Renée sleeps beside anything on two legs. She even tried to proposition me when I threatened to arrest her for the murder of Horace Brooksfield."

"I thought she was related to you!" Amelia exclaimed flabbergasted.

"She's not related to me. Can you believe she told some people I was her brother? And she tried to kiss me, on the lips. Disgusting!"

"But she said she was your sister," Amelia protested. "The woman claimed kinship by being my half-sister, but the truth is she was married to my half-brother, Titus. Titus died and any relationship with her died too."

"Did you kill your brother Titus too?" Amelia demanded.

"No, I didn't kill Titus. He disappointed Dad in the end. He died in a bank robbery. It seemed my pretty boy, do no wrong brother, financed his lifestyle robbing banks," Brad laughed.

"Did you kill Jack and Sammy?"

"I didn't mean to kill your boy. Please believe me, Amelia; I would never harm your son. I almost killed myself when Sam was killed. I didn't know he was in the car," Brad confessed with horror on his face begging her to believe him.

"You killed my baby? You monster! I hate you. Did you hear me you creep? I hate you!" Amelia screamed hitting his chest.

Brad sought to cover his head and Katha saw her move. Katha managed to break free and kicked his feet from under him kicking the gun away as well. Terrence and Lily then managed to tie him up quickly with Terrence's belt.

"I did all of this for you, my Angel, my Amelia, don't hate me. Please don't hate me," Brad pleaded. "I loved our little boy Sammy."

"Ours? He wasn't yours. Don't you dare say his name, you cretin."

"I'm sorry. Please, Amelia, my Angel, forgive me. I tried to kill myself after your boy died. Fate intervened and my cousin saved me. He told me if someone loved you, then they could forgive you and Dr. Jones told me the same thing. It was like I was reborn. Of course my cousin didn't know it was you though," Brad explained, "You do forgive me, don't you my love?"

"Of course she does, Brad. Don't you, Amelia? Since we are all family now you'll want to tell us where you took Rose," Lily replied, appeasing Brad and patting Amelia's hand.

"He took Rose? He has Rose?" Amelia demanded.

Lily nodded.

"I forgive you Brad. You love me, correct? So you wouldn't want me to be unhappy. Now would you?" Amelia winningly asked.

"I do love you, my Angel. You are my reason for living," Brad replied smiling happily, bathing in his Angel's light of goodness.

"You'll bring Rose to me, won't you?" Amelia ordered, "She's like my daughter."

"I know she's like a daughter to you and I'll bring her to you I promise. I didn't hurt her. She likes me. She wants me to be her uncle soon."

"You were at it again," Silas exclaimed angrily, interrupting the conversation as he came in with his gun drawn.

"Hello, cousin. Not to worry; everything is all right now. You see, you were right. Amelia loves me, so she'll forgive me," Brad replied.

"She didn't say she loved you. You fool!" protested Silas waving his gun.

Lily, Amelia, Katha and Terence looked on in surprise.

"Well don't look so shocked. Sit all of you," Silas demanded.

"I'm already sitting young man," Terrence complained. "And so is Lily."

"Then you two sit, Katha and Amelia," Silas commanded, "And you two remain seated."

"You are his cousin?" probed Lily and Katha shocked.

They had seen no resemblance to Brad and they now worried about the gun Silas still had drawn.

"I guess I can answer some of your questions. Yes, Brad is my cousin. Did he tell you he is adopted? My uncle dallied with another woman and the result was Brad. My uncle adopted him with my aunt. My aunt never had a clue that he was her husband's spawn, but enough family history. It's too bad we've come in on a murder-suicide. It's too hard as a police officer to come upon these scenes," Silas smirked, than sadly shook his head.

"What does he mean he came in on a murder-suicide?" asked Amelia.

"What, you think you can get away with murdering us all, and making one of us the killer? Who do you plan to make the murderer?" demanded Lily, trying to stall so Emmett could come out into the room.

"Looking for that nitwit police officer, Rogers? You're going to be waiting a long time," explained Silas laughing. "Let's put it this way. I didn't use the facilities. I checked on my earlier handy work. Emmett Rogers is still out cold, and will be another of your victims, Crown attorney Kelly. It's a terrible shame, how you hid your homicidal tendencies all this time and then snapped."

"No one will believe this. Why did you do this anyway? I thought you were one of the good guys?" protested Lily.

"I am one of the good guys. I was entrusted by my Uncle Kelvin to look after my cousin and I do my job. He needs looking after and he's family."

"If you looked after your cousin, how did he murder so many people?" Lily inquired with sarcasm, "You say you were entrusted to look after Brad by your uncle? What happened to him? Did Brad murder him too?"

"Don't be ridiculous, Brad wouldn't kill his father," Silas argued, as he looked over at Brad for confirmation.

Seeing Brad's head go down in shame, he continued, "Oh my God, she's right! You did kill Uncle Kelvin."

Silas looked thunderstruck and extremely angry. That worried Lily.

"What the hell is wrong with you?" Silas questioned, "Does family mean nothing to you? After everything we've done to protect you? Is all of this about your obsession with my girl? You understood how I felt about Amelia. How could you?"

"She is mine. I told you she's my Angel!" ranted Brad.

"Your Angel? The one you always rave about? Amelia's that Angel? When did you decide she was your Angel? Was it the summer Amelia and I met? Did you decide then and there you needed to have what I wanted?" Silas angrily exclaimed.

Pausing trying to get his anger under control but not succeeding Silas continued, "Of course it was you. You always wanted what I wanted. You took my best toys when we were small and claimed they were yours. I let you keep them. Anything you wanted was yours for the asking. I loved you like a brother. I felt sorry you were stuck with your father and Titus, the wonder boy. Now I must clean up your messes again. Why, Brad why? Why do you push me this way and test my loyalty? It isn't necessary, you are my family. I'll pick you. Always! Now because of your foolishness Amelia's going to die, and not just Amelia, but all of them. Does cleaning up after you never end? Now I must kill a teenage girl to protect you. I assume she's back at your apartment?"

Brad nodded strangely submissive. Silas then untied Brad and held the gun on Lily, Katha and Terrence.

"It's time for me to finish this. I'm sorry, Amelia, I did love you. I'll make your death as painless as possible."

"No! No she won't die! If Amelia dies, I die!" exclaimed Brad. Brad had only registered the words that Amelia would die. Brad then grabbed Silas' gun as it went off with a huge bang.

~0~

Chapter 25   - Slipping the Bonds

A short time ago at Brad's house,
one street over from Lily's

Rose and Carol

Rose slipped the bounds off her feet

and wrists. She rubbed her wrists, as she felt
the rope burns. She unfurled herself slowly,
and walked to the door, seeking a way out of
the house. She hesitated at the door for a
moment looking both ways for any sign of
Sergeant Detective Owens. Startled when
she heard a noise in the other bedroom in the
home, Rose cautiously peered into the room.
She wondered... What if Brad hid in the
shadows? She looked blinked and realized;
yes, she saw Carol tied up on a chair.

"Carol, how did you get here?" Rose asked, and then realized Carol had a gag across her mouth.

Rose sneaked over, removed the gag, and began to untie her friend.

"Rose, are you okay? The cop grabbed me after I came to make sure you were okay," Carol explained, "I'm supposed to be at my dad's house, but I left right after I got there. I told my dad I was sick. No one will look for me or you for that matter. You didn't tell anyone you went to your Grandma Katha's did you? We must get out of here before he comes back."

"Brad grabbed me too, right in Grandma Katha's house. Can you berate me later, so we leave before he does come back?" Rose replied annoyed.

Carol began sobbing and between sobs she asked "Are you sure you're okay?"

"Yes, silly, we're both okay."

"Well he sure moves fast. He had me all tied up and knocked out in about five seconds. We need to get out of here. He'll come back," Carol repeated worried.

"You wouldn't believe the story he told me. The guy is wacko. He is so obsessed with my aunt, I think he's killing people he believes will taint her." explained Rose, "Besides, I must go tell my mom, aunt and great-grandma before he does something else."

"Tell me about it!" demanded Carol.

"There's no time. Come on, now."

Rose peered into the hallway to see if Brad concealed himself in the passageway.

"Is the coast clear?" asked Carol.

"I think he's gone, but we better keep our eyes open," Rose replied, looking both ways again.

"Let's run over to your house now."

"Oh no, I'm not making a mistake again. I'm calling Mr. Stewart, Terrence's son, the police chief. I'm telling him everything," Rose announced.

"Well do it fast, while you walk outside to your place," Carol demanded.

Rose scanned the room and found her cell phone on the table. She grabbed it and pulled Carol with her out the front door of Brad's apartment to find they were only three houses away from Rose's house. She phoned the number she had seen Terrence dial only a few days ago.

"Hello, Mr. Stewart, Rose Brooksfield here. Uh huh... sorry, Chief Stewart...Oh, good! Then this should be easier, "Rose exclaimed. "I need some help. You won't believe what happened to Carol and me. We were kidnapped! What do you mean you knew I was missed?"

Carol urgently pulled at Rose's arm, but Rose continued to listen to what Chief Stewart said on the phone and didn't acknowledge her.

"Rose, listen to me. I remember the car parked in your driveway. The car is Sergeant Detective Owens' blue Honda accord. He drove the car in the parking lot at the Pope Hotel. My dad has an Accord too, so I can distinguish what kind of car it is," Carol urgently insisted, as they continued walking to Lily's house.

"What? What did you just say, Carol?" Rose asked, as part of what Carol said registered.

"I said the car belongs to Sergeant Detective Owens. The blue Honda parked in your mom's driveway is his. Which means Brad probably has taken everyone in your house prisoner," Carol exclaimed worried.

"You're sure? Of course you are," Rose exclaimed then she said into her cell phone before hanging up. I know who the serial killer is, and he is at my house...No! I'm not waiting...Sure, you can send your force to wrap this up, but by then I will have stopped him. I'm not letting him kill anyone else in my family."

"You shouldn't speak to the police chief that way, when you want his help."

"What was I supposed to do? A bad cop is here, in my house. There is no time to waste; he could be killing everyone in my family," Rose cried, sounding terrified but determined.

Rose lifted the garage door halfway, being careful not to make any noise and then quickly ducked under.

"Why are we in the garage?" asked Carol whispering following her in.

"My dad has a gun safe hidden in here .He showed me one time. There's a gun and bullets in here."

"Are you crazy? You can't use a gun! Wait for the cops."

"I can't wait. I'm not going to let Brad kill my mom too. I already lost a mom to prison because she was a drug addict and now a dad to this freak show. He's not killing my mom, Lily as well."

"You don't even know how to use a gun. You could be killed. Please, Rose, wait."

"I know how to use a gun. My dad believed in equality and he thought I should be able to shoot a gun. I'm going to stop him."

Removing the gun from the safe, Rose loaded it with bullets. Rose looked down the barrel as she pointed it in Carol's direction.

"Hey, watch where you point that thing," Carol exclaimed. "For the record I'm still against this, but I'm coming."

Rose and Carol crept in through the back door. Rose motioned for Carol to be quiet and cautiously follow her. As Rose and Carol neared the living room, they stopped and listen to the conversation.

"Looking for that nitwit police officer Rogers? You're going to be waiting a long time." explained Silas laughing, "Let's put it this way. I didn't use the facilities. I checked on my earlier handy work. Emmett Rogers is still out cold, and will be another of your victims, Crown Attorney Kelly. It's a terrible shame how you hid your homicidal tendencies all this time and then snapped."

"I'm not going in there. Someone has to stay outside and get help if needed. That's where I'm headed now," Carol insisted, whispering.

"Fine, then go to outside near the garage and keep watch," Rose whispered back. "I can handle Brad Owens. Direct Chief Stewart to me when he arrives.

"I don't want to leave you alone," Carol protested.

"Come out with me and wait. Please Rose it is too dangerous. Wait for Chief Stewart!"
"I'll be fine. I have the gun and someone has to stop him."

"Fine, but I don't like you doing this alone, so be careful," Carol advised, leaving extremely quietly.

Rose glanced around and found Emmett Rogers. His head was blooded and he was out cold. She slapped his face, managing to rouse him as he blinked his eyes.

"What happened?" he whispered to Rose while he rubbed his head.

"Silas hit you over the head is my guess. They are both in on it. Silas Rentford is Brad Owens' cousin, and he has been covering up for him all along while he committed crime after crime," deduced Rose.

"How do you know this?"

"It's a guess... maybe more like a hunch. But I'm sure I'm right. He'll make a move. We need to stop him now," exclaimed Rose, waving her gun.

"Where did you get the gun? You shouldn't brandish a gun you're only fifteen. Give it to me," demanded Emmett.

"I'll be able to make a perfect shot. My dad believed women should be able to protect themselves, so he used to take me to the pistol range. You don't need to worry," replied Rose whispering.

"I can't even see straight. I'm seeing double, but I can't let a child take a suspect into custody. Give me the gun."

"I'm not a child and I'm not giving you a choice.

"You said it yourself, Detective Rogers, you can't even see straight. And if you think for a moment I'm going to let those psychos harm my family anymore, you can think again. Besides, as Grandma Katha says, I'm a Kelly, and Kelly women are brave," Rose whispered, and then they both remained quiet for a moment to overhear and see the rest of the conversation.

"If you looked after your cousin, how did he murder so many people?" sarcastically inquired Lily. "You say you were entrusted to look after Brad by your Uncle? What happened to him? Did Brad murder him too?"

"Don't be ridiculous! Brad wouldn't kill his father," Silas argued, as he looked over at Brad for confirmation.

Seeing Brad's head go down in shame, he continued, "Oh my God, she's right! You did kill Uncle Kelvin. What the hell is wrong with you?" Silas questioned, "Does family mean nothing to you? After everything we've done to protect you? Is all of this about your obsession with my girl? You understood how I felt about Amelia. How could you?"

"She is mine. I told you she's my Angel," ranted Brad

"Your Angel? The one you always rant about? Amelia's that Angel? When did you decide she was your Angel? Was it the summer Amelia and I met? Did you decide then and there you needed to have what I wanted?" Silas angrily exclaimed.

Pausing trying to get his anger under control but not succeeding Silas continued, "Of course it was you. You always wanted what I wanted. You took my best toys when we were small and claimed they were yours. I let you keep them. Anything you wanted was yours, for the asking. I felt sorry you were stuck with your father and Titus, the wonder boy. Now I must clean up your messes again. Why, Brad, why? Why do you push me this way and test my loyalty? It isn't necessary, you are my family. I'll pick you. Always! Now because of your foolishness Amelia's going to die, and not just Amelia, but all of them. Does cleaning up after you never end? Now I must kill a teenage girl to protect you. I assume she's back at your apartment?"

Rose saw Brad nodded strangely submissive. She then saw Silas untie Brad and hold the gun on Lily Katha and Terrence.

"It's time for me to finish this. I'm sorry, Amelia, I did love you. I'll make your death as painless as possible."

A Penny Saved a Murder Earned

Brad registered the words that Amelia would die. He then grabbed Silas' gun as it went off with a huge bang.

Rose heard Brad yell, "No! No, she won't die! I won't let you kill her!"

Rose took a firing stance and the gun went off just as Silas' gun also fired. Rose looked on in horror, hoping against hope, that her bullet wasn't the one which seemed to hit Silas' chest. Silas lay profusely bleeding, his heart pumping the blood out of his body. His body shuttered a death rattle and he ceased breathing.

Brad cradled his cousin in his arm crying, "Wake up, Silas! Quit fooling around. You can't leave me. You are my only family. You look after me. Who will keep after me and make me good? Don't die, Silas! Please, don't leave me. Don't you die on me! Please Silas don't die! Don't go! You always looked after me, even when we were kids,

and father would lock me in the closet you'd
get me out of the dark. I should have picked
you. You should come first, but we can
change all of that if you give me a chance.
Please, don't leave me in the dark, Silas,"
begged Brad.

Brad continued anguish in every tone as he
begged, pleaded, and cajoled Silas to no
avail. He began rocking Silas's body in his
arms back and forth, a pitiful figure sitting
on the floor, his chest covered in blood from
Silas' wound. His arms clenched in an
unbreakable hold around Silas' body, as he
pulled him to his chest.

"Give it up, Owens. He's dead," Emmett
yelled.

An eerie howl emitted from Silas' lips, as he
realized what Emmett said was true. Silas
was unmoving and therefore dead. Brad
looked stunned and unseeing, as Emmett
then said in a moderated tone grabbing
Brad's hands behind his body he recited,
"You have the right to remain silent and

refuse to answer questions. Do you understand?"

Brad said nothing; he just continued staring at Silas' body.

"Anything you do say may be used against you in a court of law. Do you understand?"

Brad continued to stare at Silas.

"You have the right to consult an attorney before speaking to the police, and to have an attorney present during questioning now, or in the future. Do you understand?"

Brad continued staring at the body of his now dead cousin not responding, beyond perceiving sound. He moaned a low pitiful moan from time to time but no reply is heard from Brad.

"If you cannot afford an attorney, one will be appointed for you before any questioning if you wish. Do you understand?" Emmett continued, "If you decide to answer questions now without an attorney present, you will still have the right to stop answering at any time, until you talk to an attorney. Do you understand? Knowing and understanding your rights as I have explained them to you, will you answer my questions without an attorney present?"

"Mr. Owen appears out of it. I don't think he understands anything you said," Rose explained. "Did I kill the other one?"

"No, Rose, the bullet came from a trajectory which could only have come from Brad's gun. Glance at the wall there and you'll find your bullet."

"How could I have missed?" demanded Rose pretending that shooting off a gun was not a big deal, "Not that I wanted to be the one to kill anyone, but I thought I was a better shot."

Rose's speech was interrupted by Lily who ran at Rose with her arms wide open and hugged her.

"Rose, oh Rose," Lily cried with joy at seeing her daughter in one piece safe and home.

"I'm okay, Mom."

"I was terrified, baby. I'm so glad you are okay," Lily exclaimed wiping back tears and then running her hands down Rose's arms to convince herself Rose was real.

"Rose, oh my, I was so worried when Lily told me he had you," Amelia expressed hugging her niece.

"Baby girl, we're all glad you're okay," Katha exclaimed.

"Did he hurt you?" Lily asked checking Rose's face.

"No, Carol and I now own a few rope burns, but we will be fine."

"Rope burns? Let me see." Lily demanded, "Oh, my poor baby. You must have been terrified.

"I was fine. I told you I was fine," Rose claimed, "Besides; I was the one who tried to save you."

"So you did," Lily acknowledged.

Katha exclaimed, "You came through, like all Kelly women do in a pinch, because we are all or one…"

"And one for all!" Katha, Amelia, Lily and Rose responded at the same time, hugging one another.

"Can an old man get in on this family hug, Katha?" begged Terrence.

"I guess we could include you a little, Terrence. Sorry you felt left out of the loop," Lily apologized.

"Yes, sorry, dear," Katha apologized hugging Terrence "But you'll have to get used to it when we Kelly women are together we are one."

"I wouldn't have it any other way," Terrence responded hugging Katha back.

~0~

Chapter 26 - Life Goes On

Emmett tried to march a despondent

Brad Owens to a waiting police car. Brad inconsolable screamed and cried, fighting to stay with the body. Emmett with great difficulty got him in the back of the waiting car.

"Patrolman Barnes, Sergeant Detective Owens has confessed to the murders. He has been read his rights but he has not responded. He is to be taken to hospital for a mental evaluation. He will be treated with the utmost respect. This case won't be thrown out because of any police wrong doing. Is that clear?" demanded Emmett from Alan.

"Yes, sir. Good work, sir. The Police chief has told me to relay this message, sir. I'm repeating the edict word for word, so do not blame the messenger."

"Get to the hospital for a scan and medical attention now. You are to go with Patrolman Appleton now. Is that clear?" reiterated Patrolman Barnes. "Then I expect a full report on why a fifteen-year-old girl, fired a gun to protect an officer."

"Totally clear. Please tell the chief I'm on my way," Emmett acknowledged realizing he had no choice but to obey.

"You're in a bit of hot water, Emmett. Can I do anything?" Alan inquired.

"No, but thanks. Point me in Patrolman Appleton's direction," Emmett answered.

"Tell the chief and Patrolman Appleton I'm driving him instead," Lily exclaimed after overhearing this.

"What about your daughter? Doesn't she need you?" probed Emmett worried about Rose.

"Quit making excuses and get going, Sergeant Detective Rogers. I'm fine with Grandma Katha, Amelia, and of course Mr. Stewart," Rose demanded crossing her arms, appearing remarkably like her mother's stance.

"Kid, you can call me Emmett and so can your mother. I think you have earned the right. Are you okay, Quick Draw McGraw?" asked Emmett, "Maybe you should be checked out too."

"Who's Quick Draw McGraw? Oh wait a minute, that is from an old cartoon. Mom quotes him too; I prefer Annie Oakley. I'm fine, Emmett but thanks."

"Are you sure, pumpkin? I had planned on making a run to the hospital with both of you," Lily commented.

"Mom, I'm fine besides I'll stay with Grandma Katha. She needs me."

"Are you sure?" Lily asked.

"I'll be fine, Mom."

"Okay, we're leaving now. I'll be back soon," Lily said feeling reluctant to leave her daughter. "I love you, Rose." "Would you just go make sure the hero is okay?" Rose exclaimed. "Bye, my little heroine," Lily said to Rose.

Lily mouthed to Katha 'Keep her safe'.

"Rose, I was so scared, but I stayed in the garage. Is the drama all over now? Are we safe?" Carol enquired, coming out of the garage as Emmett left with Lily.

"Oh, I am sorry, Carol. I forgot you were there."

"You forgot I was there? Thanks a lot. I could have died for all you cared."

"Sorry, Carol. It's all over. Emmett arrested Detective Brad Owens. Don't go in the house though. Detective Silas Rentford is dead," Rose explained.

"You shot him?" Carol queried shocked, her hand to her mouth.

"No, I tried, but I missed. I was so scared I didn't shoot straight. I thought Silas would kill them all and it would have been my fault, since I missed."

Rose started crying.

"Rose, my baby doll, you did save us. You distracted Silas," Katha cried overhearing.

"I did?" asked Rose sounding surprised.

"Yes, you did," Katha answered.

"You are a hero, Rose, or is it heroine? I can never remember," Carol responded trying to cheer up her crying friend.

"The word is heroine, Carol." Katha informed and then announced, "And you are right, Rose is a heroine."

"What can I tell my parents?" Carol asked, "They will be so mad at me,"

"Tell them the truth Carol. When they hear you were kidnapped, they'll forget most of the rest," advised Katha.

"You still didn't explain how you wound up Brad's prisoner."

"That's your fault, Rose," Carol claimed.

"My fault? How is it my fault?" Rose demanded. "I was worried about you and came to make sure you were safe. He grabbed me outside of your house because you didn't call the police," Carol explained.

"I guess then it was a little my fault. You can blame me when you tell your parents if you want, but what really happened to you?"

"Considering it was entirely your fault, I think I will," Carol insisted. "Anyway, I got off the bus to come back here; when you didn't answer he grabbed me. Was that because he had you trussed in the chair?"

"Yes, I think he had me by then. I wasn't in Grandma's house more than five minutes and he had me tousled up like a turkey," Rose replied. "And then what happened? How did you get back here?"

"I got off the bus like I said and my mom was there, she made me go home and go to my dad's."

Carol then related to Rose and Katha, what
happened when Carol got to her dad's.

"Daddy said that he had to go out and I
whined that I had just gotten there, but
Daddy did his spiel like he always does:..
And you'll be here when I get back. The
office needs me. I've got more security
contracts; I have people depending on me. I
have to go to work .he complained. So I told
him... Okay goodbye. I don't matter. You
don't want to spend time with me. So
Daddy, offered to bring me a present. Like
presents were all I wanted? Why doesn't he
understand I want to see him more often?"
Carol bemoaned.

"Parents don't always understand that work
takes time away from loved ones. They
think there will always be time for family.
I'm sure Gerald loves you, Carol," Katha
answered.

"He did promise to take me to opening day
at the fair, this weekend. I hope his work
doesn't get in the way ,again!" Carol
answered, "After he promised me to take me
he said he loved me and he would come
back for me in a few hours. Do you think
he'll be so mad he won't take me to the
fair?"

"I'm sure he'll be so happy you are safe and he'll let all the anger go," Katha reassured.

"What Grandma Katha means is she will make sure he does," Rose said conspiratorially as Katha smiled.

"So what happened next, Carol?"

"So after my dad left I called a taxi. I took the cab to your grandma's house. Brad said you were hurt and needed me. I was such a fool to believe him. I tried to get away but he clocked me. When I woke up I was tied to a chair."

"Carol, I think we need to get you checked out at the hospital, if you were unconscious." Katha insisted, "I'll tell your parents to meet us there."

"I don't want to go to the hospital," Carol complained, "I don't need to go there. My head hurts a little, but I'll be fine."

"Head injuries can be more serious than people know. I think it's a good idea. Besides think of the case it will make with your mom and dad. They'll see you were kidnapped and hurt, making them reconsider becoming angry. They'll forgive you leaving without telling them."

"Fine, but I'm doing this under protest."

Katha drove them to the hospital and they found themselves there within twenty minutes. They were met by Gerald and Charlene Banks, two worried parents who stood together arm-and-arm.

"Weird they haven't got along not since the divorce, Rose."

"They were worried about you. I called them before we got in the car. Your parents love you," Katha added.

"Mom, Dad I'm so sorry, but I had to try and save Rose. That man could have killed her."

"No, we are sorry baby. If we hadn't been fighting and worried about our own concerns, you could have told us what worried you," Francine replied, poking Gerald.

"Your mother is right. Honey, are you okay? Katha said you were kidnapped and hit on the head,"

Gerald probed searching her eyes.

"Gerald, she should go in and get checked into the hospital. We're keeping her from being checked out."

"Sorry, of course you are right, Francine."

"Come on, sweetie. Let us go get you checked out by a doctor."

"Thank you, Katha. I don't know how I will ever thank you for saving my daughter," Gerald replied, shaking Katha's hand.

"The person you have to thank is my great-granddaughter. She untied herself, got free, and untied Carol, then she saved her entire family from that crazy police officer," Katha answered.

"See, what did I tell you, Gerald? Rose is a perfect friend for Carol. She's sweet she's kind and she saved our daughter."

"She wouldn't have gotten into any of this fix if it wasn't for Rose and her family."

"Gerald, Rose saved her. Take that back. Now!"

"Francine is right; you are a wonderful friend to our Carol Thank you, Rose," Gerald answered then turning to Francine he said, "Happy now, Francine?"

"I promise we'll talk some more later," Francine said to Katha.

"See you later, Rose," Carol declared, smiling as Rose gave her the thumbs up sign.

~0~

Chapter 27   - Epilogue-Should I or Shouldn't I?

Three months later

"**R**ose, the brief commitment trial is

completed. Brad Owens will be locked away for the near future. He will be taken to Pinecrest and get a suite in the forensic unit. I don't think they'll be along drawn out trial."

"Good, but what is Pinecrest?" Rose asked.

"It's a hospital for the criminal insane, here in Ontario. I do think, however, that his mind is broken. Losing his cousin Silas was the last draw for him."

"He's a serial killer. I have no pity for him. Do you want me to be sorry for him Mom? Why? He killed Dad," Rose asked shocked.

"Actually, I do feel sorry for him. What came out in his commitment trial was horrific. The terrible things that happened to him as a child and young adult broke his spirit."

"None of that excuses his behaviour. Lots of people have troubled childhoods, and they don't go crazy and kill people," complained Rose.

"I don't condone his actions, Rose, but I can still have empathy for him. Compassion is always possible."

"You are a better person than I. I don't want to ever think or hear about him ever again."

"School starts the weekend after next, which means we have two glorious weeks to have some fun, "Lily began before being interrupted.

"Can we go somewhere now, Mom? It's been so hard staying here. People still give me odd looks and frown. When they see me, they start talking in quiet whispers," Rose complained.

"The whole thing has been hard. This has been horrific, on all of us," Lily commented, looking at a vacation brochure.

"I wish Emmett would come around again. I liked him."

"You call him Emmett now, instead of Detective Rogers?" Lily asked hiding a smile.

"Yes, you heard him he told me to call him Emmett. He came around so many times to see you after the shooting. Did you say or do something? Emmett isn't coming around anymore."

"Well. yes, I did, he appeared interested in me but I'm mourning your dad," Lily admitted.

Rose stared at her mom, noticing, for the first time how sad she looked. Rose felt guilty for not realizing her mother had been suffering too. She decided her mom's pain needed to be acknowledged too.

"Mom, I've been selfish thinking about all my own pain. I know how much you loved Daddy. We both miss him so. But if there's ever a time when someone wants to like date you... you should go for it."

"I think it's too soon, but thank you, baby doll. Did anyone tell you, you are one of the most considerate, sweet daughters around?" replied Lily hugging Rose.

"Don't call me baby doll in front of other people, you make me sound five years old. Besides some people think it is a sexist comment. Please don't tell anyone I said you could date again either; it would ruin my reputation," Rose replied with a wink.

"Would you like to spend two weeks in a beautiful beach cottage with your Aunt Amelia, Katha, Terrence and say, your friend Carol and I?" questioned Lily with a smile.

"Really, Mom? Two weeks at the beach? And Carol, can come?" Rose requested excitedly.

"If her parents say she can go. Carol has been an incredible friend to you."

"No kidding, she is the best friend ever. She told off Billy Robertson and Nathan Patel," Rose admitted "She has one mean tongue. Her backhand is solid too."

"Why did you mention Carol's backhand? She didn't hit them?"

Rose nodded.

"What did Billy and Nathan do? Why did she get so mad?"

"Billy joked and said all the women in my family were black widows; even if we didn't kill we got others to kill for us. I hate him. I wanted to punch him too," Rose admitted.

"Rose, you know violence is never the answer." Lily was appalled at Billy's behaviour but worried about Rose's reaction to this kind of bullying.

"I do understand that, Mother. No hitting, no matter what, unless your person is threatened and you can't find another way," Rose parroted.

"Well, yes."

"Well, don't get mad at Carol and not let her come with us, but she threw her drink at Nathan."

"Why did she do that?" solicited Lily. "Nathan tried to cop a feel of my breast, but before I could do anything, Carol had thrown her drink at him and implied he committed a criminal offense. She requested whether she should be calling Sergeant Detective Rogers. Nathan got scared," Rose laughed.

"Nathan should have known to commit a sexual assault on someone is a criminal offense. How dare he touch you like that?" Lily replied with a furrowed brow I'll pick up the phone and..."

"Mom, it's handled. Besides, Billy appeared angry too. Billy made him apologized to me. Then he gave Nathan a black eye."

"I hope you're not glorifying a black eye. I mean, I know I'm angry, but to hit someone..."

"Violence is never the solution," repeated Rose sounding less than enthused.

A Penny Saved a Murder Earned

"Thank you for telling me this, Rose. I appreciate your confidence, but I think you should lay charges. He could do this to someone else."

"No worries, it's all good now Mom. But if it will make you happy, I could tell Emmett and see what he thinks," Rose answered, "Can I go call Carol now and invite her?"

"Sure, go ahead and call Carol. We leave the day after tomorrow," Lily yelled after her. "Make sure you tell Carol's mom and dad we will be home after Labour Day."

"I'll do that, Mom."

The doorbell rang and Rose ran quickly past Lily, pushing her out of the way to answer it. She found Carol on the doorstep, followed by Sergeant Detective Rogers.

"Come in, Sergeant Detective Rogers." Rose invited politely, spoiling it by yelling, "Mom, your cop is here!"

"Rose Brooksfield!" Lily exclaimed waving her finger at Rose.

Rose brought Carol into the living room and they began to talk in excited whispers giggling.

"Rose?" Lily called. "Yes, Mother?"

"Grandma Katha brought over some homemade molasses cookies at noon. They're in the cookie jar. Help yourself to two cookies, but leave room for dinner. Please ask Carol if she'd like to stay for dinner too, if it's okay with her folks."

"'Kay, we're going to my room."

"Brad Owens will remain under criminal psychiatric care for the rest of his life. The sentence to keep him there came down today," Emmett stated without preamble, as he stepped into the room.

"One of my colleagues called me and told me," Lily confessed.

"One less worry for you now; it's all over. He can't harm your family anymore."

"How's the head doing? I haven't seen you since you came by those few times, after the ordeal," Lily exclaimed with reproach.

"It's much better, thanks. I'm sorry I didn't call. I wanted to give you space," Emmett answered, hanging his head in regret.

"Why? Because you kissed me in the hospital waiting room?"

"Let see... your husband had just died, a serial killer, a killer – who happened to be a cop – had taken you and other family members' hostage and I kiss you? I felt like a heel for forcing my attentions on you," Emmett replied sheepishly. "And you didn't seem all that welcoming when I came to visit afterwards."

"You didn't force anything on me. I liked it," admitted Lily as Emmett smiled.

"Good," Emmett replied looking around for anyone. He then requested, "Is Amelia here?"

"You too?" asked Lily sounding disappointed at the thought of Emmett being attracted to Amelia.

"I don't think you understand!" Emmett insisted.

Lily stared at him and frowned. "You don't, do you? You like Amelia. Why did you kiss me? Go! Get the lady you want. Amelia is at her store."

"I wanted to make sure no one was around to interrupt us, when I do this," exclaimed Emmett passionately kissing her full on the lips.

Lily swooned for a moment, melting into the kiss. Drowning in the moment, she couldn't sense where she stood. It felt like she stood on thin air, or on a cloud. She deepened the kiss and so did Emmett. The whole world disappeared. She felt like tearing off her clothes then and there, but reality set in and she felt guilty. This was not right! She remembered Rose upstairs and her dead husband, Horace. She pulled out of the kiss. Her lips were swollen and she felt the need to kiss him again, but Lily was terrified. It was too soon wasn't it!? Her body was now at war with her mind. What am I thinking? My husband has been dead for only three months. I have Rose to think of, to put first. I can do this… No! I shouldn't do this! Should I? No, I shouldn't. It's just not right.

"It's too soon, isn't it?" probed Emmett, sensing the change in Lily's mood.

"Yes," Lily babbled breathlessly. "Er… uh no, it isn't. Hell, I don't know. This is all too soon. I can't believe I'm even considering having a relationship with you."

"I'll take this one day at a time. We can find out all about each other. Please? I'm attracted to you, Lily. Give me a chance? Give us a chance," Emmett pleaded boldly.

"This came totally out of nowhere. I'm a widow, I'm supposed to be thinking only of my dead husband, grieving for him, not thinking about another man." Lily complained, exasperated with herself, "I loved Horace."

"But you are attracted to me, despite yourself aren't you?" Emmett persisted taking her hand.

"Yes I am. I like you, too and yes, I'm attracted to you. If we start down this road dating, we will have to take it slow and keep it quiet for a while. I won't have any more gossip hurt my daughter, or the rest of the family," Lily answered, pulling her hand away from Emmett's, "I can't believe I'm even considering this. My husband died only three months ago."

"I wouldn't hurt them or you for the world," Emmett explained. "I respect you and them too much."

"I'm going away for two weeks for a family vacation. Rose needs this vacation and so do I. We can't begin any relationship until after our vacation."

"I think I can wait until you get back," Emmett answered hugging her again.

Emmett soundly kissed her again. Lily felt like she was flying, soaring high in the sky. Her limbs turned to Jell-O and she felt like she never had before in her lifetime. Neither Horace, nor William, had ever made her experience the world this way. What did that mean? She felt more alive in this kiss; it caressed every neuron ping in her body. She was truly lost in this moment, as the whole world faded away.

"You owe me five bucks. I told you Sergeant Detective Rogers appeared interested in my mother," Rose bragged smugly.

"You implied he was interested in your mother. You didn't tell me your mom might be interested in him," Carol complained, staring at Lily and Emmett kissing,. "Wow! Talk about a sizzling kiss. Someday I want someone to kiss me like that," Carol concluded. "It reminded me of the way Damon kissed Elena, on the Vampire Diaries."

"Well, even if she is interested in Emmett, she still loves my dad. She just needs someone to be her partner and hold her hand," Rose replied offended.

"He wants to do more than kiss," Carol answered.

"Yuck, Carol! Please don't talk about my mother that way," Rose admonished. "And she's still in love with my dad."

"Sorry. I do think he is attracted to her though."

"I had a dream about my dad."

"That's a good thing?" examined Carol worried.

"Yes, I think he wanted to tell me something important."

"What did father want to tell you?" Carol asked.

"My dad seemed so alive in the dream. He smiled the special smile he had only for me, which said he loved me. He motioned for me to come closer to him. I went. You don't know how incredibly wonderful it felt to see him again. I've missed him so much. He told

me..."I'm dead, Rosey." I nodded and he
continued. "You know this is a dream. I
don't have a lot of time to talk to you. I love
you sweetie, you and your mother Lily. I
want you to listen to me. I was a heel. Your
mother Lily, I betrayed her horribly. She
was so good to both of us and I made your
mother suffer. She needs to be happy."

"I don't want your mom to be lonely ever
again. Let her find what she needs...who she
needs. Rose. Give her a chance to be happy
when it comes."

Carol cocked her head and then shook it as
if she couldn't believe what she was hearing
then seem to accept it as she said "Wow!
Amaze balls. I mean, he talked to you from
the grave."

"He also said he sent someone for her. Do
you think he meant Sergeant Detective
Rogers? I think he is someone who might
make her happy. Someday! He told me I
should call him Emmett. Emmett will be
good to her. He'll treat my mom well and
make her happy... at least I hope so. But he's
not my dad!"

"I liked your dad, Rose, but he wasn't kind to your mom, maybe Emmett will make her happier.

"You know, Carol, although, Mom can take care of herself, I guess it would be great if someone else that could do that for her once in a while."

"It would be wonderful for your mother," Carol exclaimed. "You are generous to your mom's needs. Most kids would have hated their mom thinking about dating so soon."

"Yuck! That sounds icky!"

"That isn't what I meant to say!" Carol complained.

"Like I said, Dad wants her to be happy, so why shouldn't I? She took me on, and became my mother when she didn't have to make me her daughter. I suppose it's the least I can do," Rose continued, like she struggled with the idea, but wanted to do the right thing.

"So did you dream anything else?"

"Yes. My dad told me that he loved me again, and called me Rosebud. It was his favourite name for me. He said have a good life, be happy, and suddenly he was gone."

"Your dad is correct. My mom would be lost without my dad to do things for her. Even though they're divorced, he still comes over to fix things," replied Carol, clearly misunderstanding the comment.

"That's not quite what I meant, but I guess it's good too," Rose replied. "Let's go and leave them. This is kind of gross and liable to scare my psyche if we talk about it anymore."

Rose and Carol scampered up the stairs laughing and went to Rose's room.

"I'm excited about going to the beach with you and my family. Isn't it cool Mom requested that you come with us?" Rose exclaimed.

"I wonder how many guys will be at the beach? I'm taking my tiny red bikini," Carol commented."

"You hope the guy that was at the beach last time we went looks at you again," replied Rose giggling.

"Like you didn't like the way Giorgio looked at you?" laughed Carol.

"Did you see that loser Derek stare at us? I overheard him say to his friends we were hot."

"Yah, like we'd ever look at that guy." Carol laughed again.

"Do you remember Rebecca's slip?"

"Slip? The girl grabbed for her bikini bottoms. I felt sorry for her, but tie it in a knot, or knots," Carol answered cattily. "Remember the fireworks for Canada Day?"

"Yes, and I remember the moves Kyle tried to put on you." Carol started laughing, like she couldn't stop.

"Yes, it was funny. The way he laid afterwards in the sand. You really pushed him," Rose replied also giggling.

Downstairs Lily and Emmett heard the laughter.

"It's wonderful to hear Rose laughing again."

"She's been through a lot. Have fun at the beach. Remember though, I'll be waiting when you get back, I'll be waiting," Emmett promised. "Goodbye for now."

"Stay for dinner. I'll order Chinese, but this time, we'll skip the serial killer," invited Lily laughing.

"I'd be happy too."

THE END OR IS IT?

Look for Emmett and Lily further adventures and the rest of the Clan Kelly's fun in Book 2 of the Kelly Murder Mysteries - A Diller a Dollar a Real Dead Scholar, on sale now in e-book soon in paperback, on the next page is an excerpt from it.

~0~

Excerpt from A Diller A Dollar a Really Dead Scholar:

SNEAK PEAK - Chapter 1 - Real Life Is Worse than a Movie

'A diller, a dollar, A ten o'clock scholar; What makes you come so soon? You used to come at ten o'clock, But now you come at noon!' ~Nursery Rhyme, Author Unknown

Rose

Rose arrived early for choir with Carol, by her side. She wasn't aware of what she would have done without her constant side kick, and best friend Carol in the last few weeks. Carol had amazingly defended her making her proud to be her friend. However, the calendar said the second week of school and the whispers still continued. Gossip was continually passed around about the murders but especially at school.

Rose was tired of all of the innuendoes and speculation, she thought. Her father had died, no not simply died; he had been murdered by a serial killer. This should have garnered some sympathy, for both the circumstances of her father's death, and the manner, but all she caught was jokes about the position he had been found. Rose guessed finding him naked with his secretary; who he'd been having an affair with led to the gossip, but she was so tired of all of it. If that wasn't bad enough though, everyone had to find out this serial killer had killed many people. He had killed Rose's Great Uncle Jerry, Aunt Aerilla, and her cousins Robert and Grace before Aunt Amelia came to Happy Valley. Last year he had murdered Aunt Amelia's husband Jack and killed her little boy Sam.

Continuing on his killing spree, he had killed Aunt Amelia's employee Megan and the homeless guy Mr. Young. All of this simply because he was obsessed, horribly obsessed with Aunt Amelia, all of so senseless and stupid. She grew tired of talking about the incident. Who did she kid? She couldn't even talk about her father's death to the shrink, her mother made her visit. People came up to her at school and wanted gruesome details. Or they wanted to know more about the capture of the serial killer. Grandma Katha called him the cop in wolf's clothing, and some other names Rose didn't care to repeat. She wanted to scream. Torn Rose hated and loved Happy Valley, Ontario, both at the same time. It was after all the place she was born, but the buildings were old here and the town was dying as prosperity had flown along, with a number of businesses that employed people. Would there even be a job for Rose when she wanted one? With the loss of jobs, people's attitudes had changed or maybe they'd just revealed themselves to be small minded and frankly she was tired of it. As soon as she could she was going away to university and then she'd live in another city when she graduated, visiting Lily, Grandma Katha and Amelia regularly.

Rose just wanted to be Rose Brooksfield again...not Rose Brooksfield whose father had been murdered. Wasn't it bad enough that Her mother Lily Brooksfield, or Lily Kelly as she had always called herself, Mom now dated the cop, who had investigated her Dad's murder.

What did it mean about Mom's true feelings for her Dad, Horace, that she had moved on so quickly? Rose had encouraged Mom, but she had been rash. Mom should be thinking of her Dad not this Emmett Rogers all the time.

Now all Rose ever heard from Mom was Emmett this and Emmett that. What about Dad had she forgotten him? And if she had forgotten him... what did that mean for Rose? After all she was Lily's adopted daughter not her flesh and blood. If Mom got married to Emmett, would there be room for Rose? What would happen if Mom decided to have children with Emmett? Rose bit her lip she had to stop thinking this way as Grandma Katha declared this borrowed trouble, but still Rose worried.

Rose looked over at Carol as she flicked her long blonde hair out of her eyes. Rose thought that Carol dying her hair blonder had made Carol's eyes look bluer and her fair skin even more ivory looking. Carol seemed to be getting a lot more looks from guys too. What was up with that? Maybe

Rose should cut her long hair? She didn't want to look exactly like her best friend from the back. Maybe she should make her hair reddish brown like her mom, Lily's. Then they'd be more alike, with hair and eyes matching in colour.

Rose suddenly looked up from her thoughts as she noticed the light bulb appeared out in the hallway near the gym. How odd she thought she wished the janitor would change the bulb quickly. It was creepy here at six a.m., even with Carol at her side. As they reached the choir room, Rose was relieved to find the light on in the room. But where was Mr. Scholar the choir teacher?

"I don't understand why Mr. Scholar called a six-thirty a.m. practice and can't be here when we get to the room," complained Carol loudly.

When Rose didn't answer right away she whined. "Aren't you talking to me yet?"

"I had to catch my breath, besides my leg hurts and I have a cramp in my leg. All the fast cycling on my bike pulled a muscle or something in my leg, and now my stomach hurts."

"Why don't you walk around the room and get rid of your cramp? I'm going to sit here and snooze. Wake me up when someone comes. I don't want anyone to catch me sleeping," Carol replied.

Rose walked around the room. The cramp in her leg, didn't seem to ease and neither did her stomach cramp. Rose's shoe slipped and she surprised herself, stepping into something sticky in a dark corner of the room. Great, now something was on my brand new shoes. Icky she thought. She glanced down, that looked like blood. It couldn't be? Could it? Did someone get a nose bleed, perhaps Mr. Scholar?

She peered behind the desk looking for the source of the blood and saw to her great shock Mr. Scholar lay dead. A knife protruded in the place where his heart should have been. Rose stared for a moment, not believing what her eyes saw. How could Mr. Scholar be lying dead, his chest bared open and nothing inside of him.

It seemed so unreal, like one of those movies she watched at Anna's. If her mother had known she viewed a chop movie, Rose would be in so much trouble. As it is she'd observed the movie with her hands over her eyes but this.... This was real....Mr. Scholar had obviously been murdered brutally murdered and his organs were gone. Was it his heart? Because Rose was sure that's where the teacher had declared it was in biology. Oh my God, what if the killer was still nearby? Rose scanned the room with her eyes seeking out all the spaces in the room where someone may hide. How could Carol be sitting dozing in a chair? Carol slept waiting for the choir teacher, while he lay dead near her.

"Rose what's wrong with you? Why did you gasp?" asked Carol, waking up and noticing Rose stillness and alarm at the same time.

"Carol he's dead," Rose indicated.

"I appreciate your dad is dead and we are all sad, but why bring that up now Rose?" Carol retorted exasperated.

"Mr. Scholar is here."

"I don't see him."

"That's because he's behind the desk. He's dead," Rose replied in a whisper.

"What did he have a heart attack or something? He's awful young for that, but I understand lots of people have sudden heart attacks," rambled Carol.

"Carol can you be quiet?"

"Well good grief, blame me like that it's not my fault the guy decided to have a heart attack!"

"He didn't have a heart attack, someone has killed him and I think they took his heart."

"Don't joke around Rose. It isn't funny."

"I'm not joking."

"Oh my God and we're still in this room alone. The killer could come back and get us, if he isn't in here all ready. I want my mother!" wailed Carol texting on her cell phone and getting no answer.

"We have to get out of here. People should be in the Gym, this time of morning they practice for basketball." Rose replied thinking on her feet, "I want my mom, too."

"Call her. Call your mother. Ask her what to do! She's always got an answer," demanded Carol.

"Let's lock the door first and put a chair in front of it. No one is in here now, but they might have a key for all we know."

"I did that already. I'm calling my Mom," stated Rose dialling.

"Mommy...,"cried Rose, as Lily answered.

"What is wrong Rose? What has happened?" demanded Lily.

"Mommy," Rose began incoherently through sobs.

"Take a deep breath now. Speak slowly and clearly. Tell your mother what is wrong," demanded Lily.

"Mr. Scholar the choir teacher is dead," Rose told her through the sobs.

"What? Did he have a heart attack? Are you okay? Of course, you're not okay. Do you want me to come to the school, baby? I can be there in ten minutes." Lily exclaimed quickly.

"Mommy he's bee....nnn he's bee....nnn mur...dered. Someone took his heart I think," Rose hiccupped.

"What? Who is with you? Are you safe?" demanded Lily.

"No one's here. It's just me and Carol. We are so scared, mom. I want you here."

"It will be okay baby, tell me everything, but first is the room safe you're in? Is it locked, and blocked?"

"Yes, we locked the door and blocked the door as well for now, but I don't want to stay here Mommy. It's icky and the killer might come back."

"What did she say? What did she say we should do?" demanded Carol.

"Quiet. I want to understand what my Mom said," implored Rose to Carol, and then speaking to Lily she replied.

"Sorry, go ahead mom."

"So tell me what happened," Lily demanded.

"I had a cramp in my leg, because I rode my bike to school fast. We raced then I won. I didn't see Mr. Scholar at first. I walked over near his desk and slipped in something sticky. Mommy, his blood is all over my new shoes. It's all over my shoes!" Rose answered in horror.

"Then what did you see?" prompted Lily trying to calm her daughter.

"I saw him. His chest is wide open and it is empty. There's nothing there, but tons of blood around and in him. I think his heart is gone. A knife is stuck in his chest," Rose sputtered a torrent of words, tumbling out of her.

"Okay, here is what I need you both to do to do. First, did Carol get near the body, or step in the blood?" demanded Lily.

"No. Lucky girl, Carol's shoes are fine. Mine are a total loss."

"Okay, did you track much blood, across the floor?" inquired Lily "And does the door own a lock that you can turn?"

"Blood?" Rose asked shock setting it as she stared at her shoes.

"Focus, Rose. I know it's difficult but you need to focus."

"Okay. Yes, we blocked the door I did track blood across the floor, since I had my shoes on, and yes the lock turns and then you can shut it behind you."

"Okay then carefully. Now take off your shoes and leave them on the floor. Be careful to walk only where blood isn't in your sock feet," Lily advised. "Walking to the door, I want you unblock the entrance, and then run don't walk, where people congregate. Also remain on the phone until you observe lots of people. Then take

Carol's phone, while you still talking to me and call the police."

"I will Mom. We will run to the gym. They practice basketball there, early in the mornings."

Rose and Carol then flew down the hall and burst into the gym.

"Ladies, we are practice basketball here, would you like a detention?" shouted the coach.

"There's been a murder and we want to be with people," Carol shouted back belligerently.

"Carol Banks, if you made up something...,"threatened the coach as he then saw Rose who spoke into Carol's cell phone.

"911. How can I direct your call?" asked the Operator 'Fire? Ambulance? Police?"

"Police, please?" Rose demanded, as she felt an eerie calm come over herself and heard herself give the details from far away.

"There's been a murder at Happy Valley High school. It's the choir teacher Mr. Scholar. He's been murdered in the choir room with a knife. Oh no, I sound like a clue game and it's not funny. It's horrible! He's dead," Rose stated horrified, a chill coming over her. Rose suddenly felt light-headed, and with blurry vision, quickly fell to the gym floor.

~0~

Look for Emmett and Lily further adventures and the rest of the Clan Kelly's fun in Book 2 of the Kelly Murder Mysteries - A Diller a Dollar a Real Dead Scholar, on sale now in e-book soon in paperback. If you enjoyed this book please consider leaving me a few words at your favourite retailer.

Sincerely S. G. Lee

586
A Penny Saved a Murder Earned

www.ingramcontent.com/pod-product-compliance
Lightning Source LLC
Chambersburg PA
CBHW052344020726
47503CB00001B/105